The Chelsea Project

A Bill Conors Novel

by

Jack Stamp

TELEMACHUS PRESS

This book is a work of fiction. Names, characters, places and incidents are either the product of the author's imagination or are used fictitiously. Any resemblance to actual persons, living or dead, or to actual events or locales is entirely coincidental.

THE CHELSEA PROJECT

Cover art and design by Telemachus Press, LLC

Cover copyright © iStockphoto/313588/Brandon Clark
Cover copyright © Thinkstock/119403278/iStockphoto

Published by Telemachus Press, LLC
http://www.telemachuspress.com

Visit the author website
http://www.jackstampnovels.com

ISBN#: 978-1-938135-37-8 (eBook)
ISBN#978-1-938135-38-5 (paperback)

Version 2012.05.14

Printed in the United States of America
10 9 8 7 6 5 4 3 2 1

Dedicated to:

James & Dorothy

and

Ollie, who made the world a better place that would have been even better; if he had stayed longer

The Chelsea Project

A Bill Conors Novel

THE PROJECT
Early June

The tires screeched. He slammed forward and hit his head. His eyes blinked open, a coffee-stained rug slowly came into focus.

Sleeping through a landing, that's a first.

The plane parked at the gate and after the first wave of departing passengers, Bill Conors unbuckled the seat belt and extracted his six-foot frame from economy seat 34F. He grabbed a worn leather briefcase and carry-on bag. The flight crew had just transferred an elderly ninety-pound man into a narrow wheelchair. The chair bumped its way down the aisle, a stewardess stepped between seats, letting Conors pass. She looked into his eyes and smiled. "Is Boston home or business?"

"Home," said Conors, liking the sound of the word.

At 5:45 a.m. he scoured the empty terminal for caffeine. Giving up, he headed towards central parking and pushed through the swinging doors. The air was city air, hot, humid, with a dose of diesel. After a triathlon of hallways, stairways and escalators he slipped through the closing doors of an elevator and pressed the button next to the green bird. When the doors opened, he stepped onto the second floor and was greeted by a thousand cars, SUVs and pickups. He turned in a circle, scanned the unending rows, then lowered his bags to the ground.

"Shit."

Green swans were stenciled on cement columns for as far as he could see. He remembered them from a week earlier when he ran to his flight, but nothing else. Holding a set of keys above his head, he pressed the buttons on the remote, grabbed his bags and started walking. With the signal reaching two rows on each side, he figured no more than fifteen minutes to locate the company car.

Conors was less than a hundred yards from the elevator when the explosion occurred. The ex-marine instinctively dove to the ground.

***

"Someone trying to kill you?" asked the Chief of Airport Security.

Conors was leaning against a filing cabinet. The pudgy man behind the desk was waiting for an answer. Conors had drank two Pepsis, was wide awake and suppressing a desire to throttle the man. He pressed his palm against his right ear, hoping it would stop the ringing. It didn't.

"No," said Conors.

"Then change your accident report to say 'fire' instead of 'explosion.'"

"A fire doesn't blow out windows and cover a quarter acre with glass shards," said Conors.

The chief shrugged his shoulders. "Strange things happen. As you said, you may have hit the remote start button. The engine could have ignited a leaky fuel line."

The two men studied each other. Eventually the chief shrugged his shoulders again. "Make yourself comfortable, you're not leaving till this investigation is closed."

Conors could justify society's need for meter maids, cops and presidents as well as the next guy, but for Conors, the system fell apart when you plugged humans into the org chart. He pushed off from the file cabinet. "The fire's first, then maybe a gas tank blows. Cars don't instantaneously explode."

"That's probably what happened," said the Chief.

Conors looked for a hint of a smile, some sign the guy was kidding. There were no hints, no signs. "So the car smolders for a week and then conveniently blasts itself to smithereens on my return."

As if part of his job description, the chief shrugged his shoulders again.

Conors glanced around the room painted a dull gray a decade earlier and decided three hours was enough. He grabbed a stack of Xeroxed forms, crossed out the word 'explosion,' and tossed the report on the Chief's desk.

***

With ears still ringing, Conors sat in a rented subcompact. He glanced in the rearview mirror at the scratches on his face.

"Have to downplay my little accident, it won't play well in the rumor mill."

The car crawled through the maze of ramps that crisscrossed the airport. The barely moving traffic came to a dead stop and blocked his escape into the Ted Williams Tunnel. Stuck behind a Hilton Courtesy bus, he grabbed his cell phone, hit #1 on the speed dial and listened.

"Hi, honey."

"How's my favorite lady?" asked Conors.

"Missed you."

"Missed you in more ways than you can imagine," said Conors.

Kristin Conors laughed, Conors smiled.

"Well you'll have to keep on missing me for another day," said Kristin. "This is my night for rounds and the boys are looking forward to spending time with their dad."

Conors cradled his phone and hurriedly thumbed a battered PDA, checking to see if he had double scheduled. He hadn't. The traffic started moving, he dropped the PDA. "Good, we can plan our weekend at the cottage."

"What is the great adventurer planning for our four year olds?" asked Kristin.

"A trip to the wharfs for discarded fish. Then crabbing off the rocks."

"Claws and fish guts, the boys will be thrilled," said Kristin.

"I sense muted enthusiasm, but once we start pulling in those crustaceans, you'll be in the middle of it."

"Don't hold your breath."

An old Saab cut off Conors. He jammed on the brakes. The car in his rearview mirror screeched to a stop.

"Kristin, I've got to go."

Conors hung up as the traffic accelerated out of the tunnel and into the heart of downtown Boston and the last of the Big Dig.

Bostonians cynically refer to the Central Artery Project as the Big Dig because it slowly evolved into twenty years of graft, unending traffic jams and the most expensive public works in the history of mankind. Among its other achievements, the Big Dig managed to further tarnish the reputation of the city's drivers.

Boston traffic appears chaotic, but Conors had cracked the code as a teenager. Inertia was the force governing traffic flow. The older, the bigger, and the more dented the car, the greater the right-of-way. He avoided eye contact and was heavy on the accelerator, but the shiny subcompact lacked mass and the requisite dents. It took fifteen minutes of crawling and darting to complete three miles and then he came to a dead stop. An oversized excavator was hoisting a concrete road barrier onto a truck. He glanced at his watch, then dialed his Cambridge office.

"Good Morning, AEG," Lisa said.

"I'll be arriving soon. Let Matt know I'd like a quick debrief."

"Matt's in Chelsea and not expected till late afternoon. Should I call him back to the office?" asked Lisa.

"No, I need to visit the site anyway."

Conors pulled an illegal u-turn and said, "Call our Ford dealer and ask about any recalls that could cause a car to explode."

"What?" said Lisa as the phone went dead.

***

A solitary seagull was perched on one of the pilings that had supported bustling wharfs and piers, but now the decaying stumps picketed the Chelsea waterfront like cornstalks in a winter field. The gull took flight over abandoned derricks that once unloaded ships of their cargo, over partially salvaged oil tanks, abandoned red-bricked factories, roofless warehouses, and debris-covered roads. The gull landed on a fire-gutted factory. Seventy feet below, laborers were installing chain-linked fence along the perimeter of the 170 acres known as the Chelsea Project.

Chelsea, originally a swamp across the Mystic River from Boston, was settled in the 1600s and became the home for thousands of businesses from blacksmiths to large chemical companies, each building on top of their predecessors' waste and debris. Bill Conors saw beyond the sludge and the leaking drums and leveraged everything he owned to secretly purchase the city's waterfront. The Chelsea Project stretched from where the laborers were installing fence to the opposite end where two men were watching dozens of supervisors, geologists and field chemists disperse across the construction site.

"Thanks for staying for lunch and talking to the men," said Matt Kimani in a crisp Nigerian accent.

Conors nodded as he surveyed the site.

"Lisa mentioned that the company car self-destructed," said Kimani.

Conors nodded again.

"Have any idea what happened?" asked Kimani. He had an edge to his voice.

Kimani was the Chief Operations Officer for Conors' company. Over the last few months, the Chelsea Project was wearing on his managers. Conors didn't want them linking the explosion to the unending problems and strange accidents that had plagued the project.

"The cops thought it was a gas leak," said Conors.

A smirk slowly replaced the worried look on Kimani's face. "We'll have to keep you the hell away from the company cars."

Conors glanced at his friend. It was a guy thing. From barrooms to foxholes, it was always easier to break balls than deal with the 900 pound gorilla in the room. Conors laughed. "Hey, you're the guy who drives a pickup like you're on a damn Nigerian safari."

"I don't do anything they don't do in the commercials."

"Yeah and the local body shop is thrilled you believe everything seen on TV."

The smiling Conors scanned the pockmarked, pollution-stained land and the dilapidated buildings.

"I've managed a lot of projects, but this baby's different," said Conors. "If we're successful, this waste pit will be the nation's financial center, the most valuable real estate in the country."

The serious look returned to Kimani's face. He kicked a small chunk of broken concrete. "I used to think a ten million dollar project was enormous. Six billion keeps me awake at night."

Conors didn't say anything. He continued looking into the distance, at the dirt and debris that was going to make him an easy hundred million or put him in the poor house. What he never shared with anyone was that the likely outcome changed from day to day.

The distant groan of a straining diesel engine echoed across the site. Conors turned towards a crane lifting the remnants of an underground storage tank. The rusting tank swayed before coming to rest at the side of the deep hole, its home for the last ninety years.

"One of thirty projects underway," said Conors. "No wonder it looks different after a week on the road."`

Kimani was squinting into the sun looking past the crane as a Suburban with flashing yellow lights stopped at the main entrance gate. "Should we be expecting more hassles with the State?"

"Be crazy not to," said Conors, with no hint of the hate that simmered within his core. "That's what bureaucrats and politicians do."

"Bastards," said Kimani as three more vehicles pulled-up behind the Suburban.

THE 2ⁿᵈ OLDEST PROFESSION

"Nathaniel, for christ's sake, you can't be serious."

Nathaniel Forbes, President of the Massachusetts Senate, stood by a window in the State House's second largest office, watching the sun set. In the fading light, the antique glass distorted not only the view of Beacon Hill, but that of his reflection, making his nose appear even more prominent. He unconsciously turned the Harvard College ring on his right hand. Once his grandfather's, it was so worn the name of their alma mater was no longer discernible.

"Nathaniel!"

Forbes continued to gaze over the still busy streets, knowing that the rules of the game were changing. It had been the Commonwealth's unwritten law of 'pay-to-play'. The campaign contributions and contracts with his law firm were expected.

"Nathaniel, you can't mean it."

The accented and high pitched voice was difficult to ignore. Turning, he faced his unwanted guest, a bald, thin man perched on the edge of a Chippendale. Nigel Burn looked at the towering Forbes and fell silent.

"I certainly do mean it," said Forbes.

"How can you justify twenty grand for a few conversations?"

"That was the arrangement."

"Payment was based on the premise that you'd stop the financing of the Chelsea Project," said the red-faced Burn. "Just in case you haven't heard, Conors is going full-speed ahead."

"I made no promises," said Forbes.

Nigel Burn glanced at the floor. Burn was president of American operations for Burgess LTD, the world's largest engineering company, which was losing job after job to Conors' company. He reached deep for courage and said, "I'm not going to pay."

The slightest hint of a smile pulled at Forbes' lips. "Nigel, how many projects do you have underway in the Commonwealth?"

Burn shrugged and lied, "I don't remember, maybe two dozen."

"The correct answer is thirty-four. With all that at stake, you need a friend in the Senate."

Burn stopped breathing as he considered the barely veiled threat, understanding that one by one his projects would be shut-down for some irregularity. Nothing would be traceable to Forbes, just an unending army of dedicated civil servants doing their job. With his long bony fingers in fists, Burn rose from the chair. "In that case, I'm glad I've bought a friend."

Forbes ignored the comment and his departing visitor. Nigel Burn was an irritant that needed to be managed, but Conors was a different story. Forbes had underestimated him. He returned to the window and with fingers following the worn grain of the windowsill, he watched the residents returning home to Beacon Hill.

"Despite his good fortune at the airport, the Chelsea Project will fail miserably."

THE AGENT
Mid-June

Two runners raced across the Longfellow Bridge. It was dark, hot and humid. On the Cambridge side of the Charles River, the sweat-drenched women slowed as a taxi screeched through an intersection.

"Start coaching soon?"

"Varsity arrived this afternoon. But enough about me, how was Phoenix?"

"Hot," yelled Terry Hamlin before sprinting across the street.

The soccer coach was close on Terry's heels. "Wasn't interested in a weather report. Were you on some confidential assignment or are you just being secretive?"

Terry frowned as she glanced at her running mate. "Just because I'm not an open book, doesn't mean I'm secretive." After a couple of breaths, she decided her friend meant no harm. "I was investigating MS-13."

"What's MS-13?"

"A Salvadoran gang that's moved into the States," gasped Terry, having a hard time keeping her pace and talking.

"Thought your specialty was the mafia."

"Phoenix was a temporary assignment."

"Meet anybody?"

"Too busy," said Terry, before increasing her pace and ending the conversation.

They sprinted past MIT and crossed over the BU Bridge in silence. Approaching Commonwealth Avenue, Terry slowed as they started to go separate ways. "Still thinking of the half marathon in Gloucester?"

The soccer coach didn't slow. "Can't, I'll call when my schedule loosens up." The coach waved and turned right on Commonwealth.

Terry turned left. It had been a long day. She arrived at Logan, dropped her luggage at the apartment and then took the subway to the FBI field office. Her boss greeted her with a box of documents confiscated from a mob-owned business. She studied the papers into the early evening, locked them in the evidence room and left with a reluctant admiration for the Gallo Family. She had worked two years of late nights and weekends and hadn't uncovered a trace of their millions.

It was 9:30 when she jogged left onto Bay State Road. A white-haired man was standing on the sidewalk dressed in a button-down blue shirt and pressed chinos, a dog was wagging his tail and pulling at his leash.

She bent down with arms open. The dog ran into them and she gently squeezed the terrier. The dog whimpered, licking her neck and face as she stood. Terry, still out of breath, laughed for the first time in months. "Alex, it's so good to see you, you silly little dog."

Charles Bradfield stood silently, frowning at her spandex running outfit.

She placed the dog on the ground, and kissed the man on the cheek. "Love you, Pops."

"You shouldn't be sprinting about in your underwear. You don't want some crazed man chasing you down the street."

Terry rolled her eyes. "Don't worry, I'm sure I can outrun anyone who confuses Nike with Victoria Secret."

Pops, still frowning, extended his bent arm. Arm-in-arm they started up the steps to their brownstone apartment building.

"Did you get your birthday card?"

"Yes, it was nice of you to remember," said Pops.

"How could anyone forget a seventy-eighth birthday?" said Terry. "By the way, I picked-up a carrot cake at Bova's. Do you have time to celebrate a belated birthday."

Eyes twinkling, Pops said, "I believe I can rearrange my evening schedule."

"Pencil me in for ten."

At twenty-eight, Terry had spent half her life without a parent. The old man was the closest to a family she had had in years and he had aged over the last three months. She left him at the door to his second floor apartment and continued up the worn marble steps.

Upon making it to the fourth floor, Pop's voice echoed up the opened staircase. "Alex, we're having company, better make some ice tea."

Terry smiled.

***

She unlocked the two deadbolts and entered the four-room apartment she had called home for the last nine years. Her slender Nike-clad silhouette flashed across the mirrored back of the closing door. She shook her head.

"Damn, what am I suppose to do? Wear an overcoat in June?"

She grabbed a towel from the linen closet and tossed it over her shoulder. The red light on the answering machine was flashing, taunting with a mix of curiosity and irritation. Her circle of acquaintances had a small radius. Messages were from Pops, coworkers or the building superintendent. As she passed, she pushed the button.

"This is Vincent. Heard you were back and was wondering if we could get together. Maybe a walk on Cranes Beach?—I've missed you.—Missed you a lot."

The deep voice stopped Terry in her tracks. She closed her eyes and sighed. "Why did you have to complicate everything?"

She grimaced as she recalled the last three months, the temporary assigned cubicle, the cramped efficiency apartment, the unending work and her unsuccessful attempts to get through a day without thinking of him.

Terry listened to the message a second time. The machine clicked off and the apartment went quiet, her shaky hand hovered over the phone. Her hand slowly closed and she turned away.

THE BUSINESS

It was 7:30 in the morning. Ray Gallo pulled his Cadillac Escalade into a parking space next to an East Boston warehouse, finished his second Dunkin Donuts coffee and crushed the paper cup.

"Shit can't roll downhill forever."

Climbing out of the SUV, he tossed the cup on the ground and headed towards the old brick building. Gallo had a good stride, kept himself in shape and appeared taller than his five feet, ten inches. His dark hair was receding, but thanks to his mother he was passably handsome. There was only a slight resemblance to his father, who in a two thousand dollar Armani still looked like a longshoreman.

The outline of a weathered name, 'TAT', was barely visible on the warehouse door. According to IRS 1040 forms, the TAT tele-marketing company was Gallo's sole source of revenue. A fabrication maintained by daily visits to the warehouse. Gallo opened the door to a musty hallway with peeling tan paint, took the first door on the left and entered a large turquoise room filled with desks, computers and telephones. Being slow to wake, he was pleased by the quiet. In two hours the room would be filled with fourteen women, all yapping at once.

He made his way to his office, unlocked the door and sat at his desk. A moment later, Anna, the day supervisor, arrived with a newspaper and a report.

"Good morning, Mr. Gallo," she said in a Brazilian accent and placed the papers on his desk.

He glanced at the financial report that listed TAT receipts for the previous day. "Eighteen thousand, seven hundred and seventy two bucks, that's what I call good news."

"The girls worked real hard, you'd be proud of them," said Anna.

He nodded and picked up the Boston Herald as she left. He turned to the sports section, not for lunchtime bullshitting with the boys, but to get a measure of how the odds had played. He was half-way through the paper when the phone rang.

"Ray, this is Joey. Some asshole banker was here with a marshal. They put an orange sticker on our big excavator. They say they're repossessing it. What should I do?"

"Get it out of the state. Move it to Providence. Now!"

Gallo slammed the phone into its receiver. After years of laboring under the shadow of his father he had expanded the family's businesses. At thirty-six, Raymond Gallo was no longer just the boss's son, but his star in the organization was fading. Running both the local unions and a construction company had been very profitable, until the Feds blacklisted his company. Now, the company was bleeding money. With elbows on the desk, Gallo lowered his head in his hands. "I need a piece of that Chelsea Project."

By 9:45 the parking lot was filled with rusting Toyotas and Hondas and the clamor of voices escalated as women worked the phones. Gallo left his office and climbed the stairs to the second floor of the warehouse, the home of PPI, Prime Private Investigators.

Gallo used PPI's employees to skim the cream from the family's core businesses whenever somebody of influence, or money, was found whoring, buying drugs or making large bets. Like the compulsive gambler who once owned the East Boston warehouse. Gallo's bookie fed the gambler information on a run of fixed sporting events, but unfortunately for the gambler, the fix wasn't there when it really mattered.

He unlocked the door. The alarm wasn't set and light was coming from Eric Wills' office at the far end of the hallway. Eric lacked a
biological clock and if he was there in the morning, it meant he had
pulled an all-nighter. Gallo walked down the hallway to what was
more of a large computer room than an office.

As he entered, he stepped on a carpet of discarded pink pistachio shells.

"Jesus Eric, are you feeding the god-damn rats?"

Eric, sipping a Red Bull, never looked up from the 32" monitor.
"It beats having them eat my printer cables, and besides, the shells
prevent your private dicks from sneaking up on me."

The skinny neck topped with a crop of dirty hair caught Gallo's
attention, it always did. The high school dropout, now in his mid-
twenties, casually did things with a keyboard that Gallo couldn't
comprehend. But Gallo did understand that Eric loved what he did,
the challenge, the shadiness and even more importantly that Eric
appreciated the rewards of hacking for bucks as opposed to hacking
for bragging rights. He had a BMW that some insurance company
thought was totaled and never wanted for computer gear. For a
hacker, it didn't get any better.

"What do you have?" asked Gallo.

Eric pointed at a desk covered with disassembled computers.
"Seven preliminary reports. Let me know, if I should get into their
underwear."

"Anything good?" asked Gallo, while extracting the stapled
printouts from among the computer parts.

"The cokeheads, the lawyer and the two MDs, are still worth a
shitload. You're too late for the gamblers, your bookies vacuumed
their accounts."

Gallo started reading the report on the lawyer and was about to
sit on Eric's couch, when he reconsidered. Eric not only slept on the
sofa more than his own bed, but the guys mentioned he was screwing

Tina from the TAT evening shift. He dropped the report beside Eric. "Find out what type of law this guy practices and see me before you go."

Gallo turned to leave, the pistachio shells crunching underneath his feet. "Christ, have you ever eaten anything healthy?"

"Yeah, ate like a damn rabbit till I was eighteen, then my old lady died. The only vegetarian to die of a massive heart attack at thirty-seven," said Eric, while studying the data flashing across his monitor. Eric was still yakking when Gallo entered an office at the other end of the building and sat at a desk with the reports on the two MDs.

***

Gallo was standing, shredding reports with his back to the door when Tony and Dominic arrived. He looked over his shoulder.

"Nice of you to come to work," said Gallo.

Tony frowned. He was unshaven and tired. Tony and Dominic were sweeping the family's properties and cars. They had bitched about it until two years ago, when bugs were found in the Hanover Street Bar &Grille.

"You on the rag?" said Gallo as he fed more paper into the shredder.

Dominic laid two suitcases of electronic equipment on the floor. "Boss," Tony said. "While you were in your air-conditioned bed-room, me and Dominic were out playing janitor and won the damn lottery."

"What the hell do you mean, won the lottery?"

"We were sweeping the union offices and found three bugs. They were above the dropped ceiling."

Gallo's pulse quickened. "What did you do with them?"

"Nothing, we wanted to talk to you, first."

"Can you tell who wired the place?"

"Good stuff. Good installation. My money's on the Feds."

Gallo's eyes narrowed as he remembered how the Feds wired the barroom without tripping any alarms. He turned off the shredder and faced Tony.

"Do they know you found the bugs?" asked Gallo.

"There were no cameras and we never talk before a place has been swept. They'll just hear janitors banging wastebaskets and vacuuming."

"Yesterday, I told Iggy to work with that dickhead at the engineering company." Gallo's face turned red. He threw the last report onto an old desk. "I'll be screwed if the Feds link me to that hazardous waste."

Dominic glanced at Tony. They remained silent. Gallo didn't like bad news and they didn't like being the messengers.

"Tonight, you and Dominic get back there and pull the plug. Make sure those bugs never work again."

"Sure, Boss," said Tony.

Tony and Dominic silently busied themselves getting equipment ready as Gallo paced back and forth. The pacing slowed and Gallo sat at the desk. He slowly tore the report in half and then into quarters.

"If the Feds squeeze those union grunts, they'll sing like fucking Madonna."

ALL IN A DAY

A woman with a large paper cup in each hand marched down the hallway of a Cambridge building towards the corner office. Her hair was more gray than brown making Lisa Kelly look all of her forty-six years. Broad shoulders and the silhouette of a vending machine added to her formidable presence.

She put a coffee on her desk, continued into the corner office and placed a Pepsi in front of her boss, Bill Conors. He drank room temperature diet Pepsi, no ice, no Coke and no coffee. She often accused him of having the taste buds of an eight-year old.

Conors looked up from a desk covered with papers. "Thanks."

"Good weekend?" asked Lisa.

"Great, until a crab bit Kristin."

"She okay?"

"Yeah, but she didn't take kindly to me and the twins laughing."

Lisa looked disapprovingly.

Conors smiled. "You have a moment."

"Sure."

He grabbed his worn briefcase, pulled out a flat jeweler's box and laid it open on the desk. "What do you think?"

Lisa stared at the string of bluish gray pearls. "They're gorgeous. They certainly make up for all those practical gifts."

Lisa picked up the box. "It's an important anniversary and you're on target."

Conors nodded, trying to remember what past gifts were practical.

She handed the box back to Conors. "No one lasted six months before Kristin came along. I can't believe it's been five years."

"Five years of marital bliss and mystery vegetables," said Conors, still bothered by the practical gifts.

"Mystery vegetables?" said Lisa.

"Yeah, five years of finding vegetables in the fridge that I don't know if you bake them, boil them or eat them raw."

"Mystery vegetables," said Lisa on her way to the desk from where she controlled access to the CEO, Chairman and majority stockholder of AEG. She swiveled her chair towards the monitor and scanned the never ending emails.

Lisa was a street smart girl from South Boston who had worked for Conors since he was a rising star at Burgess LTD, a company he left in disgust before founding AEG. She was finishing the emails, when she heard Matt Kimani whistling his way down the hallway.

"Thought I'd stop by before leaving," said Kimani.

Before Matt Kimani was hired, Conors was working fourteen hour days. Since the Chelsea Project, they both were. Without looking up from her monitor, she handed him a thick folder. "How about reviewing a few acquisitions, before I start hounding you?"

"Always a good strategy," said Kimani, grabbing the folder.

"The tickets for the Sox/Yankee game are in your mailbox."

"Sure you can't use them?" asked Kimani.

Lisa looked up from her computer and over her reading glasses. "Yeah, niece's wedding, but I expect an inning by inning description."

Kimani headed for the door. "That's a deal."

She returned to her computer. Ten minutes later, she pulled her fingers from the keyboard. "Damn, the only way to make Bill's calendar work is to start scheduling Saturday meetings."

***

Conors' desk was covered with specifications and layers of blueprints. He was typing numbers into a spreadsheet when Lisa's voice came over the intercom.

"I know you wanted the afternoon to catch-up, but Greg's on line 1."

"I'll take it," said Conors. He picked up the phone.

"Have a few minutes?" asked Greg Bider, AEG's outside counsel.

Conors put down his pen. "It's your all-business voice. Why do I entertain notions of enjoying your company when you persist in being a bearer of bad news?"

"Well, invite me to Gloucester and we could talk about something other than business. It's been a year since I gave you a fishing lesson," said Bider.

"Listening to your fish stories is as painful as paying you eight hundred dollars an hour," said Conors.

Greg laughed. "Maybe, but you have to remember that striper."

Conors did remember, it was a beauty. "Doubt you called to discuss fishing when you could be charging somebody by the minute."

"This a good time for a few questions?" asked Bider.

"As good as any."

"Remember that New York City job you lost last April?"

"Do you mean the SRI job that was awarded to Burgess LTD?"

"That's the one," said Bider.

"Sure I remember. Matt thought we had the job in the bag and then all of a sudden we were out of the running."

"Well, I finally spoke to the New York City Solicitor, who had questioned why the lowest bidder wasn't selected. I now understand what transpired and have to ask a few questions."

"Fire away," said Conors.

"Did you ever have any financial difficulties while working at Burgess LTD?"

"Not unless exceeding revenue and profit goals is a financial difficulty."

"Did you ever misspend funds?" asked Bider.

"No. Why are you asking these damn questions?"

"Hold on. I have one more. Did you ever spend Burgess's funds on personal items, mischaracterize charges and then bill your clients?"

"Never. Now tell me what the hell's going on."

"It seems your old boss, Nigel Burn, knows a vice president at SRI and they had an off-the-record conversation before the contract was awarded."

After a moment of silence, Conors said, "Don't stop there."

"It appears that Burn told his contact that you embezzled funds and charged your clients to cover the theft."

Conors' jaw tightened. Burn was like a recurring cancer. The last litigation ended less than six months ago.

"Bill, are you still there?"

"It's all a lie."

"I knew what your answers were going to be, but had to ask."

"Do you think he's manufactured accounting evidence?" asked Conors.

"I doubt it. I'm betting Burn thought his little chat was going to stay between him and his buddy. But his friend shared the dirty little secret when the Solicitor put on the pressure."

"What's the likelihood he'll continue with this bullshit?"

"It's a possibility. Burn can't control himself when it comes to you and AEG."

"Then stop the asshole. Do whatever you need to do."

"I needed your approval before officially going forward, but have already started exploring different strategies," said Bider. "This time Burn may have crossed the line between civil and criminal activities."

"Get on it and don't show any mercy," said Conors.

"Don't worry. My firm doesn't practice the golden rule."

"We'll talk later," said Conors. He hung-up and stood by his desk with clenched fists.

He turned towards the windows and squinted into the afternoon sun. The last time he and Nigel Burn were face to face, Burn was snarling. Greg Bider had just caught Burn in a lie, a lie documented by a court stenographer. Burn's testimony had cost him the already weak case and the right to any future lawsuits. Conors had celebrated, believing that Burn was finally out of his life.

THE FEDS

The stocky and bald Joe DeLuca looked away from the rising sun and surveyed downtown Boston. The seventeenth floor window was his remote contact with the outside world. The world left behind when he retreated to the innards of the JFK building and the forty-three FBI agents under his command.

Six hours later he was working through his inbox when his near retirement age administrator stopped by his desk. She dropped the Field Activity Docket onto DeLuca's cluttered desk.

DeLuca peered over his reading glasses. "Anything I need to look at?"

"No, casework is slow. Thirteen brick agents doing background checks for DOD security clearances, three perimeter surveillances and routine pick-up of tapes."

"Anything else?" asked DeLuca.

"You have two memos regarding Agent Terry Hamlin. This one is a memorandum of commendation from the head of the Phoenix Office."

"Not surprised. O'Reilly was shocked when Terry uncovered how the gangs were laundering their money. The Phoenix Office had been trying to follow the drug money for a year."

"You better watch out, O'Reilly may ask for a transfer."

DeLuca smirked. "Won't happen. O'Reilly would love a dozen agents like Hamlin, but not Hamlin."

"Why?"

"The productivity of his single agents went to hell as they competed for Ms Hamlin's attention."

The administrator smiled. "I guess there's one advantage to our office of geriatric agents."

"What's the second memo?"

"Headquarters wants you to broaden Terry's experience, preferably undercover work. I'd say headquarters has plans for Agent Hamlin."

DeLuca frowned and grabbed the piece of paper. "I understand, there aren't many Ivy League lawyers in the agency, let alone a female lawyer who works her butt off. But undercover work?"

The administrator didn't answer and waited as her boss read. DeLuca looked up and handed back the memo. "Hamlin could blend into a roomful of white collar criminals, but I happen to run an organized crime squad."

"I'd accuse you of showing your paternal side, but I had the same thoughts," said the administrator. "This kid can go places and I'm sure you'll find the perfect assignment."

Deluca grimaced and returned to his paperwork.

THE SPILL
Late June

Conors eased off the throttle, pulled into the middle lane and slowed to 85. The radar detector was silent and the Super High Output Taurus was purring. He was smiling, a meeting in Amherst, another signed contract and Route 90 East was almost empty.

He switched lanes, passed a UPS truck and grabbed the ringing cell phone.

"Conors."

"Bill, this is Lisa. There's a problem in Chelsea."

"What type of problem?"

"A spill, a hazardous waste spill. Matt's on his way to the site as we speak."

"Was anybody hurt?" asked Conors.

"Don't think so."

"Where should I meet Matt? At the engineering trailer?" asked Conors.

"No, offsite at the corner of Marginal and Charles."

"Call me if you get any updates," said Conors.

He tossed the phone on the passenger seat, clicked on the hazard lights and punched the throttle. His pulse quickened, not because of the speed, cops or tickets, he was still a Federal Emergency Responder, but because everything he owned was riding on the Chelsea Project.

***

Conors pulled the overheated car to the curb and grabbed his hard-hat from the back seat. Even though half of Chelsea's street signs were missing, it wasn't difficult finding the corner of Marginal and Charles. At least fifty residents were jostling to get closer to a TV news van.

A hundred yards down the road were two trucks and a dozen men dressed in bright yellow coveralls. They wore white hardhats with the "AEG" logo. Kimani was talking and pointing.

Conors was passing the group of residents when he was hit with the stench of chemicals. He walked directly to the edge of the river bank.

"Christ," said Conors. A large mound of waste was resting on the mud. The telltale reek of naphthalene and the blue color of iron cyanide complexes meant it was from an abandoned gas manufacturing plant. During the 1800s, the plants generated thousands of tons of the waste and one of the largest had been located in the middle of the Chelsea project.

Kimani was speaking to a man wearing a blue hardhat with an Environmental Protection Agency logo when Conors approached.

Conors pointed in the direction of the river. "Matt, is that ours?"

"Negative," said Kimani.

Conors exhaled and felt a knot in his gut start to unravel.

"Our original schedule had us working on the gas plant site, but it had to be postponed. That's not our waste." said Kimani.

"Bill," said the man wearing the EPA hardhat.

Conors shook hands with Henry Gonzales, who ran EPA's regional Criminal Investigation Division. "Hi Henry."

"Do you have any suggestions on how to handle this?" asked Gonzales.

"Yeah, get the waste the hell out of here before the next tide," said Conors before turning towards Kimani. "Matt, how many empty dumpsters do we have?"

"At least a dozen."

Conors pointed to the edge of the bank. "Drop three large dumpsters by the bank and have the excavator transported here ASAP. Also put a team in the inflatable boats so we can anchor a boom and capture the floating oils."

"I might not be able to compensate you for the removal," said Gonzales.

"We'll worry about that another day. That shit is too close to the Chelsea Project." Conors headed off toward the river and his men. "Henry, see me before you leave."

"I plan on staying," said Gonzales.

Gonzales watched Conors direct the crew that grew as more men with AEG hardhats streamed into the area. The men were clearing brush adjacent to the bank for the excavator and dumpsters. Conors was on the two-way radio giving orders while the sounds of diesel trucks carrying dumpsters and a mammoth backhoe grew louder. The frenzied scene reminded Gonzales of a decade earlier, when Conors was in the middle of the action instead of pushing papers in a distant office.

***

Later that afternoon, Conors and Gonzales stood on the edge of the riverbank, observing a chemist leaning over a gaping hole in the mud. The pile of hazardous waste had been removed, but some of the toxic waste had leached into the underlying sediment. The chemist was identifying the contamination so the excavator could remove it and place it in dumpsters.

The hole was filling by the incoming tide. The chemist held a portable gas chromatograph above the mud. It sucked in air and measured vapors from the sediment. The chemist noted the instrument reading and the location in his field notebook. Then he looked up at Conors and yelled over the noise of the excavator. "No readings above background. We've got all of the waste and all of the contaminated sediment."

Conors nodded and gave the operator of the excavator the thumbs ups. "Take her home." He turned to the men maintaining the staging area. "Gentlemen, let's cleanup and cover the dumpsters."

Conors clothes had become saturated with the smell of diesel exhaust and sweat. Conors saw that Gonzales was just as hot. "Time for Gatorade."

Walking towards the staging area, Gonzales said, "Whoever did this could go to jail for a long time. Can we determine where this waste came from?"

"If you can identify gas plant sites that are currently being worked on," said Conors.

"Easy, they all had to submit remediation plans."

"Good. My men have samples of the waste and will place them in your custody. Analyze them along with a waste sample from each of the other gas plant sites. I'm betting you'll get a match."

"I'll have my chemist contact you about the analysis," said Gonzales.

Conors stopped at the back of a pickup truck, filled two plastic cups from the spigot of an orange cylindrical cooler and handed Gonzales one.

"Tastes nasty, but good for the electrolytes."

Gonzales took the cup. "Thanks."

Conors pointed at the dumpsters. "Who will be responsible for security?"

"I'll have the Chelsea Police check them during their rounds. But I have another question."

"Hold that thought," said Conors. He opened his ringing cell phone. "What's up?"

"I have a Mr. Mellon on the other line. He's the Public Health Agent for Chelsea," said Lisa.

"Patch him in."

After a couple of clicks, Conors said, "Mr. Mellon."

"Yes," said Mellon. "You're directed to immediately shut down all Chelsea Project operations."

"What the hell are you talking about?"

"We were informed that your company dumped hazardous waste into the river and put our citizens at risk."

"Mr. Mellon, you have everything ass backwards. We just saved a half mile of your river from being contaminated," said Conors. "Standing beside me is Dr. Henry Gonzales of the EPA. He's a toxicologist and an attorney. Have you heard of him?"

"Yes, he gives speeches to the Association of Municipal Health Agents," said Mellon.

"Henry, a Mr. Mellon from Chelsea is on the phone." Conors pointed at the dumpster. "Could you explain how this waste has nothing to do with the Chelsea Project?"

Gonzales took the phone. "Gladly."

Conors listened to one side of the conversation. Gonzales argued how the spill had nothing to do with the Chelsea Project and asked numerous questions. The answers that Conors couldn't hear angered Gonzales. After, a few minutes Gonzales hung up.

"It's not Mellon's decision, he's following the Mayor's orders," said Gonzales.

"Why the hell would the Mayor want to shut down the Chelsea Project?"

"Somebody in the State House is applying pressure," said Gonzales. "I'm sorry Bill, it isn't fair."

Conors' jaw clenched as he masked the rage that had simmered since he was eleven. He turned towards the river, looking, but not seeing the calm waters of the incoming tide. "Bastards run this state like a third world country."

ON THE JOB TRAINING
Early July

The only sound was the whirl of an air-conditioner neutralizing the summer heat. The morning sunlight filtered through the swaying Venetian blinds and flickered across the bedroom. The light played over the blue sheets and her sleeping lover.

Terry Hamlin lay motionless, studying the chiseled face. She had met the DEA agent at a federal training course. Initially she was curious, but not emotionally interested. At six feet, four, dark hair and eyes, he was too good looking to be taken seriously. She figured he was a jock spoiled from years of adoring women.

Her opinion gradually changed while studying him from the back of the classroom. On the last day, she and Vincent were half of a task group. They periodically locked eyes and he was always the first to look away. The seminar led to a series of dates, dinner, the theatre, time at the beach and eventually her becoming aware of desires that only increased as they were met. To her surprise she was often the initiator and the reason they missed the play or the movie.

Terry gently lifted Vincent's hand from her waist and placed it on the bed between them. She slipped from under the sheets and quietly made her way towards the kitchen. She was stark naked and comfortable. She was in her prime, had inherited her mother's figure and had sculptured it through a life of sports and running.

"Where are you going?"

Terry glanced over her shoulder. Vincent was leaning on his elbow and looking at her through half opened eyes. He dwarfed her oversized bed.

She entered the small kitchen and grabbed a dented coffee pot that used to be her father's "Brewing some java so we don't spend the entire weekend in bed."

"Paradise Lost," said Vincent.

She smiled, turned on the gas burner and returned to the bedroom. She was enjoying his admiring stare when she thought of her late aunt, the old religious spinster, who raised her. *I love you Auntie, but I can't and don't want to be you.*

She slipped under the sheets and snuggled close.

Vincent, still leaning on his elbow, looked down at her, moving his fingers lightly over her lips.

"I love you," he said.

She turned away and looked out the window.

Vincent frowned, recently his work was taking him to Boston and messing with what was left of his personal life. He gently turned her head and kissed her on the forehead. "I'm sorry, we couldn't go out last night."

"I understand, can't blow your cover," whispered Terry. "Will we ever walk Crane's Beach again?"

"Sure, but we'll have to wait till off-season." Vincent smiled. "Wearing stocking caps and overcoats is a bit much in July."

When she turned away, he took a deep breath. "I've decided this is my last undercover job. I'm going to become a desk jockey. If you want, I'll follow you wherever your career takes you."

His words took her by surprise. Terry turned and looked at him, he wasn't joking. Her eyes filled with tears. She buried her face in his chest. Vincent hugged her gently.

***

The weekend had left Terry buoyed but unsettled. Her career was everything, and a man she was falling for had offered to sacrifice his for her. She was scared and not sure she could or wanted to reciprocate.

But on Monday morning, like all mornings, her emotions had been left at home. Her colleagues sitting across the table at the Golden Dragon only saw the confident, professional and good-natured Hamlin. For the last week Terry had been assigned to the two brick agents, the agency's term for those who worked the streets.

James Munroe was slightly more senior and responsible for her training. "Trailing a car in city traffic is not easy. Doing it at night jacks it up a level."

Salvatore Amero, a junior agent and close to her age, nodded as he worked on his second helping from the buffet. Munroe and Amero spent a lot of time together, exchanging insults. Terry knew that sometime that morning she had become one of the guys.

Terry finished her Thai chicken wrap and placed her napkin on the table. Munroe took a break from an oversized bowl of mystery ingredients lurking in an oily brown sauce. "Sal is not that polished. I hope he hasn't offended you over the last few days."

Terry laughed. "Don't worry, most of the agents I have worked with are men. Besides, when I played field hockey, the other teams often had a guy or two."

"I don't think real guys play field hockey," said Amero.

A taunting smile crossed Munroe's face. "You're right, but even they probably gave Terry a run for her money."

Terry returned the smile. "They had their strengths and their weaknesses."

"Yeah, what were their weaknesses?" asked Amero.

"They were downright horrible at face-offs."

"Why was that?" asked Munroe.

"When I hit the ball they didn't know what they should protect, their heads or their nuts."

"That's an understandable dilemma," said Amero.

"I'm shocked," said Munroe. "You'd threaten a man's masculinity for the sake of a game."

"Got that right," said Terry, looking him in the eyes.

Munroe and Amero exchanged looks of shock.

"Jeez, the next time we work together, I'm wearing a cup," said Munroe.

Amero wagged his finger. "Watch your mouth Munroe. Have you ever heard of sexual harassment."

"Don't worry, fellows," said Hamlin. "I'd never bring James up on harassment charges."

Amero frowned and looked at Terry with arms raised and palms to the sky. "Why not?"

"It's obvious, I'm one of those upstanding individuals with an honest, trusting face," said Munroe.

Terry smiled. "Really. I hadn't noticed."

"Then it must be one of my more subtle strengths."

Terry hesitated. "I wouldn't call it a strength. The jury would take one look at your small feet and automatically discount you as a sexual predator."

Amero had hoisted his glass and just taken a swig of soda. He sprayed what soda didn't go up his nose across the table. The three agents laughed so hard tears ran freely and then laughed harder upon seeing they were the center of the restaurant's attention.

Terry eventually regained her composure and decided it was best to stop while ahead. "Gentlemen, I have to go to the ladies room."

As she walked away from the table, Munroe's eyes followed her. "Sorry Sal, but I'm thinking of switching partners. She's beats you at breaking balls and is a lot better looking."

"It wouldn't work," said Amero.

"Why's that?" asked Munroe.

"Remember last February's all night stakeout?"

"Yeah."

"Do you remember the steak bomb submarine sandwich, the bowl of chili and how do I say this, your flatulence driving me out of the car into sub-zero weather?"

"I don't remember it exactly that way," said Munroe.

"Well. Just imagine sitting there all night with Terry," said Amero. "You'd have to choose between gas pains or being embarrassed because she was on the sidewalk, gasping."

"Do you think Terry farts?" asked Munroe.

"No"

"I didn't think so, either." Munroe sighed. "Okay, you can still be my partner."

"Thanks."

***

At nine that evening, Terry passed a large federalist colonial, made a u-turn and stopped behind Sal's parked car.

She put the transmission in park. "Nice home."

Amero got out of his car and slid into the back seat behind Terry and Munroe. "Mercedes and SUV are in the courtyard. What's the plan?"

"He usually makes his rounds this time of night, we'll wait thirty minutes," said Munroe. "Get in position."

Amero left Terry and Munroe and moved his old Pontiac Bonneville to monitor the courtyard. Terry backed her car down the street so the house was no longer visible.

"I've been tracking this guy on paper for years," said Terry. "I thought I knew him, but right now, it doesn't feel that way."

Munroe nodded as the three agents adjusted their headsets. Twenty minutes later, Amero spoke, "Subject has entered the court-yard. He's climbing into the SUV."

"We'll take the lead," said Munroe. "Let us know when he's about to go through the courtyard gates."

"Roger," said Amero.

Munroe said, "Terry, lights on, pull away from the curb and then stop. Once he enters the road, we'll start following him."

"Now," whispered Amero into his headset.

"Go," said Munroe.

Terry quickly accelerated to twenty and then held her speed. The SUV backed into the street, its three brake lights blinked brightly before it sped away.

"Memorize that light pattern, that's what you're following," said Munroe. "And speed up, Gallo doesn't pay attention to speed limits."

Munroe was all business. Terry closed the distance and was three cars behind. Gallo traveled down Commonwealth Avenue through Allston, towards Kenmore Square.

"Subject is reversing direction. He's about to cross over the trolley tracks in front of BU. Sal, you follow him, we'll continue on," said Munroe into his headset.

"Roger."

Terry and Munroe continued East on Commonwealth.

Amero pulled up behind Gallo, waited for the light to change and then followed the SUV.

"He's taking the BU Bridge to Cambridge," said Amero.

"Roger," said Munroe then he pointed. "Turn here."

Terry ignored the 'Do Not Turn' sign and crossed the trolley tracks. The trolley brakes screeched and its horn blared. Her pulse was pounding. Munroe calmly said, "Status?"

"He just went East on Memorial Drive," said Amero.

"Roger. We'll be with you in a minute."

"Terry, you can slow for red lights but don't stop unless you have to."

Terry went through two red lights and took the right onto the BU Bridge. She pushed the accelerator hard and weaved the old Chevrolet Impala through the traffic. Seconds later they were on Memorial drive, the traffic was light and they were catching up.

Without signaling, Gallo took a turn and again reversed direction. The traffic was too light for Amero or Terry to follow without being noticed.

Munroe said, "Sal pull over and watch where he goes, we'll take the next left."

Amero pulled to the curb and watched Gallo's SUV through his rear window as it traveled west on Memorial Avenue.

Terry had taken the next left and was traveling west at seventy miles an hour.

"Subject's still going west on Memorial, but seems to be slowing," said Amero.

"We've just sighted him," said Munroe, "Sal, catch up, but stay a few hundred yards behind."

Amero was right, Gallo had slowed and Terry braked hard to maintain a distance. Then Gallo turned down a narrow passageway between two buildings.

"Sal, the subject just took a right down an alley. Pull over and run your ass down there."

"Roger," said Amero.

"Terry, pull to the curb," said Munroe.

Terry and Munroe listened to heavy breathing and the sounds of Amero's feet hitting the pavement.

Amero stopped behind one of the dumpsters lining the alley and spoke into his headset. "Subject is parked. He's sitting in the SUV, turning his head back and forth."

"What's he looking at?" asked Munroe.

"Not much, the back of some building with nothing but a door. Maybe he's waiting for somebody."

Amero was a runner, his breathing had returned to normal. He whispered into his headset, "Subject's vehicle is moving. He's headed out of the alley."

"Roger, we'll take over the tail," said Munroe. "Catch-up as soon as you can,"

***

Later that night two cars were alone in the back corner of a Burger King parking lot. The floodlight was flickering. They were leaning against the cars, each with a cup in their hand.

Munroe raised his coffee to Terry. "Good job at the wheel."

Amero saluted with his cup. "Not bad."

She was beat, her shoulders ached from gripping the steering wheel, but she smiled. "Guys, I don't own a car. The last time I drove one was three months ago and I drove under the speed limit like my late aunt taught me. I feel like I just competed in NASCAR."

Munroe raised the cup a second time. "In that case, you did a damn good job."

Terry smiled. "Do you have any idea why Gallo was gallivanting around greater Boston?"

"Gallo is all business, so I doubt it was a joyride," said Munroe. "But tonight he didn't stick to his routine of bookies and dealers."

"I can't imagine a Cambridge alleyway and a Brookline neighborhood being a joyride," said Amero as he glanced at his watch. "Jesus, it's late."

Munroe looked at his watch and yawned. "Let's return the cars tomorrow." He opened the door to the Impala. "I'll drop Terry off on the way home and we'll meet at nine to go over the report."

"What report?" asked Amero.

Munroe smiled, reached into the car, yanked the GPS unit from the dash and handed it to Terry. "The tailing report that Agent Hamlin is going to write."

Terry was exhausted and looking forward to falling into bed, but realized the night would be spent with her laptop and the GPS that had mapped their travels. "Maybe Sal should take me home, that way I won't hurt your feelings when I start calling you names."

"That's okay. Sticks, stones and names don't hurt, just typos," said Munroe.

Munroe started the car. She slid into the passenger seat, promising herself it would be the best trailing report Munroe had ever read.

LUNCH

The private dining room was on the third floor of Locke-Obers, across the Commons from the State House. It was the place Nathaniel Forbes held meetings that never happened. The place where he made deals that could never be documented or sanctioned.

On finishing his salad, Forbes surveyed the small room. Nigel Burn was sitting across the table, a waiter was silently standing in the doorway. The middle-aged waiter wanted to know if he should supply Burn with a menu. Forbes discreetly shook his head and the man disappeared.

Burn had been in the straight-backed chair for ten minutes and had received only the briefest of greetings between mouthfuls of assorted greens and sliced radishes. Forbes had watched Burn become more and more furious as he waited. Forbes broke off a piece of bread and sponged the remnants of dressing from the salad plate.

"Nigel, you asked for this meeting. What's on your mind?" said Forbes as he placed the bread in his mouth.

Burn unclenched his jaw. "I have two issues, they both relate to the hazardous waste dumping in Chelsea."

Forbes wiped his lips with a linen napkin. "Oh yes, that unfortunate mishap."

Burn frowned. "The newspapers indicate the project is shutdown, but there are no details."

"Since you were kind enough to forewarn us, my staff had ample time to exploit the situation and there are many details," said Forbes. "Which left us wondering how you knew of the spill before the authorities."

Burn winced. "Is the shutdown permanent?"

"Unlikely, there's pressure to restart," said Forbes. "But even if they were to start tomorrow, the cost of idling all those men and equipment has to be astronomical."

"What's your best guess as to how long they'll be closed?" asked Burn.

"I make it a policy not to guess. But, let me describe what transpired after the dumping made the news," said Forbes. "The Director of the Department of Environmental Protection, with my encouragement, called the Mayor and applied pressure. My staff also alerted some of the more radical environmental groups."

"Is that the extent of what can be done?" asked Burn.

"Not entirely. My firm is giving legal advice to environmental activists seeking an injunction against AEG and I'm arranging for a sympathetic judge to hear the argument."

"Is there any way of including Bill Conors in the litigation?"

Forbes looked at Burn. "Is your interest in Conors' demise, personal or professional?"

"Both."

Forbes leaned back into his chair as he continued to stare at Burn. "For the time being, my firm will add his name to the injunction," said Forbes.

Burn nodded. "There's another issue I need your advice on. But it's very confidential."

"Nigel, you made the wise decision of putting my firm on retainer. All our discussions are attorney-client privileged."

"Well, that being the case," said Burn turning to see if anyone was near the open door. "The waste dumped into the Chelsea River was from a site my company is managing. Unknown to me, a union trucker made arrangements with the mob to dump the waste."

A slight rise in Forbes' left eyebrow was the only change in the attorney's expressionless face. Burn glanced again at the doorway. "Three days later, I receive a photograph of a Burgess LTD truck dumping the waste. That night on the way to my car, I'm stopped by the mobster, Ray Gallo. He says I'll have a visitor from his construction company and suggests that I listen carefully."

"Well Nigel, I'd say the young Gallo did a good job of setting you up. Contrary to rumors he must take after his old man."

"I don't care who he takes after."

Forbes studied his client, until his dark eyes made Burn uneasy. "None of this adds up. Why would some union guy dump your waste in Chelsea?"

Burn squirmed, his throat was dry and his voice croaked. "I don't know. Maybe the guy thought he'd have more job security if our competitors go out of business."

Forbes leaned towards Burns. "I can't help, if you persist in lying. Union workers don't plot to take down one company versus another. They don't give a shit who's paying them."

Burn looked towards the floor. "You're right, it was an idea I threw out for discussion. But I never expected the mob to get involved."

"Who did you expect, the Sisters of St. Joseph?"

Burn raised his clenched hand as if he was about to hit the table. "Okay, I made a mistake. Can you fix it?"

"In case you haven't noticed," said Forbes. "I work for the citizens of the Commonwealth, not La Cosa Nostra."

Burn's jaw went slack. He had assumed the long reach of Nathaniel Forbes even extended into organized crime.

After a long pause, Forbes spoke in a low voice. "I need that picture. I want to know what we're up against."

Burn swallowed. "Thanks, I need this to go away."

Forbes pushed his chair back from the table. "My firm has spent a lot of time complicating life for Conors and AEG. Your retainer has been spent and then some. Somebody from my firm will be contacting you about the additional charges. I strongly advise you to establish a hundred thousand dollar retainer. You're going to need it."

"A hundred thousand. Bloody Christ, my division is barely breaking even."

Forbes stood. "Cheap compared to the alternative."

He and Burn parted as they left the restaurant. Forbes crossed Tremont Street and walked to the center of the Commons. He slowed his pace and turned to see if anybody was within hearing distance.

Using a prepaid cell phone, he dialed a number that rang in New York City. After a dozen rings, a raspy, heavily accented voice answered, "Privet."

"Yuri, this is your friend from Boston, I have another job for that gentleman. Hopefully, he can do better this time."

IGNITION
Late July

The monitoring pipes had been required by the Environmental Protection Agency and driven to a depth of twelve feet leaving the top eighteen inches above ground. A man kneeling by one of the pipes wiped the sweat from his eyes and scanned the horizon. It was a moonless night and he could only see a dozen feet in each direction. He decided he was still alone, clicked on the LED light strapped to his head and for the sixth time that night pumped the handle on a small hydraulic jack until the padlock snapped.

He removed the pipe cap with a monkey wrench and quietly placed the wrench and cap on the ground and then pulled a two-foot long cylinder from a backpack. The man stood the cylinder on its end and carefully pressed an electronic timer into its top. Using a nylon string, he lowered the cylinder to the bottom of the pipe. The man replaced the pipe cap, tightened it with the wrench, clicked off the LED light and disappeared into the darkness.

To exploit the confusion of a dark night, timers in six different pipes completed a circuit at 1:30:00 a.m. and sent an electrical current into the blasting caps that sat above the Semtex. The exploding blasting caps instantly transformed the plastic explosive into enough superheated gas to fill a football stadium.

The resulting pressure blew the pipes and the surrounding soil hundreds of feet into the air. A shockwave traveled at twenty times the speed of sound. It shattered steel and concrete within a 500 foot radius and all windows within a quarter mile before dissipating into a thunderous rumble felt fifteen miles away.

Within seconds, the site was transformed into an inferno with flames reaching hundreds of feet above Chelsea.

***

At 2 a.m., the phone rang. Bill Conors rolled over and started snoring. The previous evening he cooked, wrestled with the twins, put them to bed and worked till midnight. Night calls were always for his wife, some nurse with questions about a drug or a test. Sometimes more than a simple answer was needed and she'd leave for the hospital.

Kristin sat up blinking and picked-up the phone. "Hello".

"Wait a minute please." She shook her husband. "Bill, it's for you."

Speaking into the pillow, Conors asked, "Who is it?"

"The Chelsea Emergency Response Center."

***

Twenty minutes later, Conors was in his black Taurus SHO speeding towards Chelsea, pushing the channel buttons on the radio. He was bouncing between elevator music and talk show hosts when he hit on a news report.

"Our van was one of the last vehicles the police allowed onto the Tobin Bridge. We're half way across the bridge and three quarters of a mile from the fire. I'm outside the van and can feel the heat and see the blinking lights of emergency vehicles through the black smoke. Fire trucks and ambulances from surrounding cities are streaming into the area known as the Chelsea Project. Can't tell what's on fire but we do know that an explosion occurred an hour ago. We felt it in our Boston studios."

"The Chelsea Project has recently made the news for other reasons. Work on the site was shut down three weeks ago because of a hazardous waste spill. Tonight, the Chelsea Project has a much bigger and more serious problem. Some have compared the size of the Chelsea Project to the Big Dig, and that may not be the only similarity. My sources are saying the Chelsea Project is also cursed with mismanagement."

"Asshole," yelled Conors. "Get your facts straight."

The radio fell silent for a few seconds. The commentator returned, "Sorry about that delay, the wind has shifted and the smoke is coming our way. We have been ordered off the bridge. This is Tim McMann for 1010 AM on your radio dial."

***

A State Trooper was turning traffic away from the Sumner Tunnel. Conors did a U-turn, went the wrong way down a one-way street and sped across Boston's North End and the side streets of Charleston and Everett.

By 3 a.m. he was several blocks from the Chelsea Project and slowly proceeding down Williams Street. Both sides of the road were lined with emergency vehicles. Police and firemen were herding long lines of citizens down sidewalks towards an elementary school. Many had handkerchiefs over their faces, warding off smoke and the soot that was falling like big black snowflakes.

Conors put on his hazard blinkers and the white hardhat that had been sitting on the passenger seat. He continued weaving between emergency vehicles. Eventually there were no citizens and only emergency personnel. Some were talking on radios, most were rushing about. On Marginal Street, the smoke and soot became thicker and the shattered glass on the sidewalks and street glistened in the red and blue of emergency lights.

He rolled down the driver's window and glanced up at the buildings and the missing windows. Conors' grip on the steering wheel weakened, his mind went into overdrive.

"What the hell are you doing here?"

Conors turned to see a soot-covered fireman.

***

Conors and the fireman walked down Marginal Street towards the Chelsea Project and the heat. They passed more emergency equipment and shifts of firemen coming and going towards the fire. They jumped behind a parked fire truck when a Mass General ambulance sped down the crammed street, taking firemen to the hospital. Medics who were operating a triage center handed bottles of water to everyone who passed and offered Conors a gas mask that he adjusted and placed over his mouth and nose.

Conors' eyes were burning and he was drenched in sweat by the time he and the fireman reached their destination. Three lime-yellow trailers were upwind of the fire. The middle trailer had a dozen antennae and the words 'Commonwealth of Massachusetts' emblazoned across its side. He stopped and turned towards the smoke and the unseen fire beyond. A distant maze of fire hoses crisscrossed each other and snaked into a swirling blackness.

The fireman yelled, "Let's get out of this heat."

Conors followed him up the stairs, into the command center.

Inside, the fireman stood silently as a tall, gray-haired, man gave orders. The words 'COMMONWEALTH OF MASSACHUSETTS—FIRST RESPONSE' were barely visible under the soot that covered the back of his once phosphorescent-lime coat. The man was facing four uniformed men sitting at computers and wearing headsets.

"Damn right I'm serious. Evacuate the eastern quadrant of Chelsea and make sure East Boston is prepared to do the same."

The four men started issuing orders over their radios and the fireman escorting Conors approached.

"Chief O'Malley, this is Mr. Conors, the president of AEG, the company in charge of the Chelsea Project."

A black outline where he had worn a gas mask circled the chief's pale skin and faded blue eyes. "So you're the guy in charge of this fiasco?"

Conors looked the Chief in the eye. "I'm here to offer assistance. Take it or leave it."

"Want to help. Tell me what the hell is burning like the damn fires of Nagasaki."

"Where's the fire?" asked Conors.

The Chief took two big steps towards a map-covered wall. With a soot-covered finger he circled an area that was a hundred feet inland from where the Chelsea and Mystic Rivers met. He turned and glared at Conors.

Conors was familiar with every square foot of the Chelsea Project, but more familiar with heavily contaminated portions. This area he knew better than any other. Conors eyes moved from the smudged map to the Chief.

"This area has been used by assorted industries since the 1700s. The last business on the site was a fly-by-night lead recycler in the eighties. Prior to that it housed a solvent tank farm built over the remains of a municipal gas plant. The underlying soils are so heavily contaminated with high BTU waste that once ignited they would burn like Nagasaki."

The Chief nodded and turned towards the map. "What on the site would explode like a hundred tons of TNT?"

"As of yesterday, nothing," said Conors.

"What the hell do you mean, nothing?"

"For the last twenty years this portion of the site was used as a lover's lane. We razed the few remaining buildings. Heavy equipment crisscrossed the site. Wells were drilled and open-flame metal cutting equipment was employed to dismantle the tank farm."

He hesitated long enough to give the Chief a chance to ask a question. The Chief didn't.

"We never encountered any problem with fires or explosions. After we characterized the soil contamination we covered the site with 2 feet of sand. As of yesterday there was no potential for an explosion," said Conors.

The Chief studied Conors. "Are you suggesting arson?"

"Yes."

The Chief looked at the map, nodding his head. "Mr. Conors get some coffee. It's going to be a long night."

***

Chief O'Malley repeatedly called on Conors' familiarity with the site as he confined and eventually brought the fire under control. When Conors wasn't answering the Chief's questions about wastes and access roads, he was answering questions from the rest of the staff. A public relations expert kept the press and the public informed and away from the emergency responders. In the smaller trailer the PR person had a bank of TVs tuned to various stations. Conors periodically assisted him with site and operational details.

As the morning progressed, local and national media spouted hyperboles and superlatives as they repetitively showed a Chelsea woman by her clothesline full of soiled laundry, dirty-faced children standing in glass-strewn streets, clammers and fishermen angry about closed fishing grounds and experts opining about liability and health risks.

Conors forced himself to ignore the media. As daylight arrived, he assessed the damage, started making plans, contacted his men and mobilized the necessary equipment.

***

When the State Police Arson Team arrived and saw six craters, they called the FBI and Homeland Security. By late morning, the Coast Guard had discovered a pipe fragment embedded in a piling. The FBI was hopeful analysis of the projectile would indicate what type of explosive was used.

At noon, Conors was at a desk in an AEG trailer. The trailer had been far enough from the fire that everything was intact except for cracks in the Plexiglas windows. He had spent the morning negotiating with contractors and trucking companies to cleanup the aftermath of the fire.

Conors put down a water bottle and grabbed the ringing phone. "Conors."

"Around half of our Denver and San Francisco staffs will be here by tomorrow morning," said Kimani.

"Good. I've developed a response plan and can use all of them."

"What's the latest?" asked Kimani.

"The FBI mentioned something about terrorists and eco-terrorism."

"And what do you think?" said Kimani.

"Eco-terrorists are into trees, not inner cities and terrorists are into blowing-up people, not abandoned property."

After a dead silence, Conors said, "What's up?"

"I don't like it, this project has been cursed from day one."

"I didn't think MIT professors believed in curses," said Conors.

"Thanks to you seducing me with the big bucks, I'm no longer a professor and besides I'm a Nigerian. My ancestors invented Voodoo."

"I'll keep that in mind."

"Bill I'm serious. The damn state fought each and every permit, contractors walked away from multimillion dollar contracts. Then a company car blows-up, a truckload of hazardous waste magically appears and now the Chelsea Project literally explodes. What the hell is going on?"

Conors took a deep breath and exhaled. "I don't know. I've been trying to put my arms around it and always end up figuring my old boss, Nigel Burn, is behind it. Then I eliminate him as a potential suspect, not because it's below him, but because he doesn't have the brains to pull off shit like this."

"If not him, then who?"

"I have no freaking idea."

"If this shit keeps up, someone is going to get killed."

"Already happened," said Conors.

"What?"

"Last night seventeen firemen were hospitalized. The prognosis is that they'll all be fine, but an elderly woman died of a heart attack during the evacuation," said Conors.

"Now we're killing people."

"Christ Matt, we're not killing anybody. It's the goddamn bastards who are sabotaging us."

Conors got to his feet. "I hope to God, you're not talking this shit in front of our employees." He stopped when the trailer door was pushed open by an AEG supervisor.

"Bill, a State Trooper is here with a cease and desist order. He wants everybody off the site, now."

"Matt, I'll call back."

MONEY TALKS
First Week of August

"Bullshit."

Conors sat in his Cambridge office gripping a newspaper. His bloodshot eyes were locked on the front page, '*Chelsea Poisoned by the Most Toxic Compound Known to Man*'.

"There's no way that damn fire could create those levels of dioxin."

It had been a long week of battling the state and the city of Chelsea. Fortunately, Kimani had returned to his old reliable self and Conors' best ally. Chief O'Malley and a number of federal and state scientists also came to Conors' defense. Following a series of TV and radio interviews by Conors and a FBI press conference, the public understood the explosion was an act of arson, if not terrorism, and that AEG had not been negligent. Nevertheless, a second stop-work order had been issued, it lay crumpled on the floor. Lawyers were proceeding forward with injunctions and there was talk of a class-action suit. The newspaper headline was just the most recent salvo.

He shook his head and turned his chair away from the desk. A narrow slice of the Charles River was visible from his office. A flotilla of small sailboats scurried in and out of sight, disappearing and reappearing from behind the buildings that framed his view. The boats reminded him of the vacation, and the work that had to be done before he could leave.

Shoving the newspaper aside, he returned his attention to the plans for AEG's new offices. They were designed to accommodate the increased staff needed for the Chelsea Project. Before the shutdown and before losing a large project in San Francisco, he had signed a lease for the additional space. Conors was checking the plans versus contract specifications, when he was interrupted by the intercom.

"Bill, Sam Wyland is on line two," said Lisa.

Conors rested his hand on the phone wondering if he wanted to speak to Wyland. Conors had hired him to setup financing for the Chelsea Project. Wyland worked his magic and had pulled together a consortium of bankers and real estate moguls.

He picked up the phone. "Hi Sam, what do the moneymen have to say?"

"They're all spooked. We have to do some handholding."

"When?" asked Conors.

"Tomorrow, I've scheduled meetings across the country. We'll be gone about a week."

"Shit, I have a family vacation planned."

"Sorry," said Wyland.

Conors slouched into his chair, staring at the phone.

HOTEL

Tuesday, the Second Week of August

He leaned back into the hotel chair, sipping the last from an upturned bottle of Aquafina. Conors had spent the week traveling across the country answering questions from bankers, investment firms and billionaires who had been repeatedly screwed by engineering companies. Each meeting started with skeptics yelling and blustering. Each meeting ended with investors confident the Chelsea Project would be completed on schedule and on budget. Sam Wyland was ecstatic.

Conors had enjoyed the contentious meetings, but with the crazed pace coming to an end and the adrenaline receding, he was revisiting the day he left for his trip.

"Divorce," whispered Conors, while gently tapping the empty water bottle on the desk. His head hurt and his gut felt like a big hand was squeezing it. Conors grew up in a tough city, stood toe-to-toe with the toughest and made a damn tough Marine. But as he slouched, staring at the blank wall, he was more wounded than tough. He hadn't felt this vulnerable since he was a kid.

At eleven, Conors had become the man of the house. His father had run an auto repair business that competed with the new Mayor's brother. Within weeks of the election, the zoning for his father's building was reclassified as residential, the bank called its mortgage, the family lost everything and his father died mysteriously. An alleged suicide in an abandoned building, with a gun he didn't own. Conors learned early that life wasn't fair, especially when politicians were involved.

His childhood was a blur of school, afterschool jobs, fistfights, meatless casseroles and a proud mother who smelled of tobacco and cheap perfume. As a young man, he discovered there were worlds different and better than his. His dream became a future devoid of the litter-covered streets, unpaid utility bills and the nightly serenade of police sirens.

Despite his childhood, Conors considered himself a lucky man. He loved the Marines, but the service was just part of the plan. After the Marines, he earned a double major in engineering and business followed by a masters in environmental engineering and a career in the fast lane. He had many friends and female companions, the latter departing when discovering they were a distant second to his career.

He pampered his chain-smoking mother until she fell ill, shortly after he started AEG. Despite the heroic efforts of a young doctor, she died of cancer.

Months later, Conors asked the doctor to lunch. The elegant but unassuming woman was the daughter of a Virginia surgeon, had gone to the best schools and grew up touring art museums and vacationing in Europe. They fell in love and married. Conors didn't believe things could get any better, until the twins arrived. His meteoric career and the arrival of grandchildren also improved relations with the in-laws, who had reservations about an inner city kid with no track record.

Before Conors left on his cross country trip, he learned his near perfect world was more fragile than he had ever imagined. He arrived home late, planning on breaking the bad news about the canceled vacation, but didn't. He had found his wife sitting at the kitchen table, in tears, mourning the loss of a patient. For weeks, Kristin had been in the library and on the phone with colleagues researching clinical trials and unapproved treatments. Nothing worked for the little boy who had an eerie resemblance to their sons.

Conors consoled Kristin as she cried herself to sleep. The following morning, over a breakfast of coffee for Kristin and a warm Pepsi for himself, he mentioned the need to re-schedule their long-awaited vacation.

"Are you kidding?" asked Kristin.

Conors looked at his can of Pepsi. "No."

"You're serious, you're not going to Disney World?"

"That's right."

"What the hell is wrong with you," screamed Kristen.

Conors gritted his teeth. A calm voice masked a surge of adrenaline. "Nothing other than somebody blowing up the part of Chelsea I happen to own and potential bankruptcy. You know, just small shit."

"Do you know how many months I've been begging colleagues to cover my practice?" said Kristen as tears filled her eyes. "Do you know how much this trip means to the boys?"

"I need to shore up the funding for the Chelsea Project."

"You live for that damn Chelsea Project. It's going to destroy us."

"Destroy us?" said Conors. "Christ, don't you understand, if I pull this off, we, our kids and our kids' kids will never have a financial worry."

"If, if, if. What if the Chelsea Project lands us in divorce court?" screamed Kristin.

He tried to answer but the words had lodged in his throat like a chunk of raw meat while the anger in her teary eyes twisted at his gut.

The hotel maid knocked on his door. Conors ignored her and continued to gently tap the empty water bottle on the hotel desk. He never believed it was a possibility until she had mentioned the word. The word had stabbed deep because for Kristin to have said it, she had contemplated it.

He crushed the plastic bottle. "Divorce."

NO FREE LUNCH

It was tuesday night, Raymond Gallo sat at his kitchen table lost in thought, not tasting the medium-rare filet mignon or the 1999 merlot. He had been relying on TAT telemarketing, the bookies, and the drugs to cover losses from his construction business. But his luck had continued downhill. Two trucks were repossessed before he could hide them and that morning the DEA had raided his Malden operation, confiscating a half million in coke, heroin and pills.

He lost interest in the meal, cleared the table and watched the garbage disposal grind through his steak. He went to bed, slept restlessly and woke to a Buick commercial at 6:30 a.m. He turned off the clock radio and slowly stood.

After a shower, Gallo dressed in a polo shirt, khakis and Italian loafers without socks. He grabbed the newspaper from the sidewalk, got in the Escalade, took Storrow Drive over the Tobin Bridge to Chelsea and parked behind City Hall.

He sat in his car for fifteen minutes, allowing Jack Milligan, the union representative, enough time to leave. Gallo locked his car and entered the basement floor of City Hall, weaved his way through the empty cubicles, slipped into Milligan's office, and closed the door adorned with a Massachusetts Municipal Union plaque.

He dialed a number, knowing Caller ID would indicate the call was from Chelsea City Hall.

"AEG, Lisa Kelly speaking."

"Hi Lisa, I'm Bob Osborne calling for the Mayor of Chelsea. The Mayor would like to meet with Mr. Conors. Is he in the office today?"

"Mr. Conors is presently on travel, but returning this afternoon."

"Good, the Mayor has an earlier appointment in Cambridge and was hoping to meet with Mr. Conors this evening."

"What time were you thinking of?"

"How late will Mr. Conors be at the office?"

"He has a conference call that should end by seven and then a dinner meeting at eight."

"That will work. Pencil the Mayor in for seven, but tell Mr. Conors that if the Mayor doesn't show by seven, it's because he's running late. Mr. Conors shouldn't wait."

Gallo hung up the phone and wiped it with a handkerchief, smudging any fingerprints. He did the same with the door knob and left the office.

***

Gallo drove to Revere, spent a couple of hours at Consolidated Construction and then headed towards East Boston. He was locking the SUV when Dominic opened the warehouse door.

"Getting pizza. Want anything?" asked Dominic.

Gallo needed something in his stomach. He pulled a fifty-dollar bill from a wad and handed it to Dominic. "Good idea, we're in for a long afternoon. Is Eric here?"

"Asleep on the couch."

"Get that caffeine shit he drinks. I want him awake."

"The office is boiling and the computers are crashing. He's been yelling and throwing things."

Gallo looked at the warehouse and shook his head. "Get your ass back here as soon as you can."

"Sure. What type of pizza you want?"

"I don't care, something with meat on it and pick-up a few bottles of Coke."

He entered the warehouse, passed by the door to TAT and climbed the stairs to PPI. By the time Gallo made it to the second-floor his polo shirt was sticking to his back. He looked at the thermostat. It registered eighty-seven degrees.

He walked down the hall to Eric's computer room. It was a disaster, with scattered papers and manuals everywhere. Two fans were blowing air at opposite sides of a disassembled computer and Eric was asleep on the couch.

"Looks like a crack house."

Gallo shook his head, made his way to his office, aimed a fan at his desk, and pulled a manila folder labeled 'AEG/Conors' from a green file cabinet. After learning about the Chelsea Project, he had PPI investigate Bill Conors. Dominic had stolen the family's rubbish, replacing it with bags filled with crumpled newspaper. Eric had hacked Conors' accounts and monitored his credit cards. Gallo had read Conors' email, knew their travel plans, the cars they drove, where their kids went to daycare, social security numbers and their incomes.

Dominic had also trailed Conors and his wife on a few occasions. From the surveillance pictures, Gallo determined that Conors was in reasonable shape with a thick neck and sloping shoulders. Although pretty and not looking her 36 years, Kristin Conors was too slim for Gallo's taste.

Despite his efforts, he failed to uncover any gambling or drug problems or sex addictions. Gallo was left with no leverage and had decided he'd have to play the heavy. Although not averse to threatening, Gallo preferred squeezing those who had something to hide. People like Conors were unpredictable.

He got to the end of the file and flipped to the beginning, hoping he had missed something.

***

An hour later, Gallo was still at his desk and had read the file twice. Three open pizza boxes were spread across a nearby table. Eric sat across from him washing down a third piece of anchovy pizza with his second can of Jolt soda. Dominic, with feet on his desk, was drinking from a two-liter bottle of Coke. The smell of garlic and fish was heavy in the hot air.

Gallo had lost his appetite, his heartburn had returned with a vengeance. He looked up from a half-eaten slice of pizza and wiped his forehead with a napkin. "Eric, you've read these files, tell me what I can use to squeeze Conors."

"Zero. I don't have anything on the bastard. He's a freaking boy scout," said Eric.

Gallo held up Conors' file. "So this has everything you know about Conors."

"Everything but his medical records."

Gallo wiped some tomato paste off his hand and threw the napkin on top of the pizza. "Well, get your ass in front of that computer and get something on this guy."

Eric ignored Gallo. He slumped into his chair, more interested in his pizza than the conversation. "I spent more time on Conors than anybody else. There's no shit on this dude. Conors is clean, or he's never been caught. Christ, the goddamn guy has high-level security clearance with the Navy. To get that, the FBI was in his underpants for six months."

Gallo was glaring at Eric. "What's this shit about clearances? That's not in Conors' file."

Eric was exhausted, he waved his hand dismissively. "Just some crap on AEG's website. He did some pollution work at a submarine base. I figured you wouldn't be interested."

He sensed movement and looked up. Gallo leaned forward, stopping when their faces were a foot apart. He grabbed the braided string necklace Eric had bought at a Dave Matthews concert and yanked it tight around Eric's neck.

"You little shit. You're going to put down that pizza and get me everything you have on Conors. And remember one thing. I'm the only one who decides what I'm interested in. Do you understand?"

Eric's bladder suddenly, felt full. Gallo continued to tighten the hold on the necklace. Eric answered in a raspy voice, "Understand."

Gallo let go. "Excellent, now find something I can use to pressure Conors."

"Sure," gasped Eric. He clumsily got up from the chair, holding his throat. He stumbled as he backed out of the office.

Lowering himself into his chair, Gallo saw Dominic staring at him. "What the fuck are you looking at?"

Dominic had seen Gallo's temper before. Once a dealer was explaining how a runner had disappeared with a grand's worth of crack when Gallo smashed the dealer's hand with a whisky bottle. Then Gallo calmly told the whimpering dealer that his head was next if he didn't have his grand within twenty-four hours.

"Nothing Ray," Dominic said. "You were just a little hard on the kid."

Gallo got to his feet.

"But I agree, you should make the decisions," said Dominic.

Gallo leaned over the desk and yelled. "I'm fucking glad you'll allow me to make the decisions. I'm also glad you feel sorry for the kid, because if you ever screw up, you'll be fucking sorry for yourself and it won't be because of what I said."

Gallo sat down.

"Get me everything that kid has on Conors," said Gallo. "And keep the idiot away or I'll kill him."

Dominic left. Gallo walked around the office and then sat at his desk. He calmly ate a slice of pizza. He felt better. There was something about the fear in people's eyes that made him feel good, made him feel in control.

***

Gallo had eaten his third slice when Dominic placed forty pages on his desk. "Here's a print-out of the AEG website, some background material and travel arrangements. You already saw the itinerary for Conors' business trip, but not his family's. After they cancelled the trip to Orlando, the wife and kids booked a flight to Washington D.C. Conors returns today, but his family isn't coming back till Friday."

Gallo remained silent.

"Eric's still searching for more info," said Domenic on his way to the door.

Gallo picked up the itinerary and committed the names of Conors' wife and kids to memory. He reviewed the print-out of the website and discovered AEG had projects across the nation. The Chelsea Project was the largest by far. A bird's-eye view of the planned construction showed the magnitude of the project.

"I've got to have a piece of this."

The information on Conors' background was old news. Conors came from Lynn. Gallo saw that as good news, because Conors would remember when the mob ruled Lynn. He'd also remember the bodies floating in Lynn Harbor and understand that a threat from La Cosa Nostra was to be taken seriously. He placed the print-out on his desk, and dialed a number.

"We're still on for tonight. Need you there before six," said Gallo

"Same plan?" asked Tony.

"Yeah."

He hung up, gathered the file and printouts and took them to the shredder. While feeding the papers, a photograph of Conors fluttered to the floor. Gallo picked it up and smiled. "You don't know it yet, but your life is about to change."

He dropped the picture into the machine. It disintegrated into confetti.

WELCOME HOME

Conors pulled the phone from the back of the seat, swiped his credit card and dialed a number.

"Where are you?" asked Lisa.

"Best guess is about 30,000 feet above Iowa."

"How's the flight?"

"Booked and I have a middle seat. I'll leave the rest to your imagination."

"Sounds like fun. When are you arriving?"

"Land about one, should be in the office by two. What's my schedule like?"

"A few calls I couldn't delegate, including an evening conference call with the San Francisco Office. More importantly, you have a potential meeting with the Mayor of Chelsea, before the Chamber of Commerce dinner."

"What meeting?"

"The mayor's office asked for a short meeting. No agenda was mentioned," said Lisa.

"Interesting."

"How were the bankers in San Francisco?" asked Lisa.

"Like the ones in New York, Chicago and Houston. Smart people who've made a lot of money and want more. Anything else on today's schedule?"

"Nope."

"What's the final word from Ford about our exploding van?" asked Conors.

"No recalls on that model."

"What about explosions?"

"The engineers in Detroit claimed this is the first they've heard of any explosions."

Conors sighed. He'd been reviewing the last few months and hoping at least the car explosion had some explanation other than what his gut had been telling him.

"Okay," said Conors. "I'm going to get some shut-eye. See you around two."

***

The plane landed on time and except for a flurry of taxis at the airport, the traffic was light. Conors stopped at a red light and jacked up the air conditioner on his old Taurus, the humidity was worse than when he had left. He glanced at the cell phone resting on the passenger seat. He finished the last of the diet Pepsi, dropped the can on the floor and stared at the phone again. The traffic light was still red. He grabbed the phone and dialed the number for his in-laws.

"Hello," said a soft voice that reminded Conors how much he missed his wife.

"Hi," said Conors.

"How's my man?" said Kristin as she sat on a bed.

"Beat."

"Better get your sleep. After eight days, it's your turn to be the pampering parent."

"That's a deal. How are the little monsters?"

"They're at the matinee, a Disney movie. Grammy and Grampy are spoiling them rotten."

The word 'Disney' stopped Conors. His wife couldn't cancel her vacation, but did cancel the trip to Disney World. She took the twins to visit her parents.

"Sounds like they're living up to their job description," said Conors.

"Bill, I miss you."

Conors hesitated. "Kristin, I'm sorry. I wish I could've been with you and the boys."

"I know. Let's not have this vacationing without daddy become a habit."

"It won't, I promise," said Conors. "I'll pick you and the boys up at Logan, on Friday."

"Don't bother. I have to go to Dana-Farber. I need to check on one patient in particular. We'll meet at home."

"Okay. It's hot in Beantown. Unless you have other plans, let's spend the last three days of your vacation in Gloucester."

"Gloucester sounds great." said Kristin.

"The office is trying to get through. We'll talk tonight."

"I love you," said Kristin listening to the dial tone. She put the phone down on a pink night table and looked around her childhood bedroom, unchanged since high school. "One hell of a vacation."

CONVERGENCE

After reviewing the computer printouts, Gallo left the East Boston warehouse, drove home and lay on a sofa lost in thought, not intending to fall asleep.

The sun was low when Gallo finally woke to an uneven stomach and the taste of pizza. He slowly got to his feet and stood by the couch. He had lost three hours and felt rushed. He changed into chinos and a polo shirt. Instead of his beloved Italian loafers, Gallo picked a pair of shoes that added a good inch to his height, and went downstairs.

He stopped by the refrigerator. The first Coke washed away the unpleasant taste and gave him a needed hit of caffeine. He didn't remember drinking the second can, his mind wasn't in the designer kitchen, it was in Cambridge rehearsing what he would say and do.

***

Gallo drove past Copp's Hill cemetery in the North End, took a right onto Michelangelo and stopped by the last building on the dead end street. His bookie was sitting behind a dirty bulletproof polycarbonate window. Gallo tapped the horn. The bookie joined him, leaned against the SUV and passed a fat envelope with the number twenty-six penciled on the top left corner.

Gallo glanced at the envelope. "What the hell happened?"

"Some long-shot horse won at Suffolk Downs and this guy from Quincy had bet a grand at forty-to-one."

"Does he know something we don't?"

"I don't think so, this guy loses a shitload every year. He gets paid once a month and makes these long-shot bets. When he wins, he thinks he's on a streak. Last night, he lost twenty grand. Friday's envelope will look more normal."

Gallo placed the envelope in the center console and put the transmission in reverse. "If you're setting the odds right, it should look better than normal."

Fifteen minutes later he was in Cambridge, turned off Memorial Drive and drove down a long alleyway. At the very end, the alley widened into a tennis court sized box created by the massive foundations of adjoining buildings. An oversized dumpster on the right took up half the area, but he had a clear view of the black Taurus and a metal emergency exit door for the largest building.

Sunset was an hour away, but in the shadow of the high-rises it had arrived. He parked in the narrow part of the alley, blocking any car from leaving.

A few minutes later, a man in coveralls and a matching cap opened the exit door. Tony jogged across the alleyway. He pulled the passenger door open and slipped into the bucket seat next to Gallo.

"Christ, even in the shade it's hot as hell."

"Any problems?" asked Gallo.

"No, I've been going in and out of the lobby for thirty minutes. If you have a uniform and a toolbox the security people don't pay attention."

"Is that Conors' car?"

"Yeah, I checked the plates," said Tony.

Gallo opened the door and looked up. He figured at least the first eight floors were windowless, the architects apparently decided the view wasn't worth the glass.

"You're sure there's no surveillance camera?" asked Gallo.

"Yeah."

"Exits are usually monitored."

"This door was never designed to be used routinely."

Gallo pointed at the large roll-off dumpster. "The janitors must use the door for the trash."

"Not this one. I overheard the guards talking, AEG is growing and taking over another floor. The remodeling company is using this dumpster."

Gallo grimaced. "The asshole is expanding and I'm bleeding to death."

He pointed at the walkie-talkie resting on the console. "Let me know when he's leaving the lobby. I'll handle things on this side."

"Should I meet you afterwards?" asked Tony.

"No, I'm headed to Nahant when I'm finished. Just make sure nobody else comes through that door. I don't want any witnesses."

"Don't worry, Boss. Conors will be the only one."

"Conors is expecting the mayor at seven. When the mayor doesn't show, he'll leave for his dinner meeting. You better get inside."

"Okay," said Tony. He crossed the asphalt and disappeared into the building.

Gallo looked at his watch. It was 6:50 p.m. He leaned back into the tan leather seat, listening to the rush of the air-conditioner. He was wondering how his father was taking the news about the drug bust, when he glanced at the black Taurus.

"Keep focused. This guy and the Chelsea Project are the answer to my problems."

At five past seven the acidic taste of pizza returned. He swallowed hard and turned down the air conditioner. He removed a silver-plated and engraved pistol from the glove compartment and slid it into his pants pocket.

The walkie-talkie broke the silence. "Conors is headed towards the exit."

"Okay," said Gallo as the door flew open.

***

Conors was tired and hot as he passed through the utility room. The mayor had stood him up and he was headed to a Chamber of Commerce dinner and endless questions about the shutdown.

Being the first tenant in the Kendal Square Office Building, Conors had claimed the single parking space at the rear of the building. It had direct access to Memorial Drive and avoided the worst of Cambridge traffic. When he pushed the door open, he was prepared for the heat and humidity. He stopped when he saw the SUV blocking his exit.

"Christ, just what I needed."

He unlocked his car, dropped his briefcase and suit coat on the back seat and headed toward the SUV. A man stepped from the Cadillac Escalade.

Conors stopped by the dumpster. "Could you back up about fifty feet?"

The man didn't answer and headed towards Conors.

"Hey, let's move your truck," said Conors in a louder voice.

The man kept walking. "Bill."

"Do I know you?" asked Conors.

"Not yet," said Gallo as he stopped in front of Conors.

"Not yet?" said Conors.

"I have a business proposition" said Gallo, offering his hand.

Conors wearily took the hand, assuming the man was one of the small-time contractors vying for his attention.

"And you are?" asked Conors.

"Ray Gallo."

Conors hesitated. He studied Gallo's face.

Gallo smiled. "Yes, that Ray Gallo."

Conors pulled his hand from Gallo's grip. "You'll never have a business proposition I'd listen to."

"You're dead wrong." said Gallo.

Three quick strides and Conors was at the exit door. He slid the key into the lock, turned it, it spun freely. The door remained locked. He tried two more times and stopped.

"Something wrong?" said Gallo.

Conors turned around. Gallo was still by the dumpster.

"Now that I have your attention, let's talk about the Chelsea Project," said Gallo.

"Nothing to talk about. I have federal loan guarantees and your companies have been blacklisted," said Conors.

"Bullshit. Within hours, I can have a lawyer draw up papers for a new corporation."

"Can't justify a contract with some unknown company."

"More bullshit," snapped Gallo, "I just want subcontract work, the small stuff you can easily approve."

Conors headed towards the alley. "This conversation's over."

Gallo stepped into his path and pulled the gun from his pants pocket. He yanked the pistol's slide, let it fly forward stripping a cartridge from the magazine. He aimed the gun at Conors' chest.

Conors froze.

"I decide when the conversation is over," said Gallo.

Conors watched Gallo's index finger, its tension on the trigger.

"Shooting me doesn't make sense."

"Depends on whether we'll be working together."

"Sure, we can work together," said Conors.

"Fuck you," said Gallo. "You're thinking, I'll just bullshit this guy and then call the feds."

Conors stood silently. Gallo had expected him to cave. He pointed the gun at Conors' head. "Here's how it works in the real world. At best, the feds indict me. But my lawyers are twice as smart as the young DAs."

Gallo nodded towards the surrounding buildings. "No security cameras, it's my word against yours, the indictment is thrown out and you become another name on the missing persons list."

"As far as I'm concerned, this meeting never happened."

"Wrong again," said Gallo. He took a step towards Conors. "And the three reasons this meeting will continue, are Kristin, little Kevin and Jack."

Conors' jaw clenched tight.

"If I remember correctly, your family's on travel, flying home this Friday."

Conors looked away from the gun barrel and locked eyes with Gallo. "Stay the fuck away from my family."

"Sorry Bill, that's not the way it works. If we don't come to terms, some night your pretty little wife will disappear. But unlike you, she won't end up in a landfill."

Gallo's finger played with the trigger, squeezing out the last of the slack.

"Once she's hooked on heroin, she'll do anything for the next fix," said Gallo. "And when we tire of her, she'll be worth an easy hundred grand to some Mid-Eastern pimp."

Conors blinked, Gallo figured he was starting to break, then Conors unexpectedly stepped forward. "You lay a finger on my wife and I'll—"

Gallo swung his arm, the butt of the pistol whipped toward Conors' face. Conors ducked. The blow glanced off the back of his head. Gallo was left off-balance.

Conors stepped into his punch, his knuckles smashed into the side of Gallo's face. Gallo slammed into the side of the dumpster, his head stopped with a thud, he fell to the ground, the pistol clattered across the asphalt.

With fists clenched he hovered over Gallo. When he failed to move, Conors cautiously rolled him over. His eyes locked on a deep depression in Gallo's left temple, blood was oozing and matting his hair.

He looked up at the dumpster and saw the protruding steel rod used to hoist the container. He immediately placed his fingers on Gallo's neck searching for a pulse. Finding none, he pressed harder, moved his fingers and then lifted his hand from the still warm body.

He stood, breathing heavy and fast. His first impulse to call 911 was immediately abandoned. Admitting to killing a mobster would be the same as signing his own death warrant. When he reached for Gallo's pistol, he heard the sound of an engine. He glanced at the SUV and then back at the body.

He slipped the gun into his pants pocket and ran to the SUV, stopping just before grabbing the door handle. Conors backed away and stared at the handle. With the back of his hand he wiped sweat from his forehead. "Slow down, you'll make things worse than they are."

Conors looked up and down the alley terrified that someone would open a building door or drive down the alley. He pulled off his shoes and socks and quickly slid his bare feet into the loafers and slipped the socks over his hands.

He grabbed the door handle, climbed in, slammed the transmission into drive and came to an abrupt stop next to Gallo. Heaved the limp body into the passenger seat, did a U-turn and accelerated down the alleyway swerving around dumpsters and trash cans.

His heart raced as he thought of places to dump the body and SUV. He accelerated onto Memorial Drive, searching for a parking space, when he saw the construction site. He hit the brakes and pulled into the dirt lot. It was abandoned, he pushed the gas to the floor and left a cloud of dust as the SUV sped to a far corner and skidded to a stop between a foundation and a large truck trailer.

Despite the sock-covered hands, he efficiently turned off the engine, opened the driver's door and stepped to the ground as he yanked Gallo's body into the driver's seat, snapping the cover off the center console. He removed a wad of bills from the dead man's pockets and stuffed the money into his. Gallo's thin wallet contained a driver license and credit cards, he took them and tossed the wallet into the back seat.

He placed Gallo in an upright position, closed the door and ran to the passenger side. He opened the glove compartment, grabbed the owner's manual and receipts, scattered them and pens, a tire gauge and ticket stubs over the floor.

In the center console he found napkins and CDs and threw them onto the back seat. He was about to empty the contents of a fat envelope when he discovered it was stuffed with money and jammed the envelope into his pocket with the credit cards. Then he snapped the hinges to the glove compartment door, left it hanging, scattered more papers and dumped a half-drunk can of soda on the floor. He stopped and glanced about the SUV. It looked like a car ransacked during a robbery. He pushed the lock button and closed the door.

Hidden by the vehicle, he grabbed the envelope and credit cards in his left hand and slipped the sock off his hand and over the money and cards. He stuffed the sock-covered articles in his pants pocket, then held the pistol in his right hand and repeated the process.

Sweat ran down Conors' face as he surveyed the construction site from the shadows of the foundation wall. Seeing nobody, he ran to the sidewalk and forced himself to walk the quarter mile to the alleyway. Finding it empty, he sprinted to his car, opened the trunk and slipped the two bulging socks under the felt floor mat.

He took a pair of dirty socks from his carry-on luggage, yanked them on and slipped on his loafers. It was 7:50 p.m., when Conors sped down the alleyway towards Memorial Drive.

GIOVANNI

Nahant is a small town, a narrow peninsula of granite projecting southeast into Massachusetts Bay. An east wind was blowing across the peninsula, it ruffled bushes and rattled the screen door of the solarium where Giovanni Gallo was sitting, irritated and becoming more irritated as the sun slipped below the horizon.

The solarium was attached to the ocean side of a four-story stucco mansion, the spoils from a life of hard work. Giovanni, a self-made man, fought his way from an immigrant mason, to a union organizer of longshoremen, to the capo-de-capo. The journey was longer and more bloody than planned, but he had never doubted himself.

At sixty-seven, Giovanni was a squat man, with fat slowly replacing what was once an abundance of muscle. On the evening that Raymond Gallo met Conors, Giovanni sat motionless, massive hands resting on the table, unaware of the wind and the rattling door. It was Wednesday, the day he had supper with his son at exactly 8 p.m. Business was the reason for the weekly dinner, but as important was the time with his son. After the loss of his wife and the violent death of a brother twenty years earlier, Raymond Gallo was his only family. By 9 p.m. Giovanni's irritation had morphed into anger.

"Padrone."

Giovanni looked up from his untouched meal and glared at his plump housekeeper and cook. Assuntina took a deep breath. "I put dinners in the oven until Raymond comes?"

"Has he called?" asked Giovanni.

"No, Padrone."

Giovanni looked at the table setting before him, the Buccellati silverware, the linens and the cold meals. "At least he could have called and offered one of his pathetic excuses."

Assuntina reached for his plate.

Giovanni shook his head. "No, I'll eat." Then he pointed at the meal on the opposite side of the table. "Throw that on the rocks."

Assuntina hesitated and looked at the dish she had labored over, hoping Raymond would notice. She'd been secretly in love with him for years. Wednesdays were as important to her as they were for the Padrone.

"Now," bellowed Giovanni.

Assuntina jumped. Like a beaten dog she crossed the expansive lawn and slid the meat, the yellow and red peppers onto a flat rock. Before she retreated to her kitchen the veal Marsala had disappeared under a storm of flapping wings and pecking beaks. Giovanni ignored the screeching gulls and ate his cold meal. It, or the Chianti, did not sit well.

By 10 p.m. Giovanni's anger had evaporated. He had planned on telling his son how the gulls enjoyed his dinner, but under the darkening sky, the memory of the vulture-like birds bothered him. When his son repeatedly failed to answer his phone, he sent men to check. His thoughts drifted to the feds, the Columbians and the Russians. He wasn't worried about threats from within La Cosa Nostra. His ruthless climb to power had eliminated the competition and brought peace to the New England crime family

***

At midnight, Giovanni was still sitting in the solarium. Two men were standing before him.

"He ain't home," said Carlo.

"And, he ain't at the warehouse or his construction company," said Santo.

"Did you speak to his people?" asked Giovanni.

"Yeah, called the computer kid and Dominic. They don't know where he is," said Santo.

"Couldn't get in touch with his guy, Tony. He don't answer his fuckin phone," said Carlo.

"Wait at Ray's house. Call me, if he shows up," said Giovanni.

After the men left, Giovanni made three phone calls. Then he headed to bed, feeling his age.

THE VILLA
Thursday

A few minutes before sunrise, Giovanni Gallo opened a desk draw, removed a cellular phone, inserted a battery and ran his thick finger down a list of names and telephone numbers.

The previous evening Tony had waited in a utility room making sure Conors was the only one to enter the alleyway. After an hour of pretending to work, he checked the alley, found it empty, re-assembled the door lock and left. When he arrived at his East Boston apartment, he ate left over pasta, drank a couple of beers and fell asleep watching a doubleheader. Around midnight he plugged in his dead cell phone on the way to bed. At 5 a.m., he woke to the sound of the phone vibrating on his night table.

"Yeah."

"Do you know where Ray is?"

Tony recognized the heavily accented voice. He was instantly awake. "No sir. The last time I saw Ray was last night."

"Come to Nahant."

Tony said, "When?"

"Now."

***

The electric gates opened and Tony drove down the cobblestone driveway. Angie directed him to a spot next to three cars.

"Leave the keys."

Tony parked the car and glanced in the rearview mirror at the portly Angie, a decades-old friend of Giovanni's. In his younger days, Angie was a key player in the Mob, lately he spent more time with grandchildren than with the business.

He handed the keys to Angie. "How are ya?"

"Been better."

"What's going down?"

"Ray didn't show-up last night. I told the Boss, Ray was probably getting laid. He don't believe it."

"What's he want me for?" asked Tony.

Angie shrugged his shoulders and headed towards the gates. "Go wait in the kitchen."

"Wait for what?" said Tony.

Angie continued walking. "Get some coffee."

"Fungula," whispered Tony as he headed towards the stucco mansion and entered the kitchen. He was greeted by the strong smell of coffee and Assuntina closing an oven door.

Eleven years earlier, Assuntina, a cousin of Giovanni's late wife arrived not speaking a word of English and joined the Gallo household. Now at twenty-eight the heavyset cook shrouded in a flowery housedress could pass for a middle-aged woman. They routinely crossed paths when he swept Giovanni's houses for eavesdropping devices.

She pointed at the door and glared at him. "I have no beetles."

"Cool down. The word is bugs and I'm not looking for them. I just want some coffee."

She half filled a mug from a large stainless pot, clunked the mug on the counter and gestured towards a small pitcher at the end of the marble counter. "Crema."

Tony glanced at the mug and then at Assuntina. "Thanks, I take it black."

He pulled a stool to the counter, sipped his coffee and watched Assuntina knead dried fruit into a large mass of dough.

"Assuntina, what's going on?"

She turned and saw the worried look in his brown eyes. "I cook. I don't know business."

Tony placed the cup on the counter, leaned toward her and whispered, "Giovanni has never said a word to me. Why would he suddenly want to talk?"

Her eyes flickered between Tony and the marble counter, nobody asked for her opinion, her flour-covered hands fidgeted with a spatula, she shyly nodded towards the ovens. "Want some ruota?"

"Sure."

A delicious smell spread through the kitchen as Assuntina removed a ring-shaped loaf from a warming oven. She cut a generous wedge, placed it on a plate in front of Tony and filled his cup. She waited as he smelled it and then took a large bite.

"Magnifico." He licked the warm amaretto sugar glaze from his fingers. "How do you do this?"

Assuntina shrugged her shoulders. "Like all Italian women, I cook."

"My nonna, mamma and two sisters can't cook this."

He finished the last of the ruota, it was replaced with a larger piece, he picked it up and then looked at Assuntina. "No idea why Giovanni wants to see me?"

"I know nothing. I brought coffee to them when Signore Miller come."

"So it's just Giovanni and Miller?"

"No, Nico is with them."

Tony lowered the pastry on the counter. "Nico."

Assuntina looked at the ruota and frowned.

"That guy's freaking scary," said Tony.

Assuntina shook her head. "Nico's a good man."

Tony looked over his shoulder. "That's the first nice word ever said about the guy."

Assuntina wiped the counter with a white towel, tossed the pastry in a waste basket and left without saying a word.

He pushed the coffee away wondering why Nico was there. Elbows were on the counter and Tony's head resting in his palms when Angie entered the kitchen.

"Let's move it."

Angie silently led Tony through a series of darkened hallways into the solarium. Tony squinted as he walked into the morning sun. At first, he could only see the outline of three men.

A heavy slouched man sitting at the table pointed at a chair and with a thick accent said, "Sit down."

Tony could hear Angie's retreating footsteps as he sat. Despite the glare of the sun, he was cold. His eyes slowly adjusted. Giovanni was sitting in the chair. To Giovanni's left was Nico, all muscle and as big as anybody on the New England Patriots. A loose gray polo shirt covered his gun. Eight months earlier, Nico was a nobody from Chicago working for one of Giovanni's Captains. Then four Uzi-toting Columbians pinned Giovanni behind his Caddy. Nico shot his Glock three times. Three Columbians with holes in their heads fell to the ground. The fourth ran for his life. Nico's reward was the waterfront. He ruled the docks and warehouses like an Afghan warlord, ordering longshoremen around like schoolchildren.

A slender man standing to the right of Giovanni spoke. "Tony, my name is Neil Miller. I'm counsel for Mr. Gallo and I'm glad you were able to join us."

Tony nodded and Miller continued, "An important matter is at hand. Mr. Gallo's son was scheduled to dine with him last night, but never arrived. Nor did he call to explain his absence. With this background, I'd like to ask a few questions."

Tony's eyes darted between Giovanni, Nico and the lawyer. In a breaking voice he said, "Sure whatever I can do."

"When was the last time you saw Ray?"

"Last night, between six and seven."

"Where was that?"

"Cambridge. Ray was parked in an alleyway behind the Kendal Square Office Building."

"What was Ray doing in a Cambridge alleyway?" asked Miller, as he scribbled notes on a yellow legal pad.

"He was getting ready to meet Bill Conors from AEG."

Miller glanced at Giovanni and then at Tony. "What is AEG?"

"AEG is an engineering company in charge of the construction work in Chelsea," said Tony.

"When you say construction work are you referring to the waterfront project, the Chelsea Project?"

"That's the one. Ray figured he could make a fortune, if he got a piece of the action."

"Who's Bill Conors?" asked Miller.

"Conors is the guy that runs AEG."

"Did Ray know Conors?"

"No, but Ray knew a lot about him."

"Was he alone when he met Mr. Conors?"

"Yes, Sir."

"Why the hell weren't you with him?" asked Giovanni.

Tony nervously glanced between Miller and Giovanni. "Ray told me to wait inside the building and make sure nobody else entered the alleyway. He didn't want any witnesses."

"Did Ray ever have meetings like this before?" asked Miller.

"Yeah, a few times with some lawyers and doctors."

"Was there anything different about this meeting?"

"I guess the big thing was that Ray didn't have the goods on Conors."

"What do you mean?" asked Miller

"The lawyers and doctors were cokeheads or married and screwing our hookers. Ray had pictures or some leverage over them."

"Lacking the goods, as you say, how was Ray going to influence Mr. Conors?"

"Ray knew a lot about Conors and planned on using the soft touch before playing the heavy."

"How did Ray learn so much about Conors?"

"For months, Ray had Eric searching for stuff on AEG, Conors and that Chelsea Project."

"Who is this Eric that you refer to?"

"Eric Wills. He's the computer hacker who gets the dirt on people."

"Can you get the information Eric has on AEG and Mr. Conors?"

"Sure."

"Can you do that today?"

"Yes Sir."

"When you recall last night, are you confident Conors and Ray actually met?"

"Yeah. I mean, I didn't see them meet, but I left Ray in the alleyway and then Conors went out the back door into the alley. The way Ray was parked, Conors couldn't get by."

"Did you see either Ray or Conors after the meeting?"

"As I said, Ray wanted me to stay inside. After a while, I looked in the alley and both cars were gone."

"Is there anything else you remember?"

"No sir."

"Okay," said Miller. "This is my business card. Since you are associated with Mr. Gallo's companies, I am your attorney. Therefore this meeting is attorney-client privileged. As far as others are concerned, this meeting did not occur. Do you understand?"

"Yes Sir."

"Giovanni, do you have any questions?"

Giovanni stared at Tony, then shook his head.

"Tony, other than getting those documents from Eric, that will be all for today," said Miller.

As Tony was getting up from his seat, Giovanni growled, "Tell Angie, I want to see him."

Tony nodded and left.

"Assuming he's telling the truth and I believe he is," said Miller. "Mr. Conors is the last known person to have seen your son."

"Do you think the feds have Ray?" asked Giovanni.

"I don't think so. DeLuca would only arrest Ray if he had a rock-solid case and he wouldn't jeopardize it by ignoring Ray's rights to call his attorney."

Giovanni fell silent. The mere mention of the name reminded Giovanni of DeLuca's parting words, 'pezzo di merda'. Twenty-five years earlier, Joseph DeLuca, a first generation Italian-American fresh from FBI training helped convict most of La Cosa Nostra's hierarchy. DeLuca had interrogated Giovanni for days. When he didn't break, DeLuca called him a 'pezzo di merda', a piece of shit.

"Giovanni," said Miller. "Could the Columbians or Russians be involved in Ray's disappearance?"

"I have people looking into that."

"Let me know what you find out. I will check my contacts at federal court and the police stations," Said Miller. "Meanwhile, let's hope Ray shows up with a serious hangover."

"Neil, I want you on this until we find Ray."

"My first priority." Miller closed his leather attaché and headed for the door. "I'll call this afternoon."

Angie passed the sober Neil Miller in the hallway and mumbled to himself, "This place is like a funeral home, the kid better show up soon."

Breathing heavily, Angie made his way across the solarium and stopped in front of Giovanni. "You want me."

"Yeah, you and Nico go with Tony. He has papers that you'll take to Neil."

Giovanni stood and looked towards the bay. "Don't tell Neil, but after dropping off the papers, you and Nico pick-up this Conors guy."

Angie frowned. "Who the hell is Conors?"

"I have the details," said Nico.

Angie looked at Nico and then at Giovanni. "Okay, Boss."

After Angie and Nico had left, Giovanni squinted into the sun. A voice from within was telling him something. Something he didn't want to hear.

THE DELIVERY

While tony was waiting in Giovanni's kitchen, Ron Zylinski was crossing the Tobin Bridge. Ron drove trucks for a construction company and had picked up a trailer full of concrete forms in New Hampshire. His goal was to deliver them to Cambridge before the morning traffic got heavy and be fishing on the Saugus River by afternoon.

Ron maneuvered the truck down the Cambridge streets like it was a subcompact and not a 500 horsepower diesel rig with a 35' trailer. When Ron pulled onto the Cambridge site, he saw a man parking his pickup truck. Ron got the site engineer's attention when he applied the air brakes.

"Eddie, I've got the large panels."

"Leave them over there," said the man pointing to the far corner of the site.

The groaning diesel reverberated off the concrete substructure that would someday support a MIT dormitory. He negotiated holes and construction equipment and was backing up when he jammed on his brakes.

"Jesus."

Ron shook his head, yanked on the emergency brake and walked to the engineers' trailer.

A few minutes later, Eddie and Ron were headed towards his rig.

"Do I need to have my wife show you how to drive," said Eddie.

"If she can put my rig where you want it, I'd like to meet her."

"Can't work around it?"

"Nope. It's a big SUV. I figure one of your engineers own it. A laborer would have enough sense not to park there."

When he saw the SUV, Eddie said, "My engineers don't make enough to afford one of those." He recorded the SUV's license number. "Must be stolen."

When he looked up he saw Ron backing away from the SUV. "You Okay?"

"Somebody's inside."

Eddie joined the truck driver and froze when he looked into the SUV. He swallowed and grabbed the door handle. It was locked, he pounded on the window. The gray-skinned person with dried blood on his right shoulder didn't move. Eddie wasn't surprised. He dialed 911.

"This is Officer Shaunesey of the Cambridge Police Department on a recorded emergency line, what can I do for you?"

"Officer, this is Eddie Downey, the project manager for that MIT dormitory being built on Memorial Drive. I'm standing by a SUV that has a body locked inside."

"What do you mean, a body? Is the person breathing? Should I send an ambulance?"

"No officer. This person isn't breathing."

"Mr. Downey, don't touch anything and please remain at the scene. A patrol car will be right over."

***

Squad cars and white police vans surrounded the SUV like covered wagons readying for an Indian attack. An outer fence of yellow police tape encircled the army of cops taking pictures, collecting samples and dusting the SUV for prints. Ed Downey and the trucker had been interviewed by a uniformed officer and later by Lieutenant

Frank Rust, a detective from Homicide. Looking across the construction site towards the entrance, Downey could see the blinking blue lights and the laborers waiting to get to work. The crowd separated and a shiny black Ford made its way across the site and parked. Lieutenant Rust approached the car as Captain Thomas Cassidy of Homicide climbed out and together they headed towards the SUV.

"Who's the victim?"

"Don't know, waiting for the medical examiner before we move him and look for identification," said Rust.

"Who owns the vehicle?"

Red crept into Lieutenant Rust's face. "Ahh, we've looking into that."

Cassidy introduced himself to Eddie and the trucker as the lieutenant sat in the nearest squad car, typing the SUV's numbers into the wireless terminal. Moments later, Captain Cassidy was interrupted.

"Jesus, Mary and Joseph," said Lieutenant Rust.

Cassidy turned from the witnesses. "Lieutenant, are you going to tell us who owns the car or keep it a secret?"

"The SUV is owned by Raymond Gallo."

The forensic team and the officers stopped what they were doing and crowded around the SUV. Cassidy and Rust stood at the open driver's door and studied the corpse.

"Do you think it's Gallo?" asked the lieutenant.

The Captain leaned over the body, making sure he didn't touch anything. "I've, only seen him once. Same build and coloring."

Lieutenant Rust whispered to Cassidy. "Should we contact the FBI?"

"Are you certain the victim is Ray Gallo?" asked Cassidy.

"No."

"Do you have confidence in the ability of our men?"

"Yes," said the lieutenant.

"Then, we'll wait until the corpse is identified. Do you agree Lieutenant?"

Lieutenant Rust slipped a plastic pen into his shirt pocket. "Sounds good to me."

***

The medical examiner arrived, took dozens of photographs of the body, and then had the body removed from the SUV and placed on a stretcher. His technicians measured body temperature and took more photographs. Within twenty minutes the body was in a body bag, inside a van on its way to the morgue. FBI agents Joe DeLuca and Jim Johnson had to step out of the way as the van left the site.

Cassidy watched the approaching agents. Although they had known each other for years, there were no greetings or exchange of handshakes. Deluca had learned of the death from an agent who monitored police communications.

DeLuca looked Cassidy in the eye. "Thanks for the call."

"Would have called, but we're still working on the identification."

DeLuca surveyed the site. "What happened?"

"I'll make sure you get a copy of my report. But it's actually a simple story. A truck driver was here to drop off a trailer, but couldn't because a SUV was in the way. When he and the site engineer checked-out the situation, they noticed the front seat was occupied and called 911. After the squad car arrived they called homicide."

"Where are the engineer and truck driver?"

"The engineer's still on site, the truck driver's on his way to New Hampshire."

DeLuca glared at Cassidy, then shook his head.

"Going forward, we'll be working together," said DeLuca. "The Mayor agreed to joint custody of the evidence."

"There are downsides to working with us," said Cassidy as he walked towards his men. "You may have to leave your air-conditioned offices."

The FBI agents returned to their car while the Cambridge Police loaded the last of the equipment onto their trucks.

"Cassidy is an asshole," said Johnson

DeLuca nodded as he sat behind the wheel, bathing in the cool air coming from the cracked dash of the vintage Chevrolet. "Jim, I want everybody working their contacts. If the stiff is Ray Gallo, all hell is going to let loose."

Johnson pulled a cellphone from his pocket and dialed the office. He stared out the windshield. "The last time something this big went down, we were twenty years younger."

***

Assuntina lowered the flame under the sauce, ran across the kitchen and grabbed the ringing phone. "Hello, this is the Gallo residence."

"This is Captain Cassidy of the Cambridge Police Department. I'd like to speak to Giovanni Gallo."

"Wait please," said Assuntina. She put the phone on hold and rushed to the solarium.

Giovanni was forcing himself to eat lunch, a medium-rare hamburger. Assuntina's hand wavered as she pointed to the phone beside the rattan sofa. "Capitano d' Cambridge polizia."

Giovanni said "Tell him to call my lawyer."

She picked up the phone. "Please call the lawyer."

"I want an answer to a question first. You ask Mr. Gallo if he knows where his son is."

Assuntina depressed the hold button. "Padrone, he says do you know where Raymond is."

Giovanni pushed his chair from the table and walked to the phone. Assuntina watched her boss study the caller ID number.

Giovanni lifted the phone. "Yeah."

"Mr. Gallo?"

"Yeah."

"I'm Captain Cassidy from the Cambridge Police Department. This morning a man in his late thirties or early forties was found dead in a SUV registered to your son. Could you help with the identification?"

Giovanni grabbed the arm of the sofa and lowered himself into the seat.

After fifteen seconds of silence, Cassidy said, "Would that be possible?"

Gallo listened to a distant and controlled voice, his voice, answering. "Yeah."

"Be at the Cambridge City Morgue at two."

Cassidy hung up the phone, tore open a grease-stained paper bag that lay on an antiquated green desk and unwrapped a steak and cheese submarine. He looked across the desk at Lieutenant Rust and smiled.

"Today we'll discover if the devil has any compassion for his own."

TWO + TWO

The seventeenth floor conference room had been converted into a makeshift command center. Agent Nolan's voice emanated from a speaker phone sitting on an oversized and chipped Formica table.

"When I first arrived at the Cambridge Police Station they gave me the runaround, so this is a preliminary review of the evidence. The deceased is Raymond Gallo. We believe he was killed by a blow to the right temple with a blunt weapon. The time of death has to be confirmed, but we estimate eight to twelve hours prior to discovery. We don't believe Gallo was killed in his vehicle, or at the construction site. His clothing and the clotted blood on the left side of his head have traces of a white powder. No powder was found in the SUV or at the construction site."

"What's this powder?" asked Deluca.

"We won't be certain until the lab performs X-ray diffraction analysis. But spot tests indicate calcium sulfate."

"Calcium sulfate?"

"The stuff found in sheetrock and plaster."

Terry Hamlin had pulled up a map program on her laptop. Nobody paid attention. Hamlin was renowned for silently chasing leads during meetings. She nudged Amero and pointed at two locations, the construction site and the nearby alleyway Gallo had visited the night he was being tailed.

Amero raised his eyebrows and then returned his attention to the speakerphone.

Recalling that Gallo had also visited a Brookline street that evening, Terry reached under the table, found a cable and plugged it into the back of her laptop. She typed a series of passwords, connected to the FBI's mainframe and searched for any residents from the Brookline street who worked in Cambridge. In a matter of three minutes seventeen databases, including those operated by the national census, Social Security and the IRS were queried. Two individuals were identified, a Miriam Witkers, a transit employee who worked at the Fresh Pond MBTA Station and a William Conors, who worked at the Kendall Square Office Building.

She nudged Amero again and pointed at Conors' home and work addresses. Amero's eyes opened wide and was about to say something, when a commotion of loud voices came from the speakerphone.

The uproar subsided and Nolan said. "Agent Caruso just overheard a conversation. Did you know that Giovanni Gallo is visiting the City Morgue?"

"No, when's Giovanni coming?" asked Deluca.

"Now."

Deluca's face turned red as he grabbed the keys to his unmarked car and ran towards the door. "Continue without me."

"Captain Cassidy, may you roast in hell," said Agent Johnson.

"That's all for now," said Agent Nolan. "I need to get back to the evidence, before these cowboys contaminate it or lose something."

Nolan hung-up and Hamlin said, "Jim, we found something that's a potential lead or a very strange coincident."

"Let's have it short and sweet," said Johnson.

Agents Hamlin and Amero described the night they had trailed Gallo to a Cambridge alley and to a Brookline neighborhood. Johnson pulled a spiral notebook from his shirt pocket and scribbled whenever a name, address, date or other fact was mentioned. He scanned his notes and then asked, "Could this be the same Conors that was on TV, talking about that explosion in Chelsea?"

"Give me a few seconds," said Hamlin. She typed Conors' name into a search engine. "Same name and spelling as the Chelsea guy."

Hamlin's fingers kept pecking at the keyboard. "Bingo," said Hamlin. "The Conors involved with the Chelsea Project and the Conors from Brookline both work for a Cambridge company named AEG."

"Could the mob have had something to do with that explosion?" asked Amero.

Johnson shrugged his shoulders.

"This is way beyond coincidence," said Hamlin. Amero high-fived Hamlin.

Johnson quietly glanced at his notebook. He had chased thousands of hot leads during his career, most proved to be dead-ends. Johnson slipped the notebook in his shirt pocket and stood.

"Terry you're scheduled for that conference call on the Phoenix money-laundering," said Johnson. "By the way, congratulations, the Grand Jury based its findings on your evidence."

He adjusted his shoulder holster and slipped on his sport coat. "Sal and I will check out this Cambridge alleyway while you're dealing with the lawyers."

A look of disappointment shadowed Hamlin's face. Johnson smiled. "This case is just starting. You'll have plenty of time to get involved."

Johnson turned to Amero. "Get keys for a bucar, but not that gray Crown-Vic, the battery's as dead as Raymond Gallo."

THE MORGUE

Angie took a left onto a crowded Cambridge street. Neil Miller was waiting on the sidewalk, pacing back and forth. The Cadillac pulled to the curb. Miller opened the back door and slid next to his client.

"Giovanni, I'll do the talking. The police station is swarming with FBI Agents and I want to make sure this isn't a trap."

Miller said to Angie, "If you're going inside, leave your damn gun in the car."

"Boss, you want me to come?"

"Yeah," murmured Giovanni.

Angie slipped the pistol under the driver's seat. They climbed out of the Caddy, walked down a concrete walkway and through the morgue's swinging doors. A security guard glanced at them and then at two men leaning against tiled walls that were the same brown as the tiled floors.

The older of the two men spoke without offering his hand. "I'm Captain Cassidy and this is Lieutenant Rust." The captain pushed himself from the wall. "Please follow us."

"Captain, I'm Mr. Gallo's attorney," said Miller. "Before we proceed further, I need to understand the purpose of our visit."

"Fair enough. We want Mr. Gallo to look at some personal items. Then I'd like him to view the deceased."

Giovanni nodded and Miller said, "Okay Captain, let's see if we can help."

After a myriad of lefts and rights down identical tiled hallways, they entered a large room. The sidewalls consisted of large stainless steel storage drawers stacked three high. Two drawers were opened, white-jacketed technicians collected tissue samples from the cadavers. The far wall had doors to two rooms and large windows for viewing whatever took place within.

Captain Cassidy stopped at a desk in the center of the morgue and picked up a plastic bag.

"The SUV was vandalized in a manner indicative of a robbery," said Cassidy. He opened the bag and emptied its contents on the desk. "But, if it was a robbery, why were these pieces of jewelry found on the deceased?"

Giovanni stood silently with hands in his pockets. He glanced at the jewelry. Cassidy picked up a ring. "There were no ID's on the deceased, but this ring has 'RG' engraved on its inside. The Rolex has a date of 6/14/92, which would have been your son's twentieth birthday. The gold bracelet has no engravings. Are any of these items familiar to you?"

"Where's the body?" Giovanni said.

Cassidy tossed the ring onto the desk. He led them to one of the rooms with the viewing windows. An unzipped body bag was visible through the glass. The bag was opened to the cadaver's groin. They entered, the less disfigured side of a dead man's head was facing them. Cassidy positioned himself on the opposite side of the cart and studied the faces of the three men. Angie's eyes became watery. Miller left the room with a hand over his mouth.

Giovanni's face lacked expression. The previous night Giovanni had awakened and cried. He had done his mourning. Without a word, Giovanni left the room.

"Is this your son?" said Cassidy.

Miller who was standing outside the doorway said, "Obviously it is," he said. "Please leave Mr. Gallo to his grief."

Cassidy looked at Angie. Angie nodded.

Miller and Angie rushed to catch up with Giovanni.

Cassidy said to Lieutenant Rust, "Show our guests to the door. I don't want the La Cosa Nostra lost in this maze."

Lieutenant Rust jogged until he caught up to the three men. Giovanni was in the lead and without hesitation retracing his way to the exit. Rust, who had lost his way in the building on numerous occasions, stopped as Giovanni pushed open the door and left the morgue.

The three men climbed into the Cadillac.

"Neil, go back to Cassidy and get all the information the cops have on my son. I need to know everything."

Miller left and Giovanni said, "Angie, tell my capos what happened and have them check their contacts. I want to know what the streets are saying. Tell them there'll be a memorial service in Nahant. We'll be talking business."

"Sure Boss," said the teary-eyed Angie.

"Then you and Nico get this Conors."

Angie put the car in drive. "Consider it done."

The bucar arrived as Angie pulled from the curb. Deluca swerved and crowded the Caddy. Angie hit the brakes. For the first time in decades DeLuca and Gallo were face to face. Nothing was said, no gestures. Just eyes recalling a mutual history.

EVIDENCE

The blue impala made its way down the alleyway.

"Did you follow him this far?" asked Agent Johnson.

Amero backed off the accelerator. "On foot. I left the bucar on Memorial Drive."

"Did Gallo get out of the car or talk with anybody?"

"No, when he got to the end, he just sat in his SUV."

"How long?"

"A minute or two. He didn't—" Amero fell silent and put his foot on the brake. The car came to a gentle stop a hundred feet from the end of the shadow-filled alley.

"Interesting," said Johnson as the two agents stared at asphalt covered with what looked like a light dusting of snow.

***

Yellow police tape separated the bucar and an FBI van from the end of the alleyway. Agent Thomas Nolan was collecting samples of the white powder while another agent was using stereophotography to capture the footprints and tire tracks that traversed the powder-covered asphalt.

Johnson was leaning against the bucar, scribbling in his notebook. The exit door opened and Amero entered the alleyway with a middle-aged man in gray coveralls. The two men walked around the yellow tape.

"Agent Johnson, this is Mr. Ellison. He's the building super," said Amero.

Johnson shook his hand. "Mr. Ellison, can you tell me what this alleyway is used for?"

"Until recently, not much. For the last couple of weeks we've had a dumpster here for renovation work." The super pointed at a rectangular area of the asphalt free from white dust. "They picked it up this morning. We're scheduled to get a smaller one sometime tomorrow."

"Can you tell me what this white powder is?" asked Johnson.

"The tenant for the eleventh floor wants individual offices, so the contractor is using a lot of wallboard. The dumpster is where they threw the scrap. The stuff makes a mess."

"Who would have access to this alleyway?"

"Only the contractors."

"Thanks Mr. Ellison, that's all for now," said Johnson.

Mr. Ellison nodded and accidently backed into Agent Nolan. "Oops, it's a bit crowded. Mr. Conors is lucky he didn't park here today."

Johnson and Amero looked at each other.

"Did you say somebody parks their vehicle in this alleyway?" asked Johnson.

"Yeah. Mr. Conors does. He's the president of AEG, our largest tenant."

"Anybody else?"

"No. The Fire Department only approved a single space for the alleyway and it's reserved for Mr. Conors."

"Is Mr. Conors in today?" asked Amero.

"Don't know, but I can find out," said the super, reaching for his cell phone.

"No. That's okay. Thanks again, Mr. Ellison."

***

Two agents got off the mahogany paneled elevator. The reception area was empty except for the lady at the desk. Johnson presented his badge.

"Is Mr. Conors in?"

"Yes he is. Have a seat and I'll contact his office." She picked up her phone.

"No thanks, just give me directions," said Johnson.

She sat with the phone in her hand looking at Johnson. He pushed his badge closer and shook his head. She put the phone down and pointed to her left. "Go down that hall until you hit the corner office."

Lisa Kelley looked up. "Can I help you?"

Johnson flashed his badge, looking past Lisa at the closed office door. "I'm Agent Johnson from the Federal Bureau of Investigation. This is Agent Amero. We want to ask Mr. Conors a few questions."

Lisa stood. "Please wait here." She left her desk, entered Conors' office and started to close the door when she discovered Johnson's right foot holding it ajar.

She glared at Johnson, but seeing the resolve in the agent's face, skipped the lecture on manners. The agents followed and surveyed the office, the granite floor, wood paneled walls and a man with his back towards them, lying on a worn leather couch. Lisa gently shook the man's shoulder. The man didn't respond.

The third time Lisa shook her boss, the startled Conors jumped to his feet, almost knocking Lisa to the floor. Johnson started for his pistol, but hesitated enough to see that the man was unarmed.

Johnson shoved his badge in Conors' face.

"FBI Agents Johnson and Amero. We want to ask a few questions."

A cold hollowness filled Conors' gut.

Lisa stepped between the agents and Conors. "Bill's been putting in long hours."

He said in a whisper, "Sorry Lisa, must have been having a nightmare. Gentlemen, have a seat while I freshen up. Can you get our visitors something to drink?"

Conors walked up to the dark cherry wall behind his desk and pressed on a panel. The panel opened, exposing hanging clothes and a door to a bathroom. Conors closed the bathroom door behind him, turned the faucet and splashed cold water in his face and then more cold water. He leaned towards the mirror, staring into eyes that returned his gaze. His head was pounding. He looked away from the mirror, dried his face, took a deep breath and opened the restroom door. Two untouched coffees and a Pepsi were sitting on his desk.

The agents were standing. He pushed the panel and the room disappeared. He shook their hands and took their cards. "Sorry about the awkward introduction, too much work and too little sleep."

With an open hand Conors pointed at the chairs in front of his desk. "Make yourself comfortable."

Conors sat behind his desk and the agents took their seats. Johnson asked, "Do you always wake up that way or is something bothering you?"

"As I said, a combination of too much work and not enough sleep. The company's largest project was unexpectedly shut down and we're trying to stop the bleeding."

"You said you had a nightmare. What was the nightmare about?"

"Never remember dreams. Now, back to why you're here, I imagine you're checking on one of my government clearances."

"We're not interested in your clearances," said Johnson.

Conors sat back and forced himself to return Johnson's stare. He had gone head to head with the country's best lawyers and knew he had to regain control of what he guessed was becoming an interrogation. He looked away from Johnson and glanced at the two business cards lying on his desk. "Mr. Johnson and Mr. Amero, I'm confident your schedules are as tight as mine. If you tell me what's on your mind, I'll try to help."

The older agent sat deadpan and studied Conors. He was as easy to read as a chunk of granite.

"Where were you yesterday afternoon and evening?" asked Johnson.

"Here, in my office. I worked late."

"Why were you working late?"

"Catching up on paperwork and calls. Waiting for the Mayor of Chelsea."

"When did he arrive?"

"He didn't," said Conors.

"When did you leave?"

"Half past seven."

"Go home?"

"No, went to a Chamber of Commerce dinner," said Conors. "Why are you asking all these questions?"

Johnson ignored Conors' question. "Did anybody see you there or talk with you?"

"About fifty to a hundred local businessmen," said Conors.

Johnson didn't take his eyes off Conors. "Can you prove that you were working in your office last night??"

"Call Mike Evans at our California office. Our weekly conference call lasted till seven," said Conors. He handed his business card to Johnson. "Use the San Francisco number."

Johnson took the card by its edges and carefully placed it in his pocket. Conors stopped breathing. *Christ, the guy is going to dust the card for prints.*

"Do you know a Raymond Gallo?" asked Johnson.

"Do you mean the gangster?"

"Yeah, do you know him?"

"No."

"Why are you familiar with his name?"

"I read the newspapers."

"Have you ever met Raymond Gallo?"

"No."

"Know what he looks like?" asked Johnson

"No."

Johnson took a picture from his shirt pocket and slid it across the desk towards Conors. "Does this refresh your memory?"

It was a photograph of Gallo's body in an unzipped body bag. There was an ugly mass of coagulated blood under the translucent skin of Gallo's right temple.

"Who the hell is this?" said Conors. He dropped the photograph.

"That happens to be Raymond Gallo?"

"Okay, gentlemen. No explanation for your visit and now you're flashing pictures of dead mobsters. What the hell's going on?"

"You don't know?" asked Johnson.

"No I don't," said Conors.

"Do you park your car in the alleyway behind the building?"

Conors blinked. "When I drive to work."

"Did you drive today?"

"No, took the subway."

"Why?"

"Why not? I work for an environmental engineering company. Taking public transportation is an environmentally sound practice."

"Where's your car?"

"In front of my house." Conors remembered the gun and the money hidden in the trunk. He had burned his clothes, Gallo's license and Gallo's credit cards in the living room fireplace the previous night. The ashes were spread around the perennials in the backyard. After work, he planned to drive to Gloucester and toss the gun in Ipswich Bay.

"Any reason why you didn't park in the alleyway?" asked Johnson.

"No. I've been parking there for years."

"But you didn't today."

"No off-site meetings, so I didn't need my car. It was a pleasant walk to the T station."

"Thought it was hot?" pushed Johnson.

"Not at six this morning?"

"Mr. Conors, I'm heading a homicide investigation."

"Homicide?"

"Yes homicide." Johnson fell silent again and locked eyes with Conors.

Conors asked, "So, why are you here?"

Johnson didn't answer and leaned forward. "Mr. Conors, do you have any travel plans?"

"Next business trip is a week away. This weekend, I'll be at our cottage in Gloucester."

Johnson stood and turned to the door. "Gloucester's a nice place, this time of year."

"It is," said Conors. He remained sitting until the agents disappeared down the hallway.

***

After the agents left that afternoon, Conors busied himself with mindless tasks trying to mask the day with a facade of normality. When Lisa left, the exhaustion returned and he lay on the couch. He woke to a darkened office and then took the subway home.

Conors was walking down a Brookline street, it was dark, quiet. Parked cars lined both sides of the treed street. The previous evening, the closest space was two hundred yards from his home. As he walked past his car, Conors pulled on a door handle, it was still locked. He glanced inside and decided it hadn't been tampered with.

He slowly climbed the six steps to his home, inserted his key into the lock and glanced through the door's beveled glass at the control panel on the far wall. When coming or going, he and his wife automatically checked the LED lights to determine the alarm settings. He stopped, there were no status lights, no red, no green no yellow for battery backup, nothing. He removed his key and was backing away, when a shadow moved in the hallway and he heard a muffled voice. "He's seen us."

Conors jumped off the stoop and hit the sidewalk running. Using his remote he unlocked the car. Two men with pistols burst through the front door of his home. Conors was faster. The car's engine was running before the men had covered half the distance. Conors jammed the transmission into first, the tires squealed and the car fishtailed as it left the side street and sped towards the police station.

Conors double parked and rushed into the building.

"Somebody's broken into my house," said Conors.

The sergeant slid open a glass window separating him from the entrance hall. "Name and address?"

"William Conors, 120 Elmwood."

"Are you Dr. Conors' husband?"

"Yes."

"Mr. Conors, why do you believe your house was broken into?"

"I set the alarm this morning. When I arrived home, it was off and then I saw two armed men."

The sergeant dropped his pen. "When was that?"

"Five minutes ago."

The sergeant grabbed a microphone. "Squad cars 7, 10 and 11." Three different voices responded. "An ongoing B&E at 120 Elmwood. Charlie enter Elmwood from the south, Ron you enter from the north end and Luis, wait on Cedar Street. The owner spooked the perps. Two armed males."

The sergeant lowered the microphone. "There's a coffee machine by the side door. Make yourself comfortable."

Conors parked his car between two cruisers at the back of the station and returned to the small entrance room with its three blue plastic chairs. He sat, walked in tight circles, sat and walked again, his mind spinning, considering everything, Raymond Gallo, the alley and anything that could have lead the FBI to him. Nothing made sense other than the fat guys chasing him down his street were not FBI agents.

The glass window slid open. "Mr. Conors, let's take a drive."

"Did they catch them?"

"Not yet."

***

The sergeant turned down Elmwood. Three cruisers and an unmarked car were doubled parked in front of his house. The sergeant stopped next to a man wearing a sport coat.

"Thanks sergeant," said Conors.

The plainclothesman opened Conors' door. "Mr. Conors, I'm Detective James Nutley, why don't you follow me."

The detective walked down the narrow side yard that separated his house from the neighbor's. Conors followed. The detective stopped by the side of the house and pointed a flashlight towards the roof.

"Your telephone wires were cut, that's why your alarm company was unaware of the break-in."

The detective pointed the flashlight a few feet to the right. "See that plastic box, that's your alarm system's siren. It was carefully disassembled."

The detective continued through the yard and up the back steps. He pointed the flashlight at a splintered door jamb. "This is where they made their entry."

He pushed the door open and entered the kitchen. Conors followed.

"Mr. Conors, these burglars were professionals, not run-of-the-mill druggies."

The detective pointed at an opened bag of chips and Pepsi cans on the kitchen table. "To be quite honest, this is what confuses me. Typically, professionals spend only minutes in a house. These guys appear to have made themselves at home."

Conors' eyes locked on the empty Pepsi cans and the chips spread across the table. The table where he shared meals with his family. Conors stared at the table.

"Mr. Conors, you have to put things in perspective. Your house has been broken into and your space violated, but nobody was hurt. A little carpentry work, an alarm system using cellphone technology and this should never happen again."

"I've been traveling and my family's been on vacation. Maybe, they thought the house was deserted."

"I have no idea what they were thinking, and it's too late to call the forensic team," said the detective. He looked around the kitchen. "I'd like them to dust for prints. If I was to cordon off the crime scene, could you find someplace else to sleep?"

"I'll spend the night at our second home."

"Remember to make arrangements for a locksmith," said the detective as he handed Conors his card. "I'll call tomorrow, when I know more. The sergeant will drive you back to the station."

Conors left through the front door as his home was being fenced-off with yellow police tape. He slid into the passenger seat of the sergeant's cruiser. He noticed the silhouette of his neighbors looking out their windows and watched them until the police car turned the corner.

The sergeant drove to the police station and stopped behind Conors' car.

"Mr. Conors, are you awake enough to drive?"

"I'm fine, sergeant. Thanks for the help." Conors climbed out of the cruiser.

The sergeant left when he heard Conors' engine start. Conors put the car in drive and with a head full of unpleasant thoughts drove north.

***

Pitch black, but enough light reflected off the inky calm water to remind Conors he was driving along the Gloucester coast. It was past midnight and he had only seen a few cars since the highway. He took a left off Quarry Street onto a gravel road. The bumpy road led to a cottage and a doorless barn he used as a garage. He approached slowly, the car's bouncing high beams piercing the darkness.

The remoteness of the shore side house had been one of its attractions. He looked out his open window, it was black, still and hot. For the first time, Conors was thinking it was too secluded. "Calm down, only our friends know about the cottage."

He searched for anything out of the ordinary. When he turned towards the barn, something shiny flickered in the headlights. The roof leaked badly, everything in the barn was rotting or rusted. He braked.

He flicked on the car's driving lights and inside the barn, night became day. Conors saw the shiny object. It was a watch on the wrist of a towering man. The reflection disappeared when the man raised his hand and aimed a pistol at Conors.

Conors rammed the shift into reverse and popped the clutch. The spinning wheels filled the air with dirt as the car lunged to the opposite side of the yard. Without stopping, he slammed into first gear and for the second time that night floored the Taurus SHO.

He had expected to hear gunfire as he sped down the gravel road. But the man in his rearview mirror stood motionless as a dark car hurtled forward from behind the barn. Conors turned right on Quarry street and redlined the 220 horsepower SHO Taurus through each of the first three gears. The car was going over eighty when he shoved the car into fourth.

The Cadillac skidded to a stop. The gunman jumped into the passenger seat. Angie floored the car. "What the hell spooked the asshole?"

Nico braced himself with hands on the dash while the Caddy took a ninety degree turn onto Quarry Street, barely missing a car headed in the opposite direction. "How the fuck do I know?"

From the top of a hill, Nico could see Conors' taillights a quarter of a mile down the coastal street. Angie accelerated and braked hard maintaining the straightest possible line through the twisting, rolling and potholed road. Nico glanced at the speedometer. It registered 95 on one of the straightaways. He had heard Angie was a hell of a wheelman in his day. He decided the reputation was well deserved.

Conors had figured he had lost the Caddy. Then he saw headlights in the rear view mirror. The lights disappeared and reappeared as the road curved and straightened. Conors turned off his headlights, relied on his driving lights and sped through a double curve.

Angie, yelled over the screeching tires, "I don't see him. Did he take a turn?"

"There were no turns," said Nico. "The cazzo turned off his lights,"

With the distant headlights still in his rearview mirror Conors careened around another corner to find a slow moving car with teen-agers tossing beer bottles into the bushes. He swerved from lane to lane, just missing an oncoming mini-van. A half mile later, still seeing headlights in his mirror, Conors braked, downshifted and then accel-erated into a hard right onto Granite Street.

The Caddy rounded a curve. Angie caught the last flicker of Conors' brake lights and followed. Granite Street quickly forked into two smaller streets. Conors was not in sight. The Caddy slowed long enough to see skid marks from when Conors barreled down Stanley Street.

On Stanley, Conors had again floored the SHO. He knew he couldn't use the brakes and let brake lights forewarn his pursuer. A hundred feet before the first turn, he double-clutched from 5th into 2nd and yanked on the emergency brake. The tires screamed as the SHO decelerated. Conors released the emergency brake as he took a right, then immediately pulled hard left, breaking the rear end loose to make it down the hill. He continued through the intersection and sped towards downtown Gloucester.

Seconds later, not having seen Conors' brake lights or the upcoming turn, the Caddy was still speeding. Remarkably, Angie made the first turn and then accelerated hard to stop the car from fishtailing. That's when he saw the next turn and realized his mistake. He pushed the brake pedal to the floor, but the oversized rotors and discs were not enough. Nico sat helplessly as the Caddy crashed into a tall hedge. Angie jammed the car in reverse but the wheels had lost traction. Happy to be alive, Nico jumped from the car.

"I'll push."

They rocked the car loose and Nico threw himself into the pas-senger seat. Angie accelerated the Cadillac CTS down the hill, but not before a man stepped onto his porch and looked through the hole in his manicured hedge. The neighbors were pouring out of their homes, Nico bellowed, "Get the hell out of here."

Breathing heavily, Angie looked at the upcoming intersection. "How the fuck do we get to Route 128?"

***

Conors had a clear view of his car and the only entrance into the small industrial park. The Taurus was on the opposite side of the parking lot in the dark shadow of two tractor trailers. Conors' vantage point was from inside a pile of discarded cardboard that reached halfway up the wall of a warehouse. It had been an hour since the last siren and he was becoming restless. An emaciated dog with its head hanging low angled across the parking lot. Conors didn't move a muscle. When the dog disappeared between two distant warehouses, he pushed the cardboard aside and ran towards the Taurus. Upon reaching the car, he placed his hand on the front left wheel.

"Still hot, no wonder the brakes were fading."

When he had first backed between the two trucks, he had stayed in the car, but not for long. He was afraid the smell of burnt rubber and the pinging sounds from the cooling exhaust system would attract attention. That was when he spotted the cardboard.

Conors unlocked the car with his remote and slipped behind the wheel. He checked the entrance road and parking lot once more before turning the ignition key. He took the coastal route through Manchester and Beverly and then headed west to Route 1 and the Sumner Tunnel.

***

A cruiser was parked in front of the Brookline home. The officer studied the unmarked Chevrolet Caprice as it pulled alongside. The

man in the Caprice flashed his badge. "Good Morning officer. I'm
Agent DeLuca and this is Agent Johnson. We're from the Boston
office".

Deluca pointed at the yellow police tape. "Homicide?"

"Just a B&E," said the officer.

"Why all the tape for a B&E?"

"Things didn't make sense to the detective, so the forensic team
will be here first thing in the morning."

"Some politician getting special treatment."

The officer laughed. "Not this time. But you can bet your
paycheck the Police Chief will be checking into this one."

"Why's that?"

"The homeowner's wife is Dr. Conors. About seven years ago,
she saved the Chief's daughter from cancer after three doctors had
written her off. If you mention Dr. Conors name, the Chief still gets
tears in his eyes. Since then she saved two other cops. If I come
down with the big C, there's only one person I'll be calling."

DeLuca let the car inch forward. "Don't worry about cancer,
after sitting in these cars, you'll die from hemorrhoids. Have a good
night officer."

A moment later, the agents slowed before pulling onto Harvard
Avenue.

"Joe, when I saw the yellow tape, I was certain Conors was a
goner," said Johnson.

Deluca nodded. "Looks like the informant was right about the
mob wanting Conors alive."

***

"Charge it to AEG's corporate account," said Conors.

It was after 3 a.m. The clerk at the Sonesta Hotel returned the
man's Massachusetts license. "No bags, Mr. Conors?"

"No, a long day at the office, I just need a few hours of sleep," said Conors. He took the plastic room key.

The clerk watched Conors walk to the bank of elevators, expecting a hooker to join him. Conors took an empty elevator to the second floor and walked down a long corridor that paralleled the Charles River. He entered his room and locked the door. He sat on the bed, and pushed a few buttons on his cell phone.

"Bill, I've called home, your office and your cell. Where are you? Call my parents' number, my battery finally died."

Conors deleted his wife's voicemail. "Too late to call."

He removed the battery and placed it and the phone on the night table. "Besides she reads me like an open book and will start with the questions."

He turned on the TV and channel surfed. The stations all had the same interview with Captain Cassidy and the same pictures of the black SUV being towed from the construction site. He fell asleep before sunrise, wondering if no news was good news.

BAD COPS
Friday

Deluca was typing with his index fingers when Johnson arrived at 7 a.m. Johnson had two large coffees. He placed one on DeLuca's desk.

DeLuca looked up from the keyboard. "That for me?"

"Unless you have someone hiding under the desk."

DeLuca lifted the pie-shaped tab and took a sip. "Thanks"

Johnson unbuttoned his sport coat and adjusted his holster. "Last night my wife was listening to Fatty Ford's radio show and he mentioned something about a businessman being connected to Gallo's death."

"How the hell did he hear about Conors?" asked DeLuca.

"A Cambridge cop tailed the evidentiary team to the alleyway. He was standing around when the building super mentioned Conors name. I'll give five to one odds, he's Fatty's source."

"Jesus, do we have to start listening to that joker every night?"

Johnson shrugged his shoulders and sat across from DeLuca. "Changing the subject, any more thoughts about your drive-by meeting with Giovanni?"

"Yeah, one of those times when a picture is worth a thousand words. Seeing that prick reminded me how we convicted dozens of mobsters, leaving those with the best genes. A year from retirement and I'm wondering if my greatest accomplishment has been a Darwinian improvement of mob management."

"Then, be grateful he didn't have six kids." Johnson grimaced and readjusted his holster again. "What's this picture that's worth a thousand words."

"Like I told you yesterday, I wanted to see Giovanni and get a handle on how he would respond to his son's death. I got my answer."

"And?"

DeLuca sat-up straight. "Did you know that 'vendetta' is an Italian word?"

"No, but sounds appropriate."

DeLuca frowned. "Like me, Giovanni has melted into double chins and flab, but the eyes are the same. They're still filled with arrogance and hate, but now with a new purpose—revenge."

"You think all hell is going to break loose?"

"Depends. If Giovanni believes Conors is responsible for his son's murder, the only fall-out will be Giovanni's captains jockeying for position. If the Columbians, Mexicans or Russians were involved. Large scale shit will hit the fan."

Deluca took a sip of coffee and pointed at a three page memo sitting on his desk. "I read the report on your meeting with Conors. What do you make of the guy?"

"He's smart and gave all the right answers. Facts that could be checked, like the Chamber of Commerce dinner, have been verified. But Conors knows more than he's saying. I think he's dirty or at least hiding something."

"What makes you think that?"

"Remember when Agent Pallidino and I unknowingly walked in on that mob transaction and Pallidino left in a body bag?"

"Nobody forgets those things."

"Well, I never told anybody, but that night I woke up swinging and cursing. I scared the shit out of my wife." Johnson looked away.

"I ended up sleeping in the guest room for three months. I was afraid I'd hurt her."

"Didn't know that," said DeLuca.

"Well, when Conors woke, he had the same crazed look my wife had described. That guy is dealing with some serious devils."

"Anything else?"

"Just my gut."

"Should our visit be a good cop—bad cop routine."

Johnson took a slow sip of his coffee. "Two bad cops may work better. We need to pressure this guy."

***

Conors used the hotel phone to dial the in-laws. Nobody answered. He glanced at his watch. "The kids must have talked them into another breakfast at Denny's."

He dialed his wife's cell phone, not expecting an answer. His wife had a phone charger in the kitchen, her car and her office, but never remembered to pack one when she traveled. He hung up.

"Just as well, the burglary will freak her out. Better to break the news in person."

He dialed another number.

"Where are you?" asked Lisa.

"At the Sonesta."

"Some detective has been calling. What's this about a burglary?"

"Just a jimmied door, but doesn't look like anything was taken."

"Just?"

"Could you arrange for one of those latest technology alarm systems for the Brookline home?"

Conors could hear Lisa tapping a pen on her desk.

"Just a jimmied door and you want a state of the art alarm system?" asked Lisa.

"Kristin gets nervous about these things."

"Wonder why?"

"While you're at it, have a system installed in the Gloucester cottage."

The tapping became louder. "Bill, you better rehearse your line of bullshit before Kristin gets home, because it ain't selling."

"I'll see you in about twenty." Conors hung up.

When checking out, he made reservations for the weekend for himself and his family. After leaving the hotel he pulled into Yusef's Mobil and parked by the service door.

"Problems?" asked Yusef.

"Oil and filter. Can you fit me in?"

Yusef nodded. "Quiet morning."

Conors handed him the keys. "Don't know when I'll need it, so the sooner the better."

"I'll do it now."

"Thanks," said Conors as he headed for his office building.

He was used to functioning with little sleep, but was approaching his limit when he entered the lobby of the Kendall Square Office Building at 10:15 a.m. He passed a salesman bent over and fumbling through an oversized briefcase and took the first elevator. The salesman watched until the elevator indicator stopped and then flipped open his cell phone.

"The bird has returned to its nest."

"Maintain your position until we say otherwise. If he leaves, follow him."

"Roger."

***

"You look like hell."

"Not a good time for honesty," said Conors.

"How about taking the day off, you had one hell of a night," suggested Lisa

"Can't, Kristin and the kids are coming home tonight and I'm scheduled to take Monday off. By the way, did you have any luck finding an alarm company?"

"The company that services our offices has a residential division."

"That will work," said Conors.

"Could you call the Denver office? They're having troubles with the local regulators."

"Yes, but if Kristin calls, put her through."

***

There were three ways to enter and leave the Kendall Square Office Building, the lobby, the alleyway and the parking garage. The FBI had all three exits covered. By the time Amero saw Conors enter the lobby, it had already been a long day.

Twenty minutes after Amero placed his call, two agents got off the elevator and approached the AEG receptionist. "Good morning, we're from the FBI and are here to meet with Mr. Conors."

The receptionist smiled. "I'll contact Mr. Conors."

"No thanks. I know the way."

Johnson led. At Lisa's desk, DeLuca flashed his badge. "We'd like to speak with Mr. Conors."

Conors was on the phone. His door was open. He and the agents were staring at each other.

"Jesse, I have to go. Have the legal department locate the appropriate citations," said Conors. He hung up and slowly stood.

"Please come in gentlemen."

The agents entered and closed the door. Johnson spoke first. "Mr. Conors, this is my boss, Agent DeLuca. He's in charge of the Boston Office."

Conors remained behind his desk. "Nice to meet you."

DeLuca sat in the middle of the three chairs opposite Conors' desk. "Good to see you in one piece."

"What do you mean?" asked Conors, as he sat down behind the desk.

"By now, I expected you'd be in pieces on the bottom of Boston Harbor."

A long silence hung in the air. "Why would you expect me to be at the bottom of the harbor?"

"Because our informant said there's a price on you head."

"Why the hell would there be a price on my head?"

"Good question. I was hoping you'd have the answer."

Johnson had seated himself to DeLuca's right. "A little excitement in Brookline last night?"

Conors glanced at the agents, wondering how much they knew. "My house was burglarized."

"From what I understand nothing was stolen" said DeLuca. "If those guys were burglars, they better sign up for unemployment."

"Guess I spooked them," said Conors.

"Where did you go after you left Brookline?" asked Johnson.

"Why do you ask?" said Conors.

"There was some commotion up in Gloucester," said Johnson.

"Don't you have a home in that area?" asked DeLuca.

"Yes."

"A couple of cars were speeding around North Gloucester. Somebody complained about a black sedan," said Johnson.

"What's the color of your car," asked DeLuca.

"It happens to be black," said Conors.

"Interesting. Never caught the black sedan, but the Gloucester Police did stop a couple of mobsters. But, not having any reason to hold them, they let them go."

"What happened in Brookline and Gloucester confirms what the informant reported," said Johnson.

"Okay, I'll take the bait," said Conors. "What did this informant have to say?"

"He had a lot to say," said DeLuca. "One thing is that Papa Gallo wants you alive. Knowing that, last night makes sense."

"What makes sense?" said Conors.

"Take for example, the big muscle-bound goon questioned in Gloucester. Most people look at Nico and assume he's a leg-breaker, and it's true. A few months ago he put three longshoremen in the hospital. But his real talent is as a hit man. Our informants say he's an incredible marksman."

"What's this got to do with me?"

"If Gallo wanted you dead, some guy like Nico would have put a hole in your head. The reason you're still breathing is because Gallo wants answers."

"Let Gallo know I want to talk. I'll tell him what I've told you."

Johnson smiled. "Joe, when I get back to the office remind me to give old Giovanni a call."

DeLuca and Johnson looked at each other and laughed.

"This isn't the Oprah Winfrey show," said DeLuca. "The FBI and Gallo don't have daily therapy sessions."

Conors let the room fall silent. "Mr. DeLuca, you're right, this isn't some TV show. That's why I need to tell Gallo I had nothing to do with his son's death."

DeLuca leaned forward.

"Mr. Conors, I don't believe you, and Gallo won't either. The difference being that Gallo has ways to ensure he gets honest answers," said DeLuca. "If you don't cooperate with us, your last hours will be spent hanging from a meat hook with some goon questioning you with a cattle prod."

"What do you mean, you don't believe me," said Conors.

"Things don't add up. The powder on Gallo's clothing ties him to within feet of where you park your car. I think you know something about Gallo's death and you're not cooperating."

"I have been cooperating."

"You want to cooperate?" asked DeLuca.

"I have been, and intend to."

"Good. Come to our office and take a polygraph."

Conors studied the men. "If I was to take your offer, how would you get Gallo off my back?"

"As long as Gallo's breathing, he'll be after you," said DeLuca.

The agents rose together. DeLuca asked, "Are you coming with us?"

"I have a business to run."

"That's unfortunate," said Johnson.

"A grand jury has been convened and Agent Johnson will be returning with a subpoena," said DeLuca. "Stay put, we have the exits covered."

Deluca opened the door, and walked out. Johnson hesitated. "Seriously consider our offer."

The agent held his hand in the air and formed a circle with his thumb and forefinger. "Without us, your chances of survival are zilch."

Conors remained seated. "According to my understanding of probability, chances are seldom zero."

***

Conors closed the door and picked up the phone. He dialed Matt Kimani's extension and hit the key for voice mail.

"Matt, this is Bill. For reasons that Lisa will explain, I'm leaving you in charge of the company until I return. It's critical that you keep the Chelsea Project on schedule, so use any and all resources to keep it on track. Good Luck."

He felt like he was in a strong current, knowing generally what direction he was headed, but not what was around the bend. He removed a piece of stationary from his desk and started writing;

I have spoken with the FBI and they have advised me that due to a misunderstanding an organized crime boss may do me harm. They counseled me to seek protective custody. Since I am seriously considering their advice, I'm authorizing Matt Kimani, in my absence and until such time that I return, to take full responsibilities for the operation of AEG.

Conors read what he had written and then pushed the intercom button. "Lisa."

A few seconds later, Lisa appeared.

"Please sit down."

Lisa took her seat and Conors sat on her right. "Lisa, you know from the newspapers that a mobster was killed nearby. With that in mind, I'd like you to read and witness this document."

Lisa warily took the handwritten page. As she read, she turned white.

"Is this for real?"

"Yes," said Conors. He took the paper, signed it, dated it and handed it back. "Please sign under my name. If I accept the FBI's offer or if something happens to me, you'll give this document to Matt and the Board of Directors."

"If something happens?"

"Don't worry," said Conors. He gave Lisa the pen. She signed the document with a shaking hand and sat uncharacteristically silent.

"Lisa, can you pick Kristin and the kids up at the airport and take them to the Sonesta Hotel?"

She nodded.

"Good." Conors slipped a PDA into his pocket. "I'm going to the cafeteria."

He left Lisa sitting in the office and headed down the hallway to the janitor's storage room. He stuffed the janitor's cap and coveralls into a white trash bag, took the elevator to the third floor cafeteria and ordered an extra-large Pepsi.

With the soda and trash bag in hand, he entered the men's room and closed the door to a stall. He slipped into the coveralls and adjusted the plastic tabs on the sweat-stained hat so it sat low on his head.

Moments later with his head down and Pepsi in hand, Conors crossed the lobby and left. At the curb, Conors glanced over his shoulder into the glass enclosed lobby and recognized the man studying the people leaving and entering the elevators. Conors crossed the street. His eyes were darting about looking for other agents, when he saw two men in a parked Cadillac. The oversized man in the passenger seat was the hit man DeLuca called Nico.

Nico looked his way. Conors brought the large cup to his face and pretended to drink as he entered a RadioShack. He feigned interest in the cellular phone display and studied Nico. Conors could also see the agent stationed in the lobby.

"Can I help you with anything?"

A sales clerk was examining him suspiciously. Conors glanced at the Cadillac, the lobby, then the clerk. "Sure."

"How?"

Conors' ignored the question while a cruiser passed by. "You have one of those radios where you can listen to the police?"

"We have a portable scanner on sale for $89.99, with batteries. It's already programmed for local police channels."

"I'll take it."

Glancing between the agent in the lobby and Nico, Conors unzipped his overalls to get his credit card. He reconsidered and gave the salesperson cash. As he waited for his change, he saw Johnson enter the lobby, approach the other agent and walk towards the elevator.

Conors quickly left by the door on the opposite side of the store.

"Hey mister, don't you want your change?" yelled the clerk, as Conors turned down the side street.

***

Yusef was holding a brake pad in his greasy hands. He smiled and said in his Jordanian accent, "William, you look like the mechanic."

"Is the car ready?"

Yusef turned to a key covered board, selected a set and handed it to Conors.

"Thanks. Invoice the company," said Conors.

He slipped behind the wheel of the Taurus and headed for the Cambridge Parkway. The traffic moved slowly. He placed the scanner on his lap, inserted the batteries and turned it on.

"A 10-53. Three-cars at the corner of Hampshire and Webster. No injuries, need a second squad car. Who's nearby?"

Conors kept with the traffic. The scanner's reception drifted in and out. He was waiting at the intersection of Land Boulevard and O'Brien Highway when the static gave way to an announcement. "Looking for a middle-aged Caucasian who's avoiding a subpoena. He may be driving a 96 black Ford Taurus, plate number 3798-Mike-Foxtrot. Not believed to be armed, but be cautious. Repeat a 96 black Taurus, plate number 3798-Mike-Foxtrot."

He wiped the sweat from his forehead. He wasn't sure what police channel he was listening to, but assumed it was either Cambridge's or Boston's. The light changed. He took the Gilmore Bridge into Somerville and then Route 99 to the Revere Beach Parkway. In less than thirty minutes there were four small cities between him and Cambridge. He pulled into the parking lot for the Wonderland Transit Station, found an empty space and backed in.

He opened his trunk, made sure Gallo's pistol was still under the floor mat and opened a toolbox. He grabbed a screwdriver and exchanged his license plates for those on the Chevrolet Corsica parked to his right. He used a rag to wipe his prints from the plates and closed the trunk. He left the transit station, picked up Route 2 and stayed on the two-lane highway until he reached Troy, New York.

At 7:30 p.m., Conors was a hundred and fifty miles west of Cambridge in a Burger King parking lot. He had purchased a Gousha Road Atlas, a baseball cap, dungarees, two checkered wrinkle-free shirts, underwear and toiletries from the local Wal-Mart. His office clothes and the janitor's coveralls were in the Burger King dumpster with his half-eaten burger.

His new possessions, his PDA, Gallo's gun and the envelope from Gallo's SUV were stuffed in a black duffle bag. He had counted the money. Twenty-six grand in hundred dollar bills. He sat with one hand on the duffle bag and watched the sun disappear behind trees on the opposite bank of the Hudson River. He was thinking of his wife adjusting to a world of burglarized homes and a missing husband. He badly wanted to talk with her, but knew the FBI and maybe the mob could trace the call. He couldn't have either knowing where he was or whether he was alive or dead.

He turned the ignition key.

POLICE WORK
Third Week of August

Agent Deluca turned off the radio. "For at least one night, Fatty doesn't know more than the FBI."

Deluca was sitting at one end of a conference table as exhausted agents were plunking into chairs. Agent Munroe who had been out of the office asked the first question. "What's the status on Conors?"

DeLuca said, "Prior to today, Conors' story was checking out. He was away for a business trip. A call was made from Chelsea City Hall at the same time Lisa Kelly recorded the Mayor's appointment in her phone log. Conors returned from the business trip Wednesday afternoon and was on the phone with his San Francisco office till seven on the night of the murder. By eight, he was at a Chamber of Commerce dinner."

Deluca turned towards Johnson, who had just entered. "What's up with Conors' background check?"

"Squeaky clean," said Johnson.

DeLuca frowned, tossed a photocopy of a handwritten letter on the table. "Got this from Conors' assistant the day he disappeared. Anybody reading it would assume Conors had planned on cooperating with us. The letter combined with the building's surveillance video of two mobsters waiting on a side street, would argue that Gallo got him first."

"Makes sense," said Monroe.

"Yeah it did, but my gut was telling me something different," said DeLuca. "So I had Terry audit AEG's book."

Turning towards Hamlin, DeLuca said, "Terry, summarize what you've discovered so far."

"Yeah—sure," said Terry Hamlin.

"You okay?" asked DeLuca.

"Sorry, my mind was somewhere else," said Hamlin, who was having second thoughts about the email she sent the previous evening. For the first time in her adult life she had become dependent on someone and she was miserable during Vinny's frequent absences. It was affecting her work and after a particularly distracted day at the office, he called and they had had an argument. She hung up and sent an email saying she didn't want to see him again.

She pushed a strand of hair off her forehead. "The audit will take a few weeks, so I started with recent transactions. Two invoices caught my attention. One from the Sonesta Hotel, where Conors stayed after his house was burglarized. The second was from a local service station. When I paid Yusef's Mobil a visit, I discovered that at the same time Jim was trying to serve a subpoena, Conors was dressed in coveralls and picking up his car."

"That changes things," said Munroe.

"Sure does," said Deluca. "At this point we don't know who the hell we're dealing with. Was Conors caught up in some extortion, or is he a front for the mob. If he's a front, he's been smart enough to fly under the radar."

Johnson slipped a photocopy of receipts in front of DeLuca. "To further muddy the waters, someone in New York City charged a fifty-two inch plasma TV to Conors' credit card. Not exactly the type of stuff a man on the run would buy."

THE SPOUSE
Early September

Three weeks after her husband's disappearance, Kristin Conors was sitting in the dark, at the kitchen table. The kids were asleep and she had just finished a long telephone conversation. Kristin had played the role well and convinced her mother all was fine.

The phone rang. She looked at it. It kept ringing. She picked it up. "Hello"

"Hi Kristin," said Lisa Kelly.

Kristin swallowed hard. "It's good to hear your voice."

"How are you?" asked Lisa.

Kristin blinked back some tears. "Not too well."

"Want to talk?" asked Lisa.

"I don't know. I'm a mess. I'm losing it."

"What do you mean?" said Lisa.

"You name it. The kids miss their father. My medical practice is out of control. I don't know if Bill's alive or dead. If that wasn't bad enough, I'm not handling the little things either, like meals, the new alarm system. I feel as if I can't do anything right."

"Hell, that's no surprise. Bill's absence is causing all sorts of problems at AEG and there are three hundred of us," said Lisa.

Kristin wiped tears from her eyes. "What's happening at work?"

"The damn lawyers debated whether Bill's appointment of Matt to run the company had to be approved by the Board of Directors."

"What's happened to Matt?"

"Nothing. Just lawyers making money protecting us from other lawyers," said Lisa. "Since Bill is the majority stockholder they eventually blessed Matt's new role."

"I'm glad that's settled," Kristin said. "The Company was always so important to Bill."

"Enough about AEG, tell me more about you," said Lisa.

Kristen squeezed the tissue in her hand. "Lisa, I don't understand how the FBI can think Bill is a criminal."

"What's this crap about a criminal?"

Kristen took a deep breath. "We've had two meetings. The first was pleasant and I told the agents everything I knew, which was basically nothing. The second meeting occurred yesterday. I was asked in a dozen different ways, if I've been in contact with Bill and how I must notify them if I ever hear from my husband. The agents claimed a lack of cooperation would make me complicit in a crime. Then they said I may be served with a grand jury subpoena."

"Don't worry about those bozos, they can't wipe their own asses. For the last twenty years, they've been trying to nail Giovanni Gallo, a thug with a third grade education. I'd like to give them a piece of my mind."

Kristin laughed weakly, the tears flowed. "Better wait a couple of days, someone already put them in their place."

"Really, who?"

"Last night, Chief Kulchinsky of the Brookline Police dropped by to see how I was doing. I broke down in tears and told him about the FBI agents. Today, a smiling patrolman told me the Chief visited the FBI."

"Yeah?" said Lisa.

"Apparently, the Chief equated the FBI to the mob and told them they'd be spending time in his jail, if they ever again terrorized one of his citizens."

"Yahoo! Nothing better than a pissed-off Polack," yelled Lisa.

"Mommy."

Kristin turned to see her son. He was looking at her through half opened eyes. She wedged the phone under her chin and opened her arms. He crawled onto her lap. She kissed the top of his head.

"Lisa, Kevin needs attention. It was great talking with you. Thanks."

***

Lisa sat staring into Conors' empty office, tapping her pen on her desk. She had been closing up the office for the night when she called her friend. She shook her head and made a note to call Kristin in a couple of days. Her eyes again drifted to the blackness of Conors' unlighted office.

So the FBI thinks you're a criminal. I would've said they were crazy, but something was wrong, you knew you were in trouble.

She shook her head and picked up her purse. "Now I'm losing it. Bill's an environmental engineer, not a murderer."

ON THE HOUSE

It was the second day in the Cleveland bus terminal. The previous night, Conors had tried to rent a motel room. He left when the clerk demanded identification. He returned to the terminal and spent the night and morning reading discarded newspapers. The crowded terminal had emptied with a series of departing buses. He was left alone and exposed as he pretended to read *The Cleveland Stater*, a college newspaper.

Conors assumed a fugitive would make mistakes, so for hours he slouched behind newspapers revisiting his escape. He had driven west to upstate New York, backtracked to Bridgeport Connecticut and abandoned his car in the parking lot for the New York ferry. He passed a van boarding the ferryboat and slipped his company's credit card behind its license plate, hoping the card would make it to New York.

He avoided the Bridgeport train station, took a taxi to New Haven's Union Station and bought a ticket for the Amtrak to Cleveland. In the Cleveland station he came across a brochure for a two week bus tour to the West Coast and left that afternoon. In Los Angeles he spotted a group of tattooed men. Keeping his distance, he acted as if he had too much to drink, pulled out his handkerchief and his last two credit cards fell to the pavement. After another week of one-star motels and a busload of retirees, he was back in Cleveland, killing time in a bus terminal.

The crackling of the intercom interrupted Conors' thoughts. "Louisville, Kentucky arriving at Gate Nine."

Conors looked over the paper at the ticket counter, *That was my one mistake. When I was buying that west coast ticket, I should have left when the agent asked for a license. I need fake IDs.*

The departing passengers passed by Conors, without paying him any attention. He had been in need of a hair cut when he returned from his business trip. Unruly hair, the beginnings of a beard, cheap jeans and a baseball cap pulled to his ears, all made for an unremarkable presence.

After the passengers disappeared, Conors lowered the newspaper and realized he wasn't completely invisible. The scowling custodian had been circling him all morning, eyeing his pile of day-old newspapers.

Can't stay here much longer, Mr. Clean will sic a security guard on me.

He smiled at the custodian and raised the newspaper, *I'm quite the master planner, other than knowing I have to disappear from the face of the earth, I don't have a fucking clue.*

He was flipping through the paper, considering another bus tour, when an advertisement caught his attention;

Sublet studio apartment for fall semester. Walk to CSU. Will return in January, following overseas studies. $1200 for the semester. Call Seth, 216.687.2022.

Although he still had over twenty-five grand of Gallo's cash, Conors knew bus tours could quickly deplete his funds. Conors grabbed his duffle and headed towards a bank of telephones. The janitor seized the pile of newspapers. Conors popped three quarters into the phone and dialed.

"Yo," said the voice of a young man.

"I'm calling about the sublease. Is the apartment still available?"

"Yeah, you interested?"

"Yes. Is this Seth?" asked Conors.

"Yeah, Seth Kaplan. Are you a student at CSU?"

"Not exactly. I'm between jobs and thinking of going to graduate school in environmental engineering," said Conors.

"Cool. Save the universe shit."

"Yeah. I'd like to see your apartment."

"You pick the time," said Seth

"Give me the address and I'll be right over."

"7490 Central Avenue, Apartment 3D."

***

Conors paid the taxi driver and stood looking at a peeling white painted building, the carcass of a hundred year old mansion hacked into apartments. The building leaned to the left suggesting its reincarnation would be brief. He climbed the stairs and pushed open the front door. More peeling paint, but different colors. He counted seventeen mail boxes and estimated the size of the studio apartments. A man with screwdrivers in his shirt pocket and an unlighted joint in his mouth passed by and left through the front door.

Conors climbed the stairs to the third floor, each floor had four apartments. Conors figured the fourth floor had five apartments or there was a penthouse. Someone with a magic marker had hastily numbered the door. He knocked on 3D. A guy with a small rectangular patch of hair on his chin opened the door.

Conors offered his hand. "I'm Bill Smith. I called about the sublet."

Seth Kaplan hesitated, then shook his hand and said, "Come in."

Conors took a step in and stopped, there wasn't room to go any further without invading Seth's personal space. The room had a window that opened onto a fire escape, a microwave sitting by a small sink, an under-the-counter refrigerator, a twin-sized mattress, a closet-size bathroom, and a bookshelf stacked with Poly Sci books.

"Cozy," said Conors.

"Small as shit," said Seth.

"That too."

"You interested?"

Conors nodded.

"You don't look like a grad student."

"I'm not," said Conors.

"Thought you were thinking of grad school."

"Yep."

The frowning Seth eyed Conors for a second time. "You said you were between jobs. What was your last job?"

"Geologist."

"What does a Geologist do?" asked Seth.

When it came to geology, Conors figured he could con a poly sci major. "Did surveys for an oil company."

"Find any oil?"

"Nope."

"Is that why you're between jobs?"

"Pretty much," said Conors.

"How can I tell you're for real?" asked Seth.

Conors pulled out a roll of hundreds. "How do I know this is your apartment and I'm not being scammed?"

Seth pulled his eyes from the bills and yanked a thumbtack from the wall, freeing a dozen papers. He sorted through them and found a lease. Conors read it. "Does the landlord mind you subletting?"

"This is the world of absentee landlords, they're afraid their tenants will knife them. We deal with the super, Ralph."

"Does Ralph mind you subletting?"

"Ralph's a fucking pothead," said Kaplan. "Short of setting an apartment on fire, you can do anything in this dump."

"Ralph's the guy with long brown hair, screwdrivers in his pocket and an unlighted joint in his mouth?" asked Conors.

"Except for the unlighted part, sounds like Ralph."

Conors peeled off 12 bills. "Write across the lease that you have sublet the apartment to Bill Smith and we have a deal."

***

Conors spent the first day in his new home in a deep sleep. A sleep interrupted once by a frozen meal chiseled from the ice of the refrigerator's small freezer.

On the second day, Conors explored his neighborhood. Heading northwest towards Cleveland State University, the shops and stores became more upscale and busy, the old homes well maintained. East and southeast of his apartment, most factories and store fronts were covered with plywood and graffiti. Further out, the low income citizens were replaced by the homeless and addicts. That night he went to bed familiar with his neighborhood, the next step was getting to know his neighbors.

On the third day, he pushed open a dented steel door and entered Benson's Suds & Grub. The barroom was long and narrow. The left side was filled with a mix of chairs scattered among tables of different shapes, colors and sizes. On the right was a long oak bar that ran the length of the room, likely the pride of the original proprietor, now chipped, worn and stained.

Towards the back, a group of mostly black men were huddled around two tables. The bartender, a man with long graying blond hair and a blank face, watched Conors. Conors chose the stool with the fewest splits in its vinyl cushion. He sat down a couple of feet from the bartender.

"What's on draft?"

"Bud and Bud Light."

"Bud."

The bartender put a Cleveland Browns coaster in front of Conors, grabbed a heavy mug and held it under the tap. The foam was escaping over the rim when the man placed the beer on the coaster. Without a word, the bartender returned to emptying plastic bags of ice.

The head on the beer had not yet settled when someone tapped Conors on his shoulder. Conors glanced over his shoulder at a black man, over six feet, fat and in gray sweats.

"You're in my seat," said the man.

Conors glanced at the bartender, who had decided the other end of the bar needed cleaning. Conors got up, moved down two stools and returned to his beer.

The man followed, tapping him on the shoulder a second time,

"You're sitting in my seat."

Conors clenched his teeth and stood. He glanced at the men in the back, they were watching. He moved down two more stools and faced the man.

"Let me guess. This is also your favorite seat?"

The black man stood taller and moved closer to Conors. "Yeah, it is."

Conors eyes switched between the bartender who was looking the other way and his customers. They were standing.

"You have one hell of a fat ass, but didn't think you needed six stools." said Conors.

The man scowled and pulled back his left arm, telegraphing his intentions. Conors stepped forward. A right uppercut sunk into the black man's soft gut, pushing up into the diaphragm. Conors' left fist hit the same target.

The man gasped and fell against two stools. They tumbled with him to the floor.

Conors stood waiting for the man to get to his feet. He didn't.

The men in the back of the room broke into uproarious laughter.

One of the white men yelled, "Jamaal, you really beat that honky ba—aad."

"Yeah, Jamaal, now he's your bitch," yelled a black man over the laughter.

Another man yelled, "Six-stool Jamaal."

The group started chanting, "Six-Stool Jamaal."

A black got up from one of the tables and walked towards Conors. Unlike the man on the floor, this guy moved like an athlete. With adrenaline surging through his veins, Conors took a step towards the oncoming man.

The man raised his hands and smiled, showing a set of perfect teeth. "Whoa Rocky." The man turned to the bartender. "Two Michelobs."

The black man grabbed a bottle and handed it to Conors. "I'm Woolworth, have the Cadillac of beers."

Conors slowly took the beer, expecting and preparing for a sucker punch.

Still smiling Woolworth turned to the bar and pulled an Abe Lincoln from a thick roll of bills. The bartender shook his head. "They're on the house." He reached across the bar and offered his hand to Conors. "Name's Jonesey."

Conors took the hand. "Bill Smith."

The bartender nodded towards the man on the floor. "He's a jerk."

Woolworth, still smiling, said, "Come meet the guys."

Conors offered a hand to Jamaal, who was climbing to his knees. Jamaal turned away.

While Conors was meeting the guys, Jamaal left the bar.

ALL IN THE FAMILY

After a long night at the Nahant mansion the exhausted Tony lowered his bag of electronics to the floor. "We swept everything except the Boss's bedroom."

Angie looked at his watch, which read 6:15 a.m. "No problem, Giovanni doesn't talk in his sleep."

Tony yawned.

"If you're sure there's no bugs, you can get some sleep." Then Angie put his finger in Tony's face. "But, I tell ya, if Giovanni's voice ends up on the evening news, I wouldn't want to be in your sneakers."

Tony looked at the ground and gently shook his head from side to side. He didn't know what, but he knew something big was going down. He raised his eyes. "Angie, we checked every room and every telephone at least three times. Unless they have some new technology, there's nothing in this place."

"I don't want to hear this new technology, old technology shit, Are there any bugs in the place?"

Tony grimaced. "No. No bugs."

"Nothing in the great room?" asked Angie.

"No."

"And you're damn sure the Feds didn't find anything with their search warrants?"

"Angie, I've told you a dozen times, the only thing left in the warehouse was toilet paper and Ray never brought anything from the business to his house."

"Leave your phones on. I might need ya."

"No problem," said Tony. He grabbed his equipment and headed for the door.

***

Later that day, the wives were sitting at tables, scattered around the large granite patio. They made small talk as their husbands had directed, about the weather, children and grandchildren. The type of talk appropriate for a funeral.

At the opposite end of the mansion, Giovanni sat in the great room at one end of a table. It looked like the start of a typical business meeting, except for the overflowing trays of freshly baked ruota and trecce and the pungent odor of Italian coffee.

Giovanni studied the men before him. Five men sat on his left and another six on the opposite side of the table. They were the captains through which he controlled the New England La Cosa Nostra. As they had arrived, Giovanni embraced each and accepted their condolences.

Over the years, he had hand-picked all but two of his captains. They all were smart and ruthless. But he trusted them because every captain had a made man on his payroll, who secretly collected a second salary from Giovanni.

Behind the captains, Carlo and Santo stood on either side of the closed doors. Angie sat at a small corner table.

Funerals offered La Cosa Nostra an excuse for the family to meet face-to-face. But, there was also a risk and it was reflected in the tension between the men sitting around the table. It had been over a decade since all the captains were in the same room. A gathering of mobsters attracted the Feds and the captains were not happy with the attention. They had noticed the men outside the church and in the cars tailing them to the cemetery and Nahant.

With outstretched arms Giovanni started the meeting. "Benvenuti."

There was silence as the captains focused their attention on Giovanni. "I have suffered and your support eases the pain of a father who has lost his only son."

He rested his hands on the table. "It is a loss I will take to my grave, but it is my loss. Yet the death of my son is also a sign of a much greater loss for our family."

He looked at every captain as he spoke and saw tears in the eyes of a few. "La Cosa Nostra's proud history goes back to the 1800s, when our ancestors brought order to Italy and protected the people from the thieves and the barons. We were loved by those we protected and respected by our enemies. We no longer have that respect. Our enemies do business in our neighborhoods and plan to replace us."

To Giovanni's own surprise, he smashed his fist on the table with a fury that rattled the silverware and bellowed in a ponderous voice that started to break, "They kill our sons without fear."

His throat thicken. It was the first time he had talked openly about his son. His gaze fell upon the linen tablecloth, then returned to his captains.

"Someday one of you will rule this thing of ours. And I promise, what you rule will not be less. No one will look back and say I took the family down the road to decline."

Giovanni studied his captains. "Over the years we have worked with many outside the family, and we have profited. However, the Columbians, Israelis and Russians are different. While you work with them, they plot against you. They not only kill each other, they kill their wives and kids. They have no honor. It's only a matter of time before they turn on us."

His throat was dry. "If these animals were involved in my son's death, they will pay a price." He took a drink of lukewarm coffee. It felt good. "But we have a more immediate problem."

Giovanni studied his captains, trying to read their thoughts. "Twenty years ago, I brought peace to the family. It was hard and much blood was spilled. That can't happen again. If we fight amongst ourselves, we become weak while our enemies become stronger."

Giovanni stood. "I'll never let that happen."

He walked to the buffet and with his back to his guests, Giovanni opened a large wooden box that was centered on the marble top. He removed two objects from the box and turned towards the table with a small black box in one hand and the other hand behind his back. He glared across the table at one of his captains, a short man with multiple chins who filled the ornately carved chair. The captain looked at Giovanni and then nervously glanced around the table.

"Piero, do you remember how I brought peace to the family?"

"Sure, Boss. You ruled with an iron hand. It was necessary. It brought peace," said Piero.

Giovanni placed a small tape recorder on the table and slid it across the table. It came to rest in front of Piero.

"Push the play button."

"What's going on Boss?"

"Press the button," said Gallo. "Then you tell us what's going on?"

Piero again looked at his fellow captains. "What's going on?"

"Push it," bellowed Giovanni.

Piero pushed the play button. "Giovanni's too old to rule the family."

A second voice said, "Dad, could you imagine working for Ray. Thank god the moron's dead."

Piero's fat fingers fumbled with the stop button. "That's not my voice."

He looked up to see Giovanni and a pistol with a long silencer aimed at his head.

Giovanni's face was contorted. "I want to leave you with a parting thought."

Piero, pushed his chair back, but it caught in the thick rug. Giovanni leaned towards him. "While you were pretending to grieve at Raymond's funeral, your son had an accident. His brains were blown all over his little red sports car."

Piero stopped pushing at his chair and looked at his boss. Giovanni pulled the trigger. Three bullets hit their mark. A fine mist of blood settled on Fulvio and Dianno, the captains to the left and right of Piero.

Giovanni returned to the head of the table while Carlo and Santo laid the body on a spare tablecloth and carried Piero from the room. The speechless captains looked down and away from Giovanni. Some glanced nervously at the wooden box on the buffet wondering if more tape recorders would appear.

Giovanni took a bite of a ruota and continued the meeting. An hour later, the captains had taken their turns embracing Giovanni and repeating their condolences as they left him in the great room. Afterwards, Giovanni retreated to the shadows of a third floor window. Assuntina was giving his captains pastries for their trips home. Silvano, his captain from Providence, ignored the unending questions from Piero's wife and guided her to the back seat of his Mercedes.

Some of the captains drove themselves, others had drivers. In less than fifteen minutes, the cobblestone courtyard was empty. He felt alone.

Angie approached Giovanni from behind. "If any of them had doubts," said Angie. "They now know you're still in charge."

Giovanni continued looking out the window. "Since Ray was killed, I look at the world differently?"

"How's that?"

"I've always been a selfish prick," said Giovanni. "But walking out of that morgue, I realized that for thirty-six years, my life revolved around my son."

"I'm sorry Boss," said Angie.

"There's a hundred million Euros in Swiss accounts and foreign real estate. It was meant to be Ray's."

Angie put his hand on his Boss's shoulder.

"They say little things can make a difference," said Giovanni. "A butterfly flapping its wings can cause a storm."

Giovanni lowered himself into a chair. "What could I have done differently?"

TASK FORCE
Mid-September

Agent Deluca had put on eight pounds and looked and felt like shit. He was thumbing through the pages of a thick report, distracted by a throbbing headache. It was a month since Gallo's murder, it was late, he should have been home hours ago. He grimaced as another pain slashed across his forehead.

DeLuca put the report down and sunk into his chair. He looked at the tired agents sitting around the conference table. His eyes came to rest on Agent Hamlin. "Terry, a thorough report, could you summarize your findings?"

"Sure. After sheetrock particles on Gallo's clothing linked him to Conors' office building, we asked ourselves whether AEG was another company laundering mob funds. To answer this question, we studied AEG's cash flow, accounts receivable and accounts payable. The first step was to stratify the—"

"What's the bottom line?" said DeLuca.

Hamlin blinked a few times. "The bottom line is that AEG has no documented dealings with questionable companies, and if Conors or Gallo were laundering money, they weren't doing it through AEG. Their books are the cleanest I've seen."

DeLuca had mixed feelings. It was comforting that there were honest people and honest companies, but these dead-ends meant the questions of 'who and why' remained unanswered.

"Good work."

Joe DeLuca placed his agenda on top of the audit report. "It's late, so I'll be brief. I'm taking on additional responsibilities for Homeland Security. Going forward Jim Johnson will be the Case Agent for the Gallo murder and Terry Hamlin will be his backup."

The other agents gave the surprised Hamlin the thumbs-up. Her career had just taken a big step forward.

DeLuca turned to Johnson. "Jim could you give us the status on Ray Gallo and Conors?"

Johnson opened his little notebook. "The search warrant for Gallo's Newton house yielded absolutely nothing. We had mixed luck with the warehouse. While the second floor was sanitized, Gallo's telemarketing company had years of financial records that Terry is reviewing. The funeral went without event. All of Giovanni's captains came, paid their respect and left the same day, except Piero Macchia. He must've left Nahant sometime after we called off our surveillance."

Johnson flipped to the second page of his notebook. "There's been no sign of Conors. His wife's cell, business and home phones are tapped and email monitored. As of this afternoon, he has not tried to contact her. Under these circumstances, I would normally assume the mob got their hands on the missing person, asked their questions and disposed of the person's remains."

He moved the holster that was always digging into his side. "But besides Conors alleged escape in his car, there's another reason to doubt his demise. Our informants report that Giovanni's lawyer has been contacting bounty hunters, offering a sizable reward for Conors' capture."

Johnson took a swallow of Poland Spring water. "One of Conors' credit cards was used for a string of purchases in Los Angeles. However, the charges, like those made in New York, were not the type a fugitive would make. Within a month, we have Conors' credit cards showing up on both coasts."

"Is Conors using the cards to confuse us about his whereabouts?" asked Terry Hamlin.

"That's a possibility. We've dreamed up a number of hypotheticals that are equally credible."

"Anything else on Conors?" asked DeLuca.

"Yes. We were puzzled how Fatty Ford heard about Conors' license being used to purchase a ticket at a Cleveland bus terminal. Well, the answer is that when Conors skipped town, his APB was entered into the Agency's database with the FBI and the cities of Boston and Cambridge listed as contacts. When the ticket agent raised a flag, Boston & Cambridge police were automatically notified. With all those loose lips in the loop, Fatty was certain to find out."

"Was Conors in Cleveland?" asked Hamlin.

"Don't know, when our Cleveland Office interviewed the ticket agent, he couldn't recognize Conors from a picture and didn't remember the incident. Seems he flags license numbers whenever someone appears nervous. It could have been Conors, could have been someone using Conors' license or just a typo."

DeLuca leaned on the table to get to his feet. "Okay, let's close up shop."

THE SENATOR

Nathaniel Forbes was in the Senate President's office, behind his desk, his back to the large mahogany door, staring out the window.

When the mafia got their greasy hands into the Big Dig, my revenues evaporated. Then the damn Russians, who don't even own a dump truck, skimmed the rest of the fat.

Forbes squinted as the afternoon sun escaped from behind a cloud. *It won't happen again.*

The old hinges groaned and Forbes slowly turned his chair to see Jeffrey Signalli, the state senator from East Boston, enter and close the door.

The senator crossed the large office, no greetings, no emotions. They didn't like each other and they both knew it. The dirty blond, blue-eyed man lowered his athletic frame into the Chippendale.

After a moment of silence, Signalli said, "Nathaniel, you called this meeting."

Forbes picked up a worn fountain pen and turned it in his fingers. Five years earlier, Signalli, fresh from passing the bar, won a Senate seat after the incumbent died suddenly. The freshman Senator caught Forbe's attention when he became an advocate for a series of projects that had nothing to do with East Boston. When Forbes investigated, he discovered the same bank and unnamed investor were behind the projects. It took Forbes a year to learn that Giovanni Gallo was the investor.

"The Labor Committee has been busy," said Forbes.

"You know those unions. They're hard to keep happy."

"Considering their contributions to your last campaign, I'd say you're meeting the challenge."

Signalli faked a smile.

"Jeff, you may not be aware of the fact, but ever since 9/11, the Governor and I have had monthly meetings with Homeland Security and the FBI."

"I didn't know that."

Forbes nodded. "Potential threats to the Commonwealth are discussed. During the last meeting, the murder of Raymond Gallo became a topic."

Signalli worked at appearing disinterested.

"It appears the FBI knows who murdered Gallo, but chooses to do nothing about it," lied Forbes.

"Why would the FBI do that?" asked Signalli.

Forbes leaned back in his chair. "The FBI uncovered a Russian plot to eliminate La Cosa Nostra and is curious as to how it will play out."

The last of Signalli's poker face melted away. "The Russians killed Ray Gallo?"

"The Feds have two eyewitnesses," said Forbes.

The young senator shifted nervously in the antique chair. "Why are you telling me this?"

Forbes smiled knowingly. "Relax Jeff, just idle chitchat between colleagues."

Signalli gently shook his head in disbelief and Forbes decided it was time for the red herring.

"Would you mind if I interrupt our little confab, with an aside?" said Nathaniel.

"Not at all," said Signalli.

"You have managed to bruise the very sensitive ego of your fellow committee member, Senator Finnegan."

"The man's an idiot," blurted Signalli.

"An established fact, but not one known to the general public until you berated the man before TV cameras."

"My mistake."

Forbes nodded. "The next time the cameras show up at one of your committee meetings, please thank the dear senator for some imagined contribution."

"Done."

"We must have more of these chitchats," said Forbes as he lifted his phone and dialed a number.

Signalli closed the door and Forbes returned the phone to its cradle. *Pretty soon, Gallo and the Russians will be too busy to worry about a construction project in Chelsea.*

CHECKERS

Conors was sitting on the bed, his back against the wall, the stench from the previous night still in the air. He hadn't slept. First it had been the reek of garlic. Then his neighbors had consummated the Korean meal with a marathon of humping and moaning. A pillow over his head failed to compensate for the paper thin walls.

Earlier that morning he had put on the three dollar sweats purchased at the Salvation Army store and had run six miles followed by two hundred pushups and sit-ups. He spent the rest of the morning pacing or sitting on the bed. Thoughts of his family competed with the ever-evolving plans to recapture his life. He periodically glanced at his watch wanting to escape the cramped room and the negative thoughts that became his companions when alone.

***

It was unpleasant for a late September day. A cold Canadian wind blowing across Lake Erie had brought torrential rains. Conors was soaked when he entered Bensons Suds & Grub. It was crowded and rowdy. He walked to the bar.

"Jonesey," said Conors

"Regular?" asked the bartender.

Conors sat down. "Yeah."

Jonesey placed a draft in front of Conors and yelled over his shoulder. "Burger, heavy on the onions and peppers."

Conors nodded towards the guys in dungarees and work boots. "Baby shower or happy hour?"

"Neither, too windy to work the skyscrapers," said Jonesey. "My evening customers are six hours early, should be a good day."

"Hey Billy, come over and get your ass kicked," hollered an old black man from the back corner of the bar. Ulysses was a fixture at Benson's and the undisputed checkers champ. Conors pointed at the Bud tap and Jonesey poured him a second draft. He took the two beers and headed to Ulysses' table.

One of the steel workers yelled, "Ulysses has fresh blood".

"Careful, Ulysses is vicious," said another.

The eyes of the eighty-year old emaciated man twinkled as he took the beer. Ulysses had won each of the dozen games they had played. After a few games, Conors had discovered Ulysses' strategy, but preferred the deep laugh that mysteriously emanated from the hundred pound man.

Benson's clientele were used to Ulysses' checker games being brief. Discovering that wasn't the case with Conors, the regulars gathered around the table. Conors controlled the games from the start, but each time made a mistake that Ulysses exploited. By the third game, the bar was silent as the men made their moves. Upon taking Conors' sole remaining king, Ulysses broke into his signature laugh.

Conors stood and mimicked Ulysses' deep voice. "You kicked my ass so bad, I won't sit for a month of Sundays."

The regulars slapped Conors on his back and bought him and Ulysses beers. Conors smiled.

Jonesey had re-warmed his lunch and Conors was enjoying it. Being a married man, he had forgotten how good a barroom burger could be. He was sitting at a large table with a mix of construction workers and noontime regulars, including Woolworth.

"Bill, where are you from?" asked Esteban, one of the construction workers.

"Northeastern New York," said Conors.

"He's going to the University," said one of the regulars.

"After twelve years at a factory, I was laid off. Thinking of getting a degree, but I'm not sure," said Conors. "Looks like a lot of work."

"You have family back home?" asked Woolworth.

"Just an ailing mother. My wife divorced me, after I found her in bed with a neighbor."

"I would have killed the bastard," said Carmen, another steel worker.

"Broke his nose and front teeth."

"That'll teach the fucker," said Esteban.

"Not really. I have a record and the prick sued me," said Conors. "He now has the house and screws my ex-wife in my old bedroom."

"Jesus, Mary and Joseph," said Woolworth.

"Could have been worse," said Conors.

"How?" asked Carmen.

"My wife tried to get half of my severance pay. The judge figured I had paid my dues and said no."

"I can see why you left," said Woolworth

"That's not why I left. My wife's boyfriend thinks he got the raw end of the deal. He promised the local gangs a $2000 reward for my dick."

Esteban raised his beer. "Welcome to Cleveland. Looks like you'll be staying a while."

After everybody took a healthy mouthful, Carmen pointed to Woolworth. "If you need anything, check with this guy first. They don't call him Woolworth, the Department Store, for nothing."

Woolworth smiled. "DVD players, TVs, anything smaller than a car and never more than half price."

Conors knew that Woolworth was a well-connected fence and facilitator. He smiled and held up his beer. "I'll drink to that."

The talk turned to sports. Conors needed to relieve himself, but waited. When Woolworth got up, Conors followed. The restroom was empty.

Standing at the urinals beside Woolworth, Conors said in a low voice, "Woolworth. I need something and was wondering if you could help."

"I'm no god-damn pimp," slurred Woolworth

"I need IDs," whispered Conors.

"Shi-iit. Kid's stuff, I can get you a buckeye driver's license for seventy-five bucks."

"I can use one of those, but also need a California driver's license and a firearm license."

"Hell, why you need a gun license?"

"I have to go home a few times a year and need a gun to keep those punks away."

"Man you're talking high-quality documents."

"You can't help?"

"Did I say that?" said Woolworth. "They don't call me the Department Store for nothing, but it's ain't going to be cheap."

"How much?"

"Maybe a grand, I'll have to check."

Conors closed his zipper. "I need the IDs."

Woolworth laughed. "I guess, you really want to keep that dick of yours."

"Yeah," said Conors.

"Will you be here for lunch tomorrow?"

"I'll be here."

"Bring your money."

"Appreciate your help," Conors said as they headed back to their table. Conors drank the rest of his beer, made small talk with his new friends and paid his tab before leaving.

***

Three days later, Conors was at Bensons sitting across a table from Woolworth. Conors slowly checked the California Driver's license, the California firearm permit and the Mendocino Community College faculty ID. He had visited Woolworth's forger the previous day. Twice the forger had Conors change shirts and comb his hair differently, explaining that nobody gets all their IDs on the same day. The IDs had been aged by roughening the laminated surfaces to different degrees and looked more authentic than his counterfeit Ohio license.

"Credible," said Conors.

"Told you, he was top shelf," said Woolworth.

Conors nodded. He had put a lot of research into the persona captured in his new IDs, including many days at the CSU library. He searched the internet until he discovered an article about a well-liked teacher, who had a disagreement with a local community college. Professor William Slater resigned and disappeared, leaving his common-law wife behind. Slater had one hell of a midlife crisis that provided a clean slate for Conors to write his own story.

Conors raised his beer and smiled at Woolworth. "Here's to top shelf."

HARD DRIVE
Late September

Eric Wills waited at Giovanni's gates for ten minutes, then leaned on the horn. An enormous man approached from the other side of the wrought-iron gates.

"Jesus, must be Nico. Couldn't be two like him in the same state."

Nico pointed at a black box. "Next time get off your ass and use the intercom."

"Too bad the muscle-bound goon wasn't green," mumbled Eric as the gates opened. "Spielberg could have skipped the special effects when shooting the Hulk."

Nico pointed towards the right side of the courtyard and Eric parked his pride and joy, a seven year old BMW 3, between a Mercedes S500 and a Land Rover. He glanced at the cars, the mansion and the manicured grounds. "Guess I've been suffering from that big frog in the small puddle shit."

He got out of his car. Nico was waiting for him. "Let's have an ID."

"What, a ticket for not using the intercom?"

Nico stared with his hand out. Eric produced his wallet, thinking that besides a small brain the oversized moron had no sense of humor.

Nico compared Eric to the picture on his license and returned the wallet. "Turn around and put your hands on the roof of the car."

Eric shook his head and complied. Nico kicked his legs apart and frisked him.

"Okay," said Nico.

"I'm glad that's over. I thought you were going to butt-fuck me."

A big hand grabbed Eric's shoulder and spun him around. The same hand grabbed Eric by his t-shirt. Eric glanced between a pistol and Nico's black eyes.

"What did you say?" asked Nico.

"Nothing sir. Nothing. I'm sorry."

Nico slowly let go of Eric and pointed at the front door. "Once inside, go to the end of the hall and wait."

Eric started towards Giovanni's mansion, he looked over his shoulder. Nico said, "That mouth is going to get you killed."

***

Giovanni Gallo stood on the stairs overlooking his six-car garage. The consigliere for the Corleonesi family was standing by the back door of a limousine. The exquisitely tailored man had landed at Logan three hours earlier without luggage. Within the hour he would be boarding his private jet for Milan.

Giovanni said, "That's a lot of money for some ex-soldier."

The consigliere's eyes narrowed. "He was a captain in the Incursori, the elite of the Italian army. In Croatia, he got seven medals."

"Why does such a good soldier leave the army?"

The consigliere shrugged his shoulders. "Bored, money, maybe a little of both. I don't know, but he and his men do things the family can't do, things we shouldn't do."

The man climbed into the back seat and opened the tinted window. "Giovanni, you will not be disappointed."

"If I am, you'll never see the other five million."

The man shook his head and said, "Arrivederci."

The driver put the limo in gear and Giovanni walked down a long dark hallway to the solarium. He ignored the person in dungarees and a tee-shirt. After closing the door, he asked, "Who's the kid?"

Neil Miller had become fascinated with a flock of large white birds diving into the water at death-defying speeds. Miller turned from the window. "He's the computer whiz who worked for Ray."

Nico was sitting in a chair by a large table. Giovanni had asked him to spend more time as his bodyguard. Giovanni handed him a piece of paper that contained a series of numbers the consigliere had written from memory.

"A containership will be arriving next week from Italy. Pull that container before it gets to customs. A couple of Silvano's men will be there with a truck."

"Sure Boss," said Nico. He watched Giovanni lower himself into a chair. Usually, his Boss didn't get involved in the details. Nico wondered what was in the container, but was not about to ask.

Giovanni sat at the head of the table, with his back to the windows. "Neil, what have you heard about my son?"

"As I was saying before your Italian friend arrived, the Cambridge police are pursuing a number of competing theories."

"What theories?" asked Giovanni.

"One theory is that someone in the family is threatening your authority. Another is that an outside organization is making a grab for the family's business." Miller wasn't surprised when the irritated Giovanni shifted in his seat. "A third theory is that some thug didn't recognize Ray and ambushed him. Lastly, they're speculating that Conors had something to do with Ray's murder."

Convinced that the Russians had killed his son and that the FBI was cheering them on, Giovanni took a deep breath and looked at his lawyer. "I know when my captains take a piss. It's not someone in the family."

Giovanni's huge hands distorted from arthritis and years of being broken remained on the table but slowly curled into crude fists. "And anybody stupid enough to go after the family, would have talked. Nothing has been heard on the street."

The lawyer remained silent.

"What do the cops really believe?" said Giovanni.

"The police think it's a random thug or a family squabble," said Miller.

"Do you know what the Feds are doing?"

"The Cambridge police and the FBI have joint custody of the evidence related to Ray's murder, so communications are better than normal."

"Yeah," said Giovanni.

"According to my contacts, the FBI is trying to locate Conors. They have his wife's phones tapped and have asked the state police for help."

"Are the Feds trying to mislead us?"

"Don't think so, my contact says the Feds are trying to get Conors before you do."

"What can you tell me about Conors?" asked Giovanni.

"Nothing more than we have already discussed. That's why I asked Eric Wills to visit with us."

***

When Eric Wills noticed the sound of his sneakers scuffing across the granite floor, he stopped shuffling in circles and lowered himself into a chair in the dark hallway. His lifelong 'I-don't-give-a-shit' attitude had evaporated when Ray choked him. The emergency room doctor said the vocal cords in his prominent Adam's apple had suffered a trauma and the headaches were caused by bruised nerves in his neck. The day after Ray's death, he disappeared and moved to a new apartment under an alias. After a few weeks on his own, hacking and making money, his confidence had returned. Then the previous night, he woke to find Tony standing over him with the message that Giovanni wanted to see him. He had just gotten over Tony's unannounced visit, when he had the run-in with Nico. He bent forward, holding his head in his hands. *I just want to get away from these crazy people.*

The door opened without warning, it startled him. Eric looked up and saw a man he didn't recognize.

"Will you please join us," said Miller.

He followed Miller into the solarium.

Miller pointed at the end of the table opposite Giovanni and Nico. "Have a seat."

They both sat down and Miller picked up a pile of papers. "Eric, I reviewed the past research you did on Mr. Conors and his company. The depth of information was impressive."

Miller lowered the papers to the table. "When you were told about this meeting, you were asked to search for connections between the Russian mob and Conors and the Russian engineers that work at his company. Did you have any luck?"

"Yes sir. I had some."

"Did you find anything that linked the Russians that work at AEG to the Russian mob?" asked Miller.

Eric swallowed hard. After spending the night frantically hacking different databases, the only common link between the Russian engineers was that they were all hired by AEG upon graduating from MIT. "No sir, but that doesn't mean anything. The Russian government is protective of their mobsters and any journalist who investigates them doesn't live long. It's hard to find information,"

"Did Conors travel to Russia?" asked Giovanni.

"Yes sir. I was able to hack AEG's travel agency. He made eleven trips to Russia over a four year period."

Giovanni struck the table with his fist. "I knew the bastard was working with the Russians."

Eric glanced at Miller, then back at the red faced Giovanni. His pulse raced. Twice, he started to open his mouth, but each time surrendered to the growing fury in Giovanni's eyes. He didn't mention that Conors' trips to Russia were as part of a U.S. environmental task force.

A few questions later, Miller showed Eric to the front door. When Miller returned, Giovanni was standing.

"Neil, double the reward for Conors again. I want every bounty hunter in the country looking."

***

Giovanni called the meeting to an end and once alone tried to calm himself. He picked up his Steiner binoculars and focused on the diving birds, knowing that Northern Gannets were usually miles offshore and that the fish must be running to bring them this close.

He half-heartedly scanned the sky, trying to determine if the darker juveniles dived as expertly as the adults. Giovanni lost interest, *Raymond didn't know it, but he was putting pressure on a Russian-run business.*

He placed the binoculars on an end table. "Conors and his Russian comrades will regret the day they were born."

INK

The glass shattered, the sink turned black. A thick fluid oozed towards the drain. Conors stared at the mess, his face void of emotion. He tossed an artist paint brush into a wastebasket. "Guess I'm finished."

He glanced at the reflection in the bathroom mirror and then at a hand drawing. He took a paper towel and blotted the three leaf clover on his chest. "Can't let them get close."

***

It was another overcast afternoon in October when Conors started down the street. His goal was to get their attention, but not too soon.

He had learned from Woolworth, that there were thirteen of them, a homegrown Hispanic gang with delusions of Lincoln Navigators and bling. Three of them had jumped Conors a week earlier, two from the front, one from behind. It was quick and he didn't remember much, other than three men lying on the sidewalk. The gang claimed they were disrespected and promised revenge. Conors had stopped going to Benson's and spent his days in the apartment. Being a hermit was not part of his plan, so while they had hunted him by day, at night he cased the four block area where the gang sold drugs.

He was wearing the same grey sweats he had worn on the day he was jumped. Hood over his head and with hands in pockets, he kept a steady pace. He picked his way between trash barrels and litter, ignoring the stench of excrement. Across the street a runner handed a plastic bag to an anorexic woman in a slowly moving car and pocketed some bills in one smooth movement. He was stepping back onto the curb when he saw Conors. His eyes followed Conors while he spoke into a phone.

Conors had gotten their attention sooner than planned. He picked up his pace, the alleyway was three blocks away. He kept his head down, crossed a side street, jumped a street drain missing half its cast iron grate, and onto the sidewalk,

"Hi honey, want to warm-up?"

The sweet voice came from a woman who had an inch and an easy hundred pounds on Conors. She was covered in enough black leather to upholster a large SUV. She had appeared from a doorway and was blocking his way. He stepped into the gutter. "You'll be in my dreams till payday."

She ran her hands through her hair and winked. "Tell me when and I'll clear my calendar."

Ahead, on the opposite side of the street, four gangbangers poured out of a house. Like the runner, they wore black rapper clothes, apparently purchased with the notion they might unexpectedly grow six inches.

They spotted Conors, two of them pointed and started arguing, one talked on his phone, the fourth with his arm in a sling, pulled a pistol from the wheel well of a burned-out car. Conors recognized the kid. The kid slipped the gun into his sling and the gangbangers angled their way across the street.

He had misjudged, it was happening too fast. He needed to get past the brick building, that Woolworth said was the stash house, and to the alleyway. He picked up his pace. The gangbangers picked up theirs. They were less than fifty feet away and closing. Conors slipped the safety on Gallo's pistol to the off position.

They were close enough that Conors could feel the fear, theirs and his. The kid with the phone to his ear stopped suddenly and yelled something in Spanish. The bangers sprinted to their side of the street and huddled as if they were discussing the weather. The kid with the sling dropped the gun into a trash barrel.

Conors kept his stride and glanced about, not understanding the source of his good fortune until the black and white turned the corner. The cruiser slowed, the two cops studied Conors. He looked straight ahead. Seconds earlier Gallo's gun was comforting, now the weapon weighed in his hand. He waited for the cop to roll down the window. The cop didn't, the cruiser crawled by and stopped by the gangbangers.

Conors was a block from the alley when a tall Hispanic descended the steps of the stash house on the opposite side of the street. He was dressed in the same black clothing, but apparently wasn't anticipating a growth spurt. The man's gaze flitted between the cruiser and Conors.

The cruiser lingered and Conors made his way to the alleyway, took a few steps down the alley so he was no longer visible to the cops and turned around. He locked eyes with Manny, the leader of the gang. Conors held the stare until the anger was visible in Manny's face and then Conors slowly walked away.

Being the first time he had seen the neighborhood in daylight, Conors compared the alleyway to Google Maps. There was more debris than in the satellite picture, but the important things were the same, the alley lead to a street lined with abandoned tenements. By the time Conors reached the tenements, Manny and his soldiers were gathering at the end of the alley. Conors stopped in the middle of the empty street. There were nine of them. Manny took up the rear and they proceeded cautiously towards Conors looking for an ambush. There was yelling and bravado as they made their way.

When they were a hundred feet away, Conors pulled the sweat-shirt over his head and placed a large Bluetooth earpiece in his left ear. He was bare-chested with a cell phone in his left hand and Gallo's engraved and silver-plated gun in his right hand pointing at the ground.

The older ones were silent while the younger thugs laughed at Conors.

"Homie is a homo," said the kid with the broken arm.

The kid beside him pointed at Gallo's gun. "I want that piece."

"Shut-up," said Manny as he pushed his way to the front. He saw the shamrock-surrounded swastika and froze. Manny had spent time in the federal system and knew tattoos.

"What?" asked the soldier who had followed Manny to the front.

"Aryan Brotherhood," said Manny.

They had stopped, leaving fifty feet between them and Conors. Conors adjusted the earpiece. "Yeah, the tall one."

Conors saw the effect he had hoped for and slowly waved at the windowless buildings behind him. "Manny, two scopes are on your forehead, so tell your girls not to make any sudden moves."

They glanced at the tenements realizing they had walked into an ambush. The smarter ones looked for doorways and other escapes. The others glared at Conors.

"I'm just passing through and your pussies jump me," said Conors.

The kid with the sling took a step towards Conors. Manny grabbed him by the collar and yanked him back.

Conors raised his cell phone above his head. "I've sent pictures of all of you and your fat bitches to my brothers. If anything ever happens to me or if I ever again see any of you and you're not running in the opposite direction, the Brotherhood will hear how you disrespected them."

"We'd never disrespect the Brotherhood," said Manny.

Conors face turned red. He yelled, "You already have."

Manny flinched.

Conors pointed at the gangbangers. "Tell them to leave."

"You heard him," said Manny. The thugs slowly turned and strutted down the alley, trying to look as if they weren't relieved.

Manny started to follow.

"Not you," said Conors.

Conors waited till the gang was half way down the alleyway, picked up his sweatshirt and slipped it over his head. He walked towards Manny until their faces were inches apart. "If I wasn't trying to fly below the radar, I'd cut off your cohunes, make you eat them and then things would really get bad."

Manny stood silently.

"Get the fuck out of here."

Manny turned and walked down the alley.

Conors slipped the broken phone and earpiece, he had bought at a pawnshop for three bucks, into his pocket. He clicked the safety on Gallo's pistol and walked away from the departing Manny.

INBOX

It was early morning, Agent Johnson placed a bottle of water on DeLuca's desk.

"What's this?" said DeLuca. "The doctor yanked you off the coffee, not me."

Johnson sat down. "Drink-up. After a couple of days, it becomes a habit."

"I already have a life-long caffeine habit."

"I know, by lunch you're pacing like a greyhound at Wonderland, with eyes bulging like a teenager who's seen his first set of tits."

DeLuca reached for the bottle. "That's a lovely picture."

"The words vivid and accurate come to mind, not lovely," said Johnson.

DeLuca took a tentative sip of water and slowly screwed the cap on. He glanced at his smiling friend, then at the plastic bottle, *Maybe I should try this stuff.*

He put the bottle beside two empty cups. Johnson said, "Been here a while?"

Pointing at a pile of papers, Deluca said, "Since 9/11, this job has been in computer-driven overdrive. I can't make a dent in the damn inbox."

"Want some help? I have time later this week."

DeLuca hesitated, then said, "That would be great." He grabbed the top half of the pile and handed it to Johnson.

"Any success on the docks?" asked DeLuca.

"I never appreciated the challenges that Customs faces," said Johnson. "The Italian ship fingered by the informant was loaded with fifteen hundred containers. They open at most two percent of them and only look at a few items near the door. They'd shut down international trade if they did a hundred percent check."

"Sounds like port protection is a lost cause," said DeLuca.

"Not quite, the Port Authority screens containers for radiation, has a prioritized list of companies and countries and encourages the longshoremen to be on the lookout for anything out of the ordinary," said Johnson. "But the dockworkers weren't helpful yesterday."

"Why was that?"

"Nico Martarazzo. The bastard shadowed our entire visit, filling in for the union representative, who happened to get sick upon our arrival. Not a single longshoreman had the balls to be seen talking with us."

DeLuca frowned. "That guy's on the fast track."

"That's what happens when you save the boss's life."

"Didn't believe that story until it was verified by the third informant," said Deluca. "Our boy Nico must be one hell of a shot."

"Do we know where he was before working for Silvano?" asked Johnson.

"The mob in Chicago, he left when the local cops turned up the heat."

"Chicago makes sense, the dockworkers treat him like he was Al Capone."

"I'd love a couple of hours to question that monster," said DeLuca

"He doesn't look like the talkative type."

DeLuca sighed. "Did Terry discover anything new on Conors?"

"No, she's been reviewing the Grand Jury depositions for that Phoenix case. She'll be back on Conors' by the end of the week."

"I got another email from headquarters. Some desk jockey in Human Resources is hounding me to broaden Terry's experience," said DeLuca. "We have to get her out of the office, without putting her in the line of fire."

Johnson shrugged. "We'll think of something."

THE DICK
Late October

His eyes danced between the Little Debbie cream filled cookie and the bag of Cheese Curls lying on the dash. Daryl Dickson decided he didn't have time for another oversized cookie and grabbed a handful of Curls. He washed them down with a swig of generic cola and opened the door of the old Chevy van.

He stood and looked up and down the street. It was mid-morning and the street was mostly empty. A dozen men lingered at street corners and in doorways of closed businesses. Dickson ignored them. Before a forced early retirement, he was a Police Detective who worked these same streets. He figured his street smarts, being over six feet and the pistol under his jacket, tilted the odds in his favor.

He closed the squeaky door to the gray van and crossed the street. He'd already been to laundromats, barbers, convenience stores, luncheonettes and the post office. With eyes darting back and forth, he marched down the sidewalk, avoiding the unconscious drunk lying on the sidewalk and opened the door to Benson's Suds & Grub.

The smell of spilled beer greeted him. It was familiar and welcoming. The scowling patrons weren't. He headed to the back, towards a small group of men holding longneck bottles of Bud. Two men were playing checkers.

"Cleveland's finest," said an old black man, shaking a handful of checkers.

"You guys should be more friendly. I could be a tourist seeking the highlights of C-Town," said Dickson. The locals assumed he was still with the force, he did nothing to correct their error.

He flashed a picture in front of the old checker player. "Ever see this person?"

The old man looked away from Dickson and shook his head.

Dickson stuck the picture in the face of the only white man, other than the bartender. "Have you seen this guy?"

The guy smiled. "Lose your boyfriend."

The men broke into laughter and hoots. Dickson ignored the commotion and focused on the faces as they glanced at the picture.

"Once your boyfriend goes black, he ain't coming back."

Dickson smiled at the man and turned towards the bar, murmuring, "When I was thirty-five pounds lighter and still drinking, I would have pounded the shit out of these losers. I prefer the new me, high on Twinkies and loveable."

The bartender was drying a pilsner glass. Dickson guessed it was the same one he was drying when he entered the bar. He held the picture under the bartender's nose. "This guy ever come by?"

The bartender was shaking his head before he saw the photograph. Dickson turned quickly and stuck the picture in the face of a big fat guy sitting at the bar. The man hesitated, then a smile crossed his face.

"Is that a picture of you? All you honkies look the same."

The bar broke into a laughing uproar.

Dickson studied the big man's face and then left without a word.

He was halfway across the street when he raised the picture to his lips and kissed it.

CONTINGENCY

"I'm screwed."

Conors was sitting on the edge of his bed staring at the crumpled piece of paper on the cracked linoleum floor. There wasn't a computer in his neighborhood, never mind an internet connection. So every afternoon he'd leave Bensons, head to the CSU library, track the Boston news and search for any mention of AEG, the mob or his name. The previous day, a librarian had asked for a student ID and quietly called the campus police when he couldn't produce one. Conors had offered to leave, but the police had other ideas. Conors left them on the other side of an upturned bookcase and sprinted across campus and away from the only connection to his past life.

He knew he couldn't risk returning to CSU. He picked up and slowly straightened the paper, the last article he had printed before running from the library. He scanned the headline.

Class Action Lawsuit:
AEG sued for Dioxin Pollution of Chelsea

"One hundred percent crap," said Conors. "But if it goes to trial, they'll bankrupt me and my company."

He squashed the paper into a ball and let if fall to the floor. He glanced around the cold, musty-smelling apartment and then rested his head in his hands. Two and a half months without hearing his wife's voice, or wrestling with his sons, seemed like a lifetime. For the first time, he had skipped his morning run, the push-ups and sit-ups.

Conors stood, put on his baseball cap and left.

***

After leaving Benson's Suds & Grub that morning, Dickson moved his van 500 feet down the street and patiently watched the pedestrian traffic ebb and flow. The Bushnell scope lying on the dash was already focused for the front door of the barroom. The van's floor was speckled with aluminum foil. He popped another Hershey Kiss into his mouth and scanned the sidewalks.

It was noon and women in their Marriott and Hyatt outfits were exiting a bus after a morning of making beds. Passing through the gossiping Hispanic women was a man wearing a black baseball cap and a green vest. Dickson dropped the bag of candy on the passenger seat and studied the man as he crossed the street. The guy didn't have the gangbanger strut and wasn't dragging his ass like some laborer. Dickson grabbed the scope and zeroed in on the face.

"Bingo."

The man entered Benson's and Dickson floored the old van, stopping with two wheels on the sidewalk in front of the bar. Dickson rushed into Benson's. The man with the green vest and black cap was hunched over the bar. Dickson grabbed his handcuffs, pushed the man hard against the bar and yanked the man's right hand behind him.

He let go of the hand as fast as he had grabbed it and pulled the cap off the man's head. Woolworth turned and pointed at the cuffs. "I'm no longer into that shackles and whips shit."

"Christ," said Dickson. He dropped the cap and ran towards the back of the bar, pushing open the door to the restroom. The doorless stall and the two urinals were unoccupied.

He ran through the storage room, kicking cardboard boxes out of the way, empties clattered to the floor, he pushed open the back door. He looked up and down the deserted alley.

To the applause of the drinkers, he sprinted back through the bar and jumped into the van. He sped down the street in the direction Conors had come from and took his first left. Dickson worked on catching his breath as he drove, glancing down alleyways and side streets.

He caught a glimpse of Conors in his rearview mirror, sprinting down a street on the opposite side of the main drag. "Jesus, that bastard's fast."

He pulled a bumpy U-turn using both sidewalks, and floored the van. Barely slowing, he crossed two lanes of traffic and saw Conors turn down a side street. Within seconds Dickson's van screeched around the corner. He had expected to see Conors. Dickson hit the brakes, stopping in the middle of the street.

***

Conors' apartment building was the second building on the street. He had slammed the front door shut just before the van screeched around the corner. He ran up the stairs to the third floor hallway and looked outside, keeping his body pressed against the wall.

The man was out of the van, stopping people, holding up a piece of paper and asking questions. Conors assumed it was the picture the man had shoved in the face of his friends at Benson's.

Conors lowered himself to the floor and crawled to his apartment. He grabbed a business card tacked to the back of the door and dialed a number on a prepaid cell phone.

"Cleveland Yellow Cab," said a man with a Pakistani accent.

"I need to be picked up immediately. Is that possible?"

"Yeah, it's slow."

"333 Davis, I'll be waiting in the hallway of the apartment building."

"Five minutes," said the Pakistani.

Conors hung up, returned to the hallway and raised his head high enough to look out the window. The van was still in the middle of the street. He crawled to a corner window and looked further down the street. The sweat ran down the side of his face. There was no sign of the man. He crawled back to his room, grabbed a duffle bag that had been packed since arriving in Cleveland and yanked open the window. He lowered himself to the fire escape, raced to the bottom and disappeared down the alleyway.

He got to 333 Davis as the taxi driver was leaving. He pounded on the trunk of the accelerating taxi and it came to a jerking stop. He slid into the back seat and handed the driver thirty bucks. "1550 Superior Avenue, I'm late for my appointment."

"Yes sir."

***

The taxi pulled to the curb in front of a motel. Conors entered the one story building, walked past the registration desk, out the back door, across the motel parking lot and a narrow street and entered the back entrance of the bus station. He went directly to the schedule board. There was an hour and twenty-five minutes till the next departure.

He studied the mostly empty station and then with Gallo's money and his Bill Smith driver's license bought a round trip ticket to Cincinnati. He returned the Bill Smith license to his wallet and headed to the men's room. The restroom had an S-turn passageway designed for privacy without the congestion of swinging doors. The restroom was big, dirty and like the curving entry walls, covered with graffiti.

He went to the sink and pulled a toiletry bag from his duffle. With an electric trimmer he transformed his scruffy whiskers into a manicured beard and mustache. Then he entered a stall and replaced his cheap jeans and flannel shirt with a pair of chinos, a light blue button down shirt and an L.L. Bean barn jacket that had been neatly folded and stored in the duffle bag for months.

Finding the waste paper receptacles too small for his discarded clothing, he left them in the unlocked janitor's closet. He studied himself in the mirror and murmured, "Enjoy your sabbatical, Professor Slater."

Professor Slater approached a different ticket agent, purchased a roundtrip ticket to Akron and then chose a bench with a view of the bus he'd be boarding. He sat down with his duffle bag between his legs and pretended to read a discarded newspaper. Forty minutes later, a woman's voice made an announcement over the PA system "All passengers with tickets for Akron should board at Gate 6B."

Conors was about to get up when the man who had chased him from Benson's entered the station. He crossed the terminal, glancing at the people he encountered on his way to the ticket counter. After a short discussion, the agent pointed at Gate 6B.

Conors stood and angled towards the exit. Dickson spotted Conors and started towards him. Conors turned and entered the men's room for the second time. He dropped his duffle bag in the center stall so it would have blocked the view of his feet, closed the door from the outside and hung his jacket over the top of the door.

When Conors leaned against the wall next to the entrance, he remembered Gallo's gun was hidden in the lining of the duffle bag. Needing to improve his odds, he quietly opened the janitor's closet and grabbed a long handled dustpan. He returned to the wall next to the entrance, raised the dustpan above his head and held his breath.

The first thing Conors saw was the gun. The man fell for the trap and crouched to look into the stall. Conors swung hard. The sheet metal contraption hit the back of the man's head. The dust pan broke into pieces. The man fell to the floor, the gun, a pair of hand-cuffs and parts of the dustpan clattered across the gray tiles.

Conors grabbed the unconscious man's arms and dragged him to the janitor's closet. He returned for the gun and the cuffs. He secured one end of the cuffs to the man's left hand, and the other end to sink's drain pipe. He released the magazine from the gun and dropped it and the gun into a mop bucket filled with blackish water. Conors frisked the unconscious man and found a set of keys, a cell phone and a wallet. He pocketed the keys, dropped the phone into the bucket and opened the wallet. He found a business card.

"Daryl L. Dickson, Private Detective."

Conors looked at the man on the floor. "Mr. Dickson, that's good news. I thought you were a cop."

The men's room speakers blared, "Final boarding for Akron. Last call."

Dickson moaned. Conors dropped the wallet into the bucket, grabbed his belongings and ran. Entering the terminal, he glanced at the exit and the boarding gate. He had seconds to choose between the streets of Cleveland and the bus.

***

Conors was the last passenger on and handed his ticket to the disin-terested driver. His heart was racing, blood was pulsing through his temples. He made his way towards the back of the bus as it acceler-ated across the parking lot. He stopped half way down the aisle and sat by himself.

The brakes screeched and the old diesel groaned as the bus weaved its way through the traffic. He glanced at the city streets and the empty sidewalks. He turned from the window and opened the bus schedule the ticket agent had given him.

Cleveland, OH to Akron, OH
Bus	Departs	Arrives	Duration
4418	2:25pm	3:15pm	50m

Fifty minutes was more than he liked, but Conors had figured it would take Dickson a while to free himself. He was folding the schedule when he dropped it to the floor and hurriedly searched his pockets. He pulled out Dickson's key and stared at the General Motors key and a worn house key.

No keys for the handcuffs.

He angrily squeezed the keys in his hand until it hurt. He took a deep breath and pushed the keys between the two seat cushions. He opened his duffle and turned on the Garmin GPS he had purchased from a Cleveland pawnshop at the same time he bought a cell phone. Unlike the phone, the GPS worked and he faithfully charged it once a week. He turned it on. It showed him traveling south on Route 77. He clicked through a few menus and the device displayed nearby bus stations, the Cleveland terminal he had just left, a terminal for a small bus line and the Akron terminal.

Conors spent the following forty minutes monitoring the bus's progress on the small GPS, concerned that any moment a state trooper might force the bus over. When initially planning his departure from Cleveland he had avoided buses and trains. He disliked being stuck onboard until the next scheduled stop where a greeting party of police could be waiting.

When he was exactly 5.2 miles from the Akron terminal, Conors slipped the GPS into his pocket. He unzipped his duffle bag and removed a small bubble-wrapped container he had purchased over the internet. He unwrapped it and used a handkerchief to put the thin-glassed cylinder of ammonium sulfide in his jacket pocket. He stood and went to the restroom at the rear of the bus. He passed an older gentleman and a young man with an iPod and earphones. Both were asleep or at least had their eyes closed.

He entered the restroom and with the door partially opened, used his handkerchief to place the cylinder between the door and the jamb. He left, closing the door hard. The thin glass splintered, releasing a liquid.

Making his way back to his seat, he passed the elderly man who was now up and on his way to the restroom. The smell of hydrogen sulfide and ammonia had begun to spread. Some passengers were already sniffing, others rubbing their eyes, when the old man opened the door.

The man with the iPod woke to see the elderly man holding the restroom door. "Jee-sus, what kind of dog food have you been eating?"

Conors eyes started to burn. He slipped the strap to his duffle bag over his shoulder and then helped the stunned old man. He led him towards the front of the bus and yelled, "Stop, this man needs fresh air."

Within seconds the stench had dispersed throughout the bus.

"Let me out, let me out now," screamed a young woman who was making her way to the door.

A lady was shaking her dazed husband. "Harold, is this a terrorist attack?"

"We're being poisoned?" screamed another.

"Stop this freaking bus, before I do," bellowed a man in coveralls.

"Sit down," yelled the teary-eyed driver as he swerved from the passing lane to the breakdown lane. After screeching to a stop, the driver opened the door and the passengers poured onto the roadside coughing and hacking. Conors and the elderly man were the first to leave. Conors sat the man on the grass as the passengers gathered between him and the bus. He backed away looking at the commotion he had created for less than two bucks and a kid's stink bomb.

When the driver stuck his head in the bus to investigate, Conors walked the hundred feet to the highway exit. A few minutes after walking down the exit ramp, he was on a busy sidewalk heading towards Akron University.

***

Conors sat at a table in the back of the luncheonette reviewing the scheduled stops between Akron and Buffalo. He was not visible from the street, but had a clear view of the ChinaTravel Bus Lines terminal. The small concrete block building was manned by a Chinese mechanic who serviced the old buses and sold tickets to students and restaurant workers.

He had purchased a grease-stained ticket with Chinese characters stamped on it and then crossed the forty feet of asphalt to the luncheonette. His bus was scheduled to leave in twenty minutes. Passengers were boarding early.

Conors was sipping the last of a diet Pepsi when a gray van came to a jerking stop. He nearly dropped the can when Dickson climbed out of the vehicle and rushed into the ChinaTravel terminal. Conors pushed opened the luncheonette door and made a break for the adjacent warehouses. He was passing Dickson's van when he heard the running engine.

Conors slid to a stop, yanked on the handle and the driver's door flew open. He climbed in, threw his duffle on the passenger seat, jammed the transmission in drive and floored the van.

The van was rounding the corner when Conors glanced in the side-view mirror. Dickson was holding a gun. If he was shooting, Conors couldn't hear the shots over the floored engine and screeching tires.

Conors slowed to the 30 mph speed limit as he left the warehouses behind and approached the university campus. With a sweep of his arm he cleared the dash of candy wrappers, leaving the wet contents of Dickson's wallet drying on the heater vent. Attached to the dash was a large GPS displaying local bus terminals and train stations.

The traffic slowed to a crawl. Conors caught every light, spending one long red light beside an Akron police car. At the next light, he unfolded the ChinaTravel Bus line schedule and typed an address into Dickson's GPS. A female voice directed him to take a left.

Six turns and fifteen minutes later, the GPS announced, "You have reached your destination."

At a Giant Eagle supermarket, he pulled into the lot and parked between two cars. When he tried to turn off the van, he discovered there were no keys in the ignition. Leaning over, he saw wires hanging from underneath the dash. He yanked on them and the engine died.

Conors took Dickson's IDs from the dash, put them in his pocket, and then picked a telescope off the floor and smashed the GPS screen. He checked his watch, grabbed his duffle and walked to the Chinese restaurant on Market Street. The bus was scheduled to stop in three minutes.

ALL WET

The cruiser turned into the parking lot. The two officers saw a disheveled man with a bruised and scratched face. He was pacing in front of the ChinaTravel bus terminal. They approached slowly.

The cruiser stopped in front of Dickson. The driver asked, "Are you the person that reported a stolen van?"

"No, I'm the person who reported a stolen van twenty-seven minutes ago," said Dickson. "But it's okay, you needed time for the donuts to settle."

The patrolman in the passenger seat grabbed a clipboard and opened his door murmuring, "Going to be a long afternoon."

The officers approached Dickson. The driver asked, "Were you dragged through a mud puddle before or after your car was stolen?"

"Before and it wasn't a mud puddle, it was a bucket of mop water."

"What's your name, sir?" asked the officer with the clipboard.

"Daryl Dickson."

"You have any ID?"

"It's in the van that I reported stolen twenty-eight fucking minutes ago."

"Were your keys in the van when it was stolen?"

"Nope."

"Can you show us your car keys?"

Dickson shook his head. "Now, stop playing Inspector Clouseau and activate the damn LoJac transmitter on my van. I'd like to find it, before it ends up in one of the Great Lakes."

"If the keys weren't in the car, and you don't have the keys on your person, how were you operating the vehicle before the alleged theft?"

"What do you mean alleged?" growled Dickson.

The two officers glanced at each other, the driver moved closer to determine if he could smell alcohol. "Mr. Dickson, please answer the questions. How were you operating your car without a key?"

"It was hotwired," said Dickson.

"Why would you hotwire your own car?" asked the driver.

"Because the asshole who stole my car, had previously stolen my fucking car keys," yelled Dickson.

"Oh," said the driver with raised eyebrows. "Is this a lover's quarrel?"

"Yeah, I've this thing for guys who beat the shit out of me and steal my van," yelled the red faced Dickson.

The officer with the clipboard placed it on the cruiser and signaled his partner to back away. "Mr. Dickson, what's that object in your pants pocket?"

Dickson glanced at the bulge and then at the officers. "An unloaded pistol."

Both officers unholstered their guns and clicked their safeties off.

"Mr. Dickson, don't make any quick moves."

Dickson looked at the guns, then at the officers and concluded they were the shooting type, not the kind to get dirty wrestling somebody to the ground. In a conciliatory voice he said, "I won't."

"Do you always carry an unloaded gun?" asked the driver.

"Nope, it's usually loaded, but the man who stole my van dropped the gun into a bucket of water. I'm drying it out."

"Mr. Dickson, do you have a permit to carry a concealed weapon in the State of Ohio?"

"Yes."

"Let me guess, your permit is in the stolen car with the man who put your gun in a bucket of water."

"That's pretty accurate."

"Mr. Dickson, I want you to slowly put your hands on your head, kneel and then lie face first on the ground."

"You're joking."

The driver aimed his pistol at his chest. "Mr. Dickson, if you think we're joking you have a weird sense of humor."

***

Eight hours and nine stops later, the ChinaTravel bus had arrived at a combined bus and truck stop outside Buffalo. Each additional mile from Akron and each stop without a waiting police car had made Conors more confident that Dickson had lost his trail. He had wanted to change bus lines earlier, but this was the first terminal ChinaTravel shared with another bus company. The Trailways bus to Rochester would leave at 6:10 a.m., requiring a five hour layover.

Three hours intro his wait, the overcast night had masked the area in a fine mist. Determined not to be surprised again, Conors was in the shadows, a few feet from an asphalt walkway. The walkway ran down a gentle slope from a truck-stop restaurant to the bus terminal. He was behind a bush, leaning against the back, windowless wall of the restaurant. He had a clear view of the terminal.

Every hour, he had given himself a five minute break from the cold and stood in the restaurant while a waitress filled an oversized Styrofoam cup with diet Pepsi, no ice. He had carefully studied the restaurant's clientele. They were big-rig truckers who filled the parking lot with semis and tandem-trailer trucks. The truckers were served by a dozen middle-aged waitresses with trays filled with breakfasts and dinners. Some truckers apparently thought they were starting their day while others saw theirs coming to a close.

The caffeine was working. Conors was cold, but wide awake. He was leaning against the wall swirling the last of his soda, when he tossed the cup into the bushes.

"Christ, I must have a transmitter up my ass?"

His gut told him the man lurking beyond the streetlights was Dickson. Any doubt was removed when the man crossed the parking lot and entered the terminal. Conors pulled the duffle bag over his shoulder, left his hideaway and ran towards the restaurant. He kept to the bushes until he turned the corner and was out of Dickson's line of sight.

Conors yanked opened the door and walked into the din of a hundred truckers. When he was ten feet into the restaurant, he dropped his duffle to the floor and bellowed, "My 92 Ford Escort just blew its engine. Anybody have room for a hitchhiker?"

He was successful in getting the attention of the front half of the restaurant. The truckers looked up, but returned to their meals when Conors glanced their way.

He let out a long nervous breath, picked up his bag and turned to leave. On the way out he was passing a bearded trucker in a flannel shirt paying for his coffee. "I'm headed east and need some company," said the trucker. "I'm having a hell of a time staying awake."

Conors smiled. "I'm also headed east and would enjoy a good conversation."

The trucker pushed the door opened. "Follow me."

A couple of minutes later, Conors was sitting beside the trucker. The man double clutched into third. The diesel was working hard as the tandem rig accelerated to thirteen mph and passed the restaurant. Conors leaned back into the seat, when he saw Dickson peering into the restaurant window.

As the truck left the parking lot and approached the entrance ramp to Route 90, Conors glanced at the wet forest, his destination before the trucker offered him a ride. Conors turned towards the driver as he double clutched into seventh gear.

"How much does a rig like this cost?"

PIECES

Agent Deluca opened the conference room door and saw Johnson, Munroe, and Amero on one side of the table. On the opposite side, Terry Hamlin was standing and pointing at a wall mounted monitor. DeLuca stopped, his hand resting on the doorknob as he stared at the monitor. "I'll be damned."

Hamlin fell silent and Johnson moved his chair, making room for DeLuca. DeLuca sat down.

Johnson said, "Our agents in Ohio have been concentrating on ID forgers and raided some guy in Cleveland. By the time they got through a barricaded door, the forger had burned his ID blanks and erased his computers. The only evidence retrieved were pictures from his digital cameras." Johnson held up a dozen pages covered with passport-sized pictures. "These were in that pile you removed from your inbox and asked me to review."

"Why were the pictures forwarded to us?" asked DeLuca.

"Headquarter's computer has been flagging everything from Cleveland since the alleged sighting of Conors at the bus terminal."

Johnson placed one of the pages in front of DeLuca. "Yesterday I was going over the pictures and one caught my attention. I asked Terry to take a look. She zeroed in on the same picture and went one step further. She used some fancy computer software to compare the picture to our favorite fugitive. Terry could you give Joe a summary."

"Sure," said Hamlin. She placed the end of a long metal pointer on a picture at the left side of the monitor. "I acquired this photograph from Conors' AEG identification card during the audit and I got a copy of his license from the Registry of Motor Vehicles. This third picture is from the Cleveland forger."

She moved the pointer in a circular motion that encompassed the three pictures. "Unfortunately we're dealing with photographs, not video, which would have given us the greater accuracy of three dimensions."

Agent Hamlin pushed a couple of buttons on her laptop and a series of line crisscrossed the three photographs. A second later a summary table of measurements appeared on the bottom of the display. "Since I was dealing with photographs, I had to rely on a suite of facial measurements based on the distance between eyes, ears, nose and mouth. I used the FRVT criteria to estimate the error rate."

"What's a FRVT error rate?" said DeLuca.

"The geeks at the National Institute for Standards and Technology developed a Face Recognition Vendor Test or the FRVT to evaluate optical and software systems," said Hamlin.

"Enough, what are the chances the bearded guy is Conors?" asked DeLuca.

"The software has over ninety-eight percent confidence that it's William Conors."

DeLuca looked at his watch and got up from the table. "Good enough for government work. Forward Conors' pictures with and without the beard to the Cleveland Field Office and the New England Joint Task Force."

DeLuca headed towards the door. "Good work."

"Joe?" said Hamlin.

DeLuca stopped. "Yeah?"

"I'm done with the Phoenix job for the time being and was hoping to get out of the office. Maybe do some street work," said Hamlin.

DeLuca glanced at Johnson with raised eyebrows and then glanced at Hamlin. "We'll see what we can do."

SMOKE & STRIPPERS

Stefano slowly got to his knees and looked out the rear window of the grocery van. He had a clear view of the brick addition that protruded from the back of the nightclub. A half hour earlier, the Russian boss and his lieutenants had entered the office with vodka and cards. Stefano lowered himself to the floor of the van, made himself comfortable and studied his watch. He had been ready since the Russians arrived, but the operation needed to be synchronized with others across New England.

In addition to Stefano, six others were inside split between two tables at opposite ends of the nightclub. They had been frequenting the club for a week. They drank heavily, tipped generously, feigned drunkenness but never caused problems for the bouncers. The waitresses and strippers took a liking to the big-tipping Italians who were supposedly merchant marines awaiting an overdue freighter. Although this evening appeared no different, a keen eye would have noticed that their jackets hung lower and that the Italians were less boisterous and spilled more than they drank.

Maceo, the leader of the inside team, felt the cell phone vibrate. After the fourth ring, he stood and yelled, "Acclamazioni Piccardo." Piccardo, seated at the second table yelled back, "Bravo."

A bouncer turned to a fellow Russian tending bar. "Big-mouths." The bartender grimaced and shook his head. "Fucking Italians."

A few seconds before 10:50, a waitress approached Piccardo's table as the Italians pushed foam plugs into their ears and dropped to the floor. At the same time Stefano opened the back doors of the grocery van. Two shoulder-fired weapons were secured to a bracket bolted to the floor. A whooshing sound came from the weapon secured to the drivers' side of the bracket. The rocket blew-in a Plexiglas window, stunning those inside the nightclub's brick office.

Three seconds later the shock wave had dissipated and the second weapon was fired. A thermobaric rocket followed the path of the first and detonated. Molten metal and liquid fuel incinerated the contents of the brick office.

Inside the nightclub, the Italian soldiers heard the first explosion and waited for the second detonation before they jumped to their feet. The bombs did not destroy the building, but it had been badly shaken. Some lights were out. Most of the customers and strippers had been knocked to the floor. They were in shock, the screaming had not yet started. A cloud of smoke and dust filled the club.

With weapons drawn, the Italian looked to the last place they had seen their targets. Many of the Russians were getting to their feet. Two war-hardened Russians were running towards the bar, someone had pushed a shelf of liquor aside and opened a cabinet stashed with revolvers and shotguns. The deafening sound of six Berettas filled the nightclub. The Russians were dead before they hit the floor.

Piccardo had been assigned two targets. He had eliminated the first, but could not locate the second. He was moving down the bar, pushing dazed customers aside and using the mirrored wall to search for the bartender.

A fraction of a second too late, Piccardo saw the movement. Ten feet to his right, the bartender raised his head and shoulders above the bar. A bullet left the barrel of Piccardo's pistol as the bartender pulled the trigger of a sawed-off shotgun.

The bullet from Piccardo's Berretta obliterated the bartender's left eye. The Russian was thrown against the wall as the buckshot killed Piccardo and two customers.

Maceo saw the exchange of gunfire and within seconds was standing over Piccardo. His face was missing. Nobody had any identification, Interpol didn't have their prints and Piccardo would never be identified.

Maceo blew a piercing whistle and the Italians pushed through the nearest exits within sixty seconds of the explosions. They sprinted down the narrow street behind the nightclub, tossing their pistols into the back of the van and ran towards three waiting sedans. Stefano pushed an igniter into a large pad of plastic explosives located above the van's fuel tank. He locked the doors and ran.

That evening twenty-one men in SUVs and sedans scattered across the Northeast. Over a period of a week, they would enter Canada at different border crossings from Maine to Minnesota and fly out of five different Canadian airports. Eventually a Canadian bureaucrat would note a small but significant increase in the number of Italian businessmen flying between Canada and Europe.

***

It was approaching midnight. DeLuca was in bare feet and pajama bottoms, brushing his teeth. His eyes were fixed on the jiggling potbelly in the bathroom mirror. He hoisted his slipping pj's higher, it didn't improve the view. He shook his head and wondered what his wife saw in him.

His dentist had advised brushing for two minutes. He was approaching his less-demanding standard of thirty seconds when his cell phone rang. He dropped the toothbrush in the sink and ran to the bedroom, trying to answer the phone before it woke his wife. He grabbed it on the third ring, swallowed a mouthful of toothpaste and whispered, "Yeah."

"Agent DeLuca?"

"Yeah, this is Joseph DeLuca."

"Sir, this is the FBI Homeland Security Division and we have an agency-wide alert, but so far the activity is limited to New England."

DeLuca returned to the bathroom with the phone and closed the door. "What activity?"

"Within the last hour, we received independent requests from Massachusetts and Rhode Island. They both report military-like attacks in Boston and Providence. We are talking with Connecticut State Police, but at this point it's unclear as to what transpired in Hartford. Homeland Security Response Teams have been dispatched, and I was told to inform you."

"What were the targets?" asked DeLuca, with thoughts of 9/11 blazing in his mind.

"Initial indications are organized crime kingpins and their operations," said the agent. "Sir, I need to go, I have a list of calls to make. You are advised to return to your office so you can receive information as it becomes available."

"Give me a half hour," said DeLuca

He hung-up and immediately placed a call.

"What?" said the half-awake Johnson.

"Jim, this is Joe. We have to get to the office. Some major shit is going down."

"How major?" asked Johnson.

"Homeland Security has initiated an agency-wide alert," said DeLuca.

"I'll be there within the hour."

"Good, I'm stopping at Dunkin Donuts," said DeLuca. "You interested?"

"Yeah, my doctor doesn't need to know. Big, no cream, no sugar."

***

A note on Johnson's desk told him that DeLuca was in the Cyber Crime Department. Johnson made his way down a short hallway and entered a room crammed with computers and monitors. At the far end of the room DeLuca sat at a bench. He was viewing a patchwork of digital pictures on a sixty-inch wall monitor.

"What's this?" said Johnson while crossing the room. "It looks like Baghdad."

"The highlights of what I've been emailed. There's a continual stream of pictures coming from the response teams." Deluca pointed at the left hand side of the monitor. "These five were taken by a helicopter hovering over the Heritage Condominium Building and that black hole is the penthouse, once the home of Boston's Russian mob boss."

Johnson stood silently absorbing the significance and magnitude of the destruction. Deluca moved the cursor. "These are pictures of the Russian's nightclub in Boston. The email says the burned-out structure attached to the nightclub was the Russians' office."

The cursor circled the bottom pictures of a concrete building. "These were taken from the ground. It's a warehouse in Providence, an explosion blew off the top two stories."

"Jesus, how many casualties?" asked Johnson.

"No details other than there are casualties at all three locations," said DeLuca.

"Who's running the operation?" asked Johnson.

"Homeland Security has the lead. If it's solely an attack on organized crime targets we'll share in the oversight."

"Where do we go from here?" asked Johnson.

"I sent them a list of Russian sites in New England. They're checking them out. We'll sift through the rest of the information before calling in our agents," said DeLuca.

***

By 4 a.m., there was more information on the previous night's activities. DeLuca was reading a summary that had been emailed across the Bureau.

> *All available information indicates that at 22:50 hours a well planned attack was simultaneously launched across New England. The attack lasted minutes and in all cases except one, there was no trace of the perpetrators. The most modern of armament and explosives were employed in a manner necessitating a high level of training and discipline. Since all targets were Russian organized crime properties, it is assumed there was no intended threat against national interests. However, an organized military attack of this nature proves our vulnerability to a similarly implemented terrorist attack.*

Johnson was standing, reading over DeLuca's shoulder. When they finished Johnson said, "Just got off the phone with Headquarters. The explosive experts haven't cleared the areas for forensic investigations."

"Looks like our evidence teams will get a good night's sleep," said DeLuca.

Johnson lowered himself into a chair. "Still think Giovanni's behind this?"

"It has Giovanni written all over it. He was a proponent of overwhelming force, decades before Colin Powell," said DeLuca.

"Overwhelming force is right. Along with the chief, he massacred all the Indians."

"Giovanni would never trust any Russians. There'd be no omerta. He knows an arrested Russian would never remain silent."

"So the old Giovanni, just on a larger scale," said Johnson.

"It's the only thing that makes sense," said DeLuca. "Our informants claim Giovanni blames the Russians and Conors for his son's death."

"Could Giovanni's men have pulled this off?" asked Johnson.

"Doubt it. We know most of them and none have military backgrounds. Only possible exception is the mysterious Nico, who seems disciplined enough to have been a soldier. But, one or two doesn't make the army needed for last night," said DeLuca.

The Dunkin Donuts coffee was long gone. The two men were drinking from Johnson's stash of bottled water. DeLuca unscrewed a cap and took a mouthful. "The bigger question is whether any of this is traceable to Giovanni."

DOWN EAST
Early November

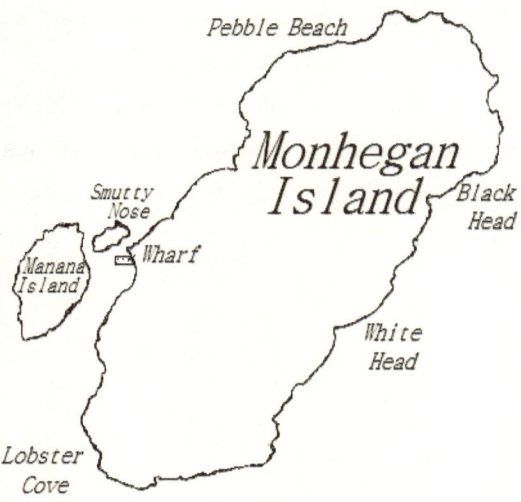

An old blue bus coasted to a stop in Rockland Maine. Conors, with a duffle over his shoulder, stepped off and stood on the sidewalk, his back to the ocean. The sun had set and the onshore wind was damp. He flipped his collar up as the bus noisily pulled from the curb. For the last three days he had crisscrossed the Northeast by trucks and buses. He was tired and in need of a shower.

There was no terminal to spend the night. This was coastal Maine, where a small white sign on a galvanized pole was the only hint of a bus stop. On the opposite side of the street was a four story wooden building, the Maritime Motor Inn. Conors crossed the street, passed by the vacancy sign and entered the lobby. He approached the elderly clerk at the desk and placed his duffle on the floor.

"How much are your rooms?"

"Fifty-five for a harbor view and forty-five for the others," said the clerk.

"I'll skip the view," said Conors.

"Will that be credit?"

"Cash, I'll pay now."

"Okay, that's forty-nine with tax, plus I need to see an ID."

Conors placed a hundred dollar bill and William Slater's driver's license on the counter. The clerk glanced at the license, suspiciously examined the hundred dollar bill, and then looked over the top of his reading glasses at Conors.

"On Saturdays, I work at the bank. If I accepted a bad bill, my boss would be on my case for a year," said the clerk. "You could give Monopoly money to the kid who works days. He wouldn't know any better."

The clerk held the bill up to the light and repositioned his reading glasses. Conors stopped breathing.

"See that little band. It's called a security thread," said the clerk. "That band tells you this is a good bill, but the kid won't take the time to look."

The exhausted and relieved Conors leaned against the counter.

"You look like you're seen a ghost," said the clerk.

"Sorry, I'm three thousand miles from home and thought my bank had given me counterfeit money."

"Won't happen at a bank. But whenever someone gives you change, hold the twenties and bigger up to the light," said the clerk.

"I'll do that," said Conors.

The clerk placed a room key, pen and a small card in front of Conors. "Sign and fill out the room card. Don't worry about the car description, I saw you get off the bus."

Conors took the pen. He had rehearsed writing his new name, the shape and angle of the letters shared no similarity with his true signature.

"Room 108 is down the hall on the left," said the clerk. He put Conors' change on the counter.

Conors picked up the key and the money. "Thanks."

The room was a muted yellow and clean. After dead-bolting the door and pulling the drapes closed, he sat on the edge of the bed and turned on the lamp. He emptied the paper currency from his wallet and held each to the light. Then he opened his duffle bag, retrieved the rest of Gallo's money and checked each bill. He had just over eighteen thousand dollars, all of it legal.

A long shower washed away the unclean feeling of buses, trucks and dirty terminals. Conors was drying himself when he noticed a paper wrapped bar of hand soap sitting on the sink. The bar was half the size of a credit card. He used to collect them, souvenirs for his boys, who helped him unpack after business trips. He picked the soap up and read the label, "Hand Soap with Lanolin." He gently returned the bar to the sink.

He dressed, shoved his duffle bag under the bed, turned on the TV and left by the back door, lost in thoughts about soap, kids and his wife. Halfway down Main Street, he found an open restaurant, the Coast Café. The small restaurant had a dozen small tables, the locals were talking with each other and the waitresses. A policeman sat alone at a back table. Conors took a seat a couple of tables away and picked up the plastic coated menu.

He ordered a fisherman's plate that turned out to be a heaping platter of fried haddock, scallops and clams. He dipped a plump clam in tartar sauce. Conors put it in his month and fondly imagined his wife's disapproving look as she silently calculated the cholesterol content of his favorite meal.

"How's everything," asked the middle-aged waitress.

Conors swallowed the clam. "Great."

"Good," said the waitress.

"What's the best way to the Port Clyde ferry, when you don't have a car?" asked Conors.

"Don't know if it's the best way, but you can hire a taxi."

"Any suggestions?"

She pointed at a bulletin board. "Yellow business card."

"Thanks," said Conors, noticing that the policeman had been listening.

After the meal, he paid at the counter in cash and left a fifteen percent tip, figuring the waitress wouldn't be pissed or remember him. He copied the telephone number from the business card onto the back of his receipt. On his way to the motel, he scouted the neighborhood in case he had to make a quick exit. He returned to his room by the motel's back door. The TV was on. The money, gun and ammo were in his duffle, undisturbed.

He took the receipt from his pocket and dialed the number. After scheduling a taxi for the morning, he turned off the light and lay on the bed. So much had happened that his escape seemed like a long time ago, yet his throbbing pulse reminded him that it was not over. He had planned on leaving Cleveland for New England in the spring. But Dickson had proven that his detailed plan was like most plans, subject to a reality controlled by others. He closed his eyes knowing he wouldn't sleep. He was on the run again.

***

The next morning he waited till eight before leaving his room. A young man was at the front desk. Conors assumed it was the kid who accepted Monopoly money. He saw the taxi in the parking lot, pushed the hotel door open and was outside before he noticed the police car.

"Mr. Slater," said a cop standing by the patrol car. "Have a moment?"

"Sure," said Conors, recognizing the officer from the previous night.

"What's your business in Rockland?"

"Just passing through," said Conors. "Taking in the scenery."

"Don't have many tourists this time of year."

"That's the idea, want to avoid the crowds," said Conors.

The cop leaned against the patrol car, silent, staring.

"Is there anything else? I have a tight schedule," said Conors.

The police officer looked at Conors, at his notebook and then back at Conors. "I guess that's it."

Conors tossed his duffle in the back seat of the taxi and slid in beside it. He closed the door and the taxi drove away. The driver looked in the rearview mirror. "Sorry about Officer Pease, we call him Dirty Harry."

"He has a way of waking you up," said Conors.

"It's nothing personal. Every night he stops by the motel to see who's checked in," said the driver. "He's looking for the next Jeffrey Dahmer."

"Hopefully, he doesn't shoot too many tourists before Jeffrey arrives," said Conors.

The driver laughed. "The jerk arrested my partner's ten-year old son for fishing from the town jetty. Jee-sus, this is Maine, that's what you want kids doing."

Once out of town, the driver hit the accelerator. The rusting Ford sedan was in need of shocks and bounced as the taxi sped down the two lane road towards Port Clyde. A few miles later, the driver took a call from his dispatcher, hung-up and pushed harder on the gas. "Have another fare at nine."

The Mainer fell silent and used his wits to keep the car in its lane. The road narrowed, the houses became closer together, closer to the road and surrounded with lobster traps, sometimes neatly stacked and other times scattered as if a tornado had dropped them.

The road narrowed more and the cab lurched through twists and turns. Conors braced his knees against the back of the front seat.

***

The sixty-five foot long Laura B was designed to be practical, not pretty. She had been built to patrol the Pacific islands during World War II and had been cruising the Gulf of Maine since her return. Although referred to as the mail boat, she also ferried cargo and passengers to and from Monhegan Island.

Once the Laura B got underway, Conors stood on the starboard catwalk and leaned against the pilot house. He grew up on the coast, served as a U.S. Marine and had a stable sea stomach. As the morning sun escaped from behind a bank of clouds Conors relaxed, something felt right about the bite of the wind and the fine spray coming over the bow. He stared into the horizon. His family was two hundred miles to the south and for the first time his plans for returning home seemed credible.

The vessel passed Hupper Island, which by Maine standards had a good number of homes. The young captain navigated a maze of ledges and barren islands as the Laura B plowed through two-foot chop. The islands became fewer and the outline of Monhegan Island could be seen seven miles to the south. The folded pamphlet supplied with his ticket included a ferry schedule, pictures, highlights and a map of the bay and the island. The pamphlet indicated the island was two miles long, less than a mile wide and home to sixty winter residents. With granite shores rising one hundred and sixty feet it had been the first landfall for many, including Giovanni da Verrazano in 1525, and John Smith in 1614.

In Muscongus Bay, five-foot easterly seas hit the Laura B broadside and the round bottom boat rolled from port to starboard and back again. Conors returned to the passengers' cabin as the sun disappeared behind thickening clouds.

The Laura B's cruising speed of less than ten knots required seventy minutes to complete the trip from Port Clyde to Monhegan. By midmorning Conors was looking at the narrow entrance to Monhegan Harbor. According to the pamphlet, the harbor's limited protection was due to a ledge called Smutty Nose that served as a breakwater and a large rock formation called Manana Island that lay a few hundred feet to the west of Monhegan. The Laura B kept Smutty Nose close to starboard and entered the harbor. Following an efficient flurry of on-deck activity the vessel was secured to the wharf. The two-man crew started to unload cargo. Conors, the only passenger, grabbed his duffle and made his way down the boarding ramp. A lone gull was on the wharf, squawking, complaining about whatever bothers seagulls on cold, overcast days.

He followed a dirt road uphill towards the village. A soggy easterly breeze greeted him, it was thick with ocean smell. Beads of moisture collected on his beard and his windbreaker. At the top of the road, he climbed the steps to an old shingled inn, stood on the porch and scanned the harbor. The Laura B was leaving. Not a person was in sight.

He ignored the closed sign and opened the door. The inn had closed for the season, but during a long telephone conversation he had convinced the manager to let him stay for two nights. The lobby was filled with stacks of rockers and cane chairs removed from the wrap-around porches. He followed a path through the shoulder high stacks to the registration counter. He was told someone would be available to show him to his room.

Conors looked about. "Hello."

When repeated attempts and a louder voice failed to produce a response, he explored the further end of the lobby and at the foot of a staircase heard a sound from above. He yelled, "Hello."

Again, hearing no answer, he shouldered his duffle and started up the stairway.

"Anybody here?"

By the time Conors arrived on the third floor, he discovered the noise, a radio tuned to the National Weather station blaring a repetitive marine forecast. He followed the sound to a utility room loaded with housekeeping materials on one side and an assortment of tools on the other. Underneath a small porcelain sink centered on the far wall was a man on his knees holding a wrench to a pipe. To be heard over the radio Conors raised his voice. "Hello."

The startled plumber turned, bouncing his head off the side of the old sink. The man slowly stood and backed away from the sink rubbing his head.

"Lordy, lordy," said the man.

The man had an athletic build, curly gray hair and a weathered face. He wore dungarees, suspenders and a flannel shirt with the top buttons undone, revealing the worn collar of long underwear. As he backed away from the sink he approached a wall of tools, including a snow rake.

He stepped hard onto the blade of the rake. The handle accelerated upwards with blurring speed. The aluminum handle smashed through the ceiling fixture and came to an abrupt stop at the back of the man's head. Fine glass splinters and powder from the fluorescent bulbs rained down on the man turning his hair white and sparkly.

The man's sun bleached blue eyes opened wide. Conors dropped his duffle and grabbed the man by the arm. He guided him to a five gallon drum of cleaning solution and helped him sit.

"Are you okay?" asked Conors.

The man was silent, touching the side of his head that had met the sink and then the back that had stopped the rake handle.

"Was, before you arrived," said the man in a Maine accent.

"Should I call a doctor?" asked Conors.

"You can call all you want. There are no doctors on the Island."

"Any medical help?"

"A few of the guys and gals are EMTs."

"How do I contact them?" asked Conors.

"Even if I needed them, I wouldn't tell you," said the old man who remained perched on the container.

"Why?" asked Conors.

"I'm expecting a headache that can be cured with a few aspirins. If the EMTs walked in here, I'd be the talk of the Island."

"Are you sure?" asked Conors.

"Yeah, I'm sure they'd make me out to be the village idiot."

The man got up and made his way to the sink. He placed both hands on the basin, leaned towards the mirror and studied the emerging bump on his forehead. His attention eventually switched to Conors' reflection in the mirror.

"Who the hell are you? The plumbing inspector or some over-sized bad-luck leprechaun?"

Conors suppressed a smile. "Neither, I'm Bill Slater looking for my room."

The man turned, Conors offered his hand. They shook and the man said, "Hi, I'm Gerald Ford."

Conors didn't know if the man was serious, but the thought that it could be his name was too much. Conors burst into laughter.

The man's poker-face melted into a wide grin.

**

Conors helped Elijah Mullen clean-up the utility room and replace the broken bulbs. Elijah opened the bar and over warm beer boiler-makers they swore to secrecy the true reasons for the bumps and bruises.

After three hours and many drinks, Conors discovered that drinking with Elijah was like peeling an onion. He assumed he'd have to strip countless layers to truly know his new acquaintance. What he did learn was that Elijah was a fourth generation Monhenganite and a Dartmouth graduate. Like his father and grandfather, he was a lobster fisherman, who practiced carpentry and plumbing during the off-season.

Before calling it a night and going their separate ways, Conors shared his hopes of finding a place on the island for the winter. Elijah suggested that he speak to his friend.

***

Late the following morning, Conors followed Elijah's directions to Rose's home and the small rental cottages. Elijah explained that in the past Rose had rented to the sternmen who helped lobstermen tend their traps. However, after one particularly rowdy tenant, she stopped renting during the fishing season, which ran from December to June.

When he approached the cottages, a lady was bent over, insulating the foundation of the main house with bales of hay. He assumed the small woman was Rose. He stopped in the road by the weathered picket fence that encircled her property.

"Ma'am."

The woman turned, she looked to be about the same age as Elijah.

"Yeah?"

"I'm interested in renting a cottage for the winter."

She returned to her work. "Don't rent during the off-season."

"Elijah mentioned that, but said I should speak to you," said Conors.

Rose, still facing her house, dropped her gardening gloves, turned, and walked towards Conors. Standing no more than a foot away, the woman looked up into his eyes and pointed a finger at him.

"Just because you're buddies with that old fool, you think you can come here and change my mind."

"No ma'am and I'm sure Elijah doesn't either. He spoke too highly of you." Conors backed up. "Sorry I bothered you."

Rose pointed a second time, but this time her finger wavered. It was stained with a multitude of paints, Conors decided she must be one of the island's year-round artists. She slowly lowered the finger that she had wielded like a weapon and started up the path towards her cottages. "Come with me."

Conors opened the gate and followed.

"See that cottage," she said.

"Yes, ma'am."

"If the well water to that cottage was left on, the pipes would freeze before Christmas."

They passed through a small stand of wind-beaten cedar trees and stopped in front of a second cottage. She waved her multi-colored hand in frustration at a small building.

"This one has a good foundation and a good roof, but the siding is falling off. The wind blows through so hard you can't keep the stove lit."

She pointed at a pile of cedar shingles to the left of the cottage. "Two years ago, a carpenter told me he'd re-shingle the cottage. A week later, when the Laura B lowered the shingles to the wharf, the carpenter climbed aboard and never returned."

She gave him a stern look. Conors figured she was deciding where he fit on the scale of humanity and hoped he'd fared better than the carpenter.

"What do you call yourself?" asked Rose.

"Bill Slater"

"Well, Mr. Slater, why do you think you could spend a winter in a cottage like this?"

"I was a Marine and bivouacked in places that make your cottage look like the Hyatt Regency."

"From the looks of your eyes, you also drink like a Marine."

Conors recalled his mother's cross-examinations. "Not usually. Last night, I tried to keep up with Elijah."

With a renewed look of irritation, Rose said, "I thought Elijah only got the old ladies drunk."

Conors sensed something was going on between Rose and Elijah that he should avoid. "If you change your mind about renting, I'd be willing to shingle the cottage," said Conors. "I'm not a finish carpenter, but worked construction during my college years."

Rose squinted and pursed her lips.

"Where you from?"

"California."

"What did you do in California?"

"Taught math at a junior college. I'm on sabbatical," said Conors.

"Married?" asked Rose.

"Common law wife for a decade. Last semester she ran off with my dean."

"Sounds awkward."

"That's why I'm on sabbatical."

Rose looked at Conors and then offered her hand.

"You shingle the cottage, pay for your propane, no wild parties unless I'm invited and you have the cottage for four hundred a month."

Conors took her hand and smiled. "Thanks ma'am. That's great."

"The name's Rose."

TRAVELING
Mid-November

Lisa Kelly checked the rental car's mirror and then switched lanes for the upcoming exit. She ignored the gray overcast skies and leafless trees and sped south on Interstate 84.

"Forty miles to New Haven. That leaves time for lunch," said Kristin Conors as she refolded the AAA map.

"Excellent, I'm dying for an old fashion, oversized, greasy hamburger," said Lisa.

"Sounds like you have plans," said Kristin.

"Matt worked in a restaurant when he was at Yale. He has talked about their hamburgers for years."

"Sounds good," said Kristin in a soft, uncertain voice. "By the way, how is Matt doing?"

"Fine," said Lisa.

Kristin became quiet again and Lisa glanced at her. "You okay?"

"Lisa, Bill's paycheck is still being deposited in our account and I'm wondering if that's right."

"It was Bill's policy to take care of the families of employees. However, you represent the largest stockholder and can change the policy. But, I'd advise against it."

Lisa passed a bus, pulled back into the travel lane and looked at the pale, tired woman in the passenger seat. Lisa adjusted the rear-view mirror so she could see Kristin as well as the traffic and asked,

"After three months, how's the world-renowned doctor standing up?"

Kristin looked out the side window. Her lower lip quivered and she spoke in an uneven voice. "I was expecting you to start probing, but was hoping you wouldn't."

As Lisa feared, the woman who spent her career consoling others had no one to turn to. "Kristin, you were there, when my husband died. I remember you asking some tough questions and it helped. I'm going to keep asking, you might as well start answering."

Kristin tried to say something, couldn't and then sobbed. Lisa handed her a handkerchief. After regaining her composure, Kristin asked, "Do you think Bill is dead?"

"No," lied Lisa. "But you have to prepare for that possibility, just like we're doing at AEG. We have to go on as if he isn't returning."

Kristin wiped more tears from her eyes and then looked out the passenger window. "I feel like a fraud. I'm always lecturing my patients about attitudes, but can't follow my own advice. I don't want to get out of bed in the morning. I don't want to go to work."

"Really, whenever I call, you seem to be at the hospital. And the kids look clean and as if they're being fed," said Lisa. "Guess, I'm just a dumb broad, I thought you were doing pretty well."

Kristin sniffed and said, "Thanks, I was hoping I didn't look like a total wreck."

***

They had lunch and then drove to the New Haven FBI Office. They waited in the lobby of the federal building for the agent who had contacted Kristin about her husband's car that had been abandoned in Bridgeport. Lisa drove stick-shift and offered to help pick up the car.

At exactly two, a man in a white shirt, tie and sport coat approached them, "Good Afternoon, I'm Agent Williams."

After some small talk the agent led Lisa and Kristin to a garage at the rear of the building. He pointed to the freshly washed and vacuumed black Taurus, a necessity after the evidence team had covered the car with powders and chemicals to detect fingerprints and blood. He had a technician attach the new license plates Kristin had obtained at his suggestion. He took the keys out of the ignition, opened the trunk, and pointed to a small tool box, ice scraper and a roll of paper towels, "These are items that were in the car at the time we took possession."

He removed the keys from the lock. "Would you please look over the car for anything that's missing?"

Without attempting to check, Kristin shook her head, "This is my husband's car. Something could be missing and I wouldn't know."

The Agent nodded, "Okay. Then please read and sign this release form?"

After Kristin signed the form, the agent carefully picked-up the piece of paper by the FBI insignia and placed it in a clear plastic envelope. He would forward the form to Boston, so the Case Agent, Terry Hamlin, would have her prints on file.

The agent offered Kristin the car keys. She didn't take them, she stood looking at him, then asked in a breaking voice, "Mr. Williams, are you aware of anything that would indicate whether my husband is or is not alive?"

He had been directed by Hamlin not to disclose any information. But looking at the woman, he thought she should know about the traces of gun powder detected in the trunk of her husband's car. But orders were orders.

"No Ma'am," said Willaims.

***

After dropping off the rental car at Hertz and slipping the clutch a few times, Lisa had Conors' old Taurus headed towards Boston.

"During lunch, you said you wanted to talk about something on the ride home," said Lisa.

Kristin kept her eyes on the road. "A friend of mine, who's in charge of the hospital's computer systems discovered that some government agency is reading my emails. He assumes they're also tapping my phone lines. I'm starting to feel like a criminal."

"Maybe they're hoping you'll become sloppy and forget to encrypt your Beef Wellington recipe."

"I'm serious," said Kristin. "Do you know if Bill ever broke the law?"

Lisa decided this was one of those rare occasions when she should use a little tact. She had been asking herself the same question and had decided that Conors disappearance would make more sense if he was a crook. She put her hand on top of Kristin's. "Kristin, I worked with your husband for ten years and never caught him in a lie, padding a bill or misleading a client. Never found him banging the receptionist or the college interns, either. If he's broken the law, he's done it when I wasn't looking."

Kristin fell silent for a few miles.

"Lisa, after your husband passed away, did you ever find yourself getting angry with him?"

"Yeah, but when I look back, I was more angry with the situation than my husband," said Lisa.

"Sometimes, after I put the kids to bed, I say dreadful things about Bill and AEG."

"Let's get this straight. He knocks you up, gives you two beautiful kids, and leaves you at least thirty million in stocks," said Lisa. "Honey, you won't get any sympathy on the talk-show circuit."

With a tear running down her right cheek, Kristin smiled and leaned against the head rest. "You're one hell of a grief counselor."

ISLAND LIFE

Rose, with envelopes in hand, closed her front door and started down the flagstone path. She passed a weathered cedar tree and came upon her tenant, shingling a rental cottage.

"Looking good."

"Thanks," said Conors. "Good grade of shingle. They're easy to work with."

He sat on an upturned milk crate with his back towards her, he used a razor knife to cut a white cedar shingle. Rose studied the cottage.

"Bill, I have a proposition."

"Yeah," said Conors.

"The other cottage is in poor shape. I'll give you a free month's rent to shingle it."

Conors stood. "I'll settle for one of those suppers I've been smelling."

Rose cocked her head and squinted at Conors, trying to look mean. "That's not my proposition."

Conors said, "Fine, a month's rent for the cottage, plus once a month you have me over for supper. I'll bring the wine."

Rose laughed. "It's a deal."

She walked down the path and turned right onto Meadow Road. The dirt road led to the Post Office. He returned to cutting and nailing shingles. When he finished the front, he moved the milk crate and picked up an old gray shingle. He turned it in his hand. It reminded him of his weather-beaten home in Gloucester and those thoughts led to others about his family. While outwardly calm, Conors was usually on a roller coaster, high when he saw a solution and down when his plans fell apart. After decades of managing projects and anticipating problems, he continually found holes in his plans for returning home. Although Maine was closer, his family seemed further away.

"Bill," yelled a man from the road.

He turned to see Elijah open the gate and make his way up the path. Conors welcomed the distraction. "Hi."

Elijah circled the cottage, inspecting the shingling. Conors was pleased to see him nodding approval. Elijah returned to the side of the cottage where Conors sat. "Hope Rosie isn't paying you by the hour."

Conors kept working. "A little slow, but unlike some people, haven't had any accidents."

Elijah frowned. "I saw Rosie go into the Post Office. Thought it was a good time to see you."

"Aren't you and Rose friends?"

"We are, she just forgets sometimes."

Conors decided not to probe any further.

"Bill. You've been jogging all over the island like a white-tailed buck during mating season. How about using that energy for something constructive?"

Conors ran every morning for a number of reasons. Besides keeping in shape, running was the fastest way to get acquainted with the Island, its seventeen miles of trails and discovering remote places for shooting.

"I assume you have a suggestion," said Conors.

"Yeah, a hundred lobster traps are sitting on the Port Clyde wharf. The dockmaster is threatening to dump them in the bay if I don't move them. Could use some help loading the traps onto the Ellie M."

"When are we leaving, Captain?"

"As soon as you can get to the wharf," said Elijah, as a quince apple hit the cottage a foot above his head. The whack of the apple startled Conors. He turned to see Rose about thirty feet away with a quince in each hand. Her front yard was full of the rock-like apples that even the crows ignored. Conors turned and whispered to Elijah, "Jesus, you'd be out cold, if she hadn't missed."

Elijah looked at the ground and whispered back, "She doesn't miss. That was a warning shot." He looked up and smiled. "Hi, Rosie."

"Don't give me one of your big hellos, Mr. Mullen. You can't come here and sweet talk me."

"Rosie, I'd never insult you with sweet talk," said Elijah, keeping an eye on Rose's left hand.

Rose's throwing arm moved back and forth. "That's right, seems you've been saving your sweet talking for Esther."

"Esther who?" replied Elijah as he looked away from Rose's eyes.

Rose threw overhand like Curt Schilling and the second apple hit the cottage inches from Elijah's head.

Elijah didn't flinch. Conors guessed it wasn't the first time the old lobsterman was a target. Rose transferred the other apple to her throwing hand.

"Rosie, you know that old widow Campbell is a friend of mine and I was just helping with some carpentry."

Rose squinted like she was looking straight into the summer sun. "From what I hear you were helping Esther with her plumbing."

"It makes me sad to see you so upset," said Elijah.

"Mr. Mullen, if you've finished your business with Professor Slater, I'd advise you to get moving."

Elijah nodded and left.

Conors returned to shingling, acting as if Rose and Elijah had exchanged pleasantries. After Rose was inside, he dropped his tools, grabbed his windbreaker and headed down Meadow Road towards the wharf.

Elijah was on the Ellie M, securing his skiff to the mooring buoy. Conors waved. Elijah returned the wave and dropped the mooring line. He casually returned to the helm and brought the Ellie M to within fifty feet of the Wharf. The old lobsterman pointed to a ladder on the windward side of the wharf. Conors climbed partially down the ladder and waited. Elijah brought the Ellie M parallel to the wharf allowing the breeze to bring her to rest against the pilings. Conors stepped on the catwalk and another step had him in the cockpit of the immaculately clean Ellie M, a forty-foot fiberglass lobster boat.

Within seconds the old man had the Ellie M underway and headed towards Port Clyde. At a cruising speed of thirty-three knots, the trip to Port Clyde was a third of the time it took the Laura B. The diesel had a throaty exhaust yet allowed for conversation at the helm.

"She's a beauty," said Conors.

Elijah nodded. "The Young brothers built it for me. They make a solid boat."

"Ellie M must have been somebody special."

"Yeah, my late wife," said Elijah.

"Sorry."

"It happened when I was forty-five so I've had time to think it through."

"Take a while?" asked Conors.

"Yeah, Ellie was my college sweetheart. We married during our junior year and had twenty-four years together."

Elijah pulled on the wheel to avoid a half-submerged timber. "She was a city girl, but took to the island like a barnacle to a rock. After learning we couldn't have kids, we did everything together. We worked hard, played harder, and traveled during the summers. You name it, we were there, Europe, the Far East, Africa, South America. In winter we pulled more pots than anybody and loved it. Ellie was not perfect and she was not always right, but she was like a drug. I was addicted to her and it took a good five years to get my head straight and out of the bottle."

"Never thought of re-marrying?" asked Conors.

"Figured when you had a marriage like we had, it was something you only do once. I have female friends, but no plans to marry."

Elijah stood to get a better view of the waters ahead. "Darn spring tides."

The entire channel between Allen and Burnt Islands was thick with yellow marsh grass riding the outgoing tide. Elijah pulled back on the throttle and scanned the grass for telltale humps that could mask another log.

"Bill, I'm sorry you got caught in the middle of that discussion with Rosie. She's one of my dearest friends, but once or twice a year, Rosie thinks she wants more of my attention. But by the end of our two week summer vacations, she sees the wisdom in having our private time. Rosie also knows about Esther. Both of them are important to me. I enjoy their company and they usually enjoy mine."

Conors decided he had heard more than he needed to know. "Elijah, when I was waiting for the Laura B, I saw a kayak behind the herring plant. Have you ever noticed it?"

"Been there about four years. You interested in it?"

"Yeah," said Conors.

"How much you willing to spend?" asked Elijah.

"Haven't thought much about it. I guess three hundred."

Elijah was silent for a few moments. "If you have a couple of hundred, I'll see what I can do."

Conors took two hundred dollars from the pocket of his windbreaker and handed it to Elijah, as the Ellie M veered around the number eight channel marker. Elijah pulled the throttle back and she slowed to three knots. The Port Clyde wharf and a stack of yellow lobster traps were straight ahead.

Following Elijah's direction, Conors removed three lines from a rope locker and secured the bow, stern and spring lines to the appropriate cleats. A gray lobster boat tied up to the wharf was taking on bait. While Elijah waited for the bait to be loaded, a white-haired woman in jeans, a flannel shirt and a figure that would make a twenty-year-old proud walked to the end of the wharf and waved. "Elijah."

Elijah gave a subtle wave. "Esther."

Esther didn't fit the picture Conors had imagined during Rose's quince attack. Conors pretended to check the spring line, turned his back to the wharf and said to Elijah, "So this is old widow Campbell?"

"I'd prefer you call her Esther," said Elijah.

Conors smiled. "Sounds like a good strategy."

After the gray boat left and its captain traded salutations with Elijah, Esther helped secure the Ellie M to the wharf and easily descended the ladder to the cockpit.

"Esther Campbell, this is Bill Slater. Bill is helping me with the traps."

"Hi Bill"

Conors shook Esther's hand. She had a good grip, eyes washed-out blue like Elijah's, and a youthful tanned face mixed with enough fine wrinkles to hint of a full life. "Nice to meet you."

"I was in the General Store and saw the Ellie M. Are you staying over?" said Esther.

"Can't," said Elijah.

Esther raised her eyebrows and stared at him. Elijah sighed. "I have to pick up an order at Rockland Marine and get these traps back to the island."

"Do you have time for some coffee and scones? I just made a dozen with the blueberries and blackberries we picked in Machias," said Esther.

Conors said, "Elijah, I can load the traps, if you want to visit with Esther."

Elijah hesitated. "Better yet, could you find your way to Rockland Marine on Harbor Street?"

Recalling the taxi trip to Port Clyde, Conors figured it would be easy to backtrack. "Yeah."

"Good. That's my red Jeep in the parking lot. The keys are under the dash on the driver's side. Tell Marty at Rockland Marine you're picking up three thousand feet of warp for Elijah."

"Warp?" asked Conors.

Elijah shook his head. "Warp is the rope used for traps."

The old jeep had roof racks, was clean and ran well. It was three months since Conors had driven and he felt a sense of freedom as he drove down the road he had traveled a couple of weeks earlier.

After an uneventful trip, Conors returned to Port Clyde and backed the Jeep down the wharf. Elijah was not to be seen, but beside the stack of lobster traps was a green polyethylene kayak, a skirt and a paddle. Conors inspected the dirty kayak and found it scratched, but sound and the gear was an unexpected bonus.

By the time Conors moved the six spools of warp from the Jeep and returned it to the parking lot, Elijah was leaving a large white house that overlooked the harbor.

Elijah joined him on the wharf. Conors said, "Thanks for the kayak."

"Here's fifty dollars. I think I could have gotten it lower, but it seemed like a fair price."

"A sea-going kayak for a hundred and fifty bucks. You must be a descendant of one of those Yankee traders."

"I am," said Elijah.

They managed to get fifty of the traps and the kayak into the cockpit of the Ellie M with Elijah explaining all the time how best to secure traps and sharing other maritime advice.

Later, the Ellie M was cruising at twenty-six knots towards Monhegan and Conors was standing by the helm enjoying a blueberry scone. Stifling a smile, he asked, "Elijah, just so I'm prepared, are we likely to encounter any more of your lady friends?"

Elijah frowned. "Not in Maine."

***

The police officer entered Rockland Marine. He approached the counter with a surly look, head cocked back, thumbs in his belt.

Marty stood by the cash register, looking as if a cockroach had slithered under the door. Both men shared a history. When they were in elementary school, Marty whipped the officer's ass on a weekly basis. Marty's only regret was that at the time he didn't know what a wedgie was.

Officer Ronald Pease maintained a chilling stare, put his two hands on the counter and leaned into Marty. Marty smiled. "Ronnie, is the rumor true that you get a hard-on when you give a parking ticket?"

Pea's eyes fluttered. He pretended not to hear.

"Who's the guy in Elijah's SUV? He looks familiar," said Pease.

Marty's jaw dropped. "You recognized him too?"

Pease nodded.

"Shit. I wasn't going to admit it. But since the law recognized him, I guess he's real. And for all these years I thought he was dead."

"Who's dead?" asked the frowning Pease.

"Elvis."

Pease turned red and left, slamming the door.

Marty watched Pease circle the Rockland Marine delivery van looking for violations.

CAREER
Mid-December

The exhausted agent was on her bed, propped-up by a mound of pillows flipping the pages of a thick report. Terry had been working seven days a week since the FBI confiscated nineteen boxes of documents from Gallo's TAT fundraising business. She had had a hard time following the money until she subpoenaed the union's books. The report in her hands described the money laundering in agonizing detail and identified the players.

She was scheduled to make a presentation to her boss in the morning and the following week to the District Attorney. She had enough evidence to convict five union leaders and Raymond Gallo. The bad news was that Ray Gallo was dead and Giovanni and his captains would walk, unless one of the union thugs turned state witness.

She glanced at the clock on the far wall and dropped the post-it covered report on the floor. "Good enough."

She rolled onto her side and looked out the bay window and down the street. The new yellow streetlamp outlined a towering and leafless maple, reminding Terry that winter had arrived. Her eyes returned to the report lying on the floor. It was her best work, Headquarters would take note, her flag was flying high.

She sighed, picked up her phone and hit autodial.

"Got home late," said Pops.

"Yeah, finishing up a report," said Terry.

"Put some grapes in your refrigerator. They're already washed."

"Thanks, I'll take them to work. But Pops, I have a question," said Terry. "I just finished an assignment. It will help my career and put some bad guys behind bars. I should be on top of the world. But I'm not."

Decades earlier the old man would have asked questions and suggested solutions. Instead he lowered himself to the couch. His dog, Alex, jumped up and lay by his master. He said, "Yeah."

"This is my dream come true. I've been told the Agency has big plans for me. I can't see giving this up to have a bunch of kids."

"That may not be all bad. Alex and I could babysit the little monsters while you shoot the bad guys."

"I'm serious, I feel like I'm going through life and missing the point."

"Not an uncommon feeling," said Pops while he wrote the word 'kids' on the message pad by the phone. He circled it.

"I'm on top of the world and I'm asking myself, isn't there more."

"You've been working long hours. We had dinner only once this week. You've had no time for exercise or your friend Vinny. You know what they say about all work and no play."

"I miss the exercise and our dinners," said Terry. Pops and Vinny had taken an instant liking to each other. She didn't want to think or talk about Vinny.

"Once you finish with this project, you should take some of that unused vacation and relax."

"I would feel a lot better, if I had gotten the goods on Conors. I'm convinced I missed something."

"I'm confident you did everything in your power," said Pops.

"I despise his type, the too good to be true businessman or the 'holier than thou' politicians."

"We all share distaste for those who abuse their positions of trust," said Pops.

"That's a great idea."

"What's a great idea?" asked Pops.

"Wingaersheek Beach," said Terry.

"What?"

"I return from DC on Wednesday night. We'll bundle up in our winter clothes and take Alex to the beach on Thursday."

"November at the beach," said Pops. "Won't need sunscreen."

"Love you Pops."

"Love you too," said the old man. He hung up, stared at the phone and remembered his late wife saying Terry was a tough woman on the outside. But a fragile girl on the inside, struggling with the cards she'd been dealt.

When Pops lost his wife, he and Terry lost their best friend. Although Terry was close to him before Greta's death, their relationship had been more formal, handshakes and pecks on the cheek. That changed the day following Greta's funeral, when Pops asked if Terry could care for Alex for the afternoon. She burst into a torrent of tears and hugged him as she sobbed. "You're my only family." Pops had patted her awkwardly on her back. While she had struggled to regain her composure, she looked up and saw tears streaming down his wrinkled cheeks. Since that day she called him Pops and hugged and kissed him like a daughter.

Pops scratched his dog behind the ear and leaned on the arm of the couch to get to his feet.

"We better stay healthy, old boy. Terry needs us."

BOOKS & BOUNTIES
Late January

At three in the morning Conors was leaning into the wind as he walked. He opened the side door to the Monhegan library, a small cedar shingled building with pale-yellow trim at the northern end of Meadow Road, across from the white schoolhouse. The room was large enough for a computer and two chairs. He placed his Hewlett Packard PDA beside the keyboard and sat at the terminal.

Although it raised hell with his sleep, the schedule yielded three hours of privacy, before the early risers came to monopolize the library's single internet connection. He entered the address for a hospital website and selected his wife's name from a list of physicians. Above a one page biography was a picture of Kristin and their two sons. Conors leaned forward and studied the picture, wondering how much his sons had grown since August.

He closely examined the smiling photograph of his wife. She was happy by nature, but he worried about how she was holding up. He leaned closer to the monitor. His body missed hers. He missed the sound of her voice, the smell of her shampoo, the feel of her smooth skin. He stared until he became aware of the underlying electronic dots that composed her picture. He blinked and the image of his wife returned. His eyes drifted and lingered on her email address, then he closed the hospital site.

After clicking on a few tabs, he opened AEG's website and found announcements for a few small contracts, but no news of the Chelsea Project class action suit. He wondered if no news was good news.

Clicking a few more keys, he entered the electronic newspaper archives he had been using to learn about the Boston mob. He was scanning an article when he stopped at a photograph entitled 'Mobsters Rule our Docks'. The picture showed Giovanni Gallo leaving a warehouse accompanied by his loyal soldier, Angelo Cassano, and another man who was a foot taller. Although his face was not clearly captured in the photograph, Conors instantly recognized the man. He read the associated article looking for information and then returned to the photograph.

"Nico Matarazzo are you as bad as the FBI claims?"

He took notes on his PDA and then typed the address for a Boston radio station and selected the Fatty Ford Show. After closing a barrage of pop-up advertisements, he turned the computer's lone speaker on and clicked the tab for archived talk shows. As he did each evening, he chose the previous day's radio show. The first hour of the show was dedicated to listeners who called in on a variety of subjects. He was fast forwarding and listening periodically when he heard,

"This guy, Conors, is the next Jimmy Hoffa."

Conors' chest tightened. He clicked the rewind button on the media player. A second later, he clicked the play button.

"The latest from the sidewalks of our drug-infested city. It looks like Giovanni Gallo is a hard man to please. After he eliminated the Russians without getting his hands dirty, Giovanni is still looking for blood. I heard from a bounty hunter and verified with others that Giovanni is still looking for Mr. William Conors. Conors is the

Cambridge businessman who allegedly met with Giovanni's son on the day of his death."

"Can bounty hunters work for the mafia," asked a member of Fatty's staff.

Fatty said, *"I asked the guy if he routinely worked for the mob and he answered no. He said technically, if a bounty hunter yields custody of a fugitive to someone other than the law, the bounty hunter is guilty of kidnapping. But he laughed and explained that this was a different situation, since the bounty was so large and because Conors wouldn't live to press any charges."*

"How much is the bounty?" asked the staffer.

"A half mil," said Fatty.

"Wow."

Fatty said, *"This guy, Conors, is the next Jimmy Hoffa."*

The words sucked the energy from Conors. He had hoped the mob wars had quenched Gallo's revenge and that given time it would be safe to return home.

He turned off the computer as he remembered Agent DeLuca's description of men being tortured as they hung from meat hooks. Conors left the library with coat in hand and made his way down the dirt road. The howling winds and the black of the night went unnoticed.

OFFICER PEASE

The Rockland Police Station consisted of three small rooms and two cells in the basement of City Hall. Officer Ronald Pease sat at the reception desk looking through the glass door. He could see the bottom three of the seven steps that lead up to the snow covered parking lot.

Pease was manning the night phones for the police station and the Department of Public Works when the midnight bell chimed. He glanced at the brass marine clock above the water cooler and turned to a new page in the telephone log. He wrote across the top, February 11.

He was halfway through his twelve hour shift. Having spent the first six hours studying for the next departmental exam, he was looking for any diversion to make the minutes pass. He removed his gun from his holster and was thinking of cleaning it when a voice came over the radio.

"Pease."

Pease picked up the mike. "This is Officer Pease, come in Unit 03."

"Skip the protocol shit, we're the only ones awake in all of Rockland."

"What do you want?" said Pease.

"Can't see past my damned hood. I've pulled into the Marina parking lot."

"Yeah?" said Pease.

"I'm staying here until the snow backs off."

"Get comfortable. The city's plows pulled off the road south-west of here for the same reason. They report that it's gotten worse not better."

"Over," was the response from the patrol car.

Pease dropped the mike on the desk, returned his pistol to its holster, stood and stretched. He walked in circles around the reception area, yawning. He stopped in front of the cluttered bulletin board he had checked the previous morning. Other than the monthly duty assignments, not much had changed.

He yawned again and started to turn from the board, when he noticed a new All Points Bulletin. He looked closer.

"Holy Shit."

GUNS & BUGS

The fourteen foot seas kept the lobster boats at their moorings, pounded Monhegan's ice-covered shores and blanketed the island in a deafening roar that muffled the gunshots.

Below the wind bent trees, Conors was crouched on a small ridge, hidden by the underbrush. Squinting into the wind, he squeezed the trigger, then threw himself to the ground, and rolled into a depression between two granite outcroppings. Seconds later, he was fifteen feet to the left, he glanced over the top of the ledge and took another shot, then dove for cover. The left pocket of his green parka caught the stub of a broken branch. He jerked to a stop. A second passed before the pocket tore and let him fall to safety.

Conors was lying on the cold ground, breathing heavily, looking up at the swaying treetops and the gray sky. A branch catching his pocket was one of those unforeseen events that could cost him his life.

He stood and was hit with a blast of wind, the goose down escaped from his torn parka and disappeared. Shaking his head, he engaged the safety mechanism on Raymond Gallo's gun and checked for dirt and debris. If his count was correct he had discharged the firearm ten times. He released the magazine from the silver-plated Ruger model P89 pistol, it and the chamber were empty.

When he was a marine, Conors had trained with both a Beretta M-9 and a .45-caliber pistol. The Ruger was more refined. He slid the magazine into the pistol frame and slipped the gun into the inside pocket of his parka. He climbed to the top of the ridge, collecting discharged shells as he approached the target, a plastic bag tied to a tree trunk. Conors had salvaged the empty cow-manure bag from Rose's rubbish.

February's weather had been bad for lobstering but good for shooting. The winds had masked most of the noise from the gun-shots and what remained was blown over the empty Atlantic. He checked the target. Seven bullets had penetrated the silhouette of the black cow at the center of the white bag. Two more had just missed. There was no sign of the tenth slug.

He dropped the empty shells down a small crevice in the middle of the forest the islanders called Cathedral Woods. He listened to the metallic sound as the shells hit the distant bottom. Conors removed the target from the tree and placed it under a flat rock that concealed four similar bags. He looked around and concluded nothing was amiss. He negotiated his way through a hundred yards of thick underbrush that separated his training area from the Blackhead Trail. Once on the path he resumed his run and headed towards his cottage.

***

A week later a four-foot swell rocked the Ellie M. After three months as a sternman, Conors instinctively countered the movement. It was hard work, but he was paid two hundred a day. More than he could ever spend on the small island.

Elijah gaffed a buoy by its rope and pulled enough slack to feed the rope through the hydraulic winch. The rope became taut, the winch lifted the traps from the bottom and slowed. The traps were in eighty feet of water, Conors took a moment to rest.

The first trap broke the surface and Elijah yelled over the groaning winch, "Full House." The lobsters clattered against each other as Conors yanked the trap onto the starboard gunwale. He slid it and the buoy towards the stern, making room for the next two traps. Moments later the second and third traps broke the surface and Conors pulled them from the water.

Elijah opened the wire doors to the third trap as Conors opened those on the first and second. The catch from December through February had been average. The first week of March was among the best Elijah had seen.

"Seven keepers and one short," said the smiling Elijah. He threw the undersized lobster overboard.

"Nine keepers, and a jumbo," said Conors while he slipped an elastic band over the claws of the largest lobster.

Elijah dropped a lobster into a plastic tank of saltwater. "The other day when dining with Esther, a Rockland cop asked what you were doing on Monhegan. I told him you were my sternman. Assume you're okay with that."

An unconvincing smile crossed Conors' face. He turned aft, busied himself with a lobster. "Unless you're planning on firing me."

Elijah's eyebrows rose as he noted the change in his friend's behavior. He studied his sternman for a few seconds and then slipped the transmission into forward. "The tanks are full, let's head to Port Clyde."

As the Ellie M cruised towards the mainland, Conors sat on the stern.

***

They dropped the day's catch at the wholesalers. Conors slipped out of his yellow slickers and put on a L.L. Bean parka with duct tape over a torn pocket. He took the helm and headed towards Monhegan while Elijah read the Rockland Courier Gazette. Thirty minutes later they passed Smutty Nose. Conors turned the wheel over to Elijah and went forward to pick up the mooring buoy.

The Ellie M passed a small boat partially filled with water. Conors rented the 1976 Boston Whaler from an islander who no longer wintered on the island. The flexibility to leave the island on his schedule was worth the hundred dollars a month. He decided he'd better bail it out before the next storm.

"Is that our bait on the wharf?" asked Elijah

"Yeah. Let's get it now, so we can have a clean start in the morning?"

Elijah changed course towards the wharf. Conors noticed a man in jeans and a heavy coat shooting pictures. Conors pulled his cap low and kept his head down. Elijah had forewarned him that during the summer you didn't dare take a leak over the side for fear of being caught on film. Conors figured the guy was a few months early and the first of many tourists. The Ellie M came alongside the wharf and Conors slipped bow and stern lines around the pilings. He heard the clicking sound of a camera.

"Is this a lobster boat?" asked the man.

Passing by Elijah, Conors heard him mumbling, "No it's a nuclear submarine."

A few minutes later, Conors had the hundred pound crates on the deck of the Ellie M and was untying the bow line when the man asked, "Can I have a ride. I've never been on a lobster boat."

Elijah lifted the brim of his cap to get a better look at the man. After staring, he spoke in a slow Maine accent Conors had never heard. "Stopped taking tourists a few years back. If they weren't getting sick they were falling overboard. Lost a couple once and spent a week dragging for their bodies. Just, not worth the trouble."

The man fell silent. Conors worked to suppress a laugh and pulled the lines from around the piling and into the cockpit. The Ellie M backed away from the dock and headed to its mooring.

Conors grabbed the boathook and headed towards the bow. The Ellie M turned into the wind and Conors found himself looking into a telephoto lens.

PLANTS

Vinny had been home less than ten minutes when there was a knock on the door. He instinctively grabbed his pistol and glanced at the small surveillance monitor. He recognized the man in the hallway and returned the gun to the kitchen counter.

He unlocked the deadbolts and opened the door to his Somerville apartment.

"Large pizza. Fourteen bucks," said a man with his cap on backwards.

Vinny took the pizza and handed the man a rolled-up bill. "Keep the change."

He closed the door, locked the deadbolts, placed the pizza box on the counter and opened it. It was cold. He tore the uncut pizza towards the center, exposing a small Ziploc bag. He freed the plastic bag and removed a 2 gigabyte flash drive identical to the one he had wrapped in the twenty dollar bill.

Vinny tossed the flash drive on the counter beside his gun and glanced at the pizza.

"Never liked thick pizza."

After closing the box, he bent it in half and stuffed it into the wastebasket. Every two weeks the same deliveryman exchanged a flash drive loaded with pornography for another drive in which a report had been encrypted into the pictures.

Vinny opened the refrigerator, it was nearly empty. He grabbed a bottle of red wine, some brie and the heels from a loaf of wheat bread.

"Damn," murmured Vinny. He dropped the moldy cheese into the wastebasket, returned to the refrigerator and grabbed a jar of crunchy peanut butter. He held the bottle, bread and peanut butter in one hand, pulled a stool up to the kitchen counter and had dinner while reading a week-old Boston Herald.

The apartment consisted of two rooms, a large kitchen and an even bigger bedroom with an oversized bay window. His bed was in the windowless kitchen because the bedroom was better suited for his hobby and more importantly the bay window made him feel like a sitting duck.

Following a half bottle of wine and a peanut butter sandwich, Vinny retreated from the kitchen and turned off the grow lights and space heaters that were alternately placed across the unfurnished bedroom. He bent over neat rows of window boxes and flower pots and deadheaded the geraniums and zinnias. Tending the plants was how he dealt with the devils that had entered his life. He dropped a handful of dead flowers into a bag, wondering if he had become addicted to the adrenaline rush of working undercover for the past eleven years. He had a low threshold for boredom and had figured he couldn't trade a career of living on the edge for a desk job? But over the last few months he had convinced himself he could, if he was coming home to Terry.

He picked up a vial, scribbled a few words in a notebook, dipped a Q-tip in the vial and carefully dabbed pollen on the pistils of each orange zinnia. He knew that despite Terry's appearance, she was a flawed package. As he saw it, never meeting your mother and losing your father at fourteen justified a few hang-ups. He dropped the Q-tip into the vial and sealed it. Every day undercover, his life depended on reading people, their emotions and what they would do next. He did it very well and understood that Terry needed him as much as he wanted her.

He stood and on his way to the kitchen stretched his back. He grabbed his keys and was headed towards the door when he stopped.

"Screw the payphone."

He picked up his cell phone, dialed a number and waited as he sat on the end of his bed.

"This is Terry. Leave a message."

Like the previous two attempts from the local phone booth, he hung up. He dropped the phone on the bed and looked about his apartment. It seemed darker, the peeling paint more depressing and the un-swept floors dirtier. He resisted the temptation to throw something, walked to the fridge, opened it and grabbed the bottle of wine.

DEVIL IN THE DETAILS
March

Conors parked Elijah's Jeep in the street, entered the building and with a paper bag under his arm climbed eight flights of creaking wooden stairs. He stopped on the fourth floor and ran his fingers along the door trim until he felt the key. He unlocked the door, it noisily dragged across the threshold and he stepped into what was advertised on the internet as spacious.

He walked to the only window and looked down on the worst section of the city. "At least there's a view of the Chelsea Project."

It was cold and the sun was setting. He clicked on the light, a ceiling fixture missing its globe, one of the three bulbs flickered on. He placed the bag of sandwiches on the kitchen table and lowered himself into the less dirty of the two chairs.

He glanced at his watch and settled in for a wait in an apartment he had rented sight unseen.

***

An hour later Conors stood as the apartment door again dragged across the threshold. He approached the doorway and gave Matt Kimani a hug. They patted each other on the back as if they had just won the softball league playoffs.

Conors broke the hug and looked at Kimani. "Good to see you."

"Likewise," said Kimani as he examined his boss and friend. "Except for the beard, you look ten years younger."

Conors picked-up the box of papers Kimani had left by the door. "Yeah,"

Kimani glanced around the room. His smile disappeared. "Nice place."

"Suits its purpose," said Conors.

Kimani shook his head, his smile returned. "Tell me about this Witness Protection Program."

"Can't say much, Matt. It's so secret even other parts of the FBI are kept in the dark. That's why I told you to never admit, even to the FBI, that we've been talking," lied Conors.

"Well, nobody has asked. But I've been tempted to say something to Kristin. She's beyond upset."

Conors opened his mouth, but no words came out. He sighed.

"Can't do that Matt," said Conors. "If she knew where I was, she'd have to give up her practice, pull the kids from school and go into hiding."

Sadness settled over Conors' face. Kimani nodded.

***

Three empty Pepsi cans were on one side of the table along with the remains of two tuna sandwiches on crumpled wax paper. The rest of the table was covered with pages from a laboratory report Kimani had brought.

"Why don't you believe these dioxin numbers?" asked Kimani.

"I've never seen values this high."

Conors flipped through the report. "Dioxins are normal byproducts of fires and you'd expect to find them in the air during the Chelsea Project fire. But not at these levels."

"Could the laboratory have made a mistake?" asked Kimani.

Conors didn't answer, he was staring at an instrument print out. "This is incredible."

"What is?"

Conors turned the paper towards Kimani and pointed at a graph containing a large number of narrow peaks.

Total Ion Chromatogram for Dioxin Analysis

"Dioxin is not one compound. It's a mixture of different compounds having from one to eight chlorine atoms. Each of these peaks represents one of the seventy-five possible dioxin compounds that are summed to get the reported concentration. Do the peaks look equal in size?"

Kimani glanced at the peaks again. "As far as I can tell."

"That means each of the seventy-five compounds are present at similar concentrations."

"Doesn't sound likely, nature prefers disorder," said Kimani,

"It's equivalent to winning the lottery, twice in the same week," said Conors. "The temperature and composition of the fire determines which of the seventy-five dioxin compounds will be generated. One set of conditions can't generate equal proportions of all seventy-five."

Kimani moved the graph to get a closer look. "How did this happen?"

"Remember how the mysterious Citizens for a Clean Chelsea disappeared after releasing this report? They must have spiked the sample with dioxin standards."

"That has to be illegal," said Kimani.

"It's the only logical explanation," said Conors as he shuffled through the last section of the report. He assembled the report into a neat pile. "Matt, take this report to AEG's Chemistry Group and innocently ask what it means to have identical concentration of all dioxin compounds."

"Then what?"

"Our chemists are pretty sharp, so after flipping a few pages their eyes will be popping out of their heads. Ask them to write a data validation report that summarizes their concerns in plain English and then get a copy to our lawyer and to Henry Gonzales."

"The EPA lawyer, I met at the Chelsea spill?"

"That's him. Also send a copy to Fatty Ford."

Kimani laughed. "Are you kidding?"

"Nope, if any of Henry's bosses try to bury the report I want someone keeping the heat on."

"Do you think Fatty will be interested?"

"Yes, because when you send him the report anonymously, the cover letter will claim there is a government cover-up."

Kimani sat back in the rickety kitchen chair and smiled. "You never taught me that trick."

"Something I picked up during my recent travels," said Conors.

Four hours later Conors was in Elijah's Jeep, headed towards Port Clyde. He was making progress but still didn't know how he'd ever return to his family without getting killed or tortured. An oncoming lumber truck roared by leaving the highway dark and quiet. Conors clicked on the high beams.

ASSIGNMENT

For a change, all his agents were in the office so Joe DeLuca called a meeting. He had splurged and bought donuts and crullers.

Terry Hamlin had just finished a presentation. DeLuca watched as she returned to her seat at the opposite end of the conference table basking in the praise of her colleagues. The team had tried to poke holes in her case, but the logic was solid and he was confident the evidence would be admissible in court.

"James, update us on Conors' whereabouts," said DeLuca.

The room fell silent and James Munroe turned on the conference room laptop. Two photographs appeared on the oversized LCD that hung on the wall. He stood, and using a laser pointer, placed a red dot on a picture of a bearded man.

"Terry used facial recognition software to prove that this photograph found on a forger's camera was actually William Conors," said Munroe as he moved the pointer to the adjacent picture of a clean-shaven Conors.

"After making this discovery, our field offices and the New England Joint Task Force members were sent an all points bulletin, including both of these pictures. As a result of the APB, we got two leads."

Munroe clicked the enter key on the notebook computer and a new photograph appeared on the wall monitor. "The first lead was for a substitute high school teacher. Other than having a similar beard, the teacher proved to be a poor match, but I took a number of pictures and using the facial recognition software verified the obvious, the guy isn't Conors."

Munroe pushed a few keys on the laptop and a map of the Maine coast filled the screen. "The second lead generated by a Maine patrolman looked even less promising. The police chief, who passed along the lead, cautioned that the patrolman suffered from an overactive imagination."

Munroe placed the blinking cursor on an island. "Having only two leads, we ignored the Chief's comment and visited Monhegan Island."

"How was the golf?" asked Agent White.

"Every morning when I teed off, I felt like I was at Pebble Beach," said the straight-faced Munroe, while he feigned a slow swing with an imaginary club.

Seeing DeLuca getting hot under the collar, Johnson said, "Enough of the golf talk."

Munroe clicked a key and on the monitor appeared a picture of a fit man running down a dirt path. "I pretended to be a photographer and spent three days on the island. I positioned myself by the lighthouse that overlooks the village and used my telephoto lens to study the islanders. On the morning of the second day, I saw this Conors lookalike returning from a run. It's apparently a daily ritual, because I took this picture the following morning. He looks as if he's training competitively and is running close to six minute miles."

The picture of the man was replaced with a small cottage. "This is where he lives, next to an open field the islanders call the meadow."

Munroe quickly clicked through a sequence of photographs showing a bearded man in rubber boots walking down a dirt road, another of two men on a lobster boat and stopped with a picture of the bearded man looking into the camera. "Our man works on a lobster boat. This last picture was taken when the boat returned after a day of fishing."

Munroe enlarged the picture and focused on the face. "The software determined it's a perfect match with the forger's picture and a ninety-eight percent match with the clean-shaven William Conors."

Johnson leaned towards DeLuca. "The New England Joint Task agreement requires notification when fugitives are found."

DeLuca shook his head. "Hold off for a while, some of those troopers have loose lips."

Salvadore Amero reached across the table and grabbed the last donut, taking a big bite from the raspberry-filled ball.

"Nice going Amero, the cleaning lady was going to take that home and feed her three kids," whispered Munroe.

DeLuca looked up from the paperclip he had been bending back and forth to see Amero giving Hamlin and Munroe one of his innocent 'who me?' expressions.

"Sal, give us a rundown on Mrs. Conors' wire taps," said DeLuca.

Amero grabbed a small notebook from his shirt pocket and glanced at his notes. "Since the wire taps were approved we have taped three hundred and thirty hours of conversation. Seventy-three hours at her hospital office and the rest at her Brookline residence. We used voice recognition software to transcribe the tapes into text files and then used a word search. I listened to every conversation that contained a key word."

Amero finally understood why the smiling Hamlin was moving her fingers over her lips and wiped the confectionary sugar from his. "Dr. Conors is a tough lady in a tough situation. She's spends a lot of time convincing her parents that everything will turn out okay. She returns patients' calls during the evening, I guess after she's put her kids to bed. She has friends in the Brookline Police Department who call once a week. She puts on a good front with most people except a lady friend from AEG. No suspicious incoming calls and all of her outgoing calls are business, family, friends or ordering takeout."

"What's your gut say?" asked DeLuca.

"She has no idea what has happened to her husband or she deserves an Oscar," said Amero.

"You're confident Conors has not tried contacting her at home or work?" asked DeLuca.

"Yes, we've checked all incoming calls and emails. Should we continue to keep the taps active?" asked Amero.

"For the time being," said DeLuca, then he looked at Hamlin. "Terry, I asked you to look into that government cover-up claim that Fatty Ford has been highlighting on his radio shows. Any Luck?"

"Yes. I spoke with the AEG scientist who authored the report that Fatty has been referring to. He seemed to be a straight shooter. He called up the lab that analyzed the Chelsea Project sample and we listened as the lab director agreed with AEG's conclusion. The lab has never seen a sample with equal concentrations of all the dioxin compounds."

"What's the bottom line?" asked Johnson.

"If they convince the judge that somebody's tampered with the sample, a multi-million dollar class action against AEG could be thrown-out."

"I'm going to assume falsified lab data are not within my jurisdiction" said Deluca. He tossed the twisted paperclip on the table. "Okay, let's get back to work and catch some mobsters."

As the agents were leaving, DeLuca overheard Munroe talking to Agent White. "The ninth hole was particularly difficult but my caddy was not only beautiful, she had great advice." DeLuca shook his head, knowing that Monhegan was a granite rock in the middle of the ocean and lacked all amenities, especially a golf course.

Agent Hamlin had gathered the materials used during her presentation into a copy paper box and was about to leave.

DeLuca asked, "Terry, you have a moment?"

"Sure."

She put the tattered box on the table and sat across from DeLuca and Johnson.

"The best financial work I've seen and a solid presentation," said DeLuca.

Hamlin smiled. "Thanks."

"By the end of the week, the Justice Department will be taking over and you'll have more time on your hands."

"Yeah, I'm guessing it'll be months before I hear from them."

"Good. I've mentioned that headquarters wants you to get a first-hand appreciation for the Agency's diverse activities," said DeLuca.

Hamlin nodded.

DeLuca continued, "I don't see the need for it, but Headquarters prefers that you get some undercover experience. What do you think of the idea?"

"Wasn't your first assignment working undercover?" asked Hamlin.

"Yeah," said DeLuca.

"Did it help your career?"

DeLuca sighed. "Yeah."

"Well, I'm not crazy about the idea, but it looks like a good career move," said Hamlin. Ever since she first heard about Headquarters' plan, she had resigned herself to a stint undercover.

DeLuca looked at her and then glanced at Johnson. The previous night, he and Johnson had debated the advantages of arresting Conors versus the costs of having undercover agents monitor his activities. They were leaning towards an arrest until they decided it was a relatively safe opportunity for Hamlin to work undercover.

"Okay," said DeLuca.

Then he pointed at the monitor and the picture of Conors. "Usually we have a good handle on why a fugitive is on the run, but this guy is a mystery. Maybe he's an innocent bystander who saw something he shouldn't have. But my nightmare is that it's something else, and I don't want to wake up someday and discover that Conors is running some unknown crime family."

DeLuca stared into Hamlin's eyes as he talked. He didn't know if it was an old man's intuition or because he felt like shit, but he wished she had declined the assignment. "Jim give her the details."

Johnson flipped open a small notebook. "According to the guest register at a Rockland motel, Mr. Conors is going by the alias of William Slater. We could pick him up on some false ID charge, but based on his tendency to be uncooperative, we're unlikely to learn anything. Alternatively, if we can monitor his activities, we may have a chance of discovering who the real Mr. Conors is."

Hamlin glanced at the computer screen and Conors' face and eyes as Johnson spoke. She found Conors ruggedly good looking. A man you'd be tempted to trust. However, her specialty was white-collar crime and she knew that the worst of the criminals were the most trusted and the last to be suspected.

"We need somebody to spend a month or two monitoring Conors and learn as much as possible before we take him in," said DeLuca. "We want to know what he does, who he meets with, who he telephones. Are you sure this is something you're interested in?"

Hamlin took a deep breath and exhaled. "Yes, I'm interested."

"Okay," said DeLuca. He stood. "Jim, all yours."

"Terry, we assumed you'd say yes and I went ahead and made some arrangements. Could you stay in the DC area after your presentation to DOJ?" asked Johnson.

Hamlin hesitated, remembering she had planned some vacation time with Pops. The room fell silent. She desperately wanted to say no. Johnson was looking at her. She said, "Yes."

"Okay, you'll go to Quantico and meet with Helena Cosgrove. She'll help develop your undercover identity, a credible reason for being on Monhegan and how you'll keep in contact with the office, your family and friends. She'll also make arrangements for the day-to-day details like having the utilities and mortgage paid in your absence."

"When will I go undercover?"

"As soon as you can get your house in order," said Johnson.

THE AGENT & THE ISLAND
April

In the black of the moonless night, unseen waves splashed against rocks some fifty feet below while she stared at the stars. Other than being able to point out Orion, Terry knew nothing about the constellations. She had lived a life dedicated to good grades, weekend jobs, summer jobs and her career. Looking at the stars she could not name, she was reminded how narrow her focus had been. In some ways, she was still the driven high school student studying long hours, hoping for perfect SAT scores.

A sea breeze rustled the leafless Rugosa bushes. Even though she had a parka over her pajamas the chill convinced her to retreat. She left the rickety wooden porch and entered the small apartment, closed the slider, stood in front of the propane heater and rubbed her hands.

She had the cozy efficiency booked for two more nights. Using Munroe's strategy, she had positioned herself on Lighthouse Hill and had followed Conors' activities. Tomorrow would be her fourth day on the island.

***

It was 8 a.m. on the second day of April and the sun was already above the Atlantic Ocean. Terry watched Elijah's lobster boat clear the harbor and then waited in her apartment. Midmorning she picked up an expensive digital camera and headed down the dirt road.

Rose Kirland had just finished a painting and wasn't sure if it was ready for the gallery. Irritated by her indecision and further irritated by the knocking, she was scowling when she yanked the door open. "What do you want?"

If there was one thing Terry understood, it was the elderly. She had been raised by her aged aunt and her aunt's even older friends. Munroe had also forewarned her about the lady with an edge. After a big smile, Terry mimicked Rose's gruff tone.

"I want to rent one of your run down cottages."

Rose laughed and Terry joined her.

After Rose's hearty laughter eased into a smile, she opened the screen door wide. "Come in for a cup of tea and I'll determine if you have sufficient pedigree to reside on my estate."

***

Conors was walking down Meadow Road towards his cottage with parka in hand. The hauling of two hundred traps had been a workout but not as challenging as the February cold or March's long days of fishing. The first three weeks of March had been record-setting, then the haul started to decline. If Elijah was correct, the lobster catch would continue to decrease and they'd stop fishing the first week of May.

When he opened the gate to Rose's property, Conors heard an unfamiliar voice from behind the vacant cottage. "Can these things explode?"

"Not unless you start a fire under them," said Rose.

Conors rounded the corner of the cottage and found Rose standing over a stunning young woman. The woman was on the ground with a large propane tank in her lap. Conors, who had been moving the containers all winter, lifted the tank off the woman and effortlessly rolled it to the storage platform next to the cottage. "Is this where you want it?" asked Conors.

Rose nodded. "Professor Slater, this is Terry Mahoney, our new neighbor."

Conors had been preparing himself for an influx of visitors and summer residents, but not a neighbor this early in the season. When he offered his hand to help her up, he noted an uneasy look in her eyes and guessed she was embarrassed. "There's a trick to handling these tanks, once you've moved a few, it's easy."

She was surprised with the ease that Conors pulled her to her feet, how small her hand was in his callused palm, how much larger he was than the images in her telephoto lens. She looked into his face. The grayish blue eyes gutted her confidence and reminded her that she was no longer in her office scanning spreadsheets. She froze.

Conors had not touched the soft skin of a woman in a long time, but the sensation yielded to her silent stare. He let go and turned towards Rose. "Call, if you need help."

He disappeared between the cedar trees and into his cottage. Rose wasn't sure why, but her newest tenant was visibly shaken. Rose broke the silence. "Men are damned handy, but can make you feel inferior in the muscle department."

That night in her drafty cottage, Terry Hamlin lay awake in her bed listening to the howling wind. If asked, she'd claim it was the cold that kept her awake, but the encounter with Conors and the undercover training at the FBI Academy had taunted her until she was wide awake. After law school, she had spent four months at the Academy located on a Marine base in Quantico Virginia. She had excelled and graduated at the top of her class. However, the previous week of specialized training was a different story. She struggled with the poker-face business of undercover work and was bluntly told by a psychologist that she lacked the necessary self-awareness to assume a fictitious identity. With the knowledge that it was a relatively safe assignment, the instructors worked closely with her, making her comfortable with her new identity, which included credit cards, a license and a checking account. To ease the transition she was given the name, Terry Mahoney, the surname of the aunt who had raised her.

The shivering Terry pushed the less than inspiring thoughts of Quantico from her mind. "I'm sure Vinny's keeping warm. There's always some woman going gaga over that oversized Ken doll."

She turned on her side, angrily pulling the blanket over her head, remembering that although Vinny worked undercover, he had claimed his worst concern was a paper cut. She knew her stay on Monhegan was different, that she was merely feet from the cottage where Conors slept, a few feet from an alleged killer.

Terry had never ridden a horse, but later that night in bed, wearing her parka, long underwear and two pairs of socks, she decided a problem during undercover work was like being thrown from a horse. She reached out from her cocoon and set the alarm for four. "Tomorrow, I'll climb back into the saddle."

***

It was quarter past five, minutes before sunrise. After a diet Pepsi and a PowerBar, Conors dressed in sweats and sneakers. He pulled a stocking cap over his head and stepped outside. It was in the low thirties, he was looking at the treetops, estimating the wind, when he saw her.

He moved into the shadow of his cottage and through cedar trees observed his neighbor in loose-fitting running pants, a puffy down jacket and earmuffs. She was leaning against the fence stretching her calf muscles. Conors moved deeper into the shadows, remembering the previous afternoon and her odd behavior. He typically ran down Meadow Road towards the shore. This morning he skirted the meadow until he reached the Burnthead Trail and the far side of the island.

By six, Terry had done more stretches than she'd do in a month and had decided Munroe was wrong about Conors' daily run. She reluctantly admitted she was relieved to have missed Conors and started down Meadow Road.

Conors had pushed himself hard and sprinted the last mile. He had just slowed to a jog when he spotted Terry running in his direction. He maintained his pace and with no more than a nod continued on his way. After they passed, the woman reversed her direction and ran beside him.

"What are the best trails for a good run?" asked Terry in a cracking voice.

Conors was short of breath. "The Burnthead and Whitehead trails."

Conors slowed and took another breath. "The rest are narrow with rocks and roots."

She slowed her pace. Conors was breathing hard. Terry decided Munroe may have been right about Conors jogging every day, but wrong about Conors being a good runner. They were approaching the rope shed. Her voice wavered and cracked again, "What trails do you run?"

He glanced at Terry. Despite the haphazard layers of clothing and neon earmuffs, she was easy to look at. Yet her striking appearance was overshadowed by a nervous energy. He decided to end the conversation and scowled. "All of them."

Terry flinched and turned red. Then she took a quavering breath and blurted, "What are you trying to hide?"

The question hit too close to home. Conors stopped abruptly. She stopped in front of him. He glared into her eyes, trying to convince himself that she couldn't know his secret.

The color drained from her face. She backed up a step and spoke in a weak voice. "Are you afraid I'm going to start the Monhegan Runners Club and the jogging masses will trample your precious trails?"

He continued to study his new neighbor, wondering why she had the jitters. She blinked and backed up another step. "Mr. Slater, you're very unfriendly. I just asked for advice on a few trails."

"I'm sorry, I thought you were looking for a running companion and I don't have time for a casual jog," said Conors.

Terry's face turned red again. "You're dreaming buddy. I don't have trouble keeping up with older men."

Terry turned and ran towards the schoolhouse. She broke into a sprint and was quickly gasping for air. Conors watched her disappear down the road. He had pissed her off and he couldn't decide if that was a good or a bad thing.

She passed the school house and made it to Ice Pond before she stopped behind the remnants of an old barn. She walked in circles, gasping, feeling sick to her stomach.

When her chest stopped heaving, she sat on the cold ground and leaned against the barn. "I'm an idiot. I just tried to impress a damn fugitive."

***

For two days Terry avoided Conors and worked on her cover as an amateur photographer. She had taken college courses in photography. Playing the role of a photographer was the easiest part of her undercover work.

She had spent an hour shooting pictures at Pebble Beach on the far end of the island and was headed home when she noticed the lights on in the grocery store, the Carina, meaning the Laura B had delivered fresh food. Hoping to expand her diet beyond the frozen dinners purchased at the North End Market, she climbed the stairs and for the first time entered the store. The Carina consisted of several tables sparsely covered with produce and meat. A man in his sixties was reading the Wall Street Journal. He looked up long enough to smile.

She took her time collecting three bananas, eggs, a steak, salad greens and two yogurts. She placed them on the counter and turned to the man with the newspaper. "Excuse me, I'd like to pay for these items?"

The man smiled again. "It's the honor system. Just write what you took on the pad and your name. You can pay at your leisure or pay now, there should be enough cash in the draw to make change."

She listed the items, calculated a sum and left the proper amount of money on the counter while thinking the islanders had more faith in human nature than most.

"Thanks," said Terry.

The man noticed the camera bag hanging from her neck. "Photographer?"

"Amateur, the name's Terry."

They shook hands.

"I'm Charlie. What equipment are you using?"

"Canon Rebel."

"Really? I struggled between that model and the Nikon D70. I finally chose the Nikon because it was compatible with my lenses," said the man.

She lifted the camera bag. "Like to check it out?"

"Love to."

Terry removed the camera from its case and handed it to the man. He studied it for a few seconds, turned it on and moved through the menus and exercised the telephoto lens.

The man turned the camera off. "I'm writing an article on the impact of digital cameras on photography and will be shooting the same subject matter with digital and film. It would be interesting to compare two top-shelf digital cameras. Would you be interested?"

"Yes," said Terry, forgetting her reason for being on the island.

The man was handing the camera back to Terry when an old lady in a yellow slicker opened the door.

"Good afternoon Mary," said the man.

"Charlie," said the lady. She closed the door.

"Mary, this is Terry. I believe she's renting from Rosie."

"Oh you must know Bill Slater. He's a lovely man," exclaimed Mary.

Terry smiled, deciding that Mary may be a nice lady, but a poor judge of character. Still smiling Terry offered Mary her hand, "Yes, I've met him. How do you know Bill?"

"He helps me with the internet. He calls me the early bird, because I show-up when he's leaving," said the old lady while lowering herself into the chair beside Charlie. "I lost my seed catalog and he showed me how to use Google. Now I use Google for all my shopping."

"He's a quiet man, but a big help around the island," said Charlie. "When the Kearney's roof gave way in an ice storm, he jury-rigged a boat tarp that saved all their belongings,"

Terry nodded and forced a smile while deciding that Mary and Charlie would have vouched for both Dr. Jekyll and Mr. Hyde. "Mary, how do you and Bill access the internet?"

"Few of us have satellite hookups, so most use the library computer," said Mary. "Bill gets there early in the morning and then goes for his run before I show up at six."

Terry picked-up her groceries. "Charlie, look me up when you want to compare cameras. Nice meeting you, Mary."

Terry left the Carina and headed in the opposite direction from her cottage. Seeing nobody at the dock, she walked towards the water and dialed a number on her cell phone.

"How are things going?" asked DeLuca, who had appointed himself Terry's official contact person.

"Slow. He isn't volunteering information. But I've rented a cottage next to his."

"Remember, your job is to observe, so don't take any chances," said DeLuca. "Has he had visitors?"

"No, but I discovered Conors uses the internet at the public library. Could you send me one of those keyboard tracking programs?"

"Sure, I'll have one of the geeks send a disk and directions for loading. But there's a more pressing issue. Did you know that we added William Slater's mail to Conors' search warrant?"

"Yeah," said Terry.

"Well, his first piece of mail arrived this week and it was an LL Bean catalogue. We checked for recent purchases."

"Anything interesting?"

"He ordered an Otis gun-cleaning kit last year."

"What type of guns can the kit be used for?" asked Terry.

"Anything from a BB gun to a shotgun."

A NIGHT OUT

It was three in the morning. Conors was at the Monhegan library typing a web address from memory. After a few additional key strokes he selected his wife's name from a list of physicians at the Dana-Farber website. The picture of Kristin and the boys was missing.

He hit the down arrow and the cursor raced through the pages until stopping on a new picture of his wife. He slowly removed his hands from the keyboard deciding his wife looked tired, but damn good. He enlarged the picture and wished she had included the kids. He explored the rest of the updated website, looking for more pictures and news about his wife.

He was scanning photographs taken at a black tie fundraiser when he stopped at a group picture of the hospital's oncologists. His wife was in the middle of the gathering. He pushed the chair back.

"Shiiit."

Conors looked away from the picture and the image of a man with his arm around his wife's waist. Conors didn't notice the uneasy smile on her face. Conors knew the young man. He was the MD PhD whiz kid who had the hots for Kristin at last summer's cookout. She laughed, when he had mentioned him.

He let out a long breath. "Well Kristin, I guess eight months was your limit."

A clenched jaw masked the hurt and the fury. He shut down the computer without a second look.

***

Terry had been standing in the shadow of a large granite boulder, a monument with a plaque commemorating Captain John Smith's 1614 visit to the island. She'd been observing Conors through binoculars, trying to verify he had actually turned on the computer, but Conors had blocked her view of the monitor.

The keyboard tracking software was working too well and recording the keystrokes for every islander who used the computer. DeLuca had asked her to identify when Conors accessed the computer so they could narrow their search. This was the fourteenth night in a row that she had recorded the time her neighbor left his cottage and if she didn't fall asleep the time he returned. Every third night, she'd follow Conors to make sure the library and the computer were his destination.

Conors had finally leaned enough to one side that she had seen a small portion of the monitor and knew that the computer was on. The relieved and shivering Terry had stuffed the binoculars into her pocket and was preparing to leave when Conors unexpectedly stood.

"He can't be finished," said Terry.

When he turned sideways, she saw the blank computer monitor. She raised the binoculars again. He was in the warmth of the library's computer room and wearing a T-shirt. It was the first time she'd seen him without a parka or sweatshirt. While his arms were not as large as Vinny's, they were big and more defined. She would have preferred a hundred pound weakling.

Conors was wearing the same sweats he ran in that morning. She winced when he pulled the sweatshirt over his head. "That thing must smell like a dirty sock."

He left the library. She sank into the shadow of the boulder and sat on the frost covered grass. He stood in the dirt road as if he didn't know which way to turn. Her teeth chattered, the dampness diffused through her body. She hugged herself.

***

Terry's eyes opened slowly. Her damp clothes were on the floor next to her bed. She eventually rose to a sitting position and slipped her feet into the furry slippers Rose had given her.

"I'll come down with narcolepsy, if this guy doesn't change his sleeping habits."

She was deciding if she was hungry when she caught a glimpse of the alarm clock. It was almost noon. She jumped up and looked out her windows, making sure no one could overhear and then placed the call.

"Everything okay?" asked DeLuca.

"Yeah, no problems. Just calling to let you know that Conors was at the computer around three this morning. He didn't stay long."

"Okay." DeLuca noted the time. "Some good news, you can call off your nighttime surveillance. The geeks discovered a pattern so the computers can automatically search for when Conors logs on."

"What pattern?" asked Terry.

"The first thing he does is go to a hospital website."

"Is our fugitive a hypochondriac?"

"No, the website has a picture of Conors' wife and kids and he spends ten or so minutes looking at their picture," said DeLuca.

"Where else does he go?"

"His company's website and the websites for the Boston Herald, Boston Globe and Fatty Ford. He listens to Fatty's archived radio programs and does internet searches on the mob."

"Any other searches?"

"He searches for anything regarding his company and that big construction project in Chelsea."

"Any email?" asked Terry.

"He's not sent or received any emails since you installed the spyware."

"He may have other ways of communicating," said Terry. "A couple of days ago, I learned that Conors has a small boat moored in Monhegan Harbor."

"Do you know where he goes?"

"No idea, but the other evening he headed towards the mainland," said Terry. "Don't know if he went that far, but he wasn't back till the next day."

"That changes things. Let me think on that one," said DeLuca. "Onto other business, yesterday I got a request from DEA. Seems there's this undercover agent they need to keep happy and he wants updates on your status. This is a privilege typically reserved for family. Do you want a Mr. Vincent Balletta contacting me for updates? It's your call," said DeLuca.

Terry smiled. "Yes, Vinny's an old friend and with both of us being undercover, I can't contact him."

"Okay," said DeLuca.

"Since I don't have to report on Conors' nocturnal excursions, I'll call the same time next week," said Terry.

"Talk to you then."

She hung up, placed the phone on her dresser and sat on the edge of her bed, forcing herself not to think of Vinny, and then wondering why an allegedly innocent businessman, who spent his nights looking at family pictures, needed a gun-cleaning kit.

She stood up and went window to window separating curtains just enough to look outside. Then she let her flannel nightgown fall to the floor, grabbed an old pair of jeans and a red sweater from her closet, dressed, slipped a credit card into her pocket and stepped outside.

It was sunny, brisk and dead quiet. She stood at her doorstep listening and looking. Her cottage was next to the road, while Conors' cottage was located farther from the street and about three feet above the wetlands, the islanders called the meadow.

She took a few steps to glance down Meadow Road. Conors had put three empty propane tanks by the roadside the previous afternoon. They were gone and replaced with full ones. Terry looked at them in disbelief, she had slept through the noisy truck delivery.

She shook her head and checked the rest of the yard. Figuring the Ellie M wouldn't return for hours, she made her way towards Conors' cottage. Her long stride brought her quickly to the cedar trees that separated the dwellings. Hidden from any passerby, she had a view of Rose's house. Seeing no signs of activity she left her cover.

Terry had examined Conors' cottage and knew the lock was the same as hers. She slipped her credit card between the door and the jamb, forcing the latch bolt back into the archaic lock assembly. The door opened with a slight push. She stepped inside, closing the door.

She stood and scanned the room creating a mental picture of what it should look like when she was finished. She started on the left side of the door and proceeded around the room and the small bathroom, opening and closing draws, checking under, inside and behind furniture, looking for loose floorboards and wall panels. The cabinet by the sink was the last place she searched before a final glance around the room, knowing that if Conors had a gun, it wasn't in the cottage.

Her eyes stopped on the PDA sitting on Conors' night table. It had requested a password when she had turned it on. She planned on asking the Agency if they could override the password, but knew the geeks' first question would be what was the operating system. She crossed the room and pressed the menu button just as a loud metal clunk resounded throughout the cottage. A propane gas tank had

been dropped onto a cement pad, on the other side of the wall, eighteen inches from where she stood.

She lowered the PDA to the night table. Her pulse quickened
with the sound of a heavy security chain being pulled tight around
the tank. She saw the back of Conors' head pass by the window. He
grabbed a second tank.

She was making her way to the door when she saw the mud. It
accurately captured the tread of her running shoes. With her hand
she frantically swept it towards the threshold. She heard approaching
footsteps, abandoned the dirt, opened and gently closed the door and
then leaped off the bank into the soggy meadow.

Conors smelled of fish, and by the time he had rolled the tanks
uphill had worked up a sweat. He was lost in thought and looking
forward to a shower when he slipped the key into the door lock.

"No bugs?" asked Terry.

He turned towards the meadow to see Terry in the midst of a
stand of cattails. She had pulled one of the tall grassy plants out of
the ground, root ball and all. Her shoulder length hair was blowing in
the building wind.

"Plenty of lobsters," said Conors. "But Elijah called it a day so
he could help the Mary-Jeanne with engine problems."

He watched her snap the grass from the root ball, then forced
his eyes away and opened his door.

She ran up the bank towards Conors. "These marsh grasses
photograph beautifully."

She had forgone a bra, her stomach was flat, her legs long. He
didn't turn away, didn't know if he could. When she reached the top
of the bank and looked up, her face was a foot from his. They stared
into each other's eyes.

His grey eyes were different than she remembered. Conors
looked away first. She had the upper hand and blushed because she
was enjoying it. Conors turned to the door of his cottage and she

walked away. After a few steps she glanced over her shoulder. Conors was holding the door handle and looking at her. She blushed again and disappeared behind the cedar trees.

Conors entered his cottage and closed the door. The picture of her running up the bank was burnt into his memory. "It's been way too long."

He dropped his keys on the counter and was removing his boots when he saw the mud. "A good looking lady walks by and you're tracking muck through your house."

He placed his boots on a rubber mat and was trying to force Terry from his mind, when he saw the PDA. Conors had not touched it since the library. He stared until the PDA went into its sleep mode.

Meanwhile Terry locked her door. During the short walk to her cottage the impression of having the upper hand had evaporated. She jammed the kitchen chair underneath the doorknob, realizing that over the last few weeks, her feelings for Conors had changed from contempt, to fear, to something else.

INSIGHT

May

From evening flights approaching Logan Airport, the Chelsea Project looked like a black hole in the middle of light-polluted Boston. Invisible to these airborne travelers was a hundred watt bulb burning in a small trailer marked, 'Chelsea Project—Onsite Security'.

Under the dangling light bulb, Marty Bulger sat at a plywood table, murmuring, "AEG Surveillance Camera 22—Noon to midnight," as he printed the words on an orange label. He checked for misspellings, stuck the label on a DVD and placed it in a secure cabinet.

He glanced at his watch, put on a dark blue jacket, adjusted his cap and stood straight, making the most of his 5'1". He left the trailer with the Magnum flashlight and billy club dangling from his waist and descended two steps to the dusty gravel. He hated one-man details and was cursing his sixth straight night alone.

But Marty was wrong, he was not alone. Igor had been in the cab of an oversized bulldozer waiting for Marty to leave the trailer. From his comfortable vantage point Igor glared at the guard. "Puny midget looks like Putin."

The guard clipped a GPS monitor to his belt, turned on his flashlight and headed towards the equipment depot where AEG's trucks and heavy equipment were stored each night.

"Govno," said Igor. He had spent three nights watching the security guard and the depot had been the last place to be checked.

Igor opened the Caterpillar's door and dropped six feet to the ground. The gravel crunched under his feet.

The startled guard swept the heavy equipment with his flashlight as he jogged into the fenced area. The equipment was parked in lines and he scanned his light up and down the shadowy rows.

Igor tried to maximize the distance between himself and the guard. At first, the guard's movements seemed erratic, but Igor soon discovered that the little man was closing in and only three rows away. Igor removed his backpack and dropped it to the ground between a tracked excavator and a road grader. He crouched under the excavator and opened the long reamer blade on his service knife. He didn't have to wait long.

The sweeping beam of the flashlight stopped on the black backpack. The security guard approached and kicked it gently. He bent to grab the pack and Igor made his move.

The corkscrew shaped blade entered the security guard's neck. The nerves not severed by the initial wound were torn as Igor twisted the reamer. The guard fell to the ground, leaving the knife in Igor's hand. With adrenaline still surging, he began kicking. "You little prick. Nobody fucks with me."

When he stopped to catch his breath, Igor saw the blood on his knife, DNA evidence he couldn't be caught with. He kicked the guard again and stuffed the knife in the dying man's pocket. He dragged the limp body to an AEG pickup truck, laid it across the front seat and slammed the door shut. He retrieved his backpack and removed a cell phone with a duct-taped cylinder dangling by two wires. He turned on the phone, removed the gas cap from the truck and lowered the narrow cylinder into the tank.

***

Conors sat at an olive-green table covered with neat piles of papers embossed with the AEG logo. The right-handed Conors handled the papers with plastic gloves and used his left hand to print comments and instructions in the margins. He didn't want anybody tracing the documents to him. He used a digital camera to copy the pages and returned the camera to the side pocket of his cargo pants.

It had been exhausting, but he had faithfully visited the apartment at least once a week since his first meeting with Kimani. He never stayed the entire night, always leaving before sunrise. On his first visit, Conors had discovered the fraudulent dioxin data that resulted in a petition to dismiss the pending lawsuit. He also learned that the samples given to EPA proved that the waste dumped into the Chelsea River was from a site managed by Nigel Burn.

During his early visits to Chelsea he had walked the neighborhood of mostly abandoned buildings and identified hiding places and escape routes to Elijah's Jeep that he always parked several streets away. Recent visits included trips to the North End and Nahant, where he circled Giovanni's homes and took pictures. The trips to Chelsea had allowed him to secretly regain some control over his company and to learn more about his enemy, but he was no closer to returning home.

Conors pushed back the chair, gathered the papers into a manila folder and got up from the wobbly table that separated the kitchen appliances from the bed. He slid the folder under the mattress, where Matt Kimani would find it.

He sat on the edge of the bed. It was 2 a.m. on a bitter May night, the room was cold and he was wide awake. A long-suppressed guilt surfaced as he thought of Kimani. Conors had not been honest with him. Although he had been living a lie since the previous August, lying to an old friend was different. While the guilt ate at him, it was not why he lingered. He knew he should leave in the dark of the morning and return to Monhegan, but he was struggling with a devil that had been tempting him since he arrived. His family was thirty minutes away.

He sighed, glanced around the fifth floor apartment and returned to his reality. A sad smirk crossed his face as he admired the landlord's choice of paint, it was hard to tell where the dark mustard paint ended and the dirt began. In the corner opposite the bed, a small stove with chipped white enamel announced its presence with the sulfide smell of leaking gas. Next to the stove was a rust streaked sink. A commode was located on the other side of a half wall. The apartment's only window seemed out of place, it was white and new. AEG's insurance company replaced it after the explosion that rocked Chelsea. The window opened onto a rusting fire escape.

A cockroach skittered across the floor avoiding deep gouges as it headed towards him. Conors squashed it with his shoe and scrapped the crunchy guts onto the floor, adding to the carnage of others that had come within reach. He stood and grabbed night vision binoculars purchased from a local marine store and opened the window. Although a warehouse was between him and the Chelsea Project, the apartment was higher. He had a good view of the site and the street that ran along its north side. His side of the street was lined with abandoned buildings. On the far side, a chain link fence topped with barbed wire separated the sidewalk from the empty fields of the Chelsea Project.

The streets and sidewalks were empty. He halfheartedly scanned the Chelsea Project as thoughts drifted to family. He was considering the downsides of a visit when an unexpected movement caught his attention. He refocused the binoculars and studied the empty fields of gravel, where months earlier decaying buildings had stood. He had decided he was imagining things when somebody jumped from the shadows, raced across the site and threw himself to the ground. It happened a second time before Conors realized the person's antics were designed to avoid the rotating security camera.

Conors threw the binoculars on the bed, knocked the screen out and jumped onto the fire escape. The rusty escape creaked and groaned as he made his way down. By the time he neared the bottom, entire portions of the stairway were no longer attached to the building. When the ladder would not lower to the alleyway, he hung and fell seven feet. Once his feet hit the ground, he headed towards the security fence.

Taking deep controlled breaths, Conors flew down a frost-covered alleyway that led to another and then slowed as he came to an open lot across the street from the Chelsea Project. He knew the layout of the abandoned lot and the paths that crisscrossed through the chest-high remains of last summer's weeds and between piles of rusting and rotting debris. He stopped in the shadow of a building, where he had a view of the street and the chain link fence that sat atop a three foot high concrete wall.

He scanned the security fence and the fields beyond. The noises of the city seemed distant from the eerie silence of the darkened lot. Conors was cursing himself for leaving the night-vision binoculars when he spotted his quarry. The dim light from a distant streetlamp was enough to reveal a man in black from head to toe. He was dashing towards the fence and the security camera that was scanning the empty street. At the fence, the man gasped and sucked a deep breath through the ski mask that covered his head and neck. He leaned against the fence post that supported the rotating surveillance camera.

The man who had methodically evaded the surveillance camera was about Conors' height and in reasonable shape. Conors decided he was dealing with a professional, probably ex-military, and that the bulge near the man's left kidney was a holster.

Since the surveillance cameras periodically scanned the street, Conors was confident no one would leave a getaway car within sight of the Chelsea Project and knew the empty lot was the intruder's closest escape route. He moved deeper into the shadows and waited. Like the man in black, he studied the surveillance camera, knowing the man's next move.

When the camera rotated its focus from the street and towards the Chelsea Project, the man jumped through a jagged opening in the chain-link fence. The man was still winded and misjudged. A strand of the hardened chain link impaled his left calf, catching him in mid-air. He groaned as he came to a jerking stop, dangling upside down above the sidewalk.

Conors watched the man frantically claw his way up the chain-link fence to take the weight off his impaled leg. The man pulled himself back through the opening in the fence, placed his good foot on the ground and pulled the wire from his bloody leg.

The man in the ski mask alternated the weight between his good and bad leg while he watched the camera turn above his head. When the camera again turned from the street, the man was more careful and much slower lowering himself to the sidewalk.

Conors was certain the camera caught the limping man as he disappeared into the empty lot. Crouching in the shadow of a burnt-out minivan, Conors waited for the man to escape towards the back alley. To Conors' surprise the man stopped after entering the lot. With his back towards Conors, he leaned against the wall of a building, facing the Chelsea Project. Then Conors saw the greenish-blue light of a cell phone and heard dialing.

Believing the man was calling a getaway car, Conors moved quickly, but quietly. He was halfway across the lot when he heard one ring from the man's phone, then an explosion. Conors fell to the ground as he saw a fire erupt on the far side of the Chelsea Project. He knew instantly that no one was meant to answer the phone call.

The man was moaning as another number was being autodialed. Conors stood and listened. On the sound of the ring, he jumped over a pile of burnt tires. The second explosion occurred before his foot landed on the glass-strewn path. The lot echoed with the sound of the explosion. He kept running towards the man. The man slouched against the wall with one hand at his crotch and the other speed dialing a third number.

Conors didn't slow. The man caught a glimpse of movement, but it was too late. Conors had jumped as another explosion shook the buildings. His foot drove into the back of the man's knee. The knee gave way and slammed into the ground, leaving the man kneeling with a leg twisted at an odd angle. The screaming man managed to reach for his gun. With an arching motion, Conors chopped him in the throat. The man gasped as his head snapped backwards, but didn't drop the pistol. Conors followed with a kick, hitting the kneeling man in the groin, lifting him into the air. The gun and the man fell back to the ground.

Conors pocketed the gun and frisked the man, who had curled into a fetal position, gurgling and hissing as he tried to breathe through his crushed larynx. Finding no additional weapons, he closed the cell phone, the blue light disappeared and the man became a writhing shadow. A secondary explosion occurred, and Conors looked up to see the Chelsea Project ablaze, again.

There wasn't a trace of compassion as Conors glanced at the man, who was making gasp-like moans. With the approaching sirens becoming louder, Conors grabbed the man by the collar and dragged him to the back of the lot, then down a series of alleyways that weaved between abandoned brick buildings. At first the man resisted, then went limp.

Conors stopped at a small brick boiler room attached to a large warehouse. He let the man fall to the ground. Then Conors yanked the ski mask off the man's head and pulled it over his, the man's sweat and saliva covered Conors' face. He put his shoulder to the rusty and dented metal door and pushed as he had observed drunks doing on cold nights.

The heat from the boiler hit like a sauna and the caged ceiling lights made Conors squint. He dragged the man through the door and dropped him on the concrete floor under a light, between the boiler and a fuel tank. The smell of kerosene, the heat and the lights brought the man to his senses.

There was some rustling and Conors saw a man in an unlighted corner. The man slipped a half empty wine bottle under his coat.

"Get out of here," said Conors.

The drunk kept to the far wall as he scurried to the door and disappeared. Conors shut the door and rolled his prisoner over. The man's sweat-soaked brown hair fell on hard features. His eyes darted about, sizing up his masked captor and the surroundings. His left calf was bathed in blood from the chain link fence, his right foot was facing the wrong way. His pants and shirt were torn, his back cut from the debris-cluttered alleyways. The man moaned, turned onto his side with his hand grabbing his stomach. With no warning, the man rolled back towards Conors. His right arm and a rounded technical knife slashed towards Conors' groin.

The man was fast. Conors was faster. He stepped sideways. The man had thrown his body into the attack, his fist hit the floor. Conors stomped on the hand, shattering bones and freeing the knife. A tortured scream gargled through a battered larynx. Conors foot sunk into the man's gut forcing the air from his lungs, the scream stopped.

He angrily kicked the knife to a far corner, furious he had missed it and underestimated the man. He scanned the boiler room and saw what he needed. After robbing buildings of electrical wiring, the winos and addicts stripped the plastic covering. While Conors gathered a handful of the longer strands, the man attempted to get up. Conors pushed him to the floor, he landed face first. With a knee on his spine, Conors tied the man's hands behind his back and his ankles together. The man struggled until the plastic strands wrenched his mangled hand.

Conors rolled the man on his right side and through the slits in the ski mask stared into the man's eyes. Having the man's attention, he pulled the gun from his jacket.

"A Makarova," said Conors as he casually released the magazine, letting it fall into his other hand. He checked that it was full with twelve rounds and returned the magazine to the pistol butt.

"Have you ever been shot?" asked Conors, while moving the pistol's safety lever to the fire position. The man's face turned white, but he didn't answer. Conors aimed the gun between the man's eyes. "Answer me, asshole."

The man choked and answered in a voice further distorted with a Ukrainian accent. "Het! Het! I mean No!"

"They say it hurts more when you're shot with your own gun." Conors moved the pistol closer. "I was hoping you'd be able to tell me if it was true," said Conors.

"I have ten grand in my car. Take it all. Just let me go," answered Igor with a raspy but louder voice.

"You've never seen enough money to get out of this mess," said Conors. "Unless you answer my questions, the only way you're leaving is in a body bag."

Conors silently circled, going in and out of the man's view. Then he spoke. "What's your name?"

"Igor."

"Last name?" said Conors. The man didn't answer and Conors shoved the pistol into his groin.

"Ovsenko."

"Igor Ovsenko, you must be the guy who blew up this place the last time?"

Igor didn't answer.

"You cost me millions. For months, Chelsea was crawling with police. They uncovered my stash house and arrested four dealers. Now you're doing it again."

Igor maintained his silence. Conors moved out of view, dropped to his knees and pressed the gun barrel hard into the man's temple. "Who're you working for? The Columbians?"

"No," wheezed Igor.

"La Cosa Nostra?"

"No, No," stammered Igor.

Conors removed the gun barrel from the man's head. "The Israelis?"

"No, I don't work for the mobs. My client doesn't have anything to do with drugs."

"Who is this client?"

"If I say his name, I'm a dead man," whimpered Igor.

Conors pressed the barrel into Igor's temple for the second time and pulled the slide. Igor felt the cartridge slam into the barrel.

"Wrong, you're fucking dead, if you don't."

Igor cried and whispered, "Forbes, Nathaniel Forbes."

Conors almost dropped the gun. He'd been expecting to hear Nigel Burn or Giovanni Gallo. For nine months, they had been the target of his anger. Conors stood, backed to the wall and leaned against it, out of Igor's view, trying to grasp what he had heard.

After minutes of silently watching his prisoner, Conors opened the Velcro closure on his pants pocket, removed the digital camera he had used to copy his paperwork, turned it on and set the camera mode to movie. He remembered the manual saying it lasted a minute or two. With his back to Igor, he placed the camera on the boiler so it was aimed at Igor and pushed the record button. He turned toward his prisoner, making sure he blocked the camera from Igor's view, pointed the pistol at his prisoner and stepped away. Igor followed the pistol.

"Tell me again, who do you work for?"

"Nathaniel Forbes."

"Is that the politician?"

"Yeah, he's a Senator."

Conors lowered the gun. "How do I know you're not bullshitting?"

"I have his unlisted cell phone number on my speed dial. I've spoken to him three times this week."

Conors took the man's phone out of his pocket and flipped it open.

"Did Forbes hire you to set tonight's fires?"

Igor nodded.

"Was he involved in the big explosion and fires last August?"

"Yeah, he hired me for that job."

"How did you do it?"

"I shoved eight pounds of Semtex down some pipes."

"Where did you learn to use explosives?" asked Conors.

"I was in the Soviet Army until Ukraine declared its independence."

Conors pointed the gun at Igor. "Why would Forbes want to blow up the Chelsea Project?"

"He never tells me why," sobbed Igor.

Conors lowered the gun again. "Is the Chelsea Project, the first time you worked for Nathaniel Forbes?"

"No I worked on the Big Dig."

"What did you do?"

"Roughed-up an inspector who was getting too fussy."

The camera shut down with a click. The Ukrainian watched as Conors grabbed the camera and returned it to his pants pocket. "Insurance policy," said Conors.

He stood over Igor, trying to understand the last nine months through the lens of his new knowledge. Conors again pointed the gun at Igor. "Did you plant explosives in a car at Logan airport?"

The fear and pain left Igor's face, he looked at his masked captor as if he was some omniscient god.

"Who are you?" said Igor.

An equally stunned expression was hidden by the ski mask. Conors' attempt to process everything he was learning failed. His repeated attempts to decide what to do next failed. A single thought screamed within his head, consuming him with reality. The cold reality that thirty years after a mayor murdered his father, another politician almost did the same to his boys. The man on the floor was that politician, was that mayor, was the reason he lived his childhood in a slum, the reason for the deep unseen anger that ate at his gut.

The gun inched closer to Igor, the fear returned as Conors leaned towards him. Igor closed his eyes and sobbed.

It was the sweat. Conors first noticed the sweat on the man's lips, then the scratches and the blood as Igor's face slowly emerged from a blur of fury. Conors became aware of the smooth feeling of the trigger as his finger tightened, as the gun pushed into the temple of the man who was meant to be his murderer. Conors blinked. He blinked a second time. His trigger finger slowly loosened.

Coors stood and stepped back, staring at the gun and then looked at Igor.

"I'm going to make a few calls," said Conors. "If you've been lying, you're dead."

Igor blinked the tears from his eyes. "I'm not lying."

"We'll see," said Conors.

He left and closed the door, walked across the alley, removed the ski mask and dialed a number on Igor's cell.

"This is Officer Dominga. This line is being recorded."

Conors folded the ski mask, placed it over the phone and whispered, "This is a cellphone call. If you ask the phone company to
track the signal, you'll find the person who started the fires at the
Chelsea Project."

"Who is this?"

"Be quiet and listen. The phone will be outside a boiler room.
Your man is inside. He used this phone to set off the explosions. Be
careful, there may be more explosives."

"Who is this?"

He wiped his prints from the phone and gun and placed them
on the small sheet metal roof that hung over the boiler room door.

He made his way back to the apartment, unseen. When the
streets were full of fire trucks and onlookers, Conors made his way to
the Jeep.

THE HACK

Deep within the bowels of the Massachusetts State Police Headquarters, the door to the windowless office was closed. Robert Collins, the Joint Task Force coordinator, was hunched over the computer. He was bored and checking his investments, they hadn't changed from earlier that morning.

Collins turned his chair from the computer monitor and glanced over his paper-covered desk. He had accumulated piles of unread documents to give the appearance of a whirlwind of activity. He shook his head. "If these assholes want to pay me $147,000 a year to search the internet and talk with my girlfriend, I'll do it till hell freezes over."

Spearheading the Massachusetts component of the Joint Task Force was his third state job. He had been chosen over two State Troopers due to his father's long tenure as Chairman of Boston's Election Department and his father's relationship with the President of the Massachusetts Senate. At his past jobs he had become used to the whispered conversations, but this job had reached a new low. His acceptance by his federal counterparts was no better. After two years on the State Police payroll, he had attended a handful of irrelevant meetings and only learned of joint task force activities from the local newspapers.

He picked the Boston Globe sport section off the floor and was looking for an article he hadn't read when the telephone rang. Not recognizing the Caller ID, he cautiously picked up the phone.

"Joint Task Force, Collins speaking."

"Mr. Collins, this is Officer Ronald Pease from the Rockland Police Department."

"Yes, Officer, What can I do for you?"

"Last month, I left a couple of messages for you about an All Points Bulletin."

"Been really busy, refresh my memory."

"Well there was an APB on this guy from Cambridge. When I fingered him a few months back, I informed the FBI."

"Did the FBI check out the lead?" asked Collins as he scanned the sports section.

"I've called a dozen times and each time, they say they'll look into it. They've giving me the runaround so when I saw your name listed as part of the Joint Task Force, I decided to give you a try."

"Officer, not to come to the FBI's defense, but I'm sure you understand how busy we've all been since 9/11."

"I know and I hate to bother you, but this guy Conors is connected to the murder of that Boston mobster."

Collins dropped the newspaper, Conors was the guy Nathaniel was all hot and bothered about.

"Officer Pease, what makes you think you identified Mr. Conors?"

"Perfect match with the picture in the APB. Same hair, eyes, build and height. I know it's him."

"Do you know where he is now?"

"Well according to the first mate on the Laura B, he's still on Monhegan."

"What the hell is the Laura B?"

"The mail boat that goes to Monhegan"

"Where's Monhegan?" asked Collins as he scribbled notes.

"It's an island off the coast of Maine."

"Right now, I'm dealing with a couple of emergencies, but when I get a chance I'll contact the FBI and chase down your lead."

"Thanks. I'm coming up for review and it would look good if I helped you guys solve a murder."

"I'm sure it would. Have a good day officer."

Collins stood, put the phone in its cradle and grabbed his car keys.

FLAMES

Agent Terry Hamlin looked down on the village and across Monhegan Harbor towards Manana Island. Rose had been gardening outside her cottage and Terry was afraid her conversation would be overheard, so she headed to Lighthouse Hill. Besides great cell phone reception, it offered solitude. The islanders saw little value in trekking up the hill.

It had taken nearly an hour to make the twenty minute walk to the lighthouse. She kept running into islanders who wanted to pass the time of day. In her short stay on the island she had made more friends than in the last ten years. She wondered if it was the islanders or if she had changed.

The Laura B cruised into the harbor and her attention was drawn to the village. She studied the miniature people milling about, going about their lives, driving their rusted trucks and rowing their boats. She wondered what someone would have thought if they had stood on Lighthouse Hill watching her for the last month.

She sighed. "The hell with the last month, what would they think of a life devoted to grades and career?"

The hour chime on her watch sounded. She pulled her cell phone from her coat and hit autodial.

"How's the spy business?" asked Joe DeLuca.

"Fine, I wanted to report that Conors disappeared yesterday afternoon and just returned."

"That's very interesting. There was a murder and another explosion in Chelsea."

Terry froze.

"What was Conors wearing?" asked DeLuca.

"He wears a sweatshirt or a parka and dungarees. He had the parka on when he returned this morning."

"Is his parka green with a gray or blue pocket?"

Terry fell silent.

"Terry? Did I lose you?"

"I'm here. Conors has a green parka. He used duct tape to mend a torn pocket," said Terry.

"I'll be damn, that wino must have seen Conors. The cops assumed the drunk was delirious."

"Sounds like Conors is a murder suspect," whispered Terry.

"No. The wino claimed he saw some vigilante beat the hell out of a guy," said Deluca. "The vigilante tied up the man, a Ukrainian, and left him for the police. The cops found an unexploded device stuck in a fuel tank with the Ukrainian's prints all over it. Looks as if Conors is a candidate for the vigilante. This Conors puzzles the hell out of me."

"That's great news," said Terry.

"What?" said DeLuca. "That I'm confused?"

"No, that Conors isn't a murderer. A group of us are having a potluck dinner tonight."

***

The wind howled and sucked at the flames in the fireplace. The salt drenched driftwood snapped with bursts of blue and red. It was warm, they had drinks before dinner, more after. Conors didn't think he was drunk, but he had let his guard down and looked into her eyes. Not long, a few seconds.

Conors was in one of the two chairs in Rosie's small living room, Elijah in the other. Terry knelt by the fire, squeezing marshmallows onto a thin metal rod. Rosie was sitting on a braided rug by Elijah's feet, a glass of brandy in hand, eyelids heavy with alcohol and unusually quiet. Without warning she pointed at Conors.

"You're dead."

The coldness in her voice sucked the oxygen from the room. Conors stared at her index finger until adrenalin pierced the alcoholic fog muddling his mind. He awkwardly pretended to take his pulse and forced a smile. "Don't think so."

Rosie's face reddened. "According to the internet, Professor William Slater died of a massive heart attack."

Conors had recently discovered the obituary for the man, whose identify he had stolen. He had hoped the short paragraph would go unnoticed. It hadn't. He stared into the fire wondering why she was googling his name.

"A month ago, I was sitting on the stern of the Ellie M. covered with fish guts, feeling better than I had in a long time. That's when I decided I couldn't go home. The next day I called the newspaper and wrote my obituary."

Conors glanced at Rosie. The anger slowly left her face and she lowered her finger. Once again his well-oiled lies seemed to work.

"Why can't you go home?" asked Rosie.

Conors turned back to the fire and spoke the truth. "Things changed, like the flick of a light switch. From out of the blue, this guy arrives and flips the switch. Day becomes night, up is down, down is up and life is shit. Then I find this island and these people, who allow me to forget. Not often, but sometimes and that helps."

Other than the crack of the fire, the cottage fell silent, he felt their eyes. He got to his feet, but didn't take a step. His head spun, the room moved, he lowered himself back into the chair. "Either we're having an earthquake or I'm drunk."

"No earthquake, we're all shitfaced," said Elijah.

Seeing humor where only the drunk can, the others laughed. Conors sat wondering why after ten painfully cautious months he had drunk so much. He passed out looking at Terry.

He woke later, but didn't know how much later. The fire flickered, yellow light darted past him into the black of the room. She was close, her back towards him. He studied her through half open eyes. Terry was a stunning woman, but it was the small things that unnerved him. Her worried but inviting eyes, the way she tossed her hair over her shoulder, the uneasy smile. Small things hinting of more and begging to be explored.

"Last of the marshmallows," said Terry. "No more s'mores."

She giggled. "No more s'mores."

"No more brandy for you, girl," slurred Rosie.

Terry had been holding the rod above the flames. When the marshmallows caught fire, she pulled them from the fire, blew out the flames and clumsily placed the gooey mess between graham crackers and dark chocolate.

Rosie caught him staring at Terry and smiled. He looked away.

"The sternman's finally awake," said Rosie. "With the fishing season coming to an end, we were wondering what your plans are."

"Unless Elijah's fired me, there's still a few days before I need to make any decisions," said Conors.

"Rosie, you should know sternmen aren't the planning type," said Elijah.

"Just got used to the smell of Elijah and the herring," said Conors. "No sense rushing things."

Terry turned and reached out to Conors. She was drunk and struggling to keep her eyes open. "Have the last one, they're delicious."

Conors took the napkin and graham crackers oozing chocolate. He looked again into her bottomless eyes.

Elijah wobbled towards the fireplace and dropped a log onto the fire, it flared. Terry backed away, leaned against Conors' thigh and wrapped her arm around his calf. A jolt of electricity surged through his body. He wanted to escape from his skin, but didn't move. She rested her head on his thigh and stared at the fire through blinking eyes.

Time passed, distant voices talked, but Conors didn't follow the conversation, he repeatedly nodded off only to be awakened by the warmth of her body.

Just before midnight, a blaring noise shook him from his stupor. Three short, three long and three short blasts from a foghorn. The international distress signal was repeated, forcing Elijah and Conors to their uncertain feet. They looked at each other in horror. There was a fire on the island.

They all stumbled out the door and spent the night linking garden hoses to nearby and then distant wells as they soaked the meadow and contained a grass fire started when an ember drifted from a chimney.

Later, he lay in his bed, the stench of smoke-drenched clothes playing with his uneasy stomach, exhausted, but eyes open and wide awake.

***

The afternoon following the potluck supper was the first time the sun was seen in the month of May. Elijah and Conors were working on the boat that Conors rented. The old engine was running rough and the island's master mechanic was diagnosing the problem.

"Told you," said Elijah, pointing at a droplet of water in the bottom of a mayonnaise jar filled with gasoline. "That small amount of water will roll around in the carburetor bowl, interfere with the aspiration of the gas and make an outboard skip."

He waited to ensure no more water separated before decanting the fuel into a gas tank. He secured the cap on the tank, Elijah returned to watching Conors reattach the dual carburetors to the block of the old Evinrude.

Elijah cleared his throat. "A few years past, I had a sternman who rented from Rosie. Actually, the same cottage you rent now."

"Yeah," said Conors as he lay on his back trying to tighten a bolt under a carburetor.

"Well, he was a hellion, and once a month his girlfriend would come over from the mainland. One of those nights she was visiting, Rosie and I were on her back porch." Elijah cleared his throat again. "You know that shower in your cottage?"

Conors frowned, put the wrench down and looked at Elijah. "I use it everyday."

Elijah nodded. "Well, they got a drinking and doing things that young couples do, but unfortunately they climbed into that sheet metal showers of yours. They got a bumping around and by the time they reached a climax, it sounded like the thunderstorm of the century. When Rosie and I got around front to see what was going on, the Kearnsey boys were in the front yard with a hockey stick and a baseball bat."

"Why are you telling me this?" asked Conors.

"Well, I noticed how that pretty thing was looking at you and didn't want you kids finding yourself in a similar position," said Elijah.

"If Terry was looking at me, it was because she had too much wine," said Conors. "And if you ever hear thunder coming from my shower, it's because I dropped a bar of soap."

"Okay, just put it aside as information that could be useful," said Elijah.

Conors still had a hangover and wasn't pleased with himself. The previous evening he put himself and his plans at risk. He was haunted by what could have happened and by what he had wanted to happen. Conors picked up the wrench and turned towards the outboard engine.

TASTE OF REVENGE

Nigel Burn entered the private dining room on the third floor of Locke-Obers and approached the President of the Massachusetts Senate.

"You're late," said Nathaniel Forbes.

"Sorry," said Burn. "Just returned from London. Still trying to catch up."

Forbes studied the bald, surly man, then used a napkin to pull an envelope from an inside pocket of his suit coat. He slid it across the table.

"The police recently forwarded this to my attention," said Forbes.

Burn pointed at the envelope. "Is this the reason for our mysterious meeting?"

Forbes nodded.

Burn picked the envelope up, opened it and unfolded a piece of paper. "It's that All Points Bulletin for Conors that you sent me a few months ago."

"Yes, Nigel, that's correct. But this has an addition. Can you read the word typed across the very top?"

"Monhegan?"

"An island off the coast of Maine as well as the new home of your lost friend," said Forbes.

Nigel glanced again at the paper and back at Forbes. "Conors?"

"I thought you'd be more excited," said Forbes.

"What should I do with it?"

"The police are already aware of Conors' whereabouts, but I recall you mentioning another party that was interested."

Burn's eyebrows furrowed further up his long forehead.

"Well, have a good afternoon and please give those unpaid invoices some consideration," said Forbes. "You know how difficult it is to keep accountants at bay."

"Sure," said Burn.

Forbes watched Burn leave, then rested his elbows on the table and crossed his forearms. His right index finger tapped nervously as he stared at the linen tablecloth. The news of Conors being alive had caught him by surprise. He couldn't afford to have Conors return. An absent owner was the primary argument for eminent domain of the Chelsea Project. He knew that if Burn didn't pass along the information, he'd have to find another way, that couldn't be traced back to him.

***

A few minutes later Burn was in the back seat of a taxi headed towards his office. "What's the name of that mob barroom that's always in the newspapers? The bar's somewhere in the North End."

"The Hanover Grille?" said the driver in a Haitian accent.

"That's it," said Burns. "Take me there."

Fifteen minutes later, the taxi driver was double-parked in front of the Hanover Street Bar & Grille. Burn had entered the bar and left instructions to wait. The cabbie watched as the bouncer approached.

"Get the hell out of here."

The driver slipped the transmission into drive and passed on the return fare.

Burn glanced around the bar and decided the few patrons and employees were low-level thugs, who'd respect authority. Standing tall, with hands in the pockets of his Barbour trench coat, he crossed the darkened room. The man behind the bar was stacking glasses.

"I have some information for Gallo," said Burn.

The bartender placed a glass upside down on a white towel and reached under the bar with his right hand. Then he took his time emptying a jar of olives into a bowl. "I don't know what you're talking about."

Burn glanced at a stocky man entering the bar from a backroom, then turned back to the bartender. "Don't give me that shit, I know you work for Gallo and I have some information he wants."

The stocky man approached Burn. "I'm John Devito, the manager. I'm sure I can help. Please step into my office."

Burn followed Devito. He was saying, "You should teach your bartender some manners," when a hand on his back shoved him through the doorway.

"What the hell," yelled Burn.

The door slammed behind him. Devito punched him in the solar plexus. Burn's last words had emptied his lungs and Devito's punch paralyzed his diaphragm. Burn started to fall as Devito pushed him towards a large keg of beer. The keg hit Burn in the gut, he collapsed with his legs on one side, his head and shoulders on the other.

Devito yanked Burn's trench coat and shirt over his head, popping buttons. The man who had shoved Burn through the door yanked Burn's pants and boxer shorts to his ankles.

"Anything?" John Devito asked.

The other man shook his head. "No wires."

Burn slumped to the concrete floor, gasping. He was aware of the smell and stickiness of spilled beer but didn't care, he couldn't breathe.

"Who's mini-dick?" asked Devito as they looked at Burn.

The man handed Burn's wallet to Devito. Devito removed the IDs and placed them on a copy machine surrounded by boxes of wine and liquor, and pushed the start button. The machine spit out a photocopy, Devito scanned it, then stuffed the cards into the wallet crushing Burn's neatly ordered bills.

"Our guest is Nigel Burn, president of a local engineering company."

"What do you make of this?" asked the other man who had emptied Burn's coat pockets and handed Devito a folded All Points Bulletin.

John Devito shrugged his shoulders.

Burn made an unintelligible sound. He pointed to the APB and tried a second time to say something, but failed.

"Take your time Nigel, you're going to be here a while," said John.

The two men waited for Burn to catch his breath. When Burn's breathing became regular John Devito said, "Nigel, why don't you tidy yourself up."

Burn, still lying on his side, slowly raised his pants, hesitating when his bruised stomach muscles made him wince.

"Nigel, my brother's going to help you into a chair."

George Devito assisted Burn to his feet and backed him into a wooden chair. John Devito waited until the bare-chested Burn raised his head.

"Nigel you wanted to tell us something."

"I have some information for Mr. Gallo," said Burn in a whisper.

"We don't know a Mr. Gallo, but why don't you tell me anyway?" said John.

"I know where Conors is," said Burn pointing at the APB in Devito's hand.

John unfolded the APB again and scanned the print at the bottom. "He's talking about the Bill Conors who skipped town."

The two brothers looked at each other in silence.

"Nigel, it's best not to talk about some things, unless you're certain," said John.

"I know where Conors is," repeated Burn.

"A lot of people are looking for Conors, how could the president of an engineering company, know where he is?" asked John.

"The police found him."

"Why would the police tell you and not the rest of Massachusetts?"

"I worked with Conors for years."

"If you worked with Conors, why are you squealing on him?" asked George.

"He screwed me."

John smiled and shook his head. "Where is he?"

"Monhegan," said Burn.

"What?" asked John.

"Monhegan's an island off the coast of Maine." Burn pointed again at the APB. "The name's printed across the top."

John glanced at his younger brother, then held the photocopy of the license, company ID and business card inches from Burn's face. "Nigel, we know where you live. It wouldn't be a good idea to bullshit us?"

"I'm not," said Burns. "I swear I'm telling the truth."

John studied Burn, then tore open a cardboard box and pulled out a bottle of Canadian whiskey.

"Nigel, you look like hell and I run a reputable business," said John. "I can't have you walking out of my bar looking like this."

He unscrewed the top. "But if you got drunk and started a fight that would explain everything."

John handed Burn the whiskey bottle. "Nigel, start drinking and don't stop."

Burn took the bottle in his shaking hands. It felt heavy. He hesitated.

John glared at him. "Drink."

Burn took a deep swig and was taking the bottle from his mouth when John yelled, "Don't stop."

He bent his head back and poured the burning liquid down his throat. An eighth of the bottle was emptied. He stopped to catch his breath.

John took the bottle from Burn's hands. "George, call a cab. Nigel needs a ride home."

"Nigel, pull yourself together and try looking like a big time executive."

Burn tucked his buttonless shirt into his pants and straightened his coat. John took the remainder of the whiskey and poured it over Burn.

Burn stood in silence as the liquor ran down his neck.

John handed Burn his wallet and saw the glaze in Burn's eyes. "Nigel, you'll tip the cabby. He's taking you home as a favor for me."

Burn nodded.

George opened the door. "Anthony's here."

John turned to Burn. "You're going to walk out of here and straight out the front door. Then get into the cab. Understand?"

"Yeah," said Burn.

Burn staggered across the bar and left.

"Did you give Nigel's address to Anthony?" asked John.

George nodded. "And if he passes out, Anthony will dump him on the doorsteps and ring the bell."

"Good. You're in charge for the night," said John Devito. He picked up the APB. "I'm taking a ride to Nahant."

VAPORS

Conors was dressed for his morning run. He had closed the cottage door and was halfway down the path to Meadow Road, when he stopped. There was a smell of propane coming from Terry's cottage.

Conors banged on the door. "Terry, are you in there?"

He put his ear to the door and heard nothing. He tried the door, it was locked. He banged again and yelled, "Terry."

He heard a faint moan, took a step back and put his shoulder to the door. It came off its hinges, Conors and the door fell to the floor. The stench of propane was worse inside.

Terry was in her bed in a t-shirt and panties. He grabbed her in his arms, she was surprisingly light. He carried her outside and towards his cottage while she mumbled something he couldn't understand.

His cottage door was locked and he didn't want to put her on the wet ground. He hoisted her over his left shoulder and slid the key into the lock. He was turning the doorknob when he felt her stomach tighten, and then the warm vomit oozing down his neck and back. He stood on the stoop while she vomited a second and third time. When she stopped, he carried her into the cottage and placed her on his bed.

"Vinny," she mumbled.

"Terry, I'm not Vinny, I'm your neighbor. You're on Monhegan Island."

He took a dish towel from his sink and wiped the vomit from her face. Then he returned to the stoop, pulled his sweatshirt over his head, dropped it and did the same with his damp t-shirt. Seconds later he was at Rose's front door pounding until she arrived in her bathrobe. She opened her door and looked through the screen at the bare-chested Conors.

"Advertising?"

He opened her screen door. "Terry needs your help."

The spry Rose took off for Terry's cottage. Conors said, "No she's in my place," and led her through the cedar trees and pushed opened the door. "She's in my bed."

Rose entered and seeing the panty clad Terry stopped and gave Conors a cold look.

"It's not what it looks like. I was going for a run and smelled propane coming from her cottage."

"You usually run half-naked around the island?"

"Only when the girls puke all over me."

Rose didn't say anything. The cold look remained as she turned towards Terry. Conors shook his head and returned to Terry's cottage, turned off the propane and opened windows. He surveyed the damage. The door frame was split and the door would need to be rebuilt. He went to the thermostat, it was set on high. He'd ask Elijah to inspect it and the heater.

A partially eaten bowl of mussels sat on the table, uncooked mussels were in Terry's sink. After tidying up the place, he returned to his cottage with a handful of uncooked mussels and knocked.

Rose opened the door. "How's she doing?" he asked.

She stepped onto the stoop. "She's asleep now. The last thing she remembers is getting sick, turning up the heat and going to bed."

He handed Rose the mussels. "I don't know why the heater went out, but I know why she got sick."

Rose murmured, "They look healthy."

Conors pointed at the part of the mussel that attaches itself to rocks. "See that black stuff on the mussel's foot? It's creosote. My guess is that she pulled the mussels from the pilings under the wharf."

Rose shook her head. "She's in the middle of the Atlantic and finds the only polluted creatures on the island."

Conors said, "In the future, we better inspect what she brings to potluck."

"I apologize for insinuating things that weren't true," said Rosie. "I'm glad you were there, I've grown fond of the girl."

Conors nodded.

"Can you help me move her back to her cottage?" asked Rose.

"It's missing a door. I'll stay at her place until it's repaired."

***

Conors and Elijah had replaced the door jamb and Conors was holding the door in place. Elijah was kneeling next to Conors marking the location of the bottom hinge with a pencil. "You're the best smelling sternman, I've ever run across."

"Used Terry's shower and there was no choice in soap."

"Oh," said Elijah. "I thought you were finally comfortable enough to show your true colors."

"Mark that hinge before I drop something on you."

Elijah cackled.

They hung the door and then Elijah, the perpetual teacher, explained the workings of the heater while he methodically dissembled, cleaned and reassembled the entire system. It was early evening and they were checking out the heater when Rose arrived with food and drinks.

She put the sandwiches on Terry's table and twisted the tops off three bottles of Rolling Rock.

Elijah and Conors pulled chairs up to the small table. Rose raised her beer in a salute. "Thanks for all your help."

They raised their bottles and drank.

"How's the young lady?" asked Elijah.

"Embarrassed about the whole thing, but I had her laughing this afternoon." Rosie turned to Conors. "She's asleep again, can she stay the night at your place?"

"Sure."

Elijah put his beer down and slid one of the wrapped sandwiches towards himself. "When I first saw the broken door, I thought Professor Slater made a night call on an available lady."

Conors blushed. Rose shook her head and spoke as if Conors wasn't present. "They'd make a nice couple, if they weren't so headstrong."

"I don't know," Elijah said. "Take a whiff of that boy. I don't think he's her type."

Rose looked at Conors with raised eyebrows. "I make it a policy not to whiff sternmen."

"A wise strategy," said Elijah. He raised his beer again. "To a sternman who sustained the stellar reputation of the Ellie M."

***

Conors had spent the night in Terry's cottage. It was identical in layout to his, but over a few weeks she had decorated it with photographs, flowers and bowls of balsam needles. Terry reminded Conors of his wife and how she magically transformed their apartments and houses into homes. He was thinking about how stark his cottage was as he knocked on its door.

"It's unlocked."

He opened the door. "Like to pick-up some clothes."

Terry was sitting in his bed with her legs pulled underneath her. One hand rested on her ankle. She held a coffee mug with the other. Her hair was pulled over her left shoulder, his frayed flannel shirt was over her tee shirt. She was as seductive as if she had been stark naked. Conors looked away.

"Coffee may be a little strong," she said. "I was expecting you earlier."

"I'll pass," said Conors. "Never drink the stuff."

He grabbed a Pepsi from the six-pack on the counter and quickly glanced around his cottage. The sugar was in a bowl and no longer in the cardboard box. His sweatshirt and shirt were washed and drying over the heater vent. He stood by the door and opened the can. His uneasiness made her smile. "Bill, I want to thank you."

"Not needed. Anybody would have done the same."

"Well, I still want to thank you for pulling me out of the cottage. Rosie said I would have died from asphyxiation." Her voice was quavering, she bit her lip, turned away from Conors for a few seconds, then looked at him. "Thanks for saving my life."

"Rosie can be a little dramatic."

"Nice of you to downplay what you did, but I also want to thank you for something else," she said. "Something you taught me."

"What's with all this gratitude," said Conors. "Where's the sarcasm."

"The sarcasm was when I thought you were horrible."

"Horrible. Well, now we're being honest," said Conors.

"Yes, there was a time when you scared me and I thought you were horrible," She put her coffee mug on the painted night table. "But, as I learned more about you, my feelings changed. At the last potluck, I discovered I had a crush on you."

Conors forced a smile. "I thought crushes were for middle school."

Her face blushed with anger, "No, it wasn't like middle school, I had dreams of you ripping my clothes off and having wild sex."

The Pepsi can shook in Conors' hands. He put it on the counter. "Terry, let's change the subject."

"No, I need to finish. I know it was childish, but I know you had similar thoughts. I could see it in your eyes. But that wasn't why I was attracted to you," she said. "It was because the man I originally thought was horrible was actually a good man."

Conors looked towards the floor. "I'm sorry, if I made you feel uncomfortable."

"Yes, you made me feel uncomfortable, but it was good for the ego."

Conors glanced at her and then looked away.

"Last year, I met a man and he'd be long gone, if he wasn't so persistent," she said. "Because of you, I realize what I almost lost."

"Is this good man named Vinny by any chance?" asked Conors.

Terry stared at Conors. She got out of Conors' bed and stood.

"Don't worry, I haven't read your love letters," said Conors. "After you puked all over me, you were calling me Vinny."

She exhaled, not realizing she had been holding her breath. She had less than a week left and her cover was still intact. She had told DeLuca that Conors had no contacts with organized crime and appeared to be an honest man in a tough situation. DeLuca directed her to end her undercover work and return to the office.

"Yes, his name is Vinny."

"If he's catholic, you should nominate him for sainthood."

She smiled uneasily at the man across the room as the cold from the wood floor seeped through her bare feet and up her back. She shivered. The smile disappeared with a rush of guilt. She was going home while his problems were far from over. If her boss was right, Conors was a marked man. Tears filled her eyes. She walked across the room. Conors backed against the door. She gave him a hug and sobbed into his chest.

Conors let his arms hang by his side, wanting to, but not returning the hug. As she sobbed, he could feel her breasts, her legs. He could smell her and feel the heat of her body. He looked at the ceiling and closed his eyes. "Terry, let go."

Her arms loosened their grip, she turned away, still sobbing and said, "I'm so sorry."

When she let go, the feeling and the warmth went with her. He left without saying a word.

FATE

It was the middle of May and Conors' days as a sternman on the Ellie M were coming to an end. When they left the harbor earlier that morning, the trees and beach roses were budding and hinting of summer. Monhegan was undergoing a metamorphosis that quickened as the days passed. The fishermen, their boats, and traps were less visible, displaced by summer residents and brightly colored duffle bags, suitcases and bags of groceries.

As Elijah had predicted, the lobsters disappeared with the arrival of good weather. He and Conors had spent the week pulling traps and storing them in Elijah's backyard.

"Three hundred and ninety-nine—four hundred," said Elijah as Conors pulled the last trap onto the deck of the Ellie M.

"I swear these traps are heavier when they're empty," said Conors.

"Yeah, when they're full of those beautiful bugs, the traps seem to jump on deck," said Elijah.

"Considering what you see in the mirror, I guess a lobster is beautiful," said Conors.

Elijah laughed. "You should be careful, an old man's ego is a sensitive thing."

Conors disconnected the line and buoy, placed the trap on top of the head-high pile and secured it. "In the unlikely event that your ego is wounded, I know at least two women who'll nurse it back to health."

"Well, those same fine women are asking if my sternman is returning next year."

Conors dropped a buoy into a large plastic barrel, knowing that he wouldn't be fishing next year because he'd either be with his family, running his business, or he'd be dead.

"You can tell your lady friends the same that I told you. I have unfinished business that makes it unlikely."

"Fair enough. You're always welcome aboard the Ellie M. You brought good luck and I've enjoyed your company," said the smiling Elijah. "Most of the time."

Conors leaned against the pile of traps while the Ellie M rolled in the ground swell. He looked at the weathered old man.

"You got me drunk the first night on the island, then spent the winter freezing my butt in the Gulf of Maine," said Conors. "But along the way I learned a few things about fishing, repairing engines and a guy from Monhegan. I couldn't ask for a better friend."

"Neither could I."

Conors smiled.

"When are you leaving?" asked Elijah.

"Middle of next week."

Elijah nodded.

"I have this bottle of Tequila with two big cactus worms on the bottom. I've heard that once you've drunk the bottle, the worms look good enough to eat," said Elijah. "Do you believe that's true?"

"There's only one way to find out," said Conors.

***

Terry placed a damp towel over a bowl of dough and wiped her wet hands on her T-shirt. The following night would be her last on Monhegan and her last potluck supper. With her tainted mussels fresh in everybody's mind, they decided against seafood. Conors agreed to cook hamburgers, she was making the dessert.

She returned the flour and sugar to the cabinet and slipped the dirty pans into the sink of soapy water. She sat at the kitchen table, lifted a bowl of balsam needles to her face, closed her eyes and savored the smell she'd always associate with Monhegan. She was at peace and very different from the woman who stepped onto the island six weeks earlier. Her concern was no longer the next promotion, but that the new Terry Hamlin might stay on the island when she stepped onto the ferry.

Terry stood and placed the bowl of needles on a sunny windowsill. She passed a mirror that caught her image and the trace of a wrinkle escaping from the corner of her right eye. She frowned and said, "It's taken you a while to find yourself."

She was examining her left eye when a smashing sound came from Conors' cottage. She opened her door but couldn't see anybody. It was dead silent.

The sun was high and warmed her. She took a breath, the earthy smell of spring filled her lungs. Her sandals flattened the green fuzz of grass and weeds erupting from last winter's mud. A stand of cedars separated the cottages, with closed eyes and hands before her she pushed through the prickly branches. On the other side she opened her eyes, and discovered she was standing on a lone crocus. She picked up the broken flower. The purple petals were wrapped tight, a day or two from blooming. She sighed and continued towards Conors' cottage. The door was ajar.

"Bill, are you there?"

"Yeah," was the muffled reply.

"You sound terrible," said Terry as she stepped through the doorway. She still had her hand on the doorknob when she saw the splintered door jamb and stopped.

She was pulled into the cottage. A pair of thick hairy arms surrounded her, crushing her chest, emptying her lungs. Her response was instinctive. She raised her right arm and swung down while moving her hips to the left. Her closed fist sunk deep into the man's groin, he let go and fell. She started for the door. The man grabbed her ankle and yanked. She lost her balance, but caught herself on the sink and grasped a thick porcelain plate. The man yanked again, twisting her leg. She fell to the floor, landing hard and shattered her knee. She smashed the plate into the side of the man's head. His grip loosened.

Terry struggled to her feet, using the sink to put weight on her good leg. She reached for the door and then suddenly stopped. Her eyes locked on the barrel of a gun. It was a Colt 1911 with a silencer that doubled its length. Her lips started to form the word 'no'.

The bullet entered her chest and careened through soft tissue and bones. The back of her head hit the wall. She tasted gunpowder. Through the haze of smoke, her eyes met his.

The second and third shots went through her stomach and knocked her to the floor.

She stopped wondering why he was shooting. She remembered her father clapping when she won the third grade spelling bee, she saw a young girl studying in a small bedroom, a high school girl reading a valedictorian speech, Pops laughing at his dog, and Vinny holding her hand on Crane's Beach. But, then suddenly Vinny had his back to her and was walking away. She called, "Vinny!" He kept walking. She screamed, "I love you!" But he didn't hear, he was too far away.

She was still screaming when she looked down at herself and saw that things were very wrong. Her lips weren't moving.

***

Monhegan harbor could be entered from the north and south, the Ellie M had approached from the south. A few hundred yards from the wharf, Elijah slipped the transmission into neutral and let the vessel glide through the water. "That's one sinister looking boat."

Conors was sitting on an upturned bucket. He dropped an emptied bait bag into a barrel and leaned over the starboard catwalk towards the wharf. With the arrival of warmer weather a float for loading and off-loading had been attached to the south side of the wharf.

Secured to the float was a stark white boat. A muffled deep sound escaped from its exhaust pipes. It was over forty feet and designed for high speeds. It had no markings, no seats, no cushions and looked like it belonged to a drug-runner.

"Not exactly a family boat," said Conors.

Elijah sat at the helm, waiting for the boat's owner. Conors returned to cleaning herring guts from bait bags.

"Traffic jam," said Elijah as the rowboat from the Mary-Jeanne passed by.

"Afternoon Elijah," said Sam Kearney then nodded to Conors. "Bill."

"Sam," said Conors.

Kearney kept rowing. "Second time today," said Kearney. "Earlier, had to wait a good twenty minutes for a boat to leave."

Sam Kearney had reached the rocky shoreline when Elijah said, "Lordy-Lordy."

Conors turned. A man was running down Wharf Road, his white polo shirt splattered with red. This time of year fishermen and boaters were speckled with red bottom paint. But the runner's stride and the way people jumped aside dismissed the possibility of paint.

The size of the man became more apparent as he barreled towards the harbor, leaving gawking onlookers in stunned silence. It was low tide. Conors was fifty feet away when the runner reached the end of the wharf and launched himself into the air. The giant of a man fell a dozen feet to a wooden float. It rocked when he landed.

The man was in midair, when Conors recognized the contorted face. He stared at the man he had first seen ten months earlier, at his home in Gloucester. The man was unaware or unconcerned with those around him. He untied the bow and stern lines, threw them onto the deck and swung himself over the boat's five feet of free-board. He landed behind the helm and pushed the throttles for the three engines. Water shot from the exhausts and a deafening roar filled the harbor.

The bow of the boat leapt out of the water as it swerved around the Ellie M, heading south. The boat leveled onto a plane while Nico Martarrazzo navigated between moorings. By the time the boat left the harbor it was going sixty knots and accelerating. In less than a minute, the bloodied Nico had disappeared behind Manana Island.

Adrenaline was flowing, but Conors was thinking clearly. He looked at Elijah. "Get me to the float!"

Elijah was surprised the soft-spoken sternman had barked an order, but did as commanded. The Ellie M was seven feet from the float when Conors jumped. Two steps later he was across the float and at the top of the ladder, skipping the first six rungs.

Elijah watched Conors run faster than he thought possible. He noted an alarming similarity between Conors and the giant that had sped out of the harbor, a physical intensity that screamed 'get out of the way'.

Elijah secured the Ellie M and started down Wharf Road, figuring he'd be making an emergency run to the mainland. Having the fastest boat on the island, it was a routine he was accustomed to.

Conors had been training for this day since Cleveland and was in the best shape of his life. Less than three minutes after leaving the Ellie M, he cleared Rosie's picket fence. Rosie was kneeling on her lawn covered with blood, leaning against the much larger Betsy Kearney. Rosie was sobbing uncontrollably. She looked old and frail.

Conors took her bloody hand, "Rosie, what happened?" He looked for signs of a wound or broken bones.

Rosie forced a word out between sobs. "Terry." She pointed towards his cottage.

The horror hit Conors hard. He walked the few yards to his cottage. Marian, the island medic, who clerked at the North End Market, was standing by the front door. Her eyes were wet. They looked at each other. She shook her head, answering the unasked question.

Conors looked through the open door. Terry was on the floor lying on her back in a pool of blood, her eyes open. He couldn't move.

Marian gently put her hand on his arm. "Bill, I just called the State Police. They said don't touch anything."

Conors backed away from the doorway, still staring at Terry. Marian stepped between him and cottage, "It's okay, Bill."

"What happened?" asked Conors.

She led Conors from the cottage and spoke quietly. "Not sure. Rosie was walking up from the wharf. She saw some guy covered in blood running from your cottage. After finding Terry, she ran to the market yelling for help. When I examined Terry and told her we were too late, she lost it."

Conors stared into the meadow, guilt and anger building as he listened. The doubts that had lingered for months evaporated. The dead woman lying on the floor meant there was no longer any choice.

"I'll be back, I need to tend to Rosie" said Marian.

Conors turned from the meadow, disappeared behind the cottage and crouched by the stone foundation. He removed two loose stones discovered the previous fall when shingling the cottage. He pulled a plastic trash bag from underneath and opened it. Conors removed a backpack that contained gloves, Gallo's gun, ammunition, Gallo's money and his savings from lobstering. He slipped it over his shoulder and headed towards the wharf.

***

The harbor was empty of the islanders when he arrived, they had all headed towards Rosie's. He dragged his polyethylene kayak over the rocky beach and into the water. He paddled to the Boston Whaler and climbed aboard. Usually he tied the kayak to the mooring buoy for his return, this time he pulled it onboard.

Conors turned the ignition key and the old Evinrude started. He untied the mooring line, pushed the throttle and the boat sped north out of the harbor towards Port Clyde. The old outboard whined as the flat-bottomed boat skipped across Muscongus Bay.

Thirty minutes later Conors reached Port Clyde and tied the boat to a mooring buoy. He lowered the kayak into the water, slipped on his backpack and paddled ashore. He tied the kayak onto the roof racks of Elijah's old Jeep and removed the key from its hiding place under the dash.

LOOSE ENDS

"Conors gets away and a broad gets killed," said Giovanni Gallo. "Dead broads motivate cops and I don't need fucking motivated cops."

Santo and Carlo stood silently in front of their boss. Giovanni scowled. "Where's Nico?"

"Don't know," said Carlo.

"You two don't know shit."

The cell phone rang. Giovanni picked it up.

"This is John." John Devito had found a telephone booth he had never used and dialed the number Angie had given him.

"You gave us some information about an island. Things didn't turn out good. I don't want anybody connecting us to that place. I want to be one hundred percent sure. Do you understand?"

"Yes, Boss. I'll make sure. One hundred percent sure."

"Good," said Giovanni. He removed the battery and dropped the phone into a waste basket. "I hate fucking phones."

He looked at the two men. "Get out of my sight."

The men left Giovanni pacing in the solarium and retreated to the courtyard. When Angie returned from the North End, they were sitting on a bench, keeping a distance from Gallo.

Angie parked the Caddy and walked up to the men. "Did John call?"

"Yeah, the Boss told him what he's gotta do," said Santo.

"How's the Boss?"

Carlo shook his head. "He's pissed, he really wanted that Conors."

"He's pissed at the world," whispered Santo.

It had been a long day for the sixty-six year old Angie. He shook his head. "I don't need this shit."

Sighing as he lowered himself onto the granite bench opposite Carlo and Santo.

Angie's cell phone rang. He pulled the phone from his pocket, opening it on the last ring.

"Angie?"

"Where the hell are you?" said Angie. "Giovanni's not happy."

"I had a bad day," said Nico.

Angie's face turned red. "We all had a fucking bad day. Now, when the hell can I tell the Boss, you'll be here?"

"Are Carlo and Santo there?"

"Yeah, they're here for the night. The fucking question is when will you be here?" said Angie.

"Later."

"When is later?" said Angie and then he slowly lowered the phone. "Stu Cazzo, he hung-up."

He shoved the phone into his pocket. "I'm out of here."

***

Devito hung up the phone. He kicked the phone booth door and then slumped against the wall. "Somebody else screws up and I get fucked."

He stared through the graffitied and cracked Plexiglas, breathing heavily until he calmed down. He knew what to do, it wasn't the first time. He glanced at his brother's Trans AM. It had been parked behind the bar when Angie arrived. A car wouldn't work, so he opened the yellow pages that were hanging from a cable. Half the pages were missing. The one he needed was there. He dialed.

"Sal's garage."

"Sal, this is John DeVito. I need one of those rental vans."

"Sure, when do you want it?"

"Now."

"You got it."

***

Sal replaced the license plates with stolen ones. Devito tossed coveralls and gloves into the back of the van. Then Devito returned to the North End, parked behind the bar and picked up his brother, some wire, brooms, mops and plastic bags.

Thanks to the thinning traffic, ten minutes later the van pulled into an underground parking garage. George Devito sat in the passenger seat. He looked at his watch. "It's almost seven. I hope the bastard's running late."

The van went to the second level and crossed the garage towards the reserved spaces. Most of the employees in the office building had left and the garage was mostly empty.

"That's it, the off-white Lexus," said John. He slowed the van to a crawl. "Now, we have to find the cameras."

They drove up and down the rows, scanning the ceiling and walls. They stopped at the end of a row, looking directly at the sedan and on the blind side of the nearest camera. John finished buttoning his coveralls, while his lanky brother struggled into his.

"Two cameras, the one by the elevator and the one in this row," said George.

"We don't have to worry about the elevator. But we need to take that one out," said John as he pointed at the ceiling halfway down the row.

"Okay." George grabbed a plastic bag and opened the door. He climbed onto the roof of the van. John put the transmission in drive and approached the camera from its blind side.

"Stop," said George. He slipped the bag over the camera and slid down the front of the van, snapping off a windshield wiper.

"Shit," said George. He picked up the broken parts and climbed into the van. John drove to the end of the row and pulled into the space next to the driver's side of the Lexus. They opened the van's side door and leaned mops and brooms against it. John handed his brother a cigarette. "Make like you're taking a break."

At quarter past seven George removed a cigarette from his mouth. "Are you sure he leaves around seven?"

John shrugged. After Burn visited the Hanover Grille, John had taken Conors' All Points Bulletin to Nahant. Although grateful for the news, Giovanni had John track Nigel Burn to verify that the guy was legit.

"I'm sure of nothing. The first night he left at six-thirty and went to an apartment in Charlestown. He came out a short time later with some young broad yelling at him. They swore at each other for a few minutes and then he left for his home on Beacon Hill. The next two nights, he left around seven and went directly home."

***

Nigel Burn sat at his desk. He was red with anger from his necktie to the top of his bald head. Headquarters' revision to his budget was spread before him. He swept the papers off his desk, they fluttered to the floor. He stood and left the office.

His career was over and the fury built as the elevator descended to the parking garage. When the door opened he saw the janitors by his sedan.

"You bloody wetbacks, get the hell away from my car."

They jumped like puppets, unlike his mistress and wife. The workers busied themselves putting out cigarettes and loading cleaning materials into the van.

Burn approached the driver's side of his car. "If I ever see you screwing-off again, I'll have you fired."

The stocky janitor threw the last mop into the van and turned. That's when Burn felt the punch. Burn folded but stayed on his feet. When he lifted his head, he saw John DeVito. A look of frightened confusion flashed across Burn's face.

"Relax Nigel, it'll be like last time except for one minor difference."

John pushed Burn onto the plastic tarp that lined the floor of the van. His brother slipped the piano wire around Nigel's neck. John slammed the door shut.

CROSSROADS

Conors cruised down Route 95, keeping to the speed limit. Although carefully planned over many months, it was a trip he had hoped to avoid.

It took the first fifty miles to bury the emotions and clear his head of the bloody images. He told himself that if he lived through the night, he'd have a lifetime to deal with the anger and the guilt.

Three hours later the sun had set and Conors almost missed the sign for the Lynn Yacht Club. The brakes squealed as he pulled into the parking lot. He drove towards the boats at the far end and parked Elijah's jeep between an archaic Trojan powerboat and an even older Owens. The gaps between the planks suggested it was their final resting place.

He unzipped his backpack and removed an envelope containing the remainder of Gallo's money and his earnings from lobstering. Conors dropped the car key into the envelope and with a pen from the Jeep's visor printed, 'Elijah—Sorry for the inconvenience'. He reached under the dash and left the envelope where Elijah would search for the key.

Despite the warm evening, Conors put on a pair of thin black gloves, the type lobstermen used under winter work gloves. He stepped from the Jeep, slipped the backpack over his shoulders, removed the kayak and a paddle from the roof, and carried them down a concrete boat ramp. Conors lowered the kayak into the water and then glanced at the carpenter pants and grey sweatshirt he was wearing. A black running outfit was in a bureau five feet from where he had seen Terry's bloodied body. It arrived in the mail the previous week, but never made it to his backpack.

The sound of cars speeding over the causeway towards Nahant distracted Conors' attention from his clothes. He scanned Lynn Harbor. The moonless night blackened as thick clouds arrived. Conors slipped into the kayak and pushed off with the paddle. He kept the Nahant coastline to his left and paddled hard. An hour later, he came upon his first landmark, the bright lights of Northeastern's oceanographic campus. He passed the campus and let the kayak glide into calm black waters. His eyes readjusted to the darkness and he saw faint lights from the distant estates. Having his bearing, he took a hard stroke.

The paddle hit something, he almost lost his grip. He stopped. There was the splash of water as something swam away and then returned, bumping the kayak. He couldn't see it, but could hear it cutting the water as it circled. When the sound was off his stern, he paddled towards the lights.

The newspapers claimed the Mafioso Boss was holed up in his Nahant mansion since the mob war. Conors hoped they were right for a change.

Friend or foe, the creature disappeared when Conors approached the shore. He looked up at the cliff, not knowing where the seaweed-covered rocks ended and the black sky began. He paddled parallel to the shore until it had more of a slope. He climbed out of the kayak, and lifted it onto a ledge. It would take hours for the incoming tide to reach it.

Conors began his ascent. The seaweed made the rock face slippery, but Conors knew how to push and kick the rockweed aside to get a handhold and foothold. He reached the top and peered over the edge at a large shingled house, shuttered and dark. He pulled himself to the top and made his way to the right, to an estate with tall stucco walls separating the property from its neighbors. It was the estate he had painstakingly studied using Google's satellite photos and the same one he had seen from the street a few weeks earlier.

A large solarium was attached to the back of the mansion. Except for a single lamp, it was dark. Conors kept low and scanned the house and the acres of open lawn. After five minutes of not seeing any dogs or activity, he removed his backpack and took out a gun and loose ammunition. He had tried to buy a second magazine for the pistol, but the Maine gun dealer refused to honor his California ID. He tossed the pack over the cliff. Conors heard a faint slap as it hit the water.

He slipped the silver-plated Ruger into the oversized pocket of the carpenter pants and stooped as he made his way along the west side of the property to the bushes at the foundation of the four story mansion. He kept close to the building while making his way to the front, where he lay under a juniper bush. Two men were in the front courtyard. He was certain they were the thugs who chased him from his Brookline home. The one standing was armed. Conors assumed the one sitting on the bench was also carrying.

Conors backtracked to the rear of the mansion, testing the doors and windows as he made his way. He found none unlocked and approached the solarium. It was an old greenhouse re-glazed with double pane glass and connected to the house by an arched doorway. It was the size of a tennis court, stood twenty feet high at its center and was surrounded by the closely cropped lawn. He could hear a screen door on the opposite end of the greenhouse gently tapping in the light sea breeze. He crawled as close as he could, without losing the cover of the bushes. A man was sitting on a sofa with a large book lying on a coffee table. He appeared to be taking notes. When the man looked up from the book, the face was a dead match for the pictures on the internet.

A woman came into the solarium. Conors lay flat on the ground. She placed a mug in front of Gallo and left without saying a word. Conors retraced his footsteps to the shore and then crouching ran towards the stucco wall on the far side of the property. He kept to the heavy vegetation and made his way along the wall towards the opposite end of the solarium. He was fifty feet from the screen door, when Gallo stood and lifted the mug from the coffee table. Conors stopped, hidden behind a large lilac. Gallo drank while facing the ocean. Then he turned and started towards the main house.

Conors darted across the yard towards the solarium. Gallo stopped by a dining table and put the mug down. Conors dove under a shrub, ten feet from the screen door. He slipped his gloved hand over the handle of the Ruger. Gallo, returned to the coffee table, picked up the book and walked towards Conors. The book had a large white egret on its cover. Gallo stopped at a desk near the screen door and sat with his back to Conors. Gallo opened the right-hand bottom draw and placed the book inside. He heard the screen door close, swiveled in the desk chair and froze. A silver-plated and ornately engraved gun was aimed at his head.

"Who are you?" asked Gallo.

Conors hesitated. He didn't notice Gallo pressing the pager attached to his belt.

"Where did you get that gun?" said Gallo whose expression changed from fear to anger.

Conors kept the gun on Gallo and didn't answer.

"Where did you get my son's pistol?" yelled Gallo.

Conors heard distant footsteps echoing down the hallway and glanced towards the main house. Gallo reached into the open desk draw.

As quick as the old man was, Conors was quicker. He pulled the trigger. A bullet tunneled through the soft tissue of Gallo's neck. A gun slipped from Gallo's hand. He was gagging, but alive. The second shot pierced Gallo's forehead. The crime boss fell off his chair and hit the tile floor.

The sound of footsteps and voices grew louder. Spotlights flooded the backyard, making it like noontime. The kayak was no longer an option. Conors glanced towards the side yard.

He was at the screen door when Carlo and Santo entered the solarium with guns drawn. Conors shot and they dove back into the hallway. One of the men held his pistol around the corner and shot blindly, shattering panels of glass.

Conors shot once more as he opened the screen door and then sprinted towards the front of the house. The two men had split up and Santo was shooting from a side door. Conors fired twice. Santo retreated inside.

Carlo had made it to the end of the solarium. Conors stopped, crouched and shot twice. The glass shattered around Carlo, forcing him to the floor. Conors turned again to the doorway. Santo was aiming his gun. Conors pulled the trigger and emptied the magazine. The bullets missed, splintering the door jamb.

Reloading the magazine would take too long. Conors dropped the Ruger and made a dash for the front. As he rounded the corner of the mansion he saw the open gates and his chance to escape.

***

When Nico had arrived, Santo and Carlo were already running into Giovanni's mansion. He pressed a remote control, the gates opened and Nico parked his car. He heard two shots coming from the ocean side of the mansion, then more gunfire. He jogged to the end of the courtyard where the mansion abutted a steep granite outcropping, leaving just enough room for a stone stairway from the backyard.

He climbed a few steps and watched Santo and Carlo shooting. A man was running erratically, trying to be less of a target. First

Santo, then Carlo ran out of ammo. The side yard funneled the running man into the stairway. Nico, still unseen, retreated to the bottom of the stairs, stepped behind the granite ledge and waited.

Conors had cleared the first five steps when Nico, with gun in hand, stepped from behind the ledge, blocking the bottom of the stairway. Santo who was close behind Conors and reloading his gun yelled, "Kill him, he shot the Boss."

Upon seeing Nico Martarazzo, Conors understood his fate. Fury overcame fear. He lunged at Nico. Nico pulled the trigger.

Conors' ears exploded with a blast of pain, his world went black. He blindly threw a punch, hitting something he couldn't see.

Another shot and he was hit in the groin. A third deafening sound was the last he heard. His skull took a crushing blow. He fell and tumbled down the granite steps.

BROKEN

Nico watched a parade of police cars speeding in the opposite direction across the causeway. After reaching the mainland, he drove the Lincoln Town Car through the back roads of Lynn, Revere and Chelsea to the Tobin Bridge. In Boston, he followed the Summer Street exit to the docks and stopped in front of a corrugated steel warehouse. He unlocked a padlock on a truck-sized door and pushed the metal door sideways. It slid down its track, slammed to a stop and reverberated throughout the empty warehouse.

Two startled dockworkers inside the warehouse office looked up from their dinner. Nico drove halfway through the cavernous building and stopped outside a plywood office that was built three feet above the cracked and oil stained concrete floor. The front wall of the office had large windows for surveying a once bustling warehouse.

The dockworkers were waiting on the stairs. They would have avoided the place, if they had expected Nico. The muscle-bound Nico got out of the car. There was a bloody gash above his eye. He pointed at the warehouse door. "Get the hell out of here."

The men hurriedly left the warehouse. After the warehouse door was closed, Nico opened the trunk and looked at the body. Blood ran down Nico's face. He wiped it from his eyes and glared at his unconscious prisoner. "Asshole."

Conors had started to come to his senses as the car thumped through a cluster of potholes. He was hallucinating and thought he was in hell. He was hogtied with hands behind his back and tied to his ankles. A rope wrapped around his head, held a rag in his mouth. Any movement or bouncing of the car forced the rag further down his throat. After the car had taken a number of hard turns, Conors lost consciousness for the second time.

Nico grabbed the ropes, lifted the two hundred pound man from the trunk and placed him face first on the ground. He cut the cord binding Conors hands to his feet, but left the ropes around the ankles and wrists. Conors started choking. Nico pulled the rope from Conors head and the rag, used for checking engine oil, fell to the ground. Nico hoisted Conors over his shoulders and climbed the six steps to the office.

He dropped Conors on the floor and went into the bathroom. He examined the gash above his left eye, swore, wiped his face with paper towels, took five Advils and left the office. He returned with a chain, handcuffs and a padlock. He surveyed the office, crossed the room and yanked hard on a steam pipe. He tore off the asbestos insulation, secured one end of the chain to the pipe with the padlock, then dragged Conors across the room and untied the ropes from his hands. He ratcheted one of the cuffs tightly around Conors' right wrist, slipped the other cuff through the oversized master link at the end of the ten foot chain and secured the second cuff on Conors wrist next to the first. Then Nico pushed the nearby desk back so nothing except the bathroom was within a twenty foot radius of the steam pipe.

At the opposite end of the office were a convertible sofa and an extra-long twin bed. Nico opened the sofa and removed a flimsy foam mattress. He dragged it across the floor to Conors and rolled him onto it.

Nico returned to the far end of the office, opened a closet and twirled the combination on a squat safe that was bolted to the floor.

He removed a loaded Glock-21. A couple of hours earlier, an identical model had been tossed in the waters off Nahant.

He held the Glock by his side as he surveyed the interior of the warehouse. He turned the lights off, lay on the sheetless bed and placed the gun on the floor within reach.

He stared into the dark, not expecting to sleep. He had failed miserably.

***

The pain gradually woke Conors from a world of hallucinations into a reality of handcuffs and chains. It was dark and his face was burning as if his head had been dunked in a pot of boiling coffee. His ears were ringing and his head pounding.

Motivated by Agent DeLuca's description of meat hooks and cattle prods, Conors struggled to free himself. For hours he pried, pulled and explored the darkness within his reach until he heard noises and understood he wasn't alone. Then he worked quietly until the morning light filtered through the translucent roof panels that ran along the peak of the warehouse. The light changed the black of night into shadows and he saw what he had only felt with his hands. Beyond his reach, a desk, a chair, windows and a door slowly took shape.

Conors stood. Unstable on his feet, he yanked on the chain to see the far end of the office. He saw Nico laying on the bed. A mix of anger and despair sapped the last of his energy. He slumped to the mattress, the chain fell to the floor.

Nico's fitful sleep had come to an end. The sounds of moving chain through the night meant his prisoner was alive and conscious. He stood and saw that Conors was awake, sitting on the mattress, leaning against the wall. The carpeting around the steam pipe had been torn-up and the ceiling panels pushed aside.

Nico walked to the desk and looked at Conors. "They knew how to make steam pipes in the old days."

He opened the pizza box left by the dockworkers the previous night, took a piece and ate it. He yanked a Coke from a six pack and gulped it down. Then he tore the cover off the pizza box, dropped a slice on top, grabbed another Coke and walked towards Conors. He kept an eye on Conors while he placed the Coke and cardboard on the mattress. "Throw the can and you'll be drinking from the toilet bowl."

Nico made his way to the restroom, turned on the cold water and splashed his face. The water stung as it re-opened the gash above his eye. Blood swirled down the drain and the angry contorted face returned.

The sound of running water stopped and Nico walked past Conors.

"Hey, Big Boy," said Conors. "Enjoy blowing that woman's guts all over my cottage?"

Nico stopped with his back to Conors. Conors got to his feet, he was seeing double. "Guess every freak has to get his kicks."

Nico turned and charged. He bulldozed Conors into the wall, knocking the wind out of him. Nico's left hand had Conors by his throat and pressed against the wall.

Nico pulled his right arm back and put his weight into the punch. The fist brushed Conors' left ear and crashed through the wood paneling.

Nico was poised for a second punch. He glared with a distorted face, eyes filled with hate, blood pulsing out of the gash and down his face.

Conors looked into the eyes of his captor, unable to breath. Nico let go and Conors fell to the mattress. The dazed Conors lay half off the mattress, looking at the toes of Nico's shoes. When the shoes moved out of sight, he forced himself to lift his head. He saw Nico grab a gun and leave.

***

It took twenty minutes for Conors to recover from the attack. He had withstood being thrown against the wall, but knew it would have been different if Nico had hit him. Nico had wanted to kill him, but something stopped the oversized madman.

Conors slowly got to his feet, the chain allowed him to reach the restroom. He drank from a rusty faucet, then studied himself in the mirror. The left side of his face was scorched as if he had passed out in the summer sun. He decided it was gunpowder burns and then washed the matted blood from his hair. He found a deep cut in his scalp.

He returned to the mattress and ate the remnants of a slice of pizza that he or Nico had stepped on. Pieces of cheese and pepperoni and the can of Coke were scattered beyond his reach. As the day progressed, he jealously watched a rat eat the remains of the pizza.

In a fit of energy he smashed floorboards around the steam pipe and explored the ceiling above, but found no opportunity for escape. Eventually, thoughts of torture returned as Conors accepted defeat. He sat on the mattress, back to the wall, his head pounding, his right hand raised to stop the bleeding caused by the chaffing handcuffs.

The previous summer, Conors had assumed Nico was a dimwit when he stepped from the darkness of the Gloucester garage. The way Nico handled the boat in Monhegan Harbor and the simple efficiency of his jury-rigged shackles had forced Conors to reconsider. He now saw Nico as a formidable enemy. His crazed look also convinced Conors that Nico was insane. As a Marine, Conors had been trained to survive interrogations and knew he had to manage Nico as opposed to pissing him off. After hours of rehearsing different strategies, the office became dark and he wondered if he was being left to die.

Conors was drifting in and out of a troubled sleep when he heard the rumble of the warehouse door. He struggled to his feet, looked out the office windows and peered into the headlights of a car pulling into the warehouse. The shadow of a large man got out, closed the warehouse door. Conors returned to the mattress and sat down.

He heard footsteps on the stairs and the opening door. Nico flipped a wall switch and the fluorescent lights flickered on. The squinting Conors remained sitting, not wanting to appear defiant.

Nico had shaved, showered and changed his clothes. A set of stitches had replaced the slash above his eye. A roll of newspapers was in his right hand and a large Wendy's bag in the other. The crazed look was gone. Except for his size, Nico could have blended into a crowded room.

Nico walked to the desk and put down the bag and newspapers. He looked at the remains of the pizza scattered over the desk. "Looks like you had company."

He picked up the pizza box by the corners, jammed it into a wastebasket and dropped the bag of fast food within Conors' reach. The famished Conors let the bag sit by his feet.

"Where am I?" asked Conors.

"Bonaire," said Nico as he wiped the crumbs off the desk with a paper napkin.

"When are we going to the beach?" said Conors.

Nico lowered himself into the desk chair. "I'm the one who asks the questions."

He took a wallet from a desk drawer and held it so Conors could see it. "What's your name?"

Conors said, "Bill Slater."

"I'll give you some medical advice. Don't lie when I know the answers."

Conors looked at Nico and then said, "Bill Conors."

"Bingo," said Nico. "What were you doing in Nahant?"

"I wanted to talk with Giovanni."

"Why?"

"He thought I had something to do with his son's death," said Conors. "I wanted to convince him otherwise."

Nico leaned into the desk chair while studying Conors. "I guess Giovanni didn't buy your line of bullshit, so you blew his brains out."

Conors was surprised at Nico's calmness.

"Before I approached Giovanni, some men ran into the solarium and started shooting," said Conors.

"You're telling me Giovanni's bodyguards killed him?"

"Maybe it was an accident."

"Carlo and Santo were idiots," said Nico. "But even they couldn't accidentally shoot their boss twice in the same night."

Nico pulled a pair of black gloves from the drawer. "Why were you wearing these?"

Conors looked at the floor and remained silent.

"Why the hell were you wearing gloves?" asked Nico.

Conors looked up from the floor, his head was pounding. He locked eyes with Nico. "Poor circulation, my hands get cold."

Again, Nico leaned back into the wooden chair and asked, "How did you get here?"

"Since its Bonaire, I guess by boat or plane."

Nico tossed the gloves on the desk. "Don't be a wise ass."

"I don't know how I got here," said Conors. "The last thing I remember is being shot at by a couple of guys. I'm running towards the front of Gallo's house and down a stairway when you jump from behind a rock and start shooting at me."

"If I was shooting at you," said Nico. "Why the hell are you alive?"

"Guess you're a bad shot."

Nico glared at Conors and then opened one of the newspapers. For twenty minutes Conors glanced between the Wendy's bag and Nico, who continued reading. Periodically rage would flash across Nico's face. Conors was struggling to think clearly and better understand his captor.

When Nico picked up a second newspaper, Conors recognized the Boston Herald and watched the crazed look return to Nico's face. Nico glanced away from the paper and caught Conors' stare. He walked towards Conors, picked up the bag of fast food and threw it at Conors. Conors caught it, the bag tore open, French fries flew across the mattress and floor.

"Asshole, I don't poison people," said Nico. He picked the newspapers off the desk and walked to the far end of the office.

The Wendy's bag was in Conors' lap. He could smell the cold greasy fries. For some reason he believed Nico, reached into the bag and reassembled a cold cheeseburger, placing the meat and pickles on the flattened roll.

Nico sat on the sofa, leaning forward with elbows on his knees, and the newspapers at his feet. He read them twice, then picked up one of the papers, walked across the office and dropped the newspaper at Conors' feet.

Nico returned to the sofa. Conors put a half-eaten burger into the Wendy's bag, picked up the Daily Lynn Item and read the front page story.

Gangland War Continues: *It started nine months ago when mobster Raymond Gallo was murdered. The man was believed to be the anointed successor to his father, Giovanni Gallo, who ruled the New England La Cosa Nostra.*

Two months later the county's most spectacular mob war eliminated the Russian mafia in a single night. Although, no proof has been uncovered, Giovanni Gallo is believed to be the mastermind behind the five-state operation. The one-night battle not only changed organized crime in the Northeast, but because of the sophisticated armament and military tactics, the war raised serious issues regarding homeland security.

Organized crime experts believed the thoroughness of the one-night offensive made an on-going war of revenge unlikely. Yesterday, the experts were proven wrong. Last night, Giovanni Gallo, the sixty-seven year old mafia boss, was executed gangland style. He was shot twice at his Nahant estate.

Gallo's two bodyguards were also executed. They were shot in the groin, before being shot in the head. Police believe the method of execution was a message to the rest of the Gallo family.

The police have concluded that professionals were responsible for the executions.

The front page of the Lynn Item had more pictures than text. A file picture of Giovanni Gallo, another of Raymond Gallo, aerial views of the Nahant estate, and a picture of yellow chalk lines on a tile floor outlining where Gallo's body was found.

The picture on the next page confused Conors. It showed where the two bodyguards were discovered. The chalk outlining the bodyguards' sprawled bodies was at the head of the stairway. The same stairway Conors was running down when Nico jumped from behind the ledge. Conors vividly remembered the bodyguards ordering Nico to kill him and Nico shooting at him from the bottom of the stairs.

Conors touched the burnt skin on his face. "It doesn't make sense, the FBI claimed Nico was a great shot."

Conors looked up to see Nico walking towards him. Nico dropped the Boston Herald on the mattress and left.

He heard the car start and stop at the warehouse door. Conors stood and watched Nico leave and close the metal door. Conors sat on the mattress and picked up the Boston Herald. Like the Lynn

Daily Item, it had pictures of Giovanni Gallo and the murder scenes. The lead story started on the front page and continued. When he turned the page, he saw a picture and froze. A middle-aged man in a suit was handing a woman a badge and shaking her hand. His focus slowly moved from the picture to the article.

> ***FBI Agent Murdered on a Remote Island****: Terry Hamlin, an FBI agent for less than five years, was murdered while working undercover. She was a member of Boston's Organized Crime Squad. The FBI released a written statement summarizing the agent's short but dynamic career.*
>
> *Ms. Hamlin received a bachelor's degree from Tufts University and a law degree from Harvard. The twenty-eight year old woman followed in her father's footsteps and entered the Agency following graduation. Her area of expertise was financial fraud and she had played a key role in two significant cases that are still being litigated.*
>
> *Agent Hamlin was murdered yesterday on Monhegan Island, which is located ten miles off the coast of Maine. According to a member of the island's emergency medical team, the agent was known as Terry Mahoney. The FBI has not discussed the substance of Hamlin's undercover assignment.*
>
> *Although an Agent of the Organized Crime Squad, there is nothing linking Ms. Hamlin's death to the gangland slayings in Nahant.*
>
> *Agent Hamlin, like her father died in the line of duty. She leaves no surviving relatives.*

He stared at the picture. The beautiful woman, the lawyer, the FBI agent, seemed to be looking back at him. The pounding head and double vision returned, he slouched against the wall and dropped the newspaper.

***

Nico was gone less than an hour. When he opened the office door, Conors was sitting on the mattress with his back against the wall, the Boston Herald left opened at his feet. Other than glancing to see who had entered, Conors didn't move.

Nico noticed that the paper was open to the story about the FBI agent. He placed a case of beer within Conors' reach, tore the top off the cardboard box and grabbed a bottle. He sat at the desk, twisted the cap off the green bottle and studied Conors.

The beer went down fast. Nico was grabbing his second beer, when Conors looked up. Nico handed him a bottle. Conors took it and unscrewed the cap. It was a Rolling Rock, Rosie's favorite beer. He took a mouthful.

Nico sat on the edge of the desk, facing Conors. Conors took another mouthful and swallowed. "What do you want?"

"Lots of things," said Nico.

"What do you want from me?"

"Like you, my boss has read the newspapers," said Nico. "When I report in, he'll expect the missing details. I need to know what you know."

"And once I give you these details, you don't need me any-more."

Nico nodded.

"Then telling you what you want isn't in my best interest."

"I can promise you, it will be a lot worse, if you don't," said Nico.

"What way do you prefer?"

"It may surprise you, but I like clean and simple."

Conors stared at the floor. He took another mouthful of beer thinking it could be his last. The thought made him take another and soon the bottle was empty. He grabbed another green bottle and unscrewed the cap. "Start asking."

"Did you kill Raymond Gallo?"

Conors looked straight ahead at the opposite wall and nodded. "Why?"

"He wanted a piece of the Chelsea Project," said Conors. "When I said no, he threatened my family. I hit him."

Conors looked up. Nico was frowning.

"It's the truth, I've always had a good right."

Nico pointed at the stitches above his left eye. "I know."

Conors looked at Nico's wound. "I don't understand."

"Did you kill Giovanni?" asked Nico.

He turned away from Nico. "Yes."

"Why?"

"I decided that as long as Giovanni Gallo was alive, my days were numbered."

"A good call," said Nico.

Conors stared at the floor, waiting for the next question. When there wasn't one, he took a mouthful of beer and swallowed. "Why did you kill the bodyguards?"

"Personal reasons," said Nico.

"So you did kill them," replied Conors.

"Yes," said Nico. "But your fingerprints are all over the murder weapon."

Conors looked at Nico and then back towards the floor.

"Since I killed them," said Conors. "Tell me what happened?"

Nico's fingers tapped lightly on the desk for a few seconds, then he looked at Conors. "I arrived just before you shot Giovanni. I heard the shooting and then watched until I had a handle on what was happening. I recognized you at the top of the stairs and knew Santo or Carlo would kill you before you made it to the bottom. It was a great excuse."

"So you weren't shooting at me?"

Nico shook his head. "Needed to ask you a few questions."

Conors put his hand to his burnt face.

"You were coming fast. I had a hard time shooting around you," said Nico. "When I shot at Santo, you got a blast of gunpowder. To my surprise you kept on coming and that's when you made contact."

Nico pointed again at the stitches.

"I managed to get a second shot off and took out Santo before I kneed you in the balls," said Nico. "By then Carlo had arrived and saw what was happening. He started shooting as you threw another punch."

"I hit you with the butt of my pistol. You delayed my shot and almost got me killed," said Nico. "Fortunately Carlo couldn't hit the side of a barn."

Conors was frowning. "Why did you shoot them in the groin?"

Nico pushed off from the desk and walked to the office window. He looked into the dark, empty warehouse. "Personal reasons."

Conors stared at Nico's back. Conors' face turned red, but his voice stayed even. "Are personal reasons your excuse for killing the FBI Agent?"

There was dead silence. Nico put a hand on the wall above the window, just below the ceiling, and kept looking out the window. "I didn't kill her."

"That's a hard sell," said Conors. "You were covered in blood and leaving Monhegan in an awful hurry."

Conors swirled the bottle, it was empty. "She was one hell of a woman." He placed the bottle on the floor. "If I was single, I'd have been convincing her to dump her boyfriend."

"What boyfriend?" asked Nico with his back still towards Conors.

"Some guy named Vinny."

Nico stiffened, then walked out of the office, leaving the door open. Conors watched until Nico disappeared into the darkness.

Conors removed two bottles from the cardboard box. He twisted the top off one and left the other in front of the box. He took a drink. His head was still pounding, but things were starting to make sense. A hazy picture was forming.

Thirty minutes and two beers later Nico came through the doorway. Conors pointed at the unopened beer by his feet. Nico picked it up and unscrewed the cap.

"Can I ask a couple of questions?" said Conors

Nico took a deep gulp of beer and shrugged.

"Did you see me leaving my office building last August?"

Nico made his way to the desk chair. He sat and took a swig of beer. "You were masquerading as a janitor."

"Shit," said Conors. He leaned against the wall, started to take another mouthful of beer and stopped. "Why did you step into my headlights when I was driving into my garage?"

"Figured somebody stupid enough to go home when the mob was chasing him, needed help," said Nico. He put his head back and emptied the bottle.

Conors was silent for a moment. "Why?"

"I'm not a philosopher. Don't ask open-ended questions."

"Why did you help me?" asked Conors.

"Unless they're shooting at me, killing people is not in my job description."

Conors nodded, tipped his bottle and found it empty. He grabbed two more, walked to the end of his chain and offered a bottle to Nico.

Nico got out of his chair and reached for the bottle. "Thanks."

Conors returned to his mattress and took another mouthful.

"And who penned your job description?"

Nico hesitated, then looked at Conors. "DEA."

Conors exhaled as more pieces of the puzzle came together. "Like most civil servants you hide your caring side."

"Part of the job description."

"You work undercover?" asked Conors.

"Yeah," said Nico.

"Why were you on Monhegan the day Terry died?"

"Giovanni had discovered you were on the island and Carlo and Santo were on their way to pick you up. I called my contact at the FBI to relay the information to Terry. He didn't answer. I tried his backup, no answer."

"Where the hell were they?"

"I didn't know till today. After leaving you I went to the local FBI office planning on splitting some heads."

"You didn't?"

Nico shook his head. "When I was trying to contact Terry's boss, he was having emergency by-pass surgery. His backup was his best friend and consoling his wife when I called."

"Where did you get that boat?"

"I used to run a drug-intercept operation in southern Florida. I went to the DEA counterpart in Boston and pulled rank. Seas were calm and I made the hundred and eighty miles to Monhegan in a little over two hours. Fast, but not fast enough."

"Why didn't you contact the local police?" asked Conors.

"I was backup, the Staties were suppose to be there long before I arrived. But, unknown to me, my request for the State Police was delayed," said Nico. "My superiors didn't want to interfere with an FBI operation before getting approval from upstairs."

Conors' head was spinning. "Do you know what happened to Terry?"

"Yeah, after leaving Monhegan I tried to catch Carlo and Santo as they made their way back to Port Clyde on a chartered boat, but the gas hog I was driving ran out of fuel," said Nico. "While I drifted off the Maine coast, I called Angie, Giovanni's right-hand man. He had the details."

"Why did they kill her?" asked Conors.

"She walked into your cottage and surprised Carlo and Santo. Carlo grabbed her, not expecting much of a fight. Within a few seconds, she had taken him out. Santo got spooked and shot her three times."

The two men looked at each other, the bloody images of Terry burning even deeper into their memories. Conors swallowed and asked, "Nico's your undercover name?"

"Yeah."

Conors looked away, understanding and suddenly exhausted. His stomach was queasy, but he took a long swig of warm Rolling Rock and turned to Nico.

"Vinny's your real name?"

Nico didn't answer. He finished his beer and put the empty green bottle on the desk.

"Yeah."

DIFFERENT WAYS

Vinny unlocked the handcuffs. Conors tossed them on the mattress. He and Vinny shared cold French fries, the remaining cheeseburger and drank until the beer ran out.

They didn't sleep, Vinny wanted to know how Terry had spent her final days on Monhegan. Vinny hid his emotions and Conors couldn't tell if the details helped or hurt.

As Vinny ran out of questions, he shared what he had learned from Terry. Conors was surprised, that prior to Terry's investigation, the FBI considered him a possible front for the mob. With the elimination of Giovanni, Conors could return home, but didn't know how to deal with the FBI. Vinny explained that the grand jury investigation of Raymond Gallo's murder had expired, voiding outstanding warrants and subpoenas. According to the law, Conors was a free man.

They rehearsed alibis and decided to separate at daylight. No one would ever know they had crossed paths. They trusted each other, understanding that if needed they could link the other to at least two murders.

***

The sun rose on a beautiful morning with one man returning home and the other going to a funeral.

"Are you sure?" asked Conors.

Vinny kept his eyes on the road while he drove. "Besides me and Terry's adopted grandfather, the chapel will be filled with FBI agents. They'd come unglued if you showed-up."

Conors nodded. "Sorry."

They came to the end of Route 128 in Gloucester and followed the Annisquam River as it headed north. It was Kristin's day off. When they found nobody at his Brookline home, Conors assumed the family would be at the cottage.

"What does an undercover agent do when his employer dies?" asked Conors.

"Could link up with one of Giovanni's captains, but I'm thinking of a career change."

"Desk job?"

"I used to work summers at my uncle's greenhouse. Maybe, I'll start a small nursery."

"Your version of swords into plowshare."

"Yeah," said Vinny. "You going to show up at work on Monday and pretend nothing happened?"

Conors looked out the window as his hand skimmed his beardless and nicked chin. He had shaved with a bar of soap and a disposable razor found in the warehouse bathroom.

"The company's done fine without me. Another month won't hurt."

They turned onto a gravel road. Vinny saw a cottage through a stand of locust trees, pulled a U-turn and stopped the Lincoln. Conors searched for the right words. He gave up and opened the door. He put one foot on the ground and turned back to Vinny, "Let me know if I can do anything."

"There is something," said Vinny. "The next time you decapitate a local crime family, let me know, I'll leave town."

Conors smiled and saw the hint of a smirk pulling at the corners of Vinny's mouth. He got out of the car and felt the coolness of a damp morning. He closed the door. Vinny drove down the gravel road, turned and disappeared.

He knew Vinny was going to have a long trip through hell, but as Conors watched him drive off, the emotions of the last ten months left with him. Conors turned and walked towards the cottage thinking of his future, not the past.

When he reached the end of the gravel road, he saw his wife's minivan in the barn and a sprinkler watering freshly planted pansies. He stopped under a locust tree. A swing made from thick nylon rope and a large orange buoy hung from an overhead limb. He grabbed the rope and looked at the cottage in need of shingles, at the weeds, and at the yellow kayak propped against a stone wall. It was all familiar but at the same time he felt like an intruder in someone else's life. When he glanced at the blue waters of Ipswich Bay, he finally understood why. In his gut, he never believed he'd ever again see his family or this place.

He was wondering if he should knock on the door of his own home when he saw her. Kristin was walking up from the rocky shore with an empty coffee cup in her hand and a sweater over her shoulders, his sweater. She deadheaded beach roses while making her way towards the cottage. She looked tired and had lost weight, weight she didn't need to lose.

On the north side of the cottage, moss-covered cobblestones wound their way up the slope from the shore to the front yard. She was halfway up when she saw him, the cup fell and shattered into pieces. She had a blank, emotionless look of disbelief. Then tears flooded her eyes.

He ran to her, hugging her as she melted into his arms, sobbing. The familiar smell, her body, welcomed him. He kissed her gently on her head.

The months had been hard on his wife. Conors kissed her again, lightly on the nape of her neck. "I'll make everything right."

Still crying, she held him tight. Conors took a deep breath as a tear, the first since he was eleven, flowed down his cheek. "I promise, I'll make everything right."

One year later

"This is Fatty Ford. Tune-in to tonight's show for a breaking story. The once-missing Senate President, Nathaniel Forbes, was found alive, bruised and disoriented. He refuses to comment on his whereabouts for the last two weeks.

"More details tonight."

ACKNOWLEDGEMENTS

Christine, Bret, Julie, Bill, Carol, Frank, Gloria, Jane, Jim, John, Mary, Maureen, Mike, Pat, Russ, Sandy, and Scott, thanks for your support, encouragement and sound advice, it has been greatly appreciated.